Praise for Sue Grafton and *"K" Is for Killer*

"Grafton's darkest and most haunting book yet . . . Complex and masterful, *'K' Is for Killer* shows that even after 11 Millhone mysteries, Ms. Grafton is still capable of coming up with fresh twists and new approaches, making it a worthy addition to a stellar series."

—*The Baltimore Sun*

"As always, Grafton's settings are wholly convincing, from a sleazy disco to a complex water purification plant. . . . Once again proves Kinsey Millhone a worthy descendant of Philip Marlowe, et al. . . . She is hard-boiled, brave, justice-loving—a true hero, who happens to be a woman."

—*The Cleveland Plain Dealer*

"Unlike many detective series, Grafton's only seems to get better each time out. . . . Kinsey Millhone [is] the spunkiest, funniest, and most engaging private investigator in Santa Teresa, California, not to mention the entire detective novel genre."

—*Entertainment Weekly*

"Grafton's prose is lean and her observational skills keen. 'K' provided a breezy read but enough tension and misdirection to keep me enthralled throughout."

—*Chicago Tribune*

Please turn the page for more stunning reviews....

"K" IS FOR

KILLER

"K" Is for Killer

Killer

sue grafton

A Kinsey Millhone Mystery

Fawcett Columbine   New York

A Fawcett Columbine Book
Published by Ballantine Books
Copyright © 1994 by Sue Grafton

All rights reserved under International and Pan-American Copyright Conventions. Published in the United States by Ballantine Books, a division of Random House, Inc., New York, and distributed in Canada by Random House of Canada Limited, Toronto.

http://www.randomhouse.com

Library of Congress Catalog Card Number: 97-90198

ISBN: 0-449-00066-4

This edition published by arrangement with Henry Holt and Company.

Manufactured in the United States of America

First Ballantine Books Mass Market Edition: May 1995
First Ballantine Books Trade Edition: May 1997

10 9 8 7 6 5 4 3 2 1

For Mary Lawrence Young and crew . . .

Richard, Lori, and Taylor,
Lawrence,
and Mary Taylor,

and, of course, the dogs . . .

Sadie and Halley,

Toto and Emmy
Oz, Bob, Dee, Lily, and Tog,

and cats . . .

Yukio, Ace, Karmin, and Kit,

and beloved Charmin, much missed.

ACKNOWLEDGMENTS

The author wishes to acknowledge the invaluable assistance of the following people: Steven Humphrey; Susan Aharonian, treatment supervisor, and JoAnn Fults, Cater Water Treatment Plant; Larry Gillespie, Santa Barbara County coroner; Lieutenant Terry Bristol, Santa Barbara County Sheriff's Office; Detective Tom Miller, Santa Barbara Police Department; Jody Knoell, Wells Fargo Bank; Michael Creek, KMGQ; Hildy Hoffman, secretary to the mayor and council, city of Santa Barbara; Tokie Shynk, R.N., and the CCU nursing staff, Santa Barbara Cottage Hospital; Bobbie Kline, R.N., B.S., director of emergency room, Santa Barbara Cottage Hospital; and Craig Wertz, Kleen Pools, Santa Barbara.

"K" IS FOR KILLER

1

The statutory definition of homicide is the "unlawful killing of one human being by another." Sometimes the phrase "with malice" is employed, the concept serving to distinguish murder from the numerous other occasions in which people deprive each other of life —wars and executions coming foremost to mind. "Malice" in the law doesn't necessarily convey hatred or even ill will but refers instead to a conscious desire to inflict serious injury or cause death. In the main, criminal homicide is an intimate, personal affair insofar as most homicide victims are killed by close relatives, friends, or acquaintances. Reason enough to keep your distance, if you're asking me.

In Santa Teresa, California, approximately eighty-five percent of all criminal homicides are resolved, meaning that the assailant is identified, apprehended, and the question of guilt or innocence is adjudicated by the courts. The victims of unsolved homicides I think of as the unruly dead: persons who reside in a limbo of their own, some state between life and death, restless, dissatisfied, longing for release. It's a fanciful notion for someone not generally given to flights of imagination, but I think of these souls locked in an uneasy relationship with those who have killed them. I've talked to homicide investigators who've been caught up in similar reveries, haunted by certain victims who seem to linger among us, persistent in their desire for vindication. In the hazy zone where wakefulness fades into sleep, in that leaden moment just before the mind sinks below consciousness, I can sometimes hear them murmuring. They mourn themselves. They sing a lullaby of the murdered. They whisper the names of their attackers, those men and women who still walk the earth, unidentified, unaccused, unpunished, unrepentant. On such nights, I do not sleep well. I lie awake listening, hoping to catch a syllable, a phrase, straining to discern in that roll call of conspirators the name of one killer. Lorna Kepler's murder ended up affecting me that way, though I didn't learn the facts of her death until months afterward.

It was mid-February, a Sunday, and I was working late, little Miss Virtue organizing itemized expenses and assorted business receipts for my tax return. I'd decided it was time to handle matters like a grown-up instead of shoving everything in a shoebox and delivering it to my accountant at the very last minute. Talk about cranky! Each year the man positively bellows at me, and I have to swear I'll reform, a vow I take seriously until tax time rolls around again and I realize my finances are in complete disarray.

I was sitting at my desk in the law firm where I rent office space. The night outside was chilly by the usual California definition, which is to say fifty degrees. I was the only one on the premises, ensconced in a halo of warm, sleep-inducing light while the other offices remained dark and quiet. I'd just put on a pot of coffee to counteract the narcolepsy that afflicts me at the approach to money matters. I laid my head on the desk, listening to the soothing gargle of the water as it filtered through the coffee maker. Even the smell of mocha java was not sufficient to stimulate my torpid senses. Five more minutes and I'd be out like a light, drooling on my blotter with my right cheek picking up inky messages in reverse.

I heard a tap at the side entrance and I lifted my head, tilting an ear in that direction like a dog on alert. It was nearly ten o'clock, and I wasn't expecting any visitors. I roused myself, left my desk, and moved out into the hallway. I cocked my head against the side door leading out into the hall. The tap was repeated, much louder. I said, "Yes?"

I heard a woman's muffled voice in response. "Is this Millhone Investigations?"

"We're closed."

"What?"

"Hang on." I put the chain on the door and opened it a crack, peering out at her.

She was on the far side of forty, her outfit of the urban cowgirl sort: boots, faded jeans, and a buckskin shirt. She wore enough heavy silver-and-turquoise jewelry to look like she would clank. She had dark hair nearly to her waist, worn loose, faintly frizzy and dyed the color of oxblood shoes. "Sorry to bother you, but the directory downstairs says there's a private investigator up here in this suite. Is he in, by any chance?"

"Ah. Well, more or less," I said, "but these aren't actual office hours. Is there any way you can come back tomorrow? I'll be happy to set up an appointment for you once I check my book."

"Are you his secretary?" Her tanned face was an irregular oval, lines cutting down along each side of her nose, four lines between her eyes where the brows were plucked to nothing and reframed in black. She'd used the same sharpened pencil to line her eyelids, too, though she wore no other makeup that I could see.

I tried not to sound irritated since the mistake is not uncommon. "I'm him," I said. "Millhone Investigations. The first name is Kinsey. Did you tell me yours?"

"No, I didn't, and I'm sorry. I'm Janice Kepler. You must think I'm a complete idiot."

Well, not *complete,* I thought.

She reached out to shake hands and then realized the crack in the doorway wasn't large enough to permit contact. She pulled her hand back. "It never occurred to me you'd be a woman. I've been seeing the Millhone Investigations on the board down in the stairwell. I come here for a support group once a week down a floor. I've been thinking I'd call, but I guess I never worked up my nerve. Then tonight as I was leaving, I saw the light on from the parking lot. I hope you don't mind. I'm actually on my way to work, so I don't have that long."

"What sort of work?" I asked, stalling.

"Shift manager at Frankie's Coffee Shop on upper State Street. Eleven to seven, which makes it hard to take care of any daytime appointments. I usually go to bed at eight in the morning and don't get up again until late afternoon. Even if I could just *tell* you my problem, it'd be a big relief. Then if it turns out it's not the sort of work you do, maybe you could recommend someone else. I could really use some help, but I don't know where to turn. Your being a woman might make it easier." The penciled eyebrows went up in an imploring double arch.

I hesitated. Support group, I thought. Drink? Drugs? Co-dependency? If the woman was looney-tunes, I'd really like to know. Behind her, the hall was empty, looking flat and faintly yellow in the overhead light. Lonnie Kingman's law firm takes up the entire third floor except for the two public restrooms: one marked *M* and one *W*. It was always possible she had a couple of *M* confederates lurking in the commode, ready at a signal to jump out and attack me. For what purpose, I couldn't think. Any money I had, I was being forced to give to the feds at pen point. "Just a minute," I said.

I closed the door and slid the chain off its track, opening the door again so I could admit her. She moved past me hesitantly, a crackling brown paper bag in her arms. Her perfume was musky, the scent reminiscent of saddle soap and sawdust. She seemed ill at ease, her manner infected by some edgy combination of apprehension and embarrassment. The brown paper bag seemed to contain papers of some sort. "This was in my car. I didn't want you to think I carried it around with me ordinarily."

"I'm in here," I said. I moved into my office with the woman close on my heels. I indicated a chair for her and watched as she sat down, placing the paper bag on the floor. I pulled up a chair for myself. I figured if we sat on opposite sides of my desk she'd check out my deductible expenses, which were none of her business. I'm the current ranking expert at reading upside down and seldom hesitate to insert myself into matters that are not my concern. "What support group?" I asked.

"It's for parents of murdered children. My daughter died here last April. Lorna Kepler. She was found in her cottage over by the mission."

I said, "Ah, yes. I remember, though I thought there was some speculation about the cause of death."

"Not in my mind," she said tartly. "I don't know *how* she died, but I know she was murdered just as sure as I'm sitting here." She reached up and tucked a long ribbon of loose hair behind her right ear. "The police never did come up with a suspect, and I don't know what kind of luck they're going to have after all this time. Somebody told me for every day that passes, the chances diminish, but I forget the percentage."

"Unfortunately, that's true."

She leaned over and rooted in the paper bag, pulling out a photograph in a bifold frame. "This is Lorna. You probably saw this in the papers at the time."

She held out the picture and I took it, staring down at the girl. Not a face I'd forget. She was in her early twenties with dark hair pulled smoothly away from her face, a long swatch of hair hanging down the middle of her back. She had clear hazel eyes with a nearly Oriental tilt; dark, cleanly arched brows; a wide mouth; straight nose. She was wearing a white blouse with a long snowy white scarf wrapped several times around her neck, a dark navy blazer, and faded blue jeans on a slender frame. She stared directly at the camera, smiling slightly, her hands tucked down in her front pockets. She was leaning against a floral-print wall, the paper showing lavish pale pink climbing roses against a white background. I returned the picture, wondering what in the world to say under the circumstances.

"She's very beautiful," I murmured. "When was that taken?"

"About a year ago. I had to bug her to get this. She's my youngest. Just turned twenty-five. She was hoping to be a model, but it didn't work out."

"You must have been young when you had her."

"Twenty-one," she said. "I was seventeen with Berlyn. I got married because of her. Five months gone and I was big as a house. I'm still with her daddy, which surprised everyone, including me, I guess. I was nineteen with my middle daughter. Her name's Trinny. She's real sweet. Lorna's the one I nearly died with, poor thing. Got up one morning, day before I was due, and started hemorrhaging. I didn't know what was happening. Blood everywhere. It was just like a river pouring out between my legs. I've never seen anything like it. Doctor didn't think he could save either one of us, but we pulled through. You have children, Ms. Millhone?"

"Make it Kinsey," I said. "I'm not married."

She smiled slightly. "Just between us, Lorna really was my favorite, probably because she was such a problem all her life. I wouldn't say that to either of the older girls, of course." She tucked the picture away. "Anyway, I know what it's like to have your heart ripped out. I probably look like an ordinary woman, but I'm a zombie, the living dead, maybe a little bit cracked. We've been going to this support group . . . somebody suggested it, and I thought it might help. I was ready to try anything to get away from the pain. Mace—that's my husband—went a few times and then quit. He couldn't stand the stories, couldn't stand all the suffering compressed in one room. He wants to shut it out, get shed of it, get clean. I don't think it's possible, but there's no arguing the point. To each his own, as they say."

"I can't even imagine what it must be like," I said.

"And I can't describe it, either. That's the hell of it. We're not like regular people anymore. You have a child murdered, and from that moment on you're from some other planet. You don't speak the same language as other folks. Even in this support group, we seem to speak different dialects. Everybody hangs on to their pain like it was some special license to suffer. You can't help it. We all think ours is the worst case we ever heard. Lorna's murder hasn't been solved, so naturally we think our anguish is more acute because of it. Some other family, maybe their child's killer got caught and he served a few years. Now he's out on the street again, and that's what they have to live with—knowing some fella's walking around smoking cigarettes, drinking beers, having himself a good old time every Saturday night while their child is dead. Or the killer's still in prison and'll be there for life, but he's warm, he's safe. He gets three meals a day and the clothes on his back. He might be on death row, but he won't actually *die*. Hardly anybody does unless they *beg* to be executed. Why should they? All those soft-hearted lawyers go to work. System's set up to keep 'em all alive while our kids are dead for the rest of time."

"Painful," I said.

"Yes, it is. I can't even tell you how much that hurts. I sit downstairs in that room and I listen to all the stories, and I don't know what to do. It's not like it makes my pain any less, but at least it makes it part of *something*. Without the support group, Lorna's death just evaporates. It's like nobody cares. It's not even something people talk about anymore. We're all of us wounded, so I don't feel so cut off. I'm not separate from them. Our emotional injuries just come in different forms." Her tone throughout was nearly matter-of-fact, and the dark-eyed look she gave me then seemed all the more painful because of it. "I'm telling you all this because I don't want you to think I'm crazy . . . at least any more than I actually am. You have a child murdered and you go berserk. Sometimes you recover and sometimes you don't. What I'm saying is, I know I'm obsessed. I think about Lorna's killer way more than I should. Whoever did this, I want him *punished*. I want this laid to rest. I want to know why he did it. I want to tell him face-to-face exactly what he did to my life the day he took hers. The psychologist who runs the group, she says I need to find a way to get my power back. She says it's better to get mad than go on feeling heartsick and defenseless. So. That's why I'm here. I guess that's the long and short of it."

"Taking action," I said.

"You bet. Not just talking. I'm sick and tired of talk. It gets nowhere."

"You're going to have to do a bit more talking if you want my help. You want some coffee?"

"I know that. I'd love some. Black is fine."

I filled two mugs and added milk to mine, saving my questions until I was seated again. I reached for the legal pad on my desk, and I picked up a pen. "I hate to make you go through the whole thing again, but I really need to have the details, at least as much as you know."

"I understand. Maybe that's why it took me so long to come up here. I've told this story probably six hundred times, but it never gets any easier." She blew on the surface of her coffee and then took a sip. "That's good coffee. Strong. I hate drinking coffee too weak. It's no taste. Anyway, let me think how to say this. I guess what you have to understand about Lorna is she was an independent little cuss. She did everything her way. She didn't care what other people thought, and she didn't feel what she did was anybody else's business. She'd been asthmatic as a child and ended up missing quite a bit of school, so she never did well in her classes. She was smart as a whip, but she was out half the time. Poor thing was allergic to just about everything. She didn't have many friends. She couldn't spend the night at anybody else's house because other little girls always seemed to live with pets or house dust, mold, or whatnot. She outgrew a lot of that as she matured, but she was always on medication for one thing or another. I make a point of this because I think it had a profound effect on the way she turned out. She was antisocial: bullheaded and uncooperative. She had a streak of defiance, I think because she was used to being by herself, doing what *she* wanted. And I might have spoiled her some. Children sense when they have the power to cause you distress. Makes them tyrants to some extent. Lorna didn't understand about pleasing other people, ordinary give-and-take. She was a nice person and she could be generous if she wanted, but she wasn't what you'd call loving or nurturing." She paused. "I don't know how I got off on that. I meant to talk about something else, if I can think what it was."

She frowned, blinking, and I could see her consult some interior agenda. There was a moment or two of silence while I drank my coffee and she drank hers. Finally her memory clicked in and she brightened, saying, "Oh, yes. Sorry about that." She shifted on her chair and took up the narrative. "Asthma medication sometimes caused her insomnia. Everybody thinks antihistamines make you drowsy, which they can, of course, but it isn't the deep sleep you need for ordinary rest. She didn't like to sleep. Even grown, she got by on as little as three hours sometimes. I think she was afraid of lying down. Being prone always seemed to aggravate her wheezing. She got in the habit of roaming around at night when everybody else was asleep."

"Who'd she hang out with? Did she have friends or just ramble on her own?"

"Other night owls, I'd guess. An FM disc jockey for one, the guy on that all-night jazz station. I can't remember his name, but you might know if I said it. And there was a nurse on the night shift at St. Terry's. Serena Bonney. Lorna actually worked for Serena's husband at the water treatment plant."

I made a note to myself. I'd have to check on both if I decided to help. "What sort of job?"

"It was just part-time . . . one to five for the city, doing clerical work. You know, typing and filing, answering the telephone. She'd be up half the night, and then she could sleep late if she wanted."

"Twenty hours a week isn't much," I said. "How could she afford to live?"

"Well, she had her own little place. This cabin at the back of somebody's property. It wasn't anything fancy, and the rent on that was cheap. Couple of rooms, with a bath. It might have been some kind of gardener's cottage to begin with. No insulation. She had no central heating and not a lot of kitchen to speak of, just a microwave oven and a two-burner hot plate, refrigerator the size of a little cardboard box. You know the kind. She had electricity, running water, and a telephone, and that was about the extent of it.

She could have fixed it up real cute, but she didn't want to bother. She liked it simple, she said, and besides, it wasn't all that permanent. Rent was nominal, and that's all she seemed to care about. She liked her privacy, and people learned to leave her pretty much alone."

"Hardly sounds like an allergen-free environment," I remarked.

"Well, I know, and I said as much myself. Of course by then she was doing better. The allergies and asthma were more seasonal than chronic. She might have an occasional attack after exercise or if she had a cold or she was under stress. The point is she didn't want to live around other people. She liked the feel of being in the woods. The property wasn't all that big . . . six or seven acres with a little two-lane gravel road coming in along the back. I guess it gave her the sense of isolation and quiet. She didn't want to live in some apartment building with tenants on all sides, bumping and thumping and playing loud music. She wasn't friendly. She didn't even like to say 'hi' in passing. That's just how she was. She moved into the cabin, and that's where she stayed."

"You said she was found at the cabin. Do the police think she died there as well?"

"I believe so. Like I said, she wasn't found for some time. Nearly two weeks, they think, from the state she was in. I hadn't heard from her, but I didn't think much about it. I'd talked to her on a Thursday night and she told me she was taking off. I assumed she meant that night, but she didn't say as much, at least not that I remember. If you recall, spring came late last year and the pollen count was high, which meant her allergies were acting up. Anyway, she called and said she'd be out of town for two weeks. She was taking time off from work and said she was driving up to the mountains to see whatever snows were left. Ski country was the only place she found relief when she was suffering. She said she'd call when she got back, and that was the last I talked to her."

I'd begun to scribble notes. "What date was this?"

"April nineteenth. The body was discovered May fifth."

"Where was she going? Did she give you her destination?"

"She mentioned the mountains, but she never did say where. You think that makes a difference?"

"I'm just curious," I replied. "April seems late for snow. It could have been a cover story if she was going somewhere else. Did you get the impression she was concealing something?"

"Oh, Lorna's not the kind who confided details. My other two, if they're going off on vacation, we all sit around poring over the travel brochures and hotel accommodations. Like right now, Berlyn's saved her money for a trip, and we're always talking about this cruise versus that, oohing and ahhing. The fantasy's half the fun is the way I look at it. Lorna said that just set up a lot of expectations and then reality would disappoint. She didn't look at anything the way other people did. At any rate, when I didn't hear from her, I figured she was out of town. She wasn't one to call much anyway, and none of us would have any reason to go to her place if she was gone." She hesitated, embarrassed. "I can tell I feel guilty. Just listen to how much explanation I'm going into here. I just don't want it to seem like I didn't care."

"It doesn't sound like that."

"That's good, because I loved that child more than life itself." Tears rose briefly, almost like a reflex, and I could see her blink them away. "Anyway, it was someone she'd done some work for, who finally went back there."

"What was her name?"

"Oh. Serena Bonney."

I glanced at my notes. "She's the nurse?"

"That's right."

"What kind of work had Lorna done for her?"

"She house-sat. Lorna looked after Mrs. Bonney's dad sometimes. As I understand it, the old fella wasn't well, and Mrs. Bonney didn't like leaving him by himself. I guess she was trying to make arrangements to leave town and wanted to talk to Lorna before she made reservations. Lorna didn't have an answering machine. Mrs. Bonney called several times and then decided to leave a note on her front door. Once she got close, she realized something was wrong." Janice broke off, not with emotion, but with the unpleasant images that must have been conjured up. After two weeks undiscovered, the body would have been in very poor shape.

"How did Lorna die? Was there a determination as to cause of death?"

"Well, that's the point. They never did find out. She was lying facedown on the floor in her underwear, with her sweat clothes strewn nearby. I guess she'd come back from a run and stripped down for her shower, but it didn't seem like she'd been assaulted. It's always possible she suffered an asthma attack."

"But you don't believe it."

"No, I don't, and the police didn't, either."

"She was into exercise? I find that surprising from what you've told me so far."

"Oh, she liked to keep in shape. I do know there were times when a workout made her wheezy and kind of short of breath, but she had one of those inhalers and it seemed to help. If she had a bad spell, she'd cut back on exercise and then take it up again when she was feeling better. Doctors didn't want her to act like an invalid."

"What about the autopsy?"

"Report's right in here," she said, indicating the paper bag.

"There were no signs of violence?"

Janice shook her head. "I don't know how to say this. I guess because of putrefaction they weren't even sure it was her at first. It wasn't until they compared her dental records that she was identified."

"I'm assuming the case was handled as a homicide."

"Well, yes. Even with cause of death undetermined, it was considered suspicious. They investigated as a homicide, but then nothing turned up. Now it seems like they dropped it. You know how they do those things. Something else comes along, and they concentrate on that."

"Sometimes there isn't sufficient information to make a finding in a situation like that. It doesn't mean they haven't worked hard."

"Well, I understand, but I still can't accept it."

I noticed that she had ceased to make eye contact, and I could feel the whisper of intuition crawling up along my spine. I found myself focusing on her face, wondering at her apparent uneasiness. "Janice, is there something you haven't told me?"

Her cheeks began to tint as if she were being overtaken by a hot flash. "I was just getting to that."

2

She reached into the brown paper bag again and pulled out a videotape in an unmarked box that she placed on the edge of the desk. "About a month ago, someone sent us this tape," she said. "I still don't know who, and I can't think why they'd do it except to cause us distress. Mace wasn't home. I found it in the mailbox in a plain brown wrapper with no return address. I opened the package because it had both our names on it. I went ahead and stuck it in the VCR. I don't know what I thought it was. A tape of some television show or somebody's wedding. I about died when I saw. Tape was pure smut, and there was *Lorna*, big as life. I just let out this shriek. I turned it off and threw it in the trash as fast as I could. It was like I'd been burned. I felt like I should go wash my hands in the sink. But then I had second thoughts. Because this tape could be evidence. It might tie in to the reason she was killed."

I leaned forward. "Let me clarify one point before you go on. This was the first you'd heard of it? You had no idea she was involved in anything like this?"

"Absolutely not. I was floored. Pornography? There's no way. Of course, once I saw what it was, I began to wonder if somebody put her up to it."

"Like what? I don't understand," I said.

"She might have been blackmailed. She might have been co-erced. For all we know, she was working undercover for the police, which they would never admit."

"What makes you say that?" For the first time, she was sound-ing "off," and I felt myself step back, viewing her with caution.

"Because we'd sue them, that's why. If she got killed in the line of duty? We'd go after them."

I sat and stared at her. "Janice, I worked for the Santa Teresa Police Department myself for two years. They're serious profes-sionals. They don't enlist the services of amateurs. In a vice investi-gation? I find that hard to believe."

"I didn't say they *did.* I didn't accuse anyone because that would be slander or libel or one of them. I'm just telling you what's pos-sible."

"Such as?"

She seemed to hesitate, thinking about it. "Well. Maybe she was about to blow the whistle on whoever made the film."

"To what end? It's not against the law to make a pornographic film these days."

"But couldn't it be a cover for something else? Some other kind of crime?"

"Sure, it *could,* but let's back up a minute and let me play devil's advocate here. You told me the cause of death was undetermined, which means the coroner's office couldn't say with any certainty what she died of, right?"

Reluctantly. "That's right."

"How do you know she didn't have an aneurysm or a stroke or a heart attack? With all the allergies she suffered, she might have died from anaphylactic shock. I'm not saying you're wrong, but you're making a big leap here without a shred of proof."

"I understand. I guess it sounds crazy to you, but I know what I know. She was murdered. I'm absolutely sure of it, but I can't get anyone to listen, and what am I supposed to do? I'll tell you something else. She had quite a lot of money at the time she died."

"How much?"

"Close to five hundred thousand dollars' worth of stocks and bonds. She had some money in CDs, but the bulk was in securities. She had five or six different savings accounts, too. Now where'd she get that?"

"How do you think she acquired it?"

"Maybe somebody paid her off. To keep quiet about something."

I studied the woman, trying to assess her powers of reasoning. First, she claimed her daughter was being blackmailed or coerced. Now she was suggesting she was guilty of extortion. I set the issue aside temporarily and shifted my focus. "How did the police react to the tape?"

Dead silence.

I said, "Janice?"

Her expression was stubborn. "I didn't take it to them. I wouldn't even show it to Mace, because he'd die of embarrassment. Lorna was his angel. He'd never be the same if he knew what she'd done." She picked up the tape and put it back in the paper bag, folding the top down protectively.

"But why not show it to the cops? At least it would give them a fresh avenue . . ."

She was already shaking her head. "No, ma'am. No way. I'd never in this world turn it over to them. I know better. That's the last we'd ever see of it. I know it sounds paranoid, but I've heard of cases like this. Evidence they don't like disappears into thin air. Get to court and it's mysteriously vanished. Period, end of paragraph. I don't trust police. That's the point."

"Why trust me? How do you know I'm not in cahoots with them?"

"I have to trust someone. I want to know how she got into this . . . blue movie stuff . . . if it's why she was killed. But I'm not trained. I can't go back in time and figure out what happened. I have no way to do that." She took a deep breath and changed gears. "Anyway, I decided if I hired an investigator, that's the person I'd give the tape to. I guess now I have to ask if you're willing to help, because if you're not, I'll have to find someone else."

I thought about it briefly. Of course I was interested. I just wasn't sure about my chances of success. "An investigation like this is likely to be expensive. Are you prepared for that?"

"I wouldn't have come up if I wasn't."

"And your husband's in agreement?"

"He's not wild about the idea, but he can see I'm determined."

"All right. Let me nose around first before we sign any contracts. I want to make sure I can do you some good. Otherwise, it's a waste of my time and your money."

"Are you going to talk to the police?"

"I'll have to do that," I said. "Maybe unofficially at first. The point is, I need information, and if we can get their cooperation, it will save you some bucks."

"I understand that," she said, "but you have to understand one thing, too. I know you feel the police here are competent, and I'm sure that's true, but everybody makes an occasional mistake, and it's just human nature to want to cover it up. I don't want you to decide whether or not you can help on the basis of their attitude. They probably think I'm crazy as a loon."

"Believe me, I'm capable of making up my own mind about things." I could feel a crick in my neck, and I took a look at my watch. Time to wind it up, I thought. I asked for her home address, her home phone, and the number at the coffee shop, making notes on my legal pad. "Let me see what I can find out," I said. "In the meantime, can you leave that with me? I'd like to get myself up to speed. The meter won't actually start ticking until we have a signed contract."

She glanced down at the paper sack beside her but made no move to lift it. "I guess so. I suppose. I wouldn't want anybody else to get their hands on the tape. It'd kill Mace and the girls if they knew what was in here."

I crossed my heart and held my hand up. "I'll guard it with my life," I said. I didn't think there was any point in reminding her that pornography is a commercial venture. There were probably thousands of copies of the tape in circulation. I tucked the notes in my briefcase and snapped the lid down. She stood up when I did, hefting the bag to one hip before she passed it over to me.

"Thanks," I said. I picked up my jacket and my handbag, setting them on top of the bag, juggling the armload of items as I turned off lights. She followed me across the hall and watched me uneasily as I locked up. I glanced back at her. "You're going to have to trust me, you know. Without that, there's no point doing business together."

She nodded, and I caught a glimpse of tears in her eyes. "I hope you remember Lorna really wasn't like what you see."

"I'll remember," I said. "I'll get back to you as soon as I know anything, and we'll work out a game plan."

"All right."

"One more thing. You're going to have to tell Mace about the tape. He doesn't have to see it, but he should know it exists. I want complete honesty among the three of us."

"All right. Anyway, I've never been good at keeping secrets from him."

We parted company in the little twelve-car parking lot behind the building, after which I drove home.

Once in my neighborhood, I had to circle the block before I snagged a semilegal spot half a block away. I locked my car and walked to my place, toting the paper sack like a load of groceries. The night was downy and soft. The street was darkened by trees, the bare branches woven overhead in a loose canopy. The few stars I saw were as bright as ice chips flung across the sky. The ocean rumbled along the winter beach half a block away. I could smell salt, like woodsmoke, on the still night air. Ahead of me, a light glowed in the window of my second-story loft, and I could see the wind-tossed pine boughs tapping at the glass. A man on a bicycle passed me, dressed in dark clothes, moving quickly, the heels of his cycling shoes marked by strips of reflector tape. He made no sound except for the soft hum of air through his spokes. I found myself staring after him, as if he were an apparition.

I pushed through the gate, which swung shut behind me with a comforting squeak. When I reached the backyard, I glanced at my landlord's kitchen window automatically, though I knew it would be dark. Henry had gone back to Michigan to see his family and wouldn't return for another couple of weeks. I was keeping an eye on his place, bringing in his newspaper and sorting through his mail, sending on anything that seemed critical.

As usual, I found myself surprised at how much I missed him. I'd first met Henry Pitts four years ago when I was looking for a studio apartment. I'd been raised primarily in trailer parks, where I lived with my maiden aunt after the death of my parents when I was five years old. In my twenties, two brief marriages did little to promote my sense of permanence. After Aunt Gin's death, I moved back into her rented trailer, retreating into the solace of that compact space. I had by then left the Santa Teresa Police Department, and I was working for the man who taught me much of what I know now about private investigation. Once I was licensed and had set up an office of my own, I occupied a series of single- and double-wides in various Santa Teresa trailer parks, the last of these being the Mountain View Mobile Home Estates out in the suburb of Colgate. I probably would have gone on living there indefinitely except that I'd been evicted along with a number of my neighbors. Several parks in the area, the Mountain View among them, had converted to "seniors, 55 and older only," and the courts were in the process of reviewing all the discrimination suits that had been filed as a result. I didn't have the patience to wait for an outcome, so I began to make the rounds of the available studio rentals.

Armed with newspaper ads and a map of the city, I drove from one sorry listing to the next. The search was discouraging. Anything in my price range (which ran all the way from very cheap to extremely modest) was either badly located, filthy dirty, or in complete disrepair. Let's don't even talk about the issues of charm or character. I chanced on Henry's ad posted at the Laundromat and checked it out only because I was in the area.

I can still remember the day I first parked my VW and pushed my way through Henry's squeaking gate. It was March, and a light rain had varnished the streets, perfuming the air with the smell of wet grass and narcissus. The flowering cherry trees were in bloom, pink blossoms littering the sidewalk out in front. The studio had been a single-car garage converted into a tiny "bachelorette," which almost exactly duplicated the kind of quarters I was used to. From the outside the place was completely nondescript. The garage had been connected to the main house by means of an open breeze-way that Henry had glassed in, most days using the space to proof mammoth batches of bread dough. He's a retired commercial baker and still rises early and bakes almost daily.

His kitchen window was open, and the smells of yeast, cinnamon, and simmering spaghetti sauce wafted out across the sill into the mild spring air. Before I knocked and introduced myself, I cupped my hands against the studio window and peered in at the space. At that time, there was really only one large room seventeen feet on a side, with a narrow bump-out for a small bath and a galley-style kitchenette. The space has been enlarged now to accommodate a sleeping loft and a second bathroom above. Even then, in its original state, one glance was all it took to know that I was home.

Henry had answered the door wearing a white T-shirt and shorts, flip-flops on his feet, a rag tied around his head. His hands were powdered with flour, and he had a smudge of white on his forehead. I took in the sight of his narrow, tanned face, his white hair, and his bright blue eyes, wondering if I'd known him in a life before this one. He invited me in, and while we talked, he fed me the first of the countless homemade cinnamon rolls I've consumed in his kitchen since.

Apparently he'd interviewed just about as many applicants as I had landlords. He was looking for a tenant without kids, vile personal habits, or an affinity for loud music. I was looking for a landlord who would mind his own business. I found Henry appealing because at his eighty-some years, I figured I was safe from unwanted attentions. I probably appealed to him because I was such a misanthrope. I'd spent two years as a cop and another two years amassing the four thousand hours required to apply for my private investigator's license. I'd been duly photographed, finger-printed, bonded, and credentialed. Since my principal means of employment involved exposure to the underside of human nature, I tended even then to keep other people at a distance. I have since learned to be polite. I can even appear friendly when it suits my purposes, but I'm not really known for my cute girlish ways. Being a loner, I'm an ideal neighbor: quiet, reclusive, unobtrusive, and gone a lot.

I unlocked my door and flipped on the downstairs lights, shed my jacket, turned on the TV, pressed the power button for the VCR, and slid Lorna Kepler's video into the machine. I don't see any point in going into excruciating detail about the contents of the tape. Suffice it to say the story line was simple and there was no character development. In addition, the acting was atrocious and there was much simulated sex of a sort more ludicrous than lewd. Maybe it was only my discomfort at the subject that made the whole enterprise seem amateurish. It surprised me to see the cred-its, which I rewound and read again from the beginning. There was a producer, a director, and an editor whose names sounded real: Joseph Ayers, Morton Kasselbaum, and Chester Ellis. I put the tape on hold while I jotted them down, then reactivated the play button and let the tape roll again. I expected the actors to have monikers like Biff Mandate, Cherry Ravish, and Randi Bottoms, but Lorna Kepler was listed, along with two others—Russell Turpin and Nancy Dobbs, whose quite ordinary names I made note of in pass-ing. There didn't seem to be a writer, but then I suppose porno-graphic sex really doesn't require much in the way of scripting. The narrative would make bizarre reading in any event.

I wondered where the film had been shot. Given what I imag-ined to be a pornographic film budget, no one was going to rent the locations or apply for any permits. For the most part, scenes took place in interiors that could have been anywhere. The lead actor, Russell Turpin, must have been hired solely on the basis of certain personal attributes that he displayed fore and aft. He and Nancy, ostensibly husband and wife, were sprawled naked on their living room couch, exchanging bad dialogue and subjecting each other to various sexual indignities. Nancy was awkward, her gaze straying to a spot at the left of camera where someone was clearly mouthing the lines she was supposed to say. I've seen elementary school pageants with more talent in evidence. Whatever passion she conjured up looked like something she'd learned from watching other pornographic film clips, the chief gesture being a lascivious lip licking more likely to cause chapping than arousal, in my opinion. I suspect she was actually hired because she was the only one who owned a real garter belt in this age of panty hose.

Lorna was the prime focus, and her appearance was staged for maximum effect. She seemed oblivious of the camera, her movements fluid and unhurried, her expertise undisguised. Her looks were elegant, and in the early moments of her role it was difficult to imagine the misbehaviors that would soon emerge. At first, she was cool and seemed to be secretly amused. Later, she was shameless, controlled, and intense, totally focused on herself and whatever she was feeling.

Early in the viewing, I was inclined to fast-forward past any scene not involving her, but the effect became comical—*The Perils of Pauline* with sex parts flapping back and forth. I tried to watch with the same detachment I affect at homicide sites, but the mechanism failed and I found myself squirming. I do not take lightly the degradation of human beings, especially when it's done solely for the financial gain of others. I've heard it said that the pornography industry is larger than the record and the film industries combined, staggering sums of money changing hands in the name of sex. At least this video had little violence and no scenes involving children or animals of any kind.

While there wasn't much story to speak of, the director had made an attempt to create suspense. Lorna played a sexually demonic apparition and as such stalked both husband and wife, who ran stark naked through the house. She was also sexually abusive to a repairman named Harry, who showed up in the film during one of the parts I skipped the first time. Often Lorna's appearances were heralded by smoke and her diaphanous gown was blown skyward by a wind machine. Once the action began, there were many close shots, lovingly detailed by a cameraman with a passion for his zoom lens.

I flicked the tape off and rewound it, turning my attention to the packaging. The production company was called Cyrenaic Cinema with a San Francisco address. Cyrenaic? What did that mean? I pulled my dictionary from the shelf and checked the reference. "Cyrenaic—of the Greek school of philosophy founded by Aristippus of Cyrene, who considered individual sensual pleasure the greatest good." Well, *someone* was literate. I tried directory assistance in the 415 area code. There was no telephone number listed, but the address might be good. Even if Janice and I came to an agreement, I wasn't sure she'd want to fund a trip to San Francisco.

I sorted through the files she'd given me, separating out the news clippings from the police reports. I read the autopsy report with particular care, translating the technicalities into my sketchy layman's understanding. The basic facts were about as distasteful as the film I'd just seen, without the leavening influence of all the corny dialogue. By the time Lorna's body was discovered, the process of decomposition was virtually complete. Gross examination revealed precious little of significance, as all the soft tissue had collapsed into a greasy mass. Maggots had made hasty work of her. Internal examination confirmed the absence of all organs, with only small amounts of tissue left representing the GI tract, the liver, and the circulatory system. Brain tissue was also completely liquefied and/or absent. Osseous remains showed no evidence of blunt force trauma, no stab or gunshot wounds, no ligature, no crushed or broken bones. Two old fractures were noted, but neither apparently pertained to the manner of her death. What laboratory tests could be run showed no drugs or poisons in her system. Complete dental arches were excised and retained, along with all ten fingers. Positive identification was made through dental charts and a residual print from the right thumb. There were no photographs, but I suspected those would be attached to her department file. Postmortem glossies would hardly have been passed along to her mother.

There was no way to pinpoint date or time of death, but a rough estimate was made from several environmental factors. Countless people interviewed testified as to her night owl tendencies. It was also allegedly her habit to jog shortly after she got up. As nearly as the homicide investigators could establish, she'd slept late as usual on that Saturday, April 21. She'd then pulled on her sweats and had gone out for a jog. The Saturday morning paper was in, as was the mail that had been delivered late that morning. All the mail and newspapers after the twenty-first were piled up unopened. Idly I wondered why she hadn't left for her trip Thursday night as planned. Maybe she'd finished out the work week on Friday, intending to take off Saturday morning once she was showered and dressed.

The questions were obvious, but it was useless to speculate in the absence of concrete evidence. While the cause of death was undetermined, the police had proceeded on the assumption that she'd been struck down by a person or persons unknown. Lorna had lived alone and in singular isolation. If she'd cried out for help, there had been none within range of her. I'm single myself, and though Henry Pitts lives close by, I'm sometimes uneasy. There's a certain vulnerability attached to my work. I've been variously shot, pummeled, punched, and accosted, but I've usually found a way to outmaneuver my attackers. I didn't like the idea of Lorna's final moments.

The homicide detective who'd done all the grunt work was a guy named Cheney Phillips, whom I ran into from time to time. The last I'd heard, he'd moved from homicide to vice. I'm not really sure how law enforcement agencies in other cities work, but in the Santa Teresa Police Department, officers tend to be rotated every two to three years, exposing them to a variety of responsibilities. This not only ensures a well-balanced department, but allows the opportunity for advancement without an officer's having to wait for the death or retirement of division-entrenched colleagues.

Like many cops in town, Phillips could usually be found in a local watering hole called CC's, which was frequented by attorneys and a variety of law enforcement types. His supervisor on the case had been Lieutenant Con Dolan, whom I knew very well. I was somewhat skeptical that Lorna's role in a low-budget movie was related to her death. On the other hand, I could see why Janice Kepler wanted to believe as much. What else are you going to think when it turns out your late and favorite daughter was a pornographic film star?

I was restless, nearly itchy with an overdose of caffeine. I'd probably sucked down eight to ten cups of coffee during the day, the last two that evening while I was talking to Janice. Now I could feel stimulants, like sugarplums, dancing in my head. Sometimes anxiety and caffeine have the same effect.

I checked my watch again. It was after midnight by now and well past my bedtime. I pulled out the phone book and found the number for CC's. The call took less than fifteen seconds. The bartender told me Cheney Phillips was on the premises. I gave him my name and had him give Cheney the message that I was on my way. As I hung up the phone, I could hear him yelling to Cheney across the din. I grabbed my jacket and my keys and headed out the door.

3

I drove east along Cabana, the wide boulevard that parallels the beach. When the moon is full, the darkness has the quality of a film scene shot day for night. The landscape is so highly illuminated that the trees actually cast shadows. Tonight the moon was in its final quarter, rising low in the sky. From the road I couldn't see the ocean, but I could hear the reverberating rumble of the tide rolling in. There was just enough wind to set the palm trees in motion, shaggy heads nodding together in some secret communication. A car passed me, going in the opposite direction, but there were no pedestrians in sight. I'm not often out at such an hour, and it was curiously exhilarating.

By day, Santa Teresa seems like any small southern California town. Churches and businesses hug the ground against the threat of earthquakes. The rooflines are low, and the architectural influence is largely Spanish. There's something solid and reassuring about all the white adobe and the red tile roofs. Lawns are manicured, and the shrubs are crisply trimmed. By night the same features seem stark and dramatic, full of black-and-white contrasts that lend intensity to the hardscape. The sky at night isn't really black at all. It's a soft charcoal gray, nearly chalky with light pollution, the trees like ink stains on a darkened carpet. Even the wind has a different feel to it, as light as a feather quilt against the skin.

The real name for CC's is the Caliente Cafe, a low-rent establishment housed in an abandoned service station near the railroad tracks. The original gasoline pumps and the storage tanks below had been removed years before, and the contaminated soil had been paved over with asphalt. Now, on hot days the blacktop tends to soften and a toxic syrup seeps out, a tarry liquid quickly converted into wisps of smoke, suggesting that the tarmac is on the verge of bursting into flames. Winters, the pavement cracks from dry cold, and a sulfurous smell wafts across the parking lot. CC's is not the kind of place to encourage bare feet.

I parked out in front beneath a sizzling red neon sign. Outside, the air smelled like corn tortillas fried in lard; inside, like salsa and recirculated cigarette smoke. I could hear the high-pitched whine of a blender working overtime, whipping ice and tequila into the margarita mix. The Caliente Cafe bills itself as an "authentic" Mexican cantina, which means the "day-core" consists of Mexican sombreros tacked above the doors. Bad lighting eliminates the need for anything else. Every item on the menu has been Americanized, and all the names are cute: Ensanada Ensalada, Pasta Pequeño, Linguini Bambini. The music, all canned, is usually played way too loud, like a band of mariachis hired to hover at your table while you try to eat.

Cheney Phillips was sitting at the bar, his face tilted in my direction. My request for an audience had clearly piqued his interest. Cheney was probably in his early thirties: a white guy with a disheveled mop of dark curly hair, dark eyes, good chin, prickly two-day growth of beard. His was the sort of face you might see in a men's fashion magazine or the society section of the local papers, escorting some debutante decked out like a bride. He was slim, of medium height, wearing a tobacco-brown silk sport coat over a white dress shirt, his pants a pleated cream-colored gabardine. His air of confidence suggested money of intimidating origins. Everything about him said trust fund, private schools, and casual West Coast privilege. This is pure projection on my part, and I have no idea if it's accurate. I've never really asked him how he ended up a cop. For all I know, he's third-generation law enforcement with all the women in his family doing jail administration.

I eased up onto the bar stool next to his. "Hello, Cheney. How are you? Thanks for waiting. I appreciate it."

He shrugged. "I'm usually here until closing time anyway. Can I buy you a drink?"

"Of course. I'm so wired on coffee I may never get to sleep."

"What's your pleasure?"

"Chardonnay, if you please."

"Absolutely," he said. He smiled, revealing first-rate orthodontic work. No one could have teeth that straight without years of expensive correction. Cheney's manner was habitually seductive and never more so than in a setting such as this.

The bartender had been watching our interchange with an exaggerated late night patience. In a bar like CC's, this was the hour when the sexually desperate made their last minute appeals for company. By then enough liquor had been consumed that potential partners, who earlier had been rejected as unworthy, were now being reconsidered. The bartender apparently assumed we were negotiating a one-night relationship. Cheney ordered wine for me and another vodka tonic for himself.

He checked back over his shoulder, doing a quick visual survey of the other patrons. "You ought to keep an eye on all the off-duty police officers. Last call, we go out in the parking lot and pass around a Breathalyzer, like we're copping a joint, make sure we're still sober enough to drive ourselves home."

"I heard you left homicide."

"Right. I've been doing vice for six months."

"Well, that suits," I said. "Do you like it?" He'd probably been moved to vice because he still looked young enough to have some.

"Sure, it's great. It's a one-man department. I'm the current expert on gambling, prostitution, drugs, and organized crime, such as it is in Santa Teresa. What about you? What are you up to? You probably didn't come down here to chat about my career in law enforcement." He looked up as the bartender approached, halting further conversation until our drinks had been served.

When he looked back, I said, "Janice Kepler wants to hire me to look into her daughter's death."

"Good luck," he said.

"You handled the original investigation, yes?"

"Dolan and me, with a couple more guys thrown in. This is the long and short of it," he said, ticking the items off his fingers. "There was no way to determine cause of death. We still aren't absolutely certain what day it was, let alone what time frame. There was no significant trace evidence, no witnesses, no motive, no suspects . . ."

"And no case," I supplied.

"You got it. Either this was not a homicide to begin with or the killer led a charmed life."

"I'll say."

"You going to do it?"

"Don't know yet. Thought I'd better talk to you first."

"Have you seen a picture of her? She was beautiful. Screwed up, but gorgeous. Talk about a dark side. My God."

"Like what?"

"She had this part-time job at the water treatment plant. She's a clerk-typist. You know, she does a little phone work, a little filing, maybe four hours a day. She tells everybody she's working her way through city college, which is true in its way. She takes a class now and then, but it's only half the story. What she's really up to is a bit of high-class hooking. She's making fifteen hundred bucks a pop. We're talkin' substantial sums of money at the time of her death."

"Who'd she work for?"

"Nobody. She was independent. She started doing out-call. Exotic dance and massage. Guys phone this service listed in the classifieds, and she goes out and does some kind of bump-and-grind strip while they abuse themselves. The game is you can't make a deal for more than that up front—Undercover used to call and pull that 'til everybody wised up—but once she's on the premises, she can negotiate whatever services the client wants. It's strictly their transaction."

"For which she gets paid what?"

Cheney shrugged. "Depends on what she does. Straight sex is probably a hundred and fifty bucks, which she ends up splitting with the management. Pretty quick, she figures out she has more on the ball, so she bags the cheap gigs and moves up to the big time."

"Here in town?"

"For the most part. I understand they used to see quite a bit of her in the bar at the Edgewater Hotel. She also cruised through Bubbles in Montebello, which you probably heard was closed down last July. She had a penchant for the places where the high rollers hung out."

"Did her *mother* know this?"

"Sure she did. Absolutely. Lorna was even picked up once on a misdemeanor for soliciting an undercover vice officer at Bubbles. We didn't want to rub her mother's nose in the fact, but she was certainly informed."

"Maybe it's just beginning to sink in," I said. "Someone sent her a copy of a pornographic film in which Lorna loomed large. Apparently that's what prompted her to come see me. She thinks Lorna was either blackmailed into it or working undercover."

"Oh, yeah, right," he said.

"I'm just telling you her assumption."

Cheney snorted. "She's in denial big time. Have you actually seen this tape?"

"I just saw it tonight. It was pretty raunchy."

"Yeah, well, I'm not sure how much difference it makes. The kind of stuff she was into, it really doesn't surprise me. How's it supposed to tie in? That's the part I don't get."

"Janice thinks Lorna was about to blow the whistle on someone."

"Oh, man, that lady's seen too many bad TV movies. Blow the whistle on who, and for what? Those people are legitimate . . . in some sense of the word. They're probably scumbags, but that's not against the law in this state. Look at all the politicians."

"That's what I told her. Anyway, I'm trying to figure out if there's enough to warrant my taking on the job. If you guys couldn't come up with anything, how can I?"

"Maybe you'll get lucky. I'm one of life's eternal optimists. Case is still open, but we ain't had jackshit for months. You want to look at the files, it can probably be arranged."

"That'd be great. What I'd really like to see are the crime scene photographs."

"I'll try to clear it with Lieutenant Dolan, but I don't think he'll object. You heard he's in the hospital? He had a heart attack."

I was so startled, I put a hand to my own heart, nearly knocking my glass over in the process. I caught it before it tipped, though a little wave of wine slopped out. "Dolan had a heart attack? That's awful! When was this?"

"Yesterday, right after squad meeting, he started having chest pains. Like boom, he's in trouble. Guy looks like shit, and he's short of breath. Next thing I know he's out like a light. Everybody scrambling around, doing CPR. Paramedics pulled him back from the brink, but it was really touch-and-go."

"Is he going to be okay?"

"We hope so. He's doing fine, last I heard. He's over at St. Terry's in the cardiac care unit, raising hell, of course."

"Sounds like him. I'll try to get over there first chance I have."

"He'd like that. You should do it. I talked to him this morning, and the guy's going nuts. Claims he doesn't like to sleep because he's scared he won't wake up."

"He admitted that? I never knew Lieutenant Dolan to talk about anything personal," I said.

"He's changed. He's a new man. It's amazing," he said. "You ought to see for yourself. He'd be thrilled at the company, probably talk your ear off."

I shifted the subject back to Lorna Kepler. "What about you? Do you have a theory about Lorna's death?"

Cheney shrugged. "I think somebody killed her, if that's what you're after. Rough trade, jealous boyfriend. Maybe some other hooker thought Lorna was treading on her turf. Lorna Kepler loved risk. She's the kind who liked to teeter right out on the edge."

"She have enemies?"

"Not as far as we know. Oddly enough, people seemed to like her a lot. I say 'oddly' because she was different, really unlike other folk. It was almost admiration on their part because she was so *out* there, you know? She disregarded the rules and played the game her way."

"I take it your investigation covered a lot of ground."

"That's right, though it never came to much. Frustrating. Anyway, it's all there if you want to take a look. I can have Emerald pull the files once we get Dolan's okay."

"I'd appreciate that. Lorna's mother gave me some stuff, but she didn't have everything. Just let me know and I'll pop over to the station and take a look."

"Sure thing. We can talk afterward."

"Thanks, Cheney. You're a doll."

"I know that," he said. "Just make sure you keep us informed. And play it straight. If you come up with something, we don't want it thrown out of court because you've tainted the evidence."

"You underestimate me," I said. "Now that I'm working out of Lonnie Kingman's office, I'm an angel among women. I'm a paragon."

"I believe you," he said. His smile was lingering, and his eyes held just a hint of speculation. I thought I'd probably said enough. I backed away and then turned, giving him a wave as I departed.

Once outside, I drank in the quiet of the chill night air, picking up the faint scent of cigarette smoke trailing back at me from somewhere up ahead. I lifted my head and caught a glimpse of a man easing out of sight around a bend in the road, his footsteps growing faint. There are men who walk at night, shoulders hunched, heads bent in some solitary pursuit. I tend to think of them as harmless, but one never knows. I watched until I was certain he was gone. In the distance, low-lying heavy cloud cover had been pushed up the far side of the mountain and now spilled over the top.

All the parking spots were filled. Vehicles gleamed in the harsh overhead illumination like a high-end used-car lot. My vintage VW looked distinctly out of place, a homely pale blue hump among the sleek, low-slung sports models. I unlocked the car door and slid onto the driver's seat, then paused for a moment, hands on the steering wheel, while I contemplated my next move. The single glass of white wine had done little to temper my wired state. I knew if I drove home, I'd just end up lying on my back, staring at the skylight above my bed. I fired up the ignition and then drove along the beach as far as State Street. I hung a right, heading north.

I crossed the railroad tracks, jolting the radio to life. I didn't even realize I'd left the damn thing on. It seldom worked these days, but every now and then I could coax something out of it. Sometimes I'd bang on the dash with my fist, jarring forth news or a commercial. Other times, for no apparent reason, I'd pick up a baffling fragment of the weather. The problem was probably a loose wire or faulty fuse, which is just a guess on my part. I don't even know if radios have fuses these days. At the moment, the reception was as clear as could be.

I pressed a button, neatly switching from AM to FM. I turned the dial by degrees, sliding past station after station until I caught the strains of a tenor sax. I had no idea who it was, only that the mournful mix of horns was perfect for this hour of the night. The cut came to an end, and a man's voice eased into the space. "That was 'Gato' Barbieri on sax, a tune called 'Picture in the Rain' from the movie sound track *Last Tango in Paris*. Music was composed by 'Gato' Barbieri, recorded back in 1972. And this is Hector Moreno, here on K-SPELL, bringing you the magic of jazz on this very early Monday morning."

His voice was handsome, resonant, and well modulated, with an easygoing confidence. This was a man who made his living staying up all night, talking about artists and labels, playing CDs for insomniacs. I pictured a guy in his mid-thirties, dark, substantial, possibly with a mustache, his long hair pulled back and secured with a rubber band. He must have enjoyed all the perks of local celebrity status, acting as an MC for various charity events. Radio personalities don't need even the routine good looks of the average TV anchorperson, but he'd still have name recognition value, probably his share of groupies as well. He was taking call-in requests. I felt my thoughts jump a track. Janice Kepler had mentioned Lorna's hanging out with some DJ in her late night roamings.

I began to scan the deserted streets, looking for a pay phone. I passed a service station that was shut down for the night. At the near edge of the parking lot, I spotted what must have been one of the last real telephone booths, a regular stand-up model with a bifold door. I pulled in and left the car engine running while I flipped through my notes, looking for the phone number I'd been given for Frankie's Coffee Shop. I dropped a quarter in the slot and dialed.

When a woman at Frankie's Coffee Shop finally answered the phone, I asked for Janice Kepler. The receiver was clunked down on the counter, and I could hear her name being bellowed. In the background there was a low-level buzz of activity, probably late night pie-and-coffee types, tanking up on stimulants. Janice must have appeared because I heard her make a remark to someone in passing, the two of them exchanging brief comments before she picked up. She identified herself somewhat warily, I thought. Maybe she was worried she was getting bad news.

"Hello, Janice? Kinsey Millhone. I hope this is all right. I need some information, and it seemed simpler to call than drive all the way up there."

"Well, my goodness. What are you doing up at this hour? You looked exhausted when I left you in the parking lot. I thought you'd be sound asleep by now."

"That was my intention, but I never got that far. I was too stoked on coffee, so I thought I might as well get some work done.

I had a chat with one of the homicide detectives who worked on Lorna's case. I'm still out and about and thought I might as well cover more ground while I'm at it. Didn't you mention that Lorna used to hang out with a DJ on one of the local FM stations?"

"That's right."

"Is there any way you can find out who it was?"

"I can try. Hang on." Without covering the receiver, she consulted with one of the other waitresses. "Perry, what's the name of that all-night jazz show, what station?"

"K-SPELL, I think."

I knew that much. Thinking to save time, I said, "Janice?"

"What about the disc jockey? You know his name?"

In the background, somewhat muffled, Perry said, "Which one? There's a couple." Dishes were clattering, and the speaker system was pumping out a version of "Up, Up, and Away" with stringed instruments.

"The one Lorna hung out with. 'Member I told you about him?"

I cut in on Janice. "Hey, Janice?"

"Perry, hold on. What, hon?"

"Could it be Hector Moreno?"

She let out a little bark of recognition. "That's right. That's him. I'm almost sure he's the one. Why don't you call him up and ask if he knew her?"

"I'll do that," I said.

"You be sure and let me know. And if you're still out running around town after that, come on up and have a cup of coffee on the house."

I could feel my stomach lurch at the thought of more coffee. The cups I'd consumed were already making my brain vibrate like an out-of-balance washing machine. As soon as she hung up, I depressed the lever and released it, letting the dial tone whine on while I hauled up the phone book on its chain and flipped through. All the radio stations were listed at the front end of the K's. As it turned out, K-SPL was only six or eight blocks away. Behind me, from the car, I could hear the opening bars of the next jazz selection. I found another quarter in the bottom of my handbag and dialed the studio.

The phone rang twice. "K-SPELL. This is Hector Moreno." The tone was businesslike, but it was certainly the man I'd been listening to.

"Hello," I said. "My name is Kinsey Millhone. I'd like to talk to you about Lorna Kepler."

4

Moreno had left the heavy door to the station ajar. I let myself in and the door closed behind me, the lock sliding home. I found myself standing in a dimly lit foyer. To the right of a set of elevator doors, a sign indicated K-SPL with an arrow pointing down toward some metal stairs on the right. I went down, my rubber-soled shoes making hollow sounds on the metal treads. Below, the reception area was deserted, the walls and the narrow hallway beyond painted a dreary shade of blue and a strange algae green, like the bottom of a pond. I called, "Hello."

No answer. Jazz was being piped in, obviously the station playing back on itself.

"Hello?"

I shrugged to myself and moved down the corridor, glancing into each cubicle I passed. Moreno had told me he'd be working in the third studio on the right, but when I reached it, the room was empty. I could still hear faint strains of jazz coming in over the speakers, but he'd apparently absented himself momentarily. The studio was small, littered with empty fast-food containers and empty soda cans. A half-filled coffee cup on the console was warm to the touch. There was a wall clock the size of the full moon, its second hand ticking jerkily as it made the big sweep. Click. Click. Click. Click. The passage of time had never seemed quite so concrete or so relentless. The walls were soundproofed with sections of corrugated dark gray foam.

To my left, countless cartoons and news clippings were tacked to a corkboard. The balance of the wall space was taken up with row after row of CDs, with additional shelves devoted to albums and tape cassettes. I did a visual survey, as if in preparation for a game of Concentration. Coffee mugs. Speakers. A stapler, Scotch tape dispenser. Many empty designer water bottles: Evian, Sweet Mountain, and Perrier. On the control board, I could see the mike switch, cart machines, a rainbow of lights, one marked "two track mono." One light flashed green, and another was blinking red. A microphone suspended from a boom looked like a big snow cone of gray foam. I pictured myself leaning close enough to touch my lips to the surface, using my most seductive FM tone of voice. "Hello, all you night owls. This is Kinsey Millhone here, bringing you the best in jazz at the very worst of hours. . . ."

Behind me, I heard someone thumping down the hall in my direction, and I peered out with interest. Hector Moreno approached, a man in his early fifties, supported by two crutches. His shaggy hair was gray, his brown eyes as soft as dark caramels. His upper body was immense, his torso dwindling away to legs that were sticklike and truncated. He wore a bulky black cotton sweater, chinos, and penny loafers. Beside him was a big reddish yellow dog with a thick head, heavy chest, and powerful shoulders, probably part chow, judging by the teddy bear face and the ruff of hair around its neck.

"Hi, are you Hector? Kinsey Millhone," I said. The dog bristled visibly when I held out my hand.

Hector Moreno propped himself on one crutch long enough to

shake my hand. "Nice to meet you," he said. "This is Beauty. She'll need time to make up her mind about you."

"Fair enough," I said. She could take the rest of her life, as far as I was concerned.

The dog had begun to rumble, not a growl but a low hum, as if a machine had been activated somewhere deep in her chest. Hector snapped his fingers, and she went silent. Dogs and I have never been that fond of one another. Just a week ago I'd been introduced to a boy-pup who'd actually lifted his leg and piddled on my shoe. His owner had voiced his most vigorous disapproval, but he really didn't sound that sincere to me, and I suspected he was currently recounting, with snorts and guffaws, the tale of Bowser's misbehavior on my footwear. In the meantime I had a Reebok that smelled like dog whiz, a fact not lost on Beauty, who gave it her rapt attention.

Hector swung himself forward and moved into the studio, answering the question I was too polite to ask. "I collided with a rock pile when I was twelve. I was spelunking in Kentucky, and the tunnel caved in. People expect something different, judging from my voice on the air. Grab a seat." He flashed me a smile, and I smiled in response. I followed as he set his crutches aside and hoisted himself onto the stool. I found a second stool in the corner and pulled it close to him. I noticed that Beauty arranged herself so that she was between us.

While Hector and I exchanged pleasantries, the dog watched us with an air of nearly human intelligence, her gaze shifting constantly from his face to mine. Sometimes she panted with an expression close to a grin, dangling tongue dancing as if at some private joke. Her ears shifted as we spoke, gauging our tones. I had no doubt she was prepared to intervene if she didn't like what she heard. From time to time, in response to cues I wasn't picking up myself, she would retract her tongue and close her mouth, rising to her feet with that low rumble in her chest. All it took was a gesture from him and she'd drop to the floor again, but her look then was brooding. She probably had a tendency to sulk when she wasn't allowed to feast on human flesh. Hector, ever watchful, seemed amused at the performance. "She doesn't trust many people. I got her from the pound, but she must have been beaten when she was young."

"You keep her with you all the time?" I asked.

"Yeah. She's good company. I work late nights, and when I leave the studio, the town is deserted. Except for the crazies. They're always out. You asked about Lorna. What's your connection?"

"I'm a private investigator. Lorna's mother stopped by my office earlier this evening and asked if I'd look into her death. She wasn't particularly happy with the police investigation."

"Such as it was," he said. "Did you talk to that guy Phillips? What a prick he was."

"I just talked to him. He's out of homicide and onto vice these days. What'd he do to you?"

"He didn't *do* anything. It's his attitude. I hate guys like him. Little banty roosters who push their weight around. Hang on a sec." He slid a fat cassette into a slot and depressed a button on the soundboard, leaning forward, his voice as smooth and satiny as fudge. "We've been listening to Phineas Newborn on solo piano, playing a song called 'The Midnight Sun Will Never Set.' And this is Hector Moreno, casting a little magic here at K-SPELL. Coming up, we have thirty minutes of uninterrupted music, featuring the incomparable voice of Johnny Hartman from a legendary session with the John Coltrane Quartet. *Esquire* magazine once named this the greatest album ever made. It was recorded March 7, 1963, on the Impulse label with John Coltrane on tenor sax, McCoy Tyner on piano, Jimmy Garrison on bass, and Elvin Jones on drums." He punched a button, adjusted the studio volume downward, and turned back to me. "Whatever he said about Lorna, you can take it with a grain of salt."

"He said she had a dark side, but I knew that much. I'm not sure I have the overall picture, but I'm working on that. How long had you known her before she died?"

"Little over two years. Right after I started doing this show. I was in Seattle before that, but the damp got to me. I heard about this job through a friend of a friend."

"Is your background in broadcast?"

"Communications," he said. "Radio and TV production; video to some extent, though it never interested me much. I'm from Cincinnati originally, graduated from the university, but I've worked everywhere. Anyway, I met Lorna when I first got down here. She was a night owl by nature, and she started calling in requests. Between cuts and commercials, we'd sometimes talk for an hour. She began to drop by the studio, maybe once a week at first. Toward the end, she was here just about every night. Two-thirty, three, she'd bring doughnuts and coffee, bones for Beauty if she'd been out to dinner. Sometimes I think it was the dog she cared about. They had some kind of psychic affinity. Lorna used to claim they'd been lovers in another life. Beauty's still waiting for her to come back. Three o'clock, she goes out to the stairs and just stands there, looking up. Makes this little sound in her throat that'd break your heart." He shook his head, waving off the image with curious impatience.

"What was Lorna like?"

"Complicated. I thought she was a beautiful, tortured soul. Restless, disconnected, probably depressed. But that was just one part. She was split, a contradiction. It wasn't all the dark stuff."

"Was she into drugs or alcohol?"

"Not as far as I know. She blew hot and cold. She was nearly hyper sometimes. If you want to get analytical, I'd be tempted to label her manic-depressive, but that doesn't really capture it. It was like a battle she fought, and the down side finally won."

"I guess we all have that in us."

"I do, that's for sure."

"You knew she did a porno film?"

"I heard about that. I never saw it myself, but I guess the word was out."

"When was it shot? Any time close to her death?"

"I don't know much about that. She was out of town a lot on weekends, Los Angeles, San Francisco. Could have been one of those trips. I really couldn't say for sure."

"So it was not something you discussed."

He shook his head. "She enjoyed being tight-lipped. I think it made her feel powerful. I learned not to pry into her personal affairs."

"Any idea why she did the film? Was it money?"

"I doubt it. Producer probably cleans up, but the actors get a flat rate. At least from what I've heard," he said. "Maybe she did it for the same reason she did anything. Lorna flirted with disaster every day of her life. If you want my theory, fear was the only real sensation she felt. Danger was like a drug. She had to boost the dose. She couldn't help herself. Didn't seem to matter what anyone said. I used to talk 'til I was blue in the face. It never made any difference as far as I could see. This is just my observation, and I could be all wrong, but you asked and I'm answering. She'd act like she was listening. She'd act like she agreed with every word you said, but then it washed right over her. She went right on doing it, whatever it was. She was like an addict, a junkie. She knew the life wasn't good, but she couldn't make the break."

"Did she trust you?"

"I wouldn't say that. Not really. Lorna didn't trust anyone. She was like Beauty in that respect. She might have trusted me more than most."

"Why was that?"

"I never came on to her, so I wasn't any kind of threat. With no sexual investment, she couldn't lose with me. She couldn't win, either, but that suited us both. With Lorna, you had to keep your distance. She was the kind of woman, the minute you got involved, it was over, pal. That was the end of it. The only way you could hold on to her was to keep her at arm's length. I knew the rule, but I couldn't always manage it. I was hooked myself. I kept wanting to save her, and it couldn't be done."

"Did she tell you what was going on in her life?"

"Some things. Trivia, for the most part. Just the day-to-day stuff.

She never confided anything important. Events, but not feelings. You know what I mean? Even then, I doubt she ever really leveled with me. I knew some things, but not always because she told me."

"How'd you get your information?"

"I have buddies around town. I'd get frustrated with her behavior. She'd swear she was playing straight, but I guess she really couldn't give it up. Next thing you know, she'd be picking up guys. Twosomes, threesomes, anything you want. People would see her and make a point of telling me, worried I was getting in over my head."

"And were you?"

His smile was bitter. "I didn't think so at the time."

"Did the rumors bother you?"

"Hell, yes. What she did was dangerous, and I was worried sick. I didn't like what she was doing, and I didn't like people running in here talking about her behind her back. Tattletales. I hate that. I couldn't get them to quit. With her, I tried to keep my mouth shut. It was none of my business, but I kept getting sucked in. I'd be saying, 'Why, babe? What's the point?' And she'd shake her head. 'You don't want to know, Heck. I promise. It's got nothing to do with you.' The truth is, I don't think *she* knew. It was a compulsion, like a sneeze. It felt good to do it. If she held off, something tickled until it drove her nuts."

"You have any idea who was in her life besides you?"

"I wasn't *in* her life. I was on the fringe. Way out here. She had a day job, part-time at the water treatment plant. You might talk to them, see if they can fill you in. Most times, I never even saw her before three A.M. She might've had some other kind of life entirely when the sun was up."

"Ah. Well. Food for thought," I said. "Anything else I should know?"

"Not that I can think of offhand. If something occurs to me, I can get in touch. You have a card?"

I fished one out and placed it on the console. He looked at it briefly and left it where it was.

I said, "Thanks for your time."

"I hope I've been of help. I hate the idea someone got away with murder."

"This is a start, at any rate. I may be back at some point." I hesitated, glancing at the dog still lying there between us. The minute she sensed my look, she rose to her feet, which put her head just about level with the stool where I was perched. She kept her eyes straight ahead, gazing intently at the flesh on my hip, possibly with an eye toward a late evening snack.

"Beauty," he murmured with scarcely any change of tone.

She sank to the floor, but I could tell she was still thinking about a jaw full of gluteus maximus.

"Next time I'll bring her a bone," I said. Preferably not mine.

I headed home through the business district, following a trail of stoplights that winked from red to green. The storefronts had been secured, plate-glass windows ablaze with fluorescent lighting. The streets were bleached white with the spill of illumination. I passed a lone man on a bike, dressed in black. It was almost 1:30 A.M., traffic minimal, intersections wide and deserted. Most of the bars in town were still open, and in another half hour or so, all the drunks would emerge, heading for the various downtown parking structures. Many buildings were dark. The homeless, bundled in sleep, blocked the doorways like toppled statues. For them, the night is like a vast hotel where there's always a room available. The only price they pay, sometimes, is their lives.

At 1:45 I finally stripped off my jeans, brushed my teeth, and doused the lights, crawling into bed without bothering to remove my T-shirt, underpants, and socks. These February nights were too cold to sleep naked. As I eased toward unconsciousness, I found myself mentally replaying select portions of Lorna's tape. Ah, the life of the single woman in a world ruled by sexually transmitted diseases. I lay there, trying to think back to when I'd last had sex. I couldn't even remember, which was *really* worrisome. I fell asleep wondering if there was a cause-and-effect relationship between memory loss and abstinence. Apparently so, as that was the last thing I was aware of for the next four hours.

When the alarm went off at 6:00 A.M., I rolled out of bed before my resistance came up. I pulled on my sweats and my running shoes, then headed into the bathroom, where I brushed my teeth, avoiding the sight of myself in the mirror. One ill-advised glance had revealed a face fat with sleep and hair as stiff and matted as a derelict's. I'd snipped it off six months before with a trusty little pair of nail scissors, but I hadn't done much to it since. Now the sections that weren't sticking straight up were either flat or adrift. I was really going to have to do something about it one of these days.

Given the four hours of sleep, my run was a bit on the perfunctory side. Often I tune in to the look of the beach, letting sea birds and kelp scent carry me along. Jogging becomes a meditation, shifting time into high gear. This was one of those days when exercise simply failed to uplift. In lieu of euphoria, I had to make my peace with three hundred calories' worth of sweat, screaming thighs, and burning lungs. I tacked on an extra half mile to atone for my indifference and then did a fast walk back to my place as a way of cooling down. I showered and slipped into fresh jeans and a black turtleneck, over which I pulled a heavy gray cotton sweater.

I perched on a wooden stool at the kitchen table and ate a bowl of cereal. I scanned the local paper in haste. No surprises there. While floods threatened the Midwest, the Santa Teresa rainfall averages were down and there was already speculation of another drought in the making. January and February were usually rainy, but the weather had been capricious. Storms approached the coast and then hovered, as if flirting, refusing us the wet kiss of precipitation. High-pressure systems held all the rains at bay. The skies clouded over, brooding, but yielded nothing in the end. It was frustrating stuff.

Turning to happier items, I read that one of the big oil companies was talking about building a new refinery somewhere on the south coast. That would be a handsome addition to the local landscape. A bank robbery, a conflict between land developers and opposing members of the county board of supervisors. I scanned the funnies while I sucked down my coffee and then headed into the office, where I spent the next several hours assembling the balance of my tax receipts. Obnoxious. Having finished, I pulled out a standard boilerplate contract and typed in the details of my agreement with the Keplers. I spent the bulk of the day finishing the final report on a case I'd just done. The closing bill, with expenses, was something over two thousand bucks. It wasn't much, but it kept the rent paid and my insurance intact.

At five, I put a call through to Janice, figuring she'd be up by then. Trinny, the younger of the two daughters, answered the telephone. She was a chatty little thing. When I identified myself, she said her mother's alarm was set to go off any minute. Berlyn was making a run to the bank, and her father was on his way home from a job. That took care of just about everyone. Janice had given me the address, but Trinny filled in directions, sounding pleasant enough.

I retrieved my car from the public lot several blocks away. A steady stream of moving cars spiraled down the ramp as shoppers and office workers headed home. As I drove up Capillo Hill, the very air seemed gray, sueded with twilight. Streetlights flicked on like a series of paper lanterns strung festively from pole to pole.

Janice and Mace Kepler owned a little house on the Bluffs in a neighborhood that must have been established for merchants and tradesmen in the early fifties. Many streets overlooked the Pacific, and in theory the area should have been pricey real estate. In reality there was too much fog. Painted exteriors peeled, aluminum surfaces became pitted, and wooden roof shingles warped from the constant damp. Wind whistled off the ocean, forcing lawns into patchiness. The neighborhoods themselves were comprised almost entirely of tract housing—single-family dwellings thrown up in an era when construction was cheap and the floor plans could be purchased by mail from magazines.

The Keplers had apparently done what they could. The yellow paint on the board-and-batten siding looked as if it had been applied within the year. The shutters were white, and a white split-rail fence had been constructed to define the yard. The lawn had been replaced by dense ivy, which seemed to be growing everywhere, including halfway up the two trees in the yard.

In the driveway, there was a blue panel truck emblazoned with a large cartoon replica of a faucet. A big teardrop of water hung from the spout. MACE KEPLER'S PLUMBING • HEATING • AIR was lettered in white across the truck body. A small oblong emblem indicated that Kepler was a member of PHCC, the National Association of Plumbing, Heating, and Cooling Contractors. His state license number was listed along with the twenty-four-hour emergency repairs he provided (water leaks, sewer drains, gas leaks, and water heaters) and the credit cards he took. These days doctors don't offer services that comprehensive.

I pulled into the gravel driveway and parked my vehicle behind his. I left the car unlocked and peered briefly into the backyard before I climbed the low concrete steps to the front porch. Somebody in the family had a passion for fruit trees. A veritable orchard of citrus had been planted at the rear of the lot. At this season all the branches were bare, but come summer the dark green foliage would be lush and dense, fruit tucked among the leaves like Christmas ornaments.

I rang the bell. There were muddy work shoes by the door mat. There was only a brief pause before Mace Kepler opened the door. I had to guess he'd been alerted to watch for my arrival. Given my incurable inclination to snoop, I was happy I hadn't paused to riffle through his mailbox.

We introduced ourselves, and he stepped back to admit me. Even in his leather bedroom slippers, he was probably six feet four to my five feet six. He wore a plaid shirt and work pants. He was in his sixties, quite hefty, with a broad face and a receding hairline. His deeply cleft chin seemed to have a period buried at its center, and a vertical worry line, like a slash mark, dissected the space between his eyes. On residential jobs he probably hired younger, smaller guys to navigate the crawl space underneath the house. "Janice's in the shower, but she'll be right out. Can I offer you a beer? I'm having one myself. I just got home from a hell of a day."

"No thanks," I said. "I hope I haven't picked a bad time." I waited by the door while he lumbered toward the kitchen to fetch himself a beer.

"Don't worry about it. This is fine," he said. "I just haven't had a chance to unwind yet. This is my daughter Trinny."

Trinny glanced up with a brief smile and then went about her work, pouring a cocoa-brown batter into a nine-by-thirteen aluminum cake pan. The hand mixer, its beaters still dripping brown goo, sat on the kitchen counter beside an open box of Duncan Hines chocolate cake mix. Trinny tucked the pan in the oven and set a timer shaped like a lemon. She'd already opened a cardboard container of ready-mix fudge frosting, and I'd have bet money she'd helped herself to a fingerful. While my aunt had never really taught me to bake, she'd warned me repeatedly about the ignominy of the commercial cake mix, which she ranked right up there with instant coffee and bottled garlic salt.

Trinny was barefoot, wearing an oversize white T-shirt and a pair of ragged blue jean cutoffs. Judging from the size of her butt, she'd conjured up quite a few homemade cakes in her day. Mace opened the refrigerator door and took out a beer. He found the flip in a drawer and levered off the cap, tossing the bottle top in a brown paper trash bag as he passed it.

Trinny and I murmured a "hi" to one another. Berlyn, the older daughter, emerged from the hallway, wearing a pair of black tights with a man's white broadcloth dress shirt over them. Again, Mace introduced us, and we exchanged inconsequential greetings of the "hi, how are you" type. She was intent on rolling up her sleeves as she crossed into the open kitchen. She paused beside Trinny and held her arm out for assistance. Trinny wiped her hands and began to roll up Berlyn's sleeve.

At first glance, they were sufficiently similar to be mistaken for twins. They seemed to favor their father, both big girls and buxom with heavy legs and thighs. Berlyn was a dyed blonde, with big blue eyes framed in dark lashes. She had a clear, pale complexion and a lush full mouth, vibrant with glossy pink lipstick. Trinny had opted for her natural hair color: a double fudge brown, probably the shade Berlyn was born with. Both had bright blue eyes and dark brows. Berlyn's features were the coarser, or perhaps it was the bleached hair that gave her the appearance of tartishness. Without Lorna's delicate beauty in the family for contrast, I would have said they were pretty in a slightly vulgar way. Even knowing what I knew about Lorna's promiscuity, she seemed to have had a classiness about her that the other two lacked.

Berlyn moved over to the refrigerator and pulled out a diet Pepsi. She popped the tab and ambled out the back door onto a wooden deck that ran along the back of the house. Through the window, I watched as she settled on a chaise made of interwoven plastic strips. It seemed too chilly to be sitting out there. Her eyes caught mine briefly before she looked away.

Beer in hand, Mace moved through the kitchen toward the den, indicating that I was to follow. As he closed the door behind us, I picked up the chemical scent of baking chocolate cake.

5

The den had been added onto the house by framing in one-half of the two-car garage. Subflooring had been laid over the original concrete, and look-like-oak tongue-and-groove vinyl planks had been installed on top of that. Even with the addition of an area rug, the room smelled like motor oil and old car parts. A sofa bed, coffee table, four chairs, an ottoman, and a rolling cart for the television set had been arranged in the space. In one corner was a filing cabinet and a desk piled high with papers. All of the furniture looked like garage sale purchases: mismatched fabrics, worn upholstery, someone else's discards given another chance in life.

Mace sank onto a battered brown Naugahyde lounger, activating the mechanism that flipped the footrest into place. His mouth was crowded with bad teeth. The flesh along his jaw had softened with age, and he now had parentheses setting off the thin line of his mouth. He picked up the TV remote, punched the mute button, and then clicked his way through several channels until he found a basketball game in progress. Silently, guys bounded up and down the court, leapt, fell, and bumped one another sideways. If the sound had been turned up, I knew I'd hear the high-pitched shriek of rubber soles on the hardwood floor. The ball sailed into the basket as if magnetized, not even touching the rim half the time.

Without invitation, I perched on the nearby ottoman, arranging myself so I was in his line of sight. "I take it Janice has told you about our conversation last night." I was prepared to make soothing noises about Lorna's participation in the pornographic film. Mace made no response. A fast-food commercial came on, a fifteen-by-twenty-inch full-color burger filling the TV screen. The sesame seeds were the size of rice grains, and a slice of bright orange cheese drooped invitingly from the edge of the bun. I could see Mace's eyes fix on the picture. I'd always known I wasn't as compelling as a flame-broiled beef patty, but it was deflating nonetheless to see his attention displaced. I moved my head to the left, entering his visual frame of reference.

"She told me she wants to hire you to look into Lorna's death," he said as though prompted by someone off stage.

"How do you feel about it?"

He began to tap on the chair arm. "Up to Janice," he said. "I don't mean to sound crass, but her and me have a difference of opinion with regard to that. She believes Lorna was murdered, but I'm not convinced. It could have been a gas leak. Could have been carbon monoxide poisoning from a faulty furnace." He had a big voice and big hands.

"Lorna's cabin had a furnace? I was under the impression her living quarters were pretty crude."

A brief look of impatience flashed across his face. "Janice does the same thing. She takes everything literal. I'm just giving an *example*. Every item in that cabin was either old or broke down. You have a heater that's defective, and you can get yourself in a peck of trouble. That's the point I was trying to make. I see it all the time. Hell, that's what I do for a living."

"I assume the police looked into the possibility of a gas leak."

He shrugged that one off, hunching one beefy shoulder while he worked out a kink. "Bunged myself on the back, trying to wrench a pipe off a slab," he said. "I don't know what the police did. Point is, I think this whole business ought to be laid to rest. Seems to me this speculation about murder is just another way of keeping the subject open for discussion. I loved my daughter. She's as near perfect as you could want. She's a beautiful, sweet girl, but she's dead now, and nothing's going to change that. We got two daughters living, and we need to focus our attention on them for a change. You start hiring lawyers and detectives, all you're going to have is a lot of unnecessary expense in addition to the heartache."

I could feel my inner ears prick up. No outrage, no protest, no reference whatever to all the licking and sucking? To me, Lorna's prurient behavior left her short of "near perfect" and put her closer to "wanton." Being wild didn't make her bad, but the word *sweet* was not quite the word that leapt to *my* mind. I said, "Maybe the two of you need to have another chat about this. I told her last night you'd have to agree."

"Well, we're not *in* agreement. I think the woman's got her head up her butt, but if that's what she wants, I'm willing to go along with it. We're all of us coping any way we can. If this makes her feel good, I won't interfere, but that doesn't mean I *agree* with her on the issue."

Oh, boy. Wait until the man saw the bill for my services. I didn't want to be caught in the middle of *that* dispute. "What about Trinny and Berlyn? Have you discussed this with them?"

"It's not up to them. It's me and her make decisions. The girls live at home, but we're the ones pay the bills."

"I guess what I'm really asking is how they're coping with Lorna's death."

"Oh. I guess we don't tend to talk about that much. You'd have to ask them yourself. I'm trying to put this behind us, not keep it all stirred up."

"Some people find it helpful to talk about these things. That's how they process what they've experienced."

"I hope I don't sound like a surly so-and-so on the subject, but I'm just the opposite. I'd just as soon drop it and get on with life."

"Would you object to my talking with them?"

"That's between you and them, as far as I'm concerned. They're grown-ups. As long as they're willing, you can talk all you want."

"Maybe I'll catch them before I leave. We don't necessarily have to talk today, but I'd like to have a conversation with each of them soon. It's always possible Lorna confided something that might turn out to be significant."

"I doubt it, but you can ask."

"What hours do they work?"

"Berl mans the phone here eight to five. I got a pager, and she makes sure I know about emergencies. She keeps my books, pays the bills, and handles the deposits. Trinny's in the process of looking for work. She got laid off last month, so she's here most of the time."

"What's she do?"

The series of commercials had finally come to an end, and his attention was focused on the TV set again. Two ex-athletes in suits were discussing the game. I let the matter pass, thinking I could ask her myself.

There was a knock at the den door, and Janice peered in. "Oh, hi. Trinny said you were here. I hope I'm not interrupting." She came into the den and closed the door behind her, bringing with her the scent of shower soap, deodorant, and damp hair. She was wearing a red-and-white-checked shirt and red polyester stretch pants. "I got a regular uniform for work," she said, her glance following mine. She looked spiffier than I did, polyester or no. "Did anyone offer you a beverage?" I was surprised she didn't pull out an order pad and pen.

"Thanks, but I'm fine. Mace offered earlier." I reached into my handbag and took out the contract, which I laid on the coffee table. "I stopped by with this. I hope I'm not interrupting your supper preparations."

She waved a hand. "Don't worry about it. Trinny's taken care of that. Ever since she got laid off, it's like having live-in help. We don't eat until eight, which is hours from now anyway. Meantime, how've you been? I hope you got enough sleep. You look tired."

"I am, but I'm hoping to catch up tonight. I don't know how you work the night shift. It would kill me."

"You get used to it. Actually, I prefer it. A whole different set of people come in at night. By the way, that offer of coffee still stands if you're ever up in that area when I'm on shift." She picked up the contract, a simple one-page document spelling out the terms of our agreement. "I guess I better read this before I sign. How does this work? Is this hourly or flat fee?"

"Fifty bucks an hour plus expenses," I said. "I'll submit a written report once a week. We can touch base by phone as often as you like. The agreement authorizes my services and expenditures up to five thousand dollars. Anything beyond that, we'll discuss if the time comes. You may decide you don't want to proceed, and if so, that's the end of it."

"You'll probably need an advance. Isn't that how this is done?"

"Generally," I said. We spent a few minutes talking about the particulars while Mace watched the game.

"This looks all right to me. Honey, what do you think?"

She held out the contract for him, but he ignored her. She turned back to me. "I'll be right back. The checkbook's in the other room. Will a thousand dollars be all right?"

"That'd be fine," I said. She left the room, and I turned my attention to him. "It will save me some time if you can give me the names and addresses of Lorna's friends."

"She didn't have any friends. She didn't have enemies, either, at least as far as we know."

"What about her landlord? I'll need his address."

"Twenty-six Mission Run Road. Name is J. D. Burke. Her place was at the back of his property. I imagine he'd give you the tour if you ask him nice."

"You have any idea why she might have been killed?"

"I already told you my opinion," he said.

Janice returned to the room, catching my last remark and his response. "Ignore him. He's a pill," she said. She took a swat at his head. "You behave yourself."

She sat down on the couch with her checkbook in hand. From the glimpse I caught of the check register, it looked as though it had been a while since she'd done her subtraction. She seemed to favor rounding everything off to the nearest dollar, which made all the amounts end in zero. She wrote out the check, tore it off, and passed it over to me, making a note of the check number and the sum. Then she scribbled her name at the bottom of the contract and handed it to Mace. He took the pen and added his signature without glancing at the terms. The very gesture conveyed, not indifference, but something close to it. I've been in business long enough to smell trouble, and I made up my mind to have Janice pay me as we went along. If I waited to submit a final bill of any substance, Mace would probably get his undies in a bundle and refuse to pay.

I glanced at my watch. "I better go," I said. "I have an appointment in fifteen minutes on the other side of town." I was lying, of course, but these people were beginning to give me a stomachache. "Could you walk me out?" I asked.

Janice stood up when I did. "Be happy to," she said.

"Nice meeting you," I murmured to Mace as I departed.

"Yeah, ditto for sure."

Neither Berlyn nor Trinny was visible as we passed through the living room on our way to the door. As soon as we hit the front porch, I said, "Janice, what's going on here? Have you told him about the tape? He doesn't act like he knows, and you swore you would do that."

"Well, I know, but I haven't had a chance yet. He'd already gone to work when I got home this morning. This is the first opportunity I've had. I didn't want to mention it in front of Berlyn or Trinny. . . ."

"Why not? They have a right to know what she was up to. Suppose they have information that's relevant. Maybe they're holding something back, trying to be protective of the two of you."

"Oh. I hadn't thought of that. Do you really think so?"

"It's certainly possible," I said.

"I guess I could tell them, but I hate to tarnish her memory when it's all we have."

"My investigation may turn up worse than that."

"Oh, Lord, I hope not. What makes you say that?"

"Wait a minute. Let's stop this. I can't be effective if you keep on playing games."

"I'm not playing games," she said, her tone indignant.

"Yes, you are. You can knock off the bullshit about Lorna, for starters. The detective I talked to says you knew what she was doing because he told you himself."

"He did not!"

"I don't want to get into this 'did too, did not' stuff. I'm telling you what he said."

"Well, he's a damn liar, and you can tell him that's what *I* said."

"I'll convey your position. The *point* is, you promised to tell Mace about the video. You're lucky I didn't open my big mouth and put my foot in it. I came this close to mentioning it."

"That'd be all right," she said with caution, apparently mistaking my statement for an offer.

"I bet that'd be all right with *you*. You figure he's already hostile toward me, so what difference would it make? I can just imagine his reaction. Hey, no thanks. That's your job, and you better be quick."

"I'll raise the subject at supper."

"The sooner the better. Just don't leave me in the position of knowing more than he does. He's going to feel foolish enough as it is."

"I said I'd take care of it," she said. Her manner was frosty, but I didn't care.

We parted company on that slightly strained note.

I stopped by the bank on my way through town and deposited the check. I wasn't convinced the damn thing wouldn't bounce, and if I'd had any sense, I'd have waited until it cleared before I did any further work. I intended to head home. Under the trees, the February twilight had accumulated shadows. I was looking forward to an early supper and a good night's sleep. In the interest of efficiency, I did a detour as far as Mission Run Road in search of Lorna's former landlord. If he was home, I'd have a quick chat. If he was out, I'd leave a card with a note asking him to get in touch.

The house was a two-story Victorian structure: white frame with green shutters and a wrap-around porch. Like many such homes in Santa Teresa, this had probably been the main residence on agricultural land of considerable acreage. There was a time when this parcel would have been on the outskirts of town instead of close to its center. I could picture the orchards and fields being subdivided, other houses encroaching while owner after owner put money in the bank. Now what remained was probably less than six acres populated with old trees and the suggestion of outbuildings converted to other use.

As I moved up the walk, I could hear voices, one male, one female, raised in anger, though the subject matter wasn't audible. A door slammed. The man yelled something else, but the point was lost. I went up wooden steps that were rough with flaking gray paint. The front door was standing open, the screen on the latch. I rang the bell. I could see linoleum in the hallway and on the right, stairs going up to the second-floor landing. One portion of the hallway had been sectioned off with two accordion gates, one near the stairway, the other halfway to the kitchen. Burke had a puppy or a kid, it was hard to say. Lights were on at the back of the house. I rang the bell again. A man called out from the kitchen and then appeared, heading in my direction with a dish towel tucked in his belt. He flipped on the porch light, peering out at me.

"Are you J. D. Burke?" I asked.

"That's right." His smile was tentative. He was in his mid- to late forties, with a lean face and good teeth, though one was chipped in front. He had deep creases on either side of his mouth and a fan of wrinkles at the outer corners of his eyes.

"My name is Kinsey Millhone. I'm a private investigator. Lorna Kepler's mother hired me to look into her death. Can you spare a few minutes?"

He glanced back over his shoulder and then shrugged to himself. "Sure, as long as you don't mind watching me cook." He unlatched the screen and held it open for me. "Kitchen's back here. Watch your feet," he said. He sidestepped an array of plastic blocks as he moved down the hall. "My wife thinks playpens are too confining for kids, so she lets Jack play here, where he can see what's going on." I could see that Jack had smeared peanut butter on all the stair spindles he could reach.

I followed J.D. down a chilly hallway, made darker by mahogany woodwork and wallpaper somber with age. I wondered if the art experts could brighten the finish by cleaning away the soot, restoring all the colors to their once clear tones like an old masterpiece. On the other hand, how colorful could pale brown cabbage roses get?

The kitchen was someone's depressing attempt to "modernize" what had probably been a utility porch to begin with. The countertops were covered with linoleum, rimmed with a band of metal where a line of dark gray grunge had collected. The wooden cabinets were thick with lime-green paint. The stove and refrigerator both appeared to be new, incongruous white appliances sticking out into the room. An oak table and two chairs had been tucked into an alcove, where a bay of windows with built-in benches looked out onto a tangled yard. The room was at least warmer than the hall we'd passed through.

"Have a seat."

"I'm fine. I can't stay long," I said. Really, I was reluctant to park my rear end on seats that were sticky with little fingerprints. A short person, probably Jack, had made the rounds of the room, leaving a chair rail of grape jelly that extended as far as the back door, which opened onto a small glass-enclosed porch.

J.D. leaned toward the burner and turned the flame up under his skillet while I leaned against the doorjamb. His hair was a mild brown, thinning on top, slightly shaggy across his ears. He wore a blue denim work shirt, faded blue jeans, and dusty boots. A white paper packet marked with butcher's crayon sat on the counter, along with a pile of diced onions and garlic. He added olive oil to the skillet. I do love to watch men cook.

"J.D.?" A woman's voiced reached us from the front of the house.

"Yeah?"

"Who's at the door?"

He looked toward the corridor behind me, and I turned as she approached. "This lady's a private investigator looking into Lorna's death. This is my wife, Leda. Sorry, but your name slipped right by me." With the oil hot, he scooped up the onions and minced garlic and dropped them in the pan.

I turned and held my hand out. "Kinsey Millhone. Nice to meet you."

We shook hands. Leda was exotic, a child-woman scarcely half Burke's height and probably half his age. She couldn't have been more than twenty-two or twenty-three, small and frail with a dark pixie cut. Her proffered fingers were cold, and her handshake was passive.

Burke said, "Actually, you might know Leda's dad. He's a private investigator, too."

"Really? What's his name?"

"Kurt Selkirk. He's semiretired now, but he's been around for years. Leda's his youngest. He's got five more just like her, a whole passel of girls."

"Of course I know Kurt," I said. "Next time you talk to him, tell him I said hi." Kurt Selkirk had made his living for years doing electronic surveillance, and he had a reputation as a sleazebag. Since Public Law 90-351 was passed in June of 1968, "anyone who willfully uses, endeavors to use, or procures any other person to use or endeavor to use any electronic, mechanical, or other device to intercept any oral communication" was subject to fines of not more than $10,000 or imprisonment for not more than five years. I knew for a fact that Selkirk had risked both penalties on a regular basis. Most private investigators in his age range had made a living, once upon a time, eavesdropping on cheating spouses. Now the no-fault divorce laws had changed much of that. In his case, the decision to retire was probably the result of lawsuits and threats by the federal government. I was glad he'd left the business, but I didn't mention that. "What sort of work do you do?" I asked J.D.

"Electrician," he said.

Meanwhile Leda, smiling faintly, moved past me in a cloud of musk cologne. Any oxen in the area would have been inflamed. Her eye makeup was elaborate: smoky eye shadow, black eyeliner, brows plucked into graceful arches. Her skin was very pale, her bones as delicate as a bird's. The outfit she was wearing was a long, white sleeveless tunic, cut low on her bony chest, and gauzy white harem pants, through which her thin legs were clearly visible. I couldn't believe she wasn't freezing. Her sandals were the type that always drive me insane, with thin leather straps coming up between the toes.

She moved out onto the glassed-in porch, where she busied herself with a swaddled infant, which she lifted from a wicker carriage. She brought the infant to the kitchen table, sliding onto the bench seat. She bared her quite weensie left breast, deftly affixing the baby like some kind of milking apparatus. As far as I could tell, the child hadn't made a sound, but it may have emitted a signal audible only to its mother. Jack, the toddler, was probably off somewhere finger painting with the contents of his diaper.

"I was hoping to see Lorna's cabin, but I didn't know if you had tenants in there at this point." I noticed Leda watched me carefully while I talked to him.

"Cabin's empty. You can go on back if you want. There hasn't been a way to rent it since the body was found. Word gets out and nobody wants to touch it, especially the shape she was in." Burke held his nose with exaggerated distaste.

Embarrassed, Leda said, "J.D.!" as if he'd made a rude noise with his butt.

"It's the truth," he said. He opened the butcher's packet and took out a pillow of raw ground beef, which he plunked into the skillet on top of the sautéed onions. He began to break up the bulk meat with his spatula. I could still see the densely packed noodles of beef where the meat had emerged from the grinder. Looked like worms to me. The hot skillet was turning the bottom of the bulk ground beef from pale pink to gray. I'm giving up meat. I swear to God I am.

"Can you remodel the place?"

"Right now I don't have the bucks, and it probably wouldn't help. It's just a shack."

"What was she paying?"

"Three hundred a month. Might sound like a lot unless you compare it to other rentals in the area. It's really like a one-bed-room with a wood-burning stove I finally took out. People know a place is empty, and they'll steal you blind. They'll take all the lightbulbs if nothing else."

I noticed that in typical landlord assessment, the "shack" had been elevated to a "one-bedroom apartment." "Did someone live there before she did?"

"Nope. My parents used to own the property, and I inherited when Mom died, along with some other rentals on the far side of town. I met Lorna through some people at the plant where she worked. We got talking one afternoon, and she told me she was looking for a place with some privacy. She'd heard about the cabin and asked if she could see it. She fell in love with it. I told her, 'Look, it's a mess, but if you want to fix it up, it'd be fine with me.' She moved in two weeks later without really doing much."

"Was she a party person?"

"Not to my knowledge."

"What about friends? Did she have a lot of people back there?"

"I really couldn't say. It's way back in the back. There's like this little private dirt road going in off the side street. You want to see it, you probably ought to drive your car around and come in that way. Used to be a path between the two places, but we don't use it anymore, and it's overgrown by now. Most of the time, I didn't see if she had company or not because the foliage is so dense. Winters I might catch lights, but I never paid much attention."

"Did you know she was hustling?"

He looked at me blankly.

"Turning tricks," Leda said.

J.D. looked from her face to mine. "What she did was her business. I never considered it my concern." If he was startled by the revelation, it didn't show on his face. His mouth curved down in a display of skepticism while he poked at the cooking beef. "Where'd you hear about that?" he asked me.

"From a vice detective. Apparently, a lot of hookers work the classy hotels where the high rollers hang out. Lorna had done outcall, but she upgraded to independent."

"I guess I'll have to take your word for it."

"So as far as you knew, she didn't bring clients here."

"Why would she do that? You want to impress a fella, you'd hardly bring 'em back to some little shack in the woods. You'd be better off at the hotel. That way he'd get stuck for all the drinks and stuff."

"That makes sense," I said. "I gather she was careful to keep her private life private, so she probably didn't like to mix the two, anyway. Tell me about the day you found her."

"Wasn't me. It was someone else," he said. "I'd been out of town, up at Lake Nacimiento for a couple of weeks. I don't remember the exact timetable offhand. I got home, and I was taking care of some bills came in while I was gone and realized I didn't have her rent check. I tried calling a bunch of times and never got any answer. Anyway, couple days after that, this woman came to the door. She'd been trying to get in touch with Lorna herself, and she'd gone back there to leave her a note. Soon as she got close, she picked up the stink. She came and knocked on our door and asked us to call the police. She said she was pretty sure it was a dead body, but I felt like I ought to check it out first."

"You hadn't noticed anything before?"

"I'd been aware of something smelling bad, but I didn't think much of it. I remember the guy across the street was complaining, but it wasn't like either one of us really thought it was *human*. Possum or something. Could have been a dog or a deer. There's a surprising amount of wildlife around here."

"Did you see the body?"

"No ma'am. Not me. I got as far as the porch and turned around and came back. I didn't even knock. Man, I knew something was *wrong*, and I didn't want to be the one to find out what it was. I called 911 and they sent a cop car. Even the officer had a hard time. Had to hold a handkerchief across his mouth." J.D. crossed to the pantry, where he took out a couple of cans of tomato sauce. He took the crank-style can opener from a nearby drawer and began to remove the lid on the first can.

"You think she was murdered?"

"She was too young to die without some kind of help," he said. He dumped the contents of the first can into the skillet and then cranked open the second. The warm, garlicky smell of tomato sauce wafted up from the pan, and I was already thinking maybe meat wasn't so bad. Other people's cooking always makes me faint with hunger. Must be the equivalent of lost mothering. "Any theories?"

"Not a one."

I turned to Leda. "What about you?"

"I didn't know her that well. We put the vegetable garden back in that corner of the property, so I'd sometimes see her when I went back there to pick beans."

"No friends in common?"

"Not really. J.D. knew Lorna's supervisor out at the water treatment plant. That's how she heard we had a cabin in the first place. Other than that, we didn't socialize. J.D. doesn't like to get too chummy with the tenants."

"Yeah. First thing you know they're giving you excuses instead of the rent check," he said.

"What about Lorna? Did she pay on time?"

"She was good about that. At least until the last one. Otherwise, I wouldn't have let it ride," he said. "I kept thinking she'd bring it by."

"Did you ever meet any friends of hers?"

"Not that I remember." He turned to look at Leda, who shook her head in the negative.

"Anything else you can think of that might help?"

I got murmured denials from both.

I took out a business card and jotted my home phone on the back. "If anything occurs to you, would you give me a buzz? You can call either number. I have machines on both. I'll take a look at the cabin and get back to you if there's a question."

"Watch the bugs," he said. "There's some biggies out there."

6

I nosed the VW down the narrow dirt road that cut into the property close to the rear lot line. The lane had once been black-topped, but now the surface was cracked and graying, overgrown with crab-grass. My headlights swept along the two rows of live oaks that defined the rutted pathway. The branches, interlocking overhead, formed a tunnel of darkness through which I passed. Shrubbery that once might have been neatly trimmed and shaped now spilled in a tumble that made progress slow. Granted, my car may have seen better days, but I was reluctant to let branches snap against the pale blue paint. The potholes were already acting on my shock absorbers like a factory test.

I reached a clearing where a crude cabin loomed in the shadows. I did a three-point turn, positioning the car so I could avoid backing out. I doused the lights. The illusion of privacy was immediate and profound. I could hear crickets in the underbrush. Otherwise, there was silence. It was hard to believe there were other houses nearby, flanked by city streets. The dim illumination from streetlights didn't penetrate this far, and the sound of traffic was reduced to the mild hush of a distant tide. The area felt like a wilderness, yet my office downtown couldn't have been more than ten minutes away.

Peering toward the main house, I could see nothing but the thick growth of saplings, ancient live oaks, and a few shaggy evergreens. Even with the limbs bare on the occasional deciduous tree, the distant lights were obscured. I popped open the glove compartment and took out a flashlight. I tested the beam and found that the batteries were strong. I tucked my handbag in the backseat and locked the car as I got out. About fifty feet away, between me and the main house, I could see the skeletal tepee constructions for the pole beans in the now abandoned garden. The air smelled densely of damp moss and eucalyptus.

I moved up the steps to the wooden porch that ran along the front of the cabin. The front door had been removed from its hinges and now leaned against the wall to one side of the opening. I flipped the light switch, relieved to note the electrical power was still connected. There was only one fixture overhead, with a forty-watt bulb that bathed the rooms in drab light. There was little, if any, insulation, and the place was dead cold. While all the window-panes were intact, a fine soot had settled in every crevice and crack. Dead insects lined the sills. In one corner of the window frame, a spider had wrapped a fly in a white silken sleeping bag. The air smelled of mold, corroded metal, and spoiled water sitting fallow in the plumbing joints. A section of the wooden floor in the main room had been sawed away by the crime scene unit, the gaping hole covered over with a sheet of warped plywood. I picked my way carefully around that. Just above my head, something thumped and scampered through the attic. I imagined squirrels squeezing into roof vents, building nests for their babies. The beam of my flashlight picked up countless artifacts of the ten months of neglect: rodent droppings, dead leaves, small pyramids of debris created by the termites.

The interior living space was arranged in an L, with a narrow bathroom built into its innermost angle. The plumbing was shared between the bathroom and the kitchenette, with a dining area that wrapped around the corner to the "living" room. I could see the metal plate in the floor to which the wood-burning stove had been affixed. The walls, painted white, were dotted with daddy longlegs, and I found myself keeping an uneasy eye on them as I toured the premises. To one side of the front door was the Belltone box for the doorbell, about the size of a cigarette pack. Someone had popped the housing away from the wall, and I could see that the interior mechanism was missing. An electrical wire, sheathed in green plastic, had been cut and now drooped sideways like a wilted flower stem with the blossom gone.

Lorna's sleeping area had probably been tucked into the short arm of the L. The kitchen cabinets were empty, linoleum-lined shelves still gritty with cornmeal and old cereal dust. Karo syrup or molasses had oozed onto the surface, and I could see circles where the bottoms of the canned goods had formed rings. I checked the bathroom, which was devoid of exterior windows. The toilet was old, the tank tall and narrow. The bowl itself protruded in front, like a porcelain Adam's apple. The brown wood seat was cracked and looked as if it would pinch you in places you cherished. The sink was the size of a dishpan, supported on two metal legs. I tried the cold-water faucet, jumping back with a shriek when a shot of brown water spurted out. The water pipes began to make a low-pitched humming sound, sirens in the underground announcing the crime of trespass. The bathtub rested on ball feet. Dead leaves had collected in a swirling pattern near the drain, while black swans glided across an opaque green plastic shower curtain that hung from an elliptical metal frame.

In the main room, despite the lack of furniture, I could surmise how the space had been used. Close to the front door, dents in the pine flooring suggested the placement of a couch and two chairs. I pictured a small wooden dinette set at the other end of the living room where it turned the corner into the kitchen. To one side of the sink, there was a small cabinet with a phone jack attached just above the baseboard. Lorna probably had a portable phone or a long extension cord, which would have allowed her to keep the phone in the kitchen by day and beside her bed at night. I turned and scanned the premises. Around me, shadows deepened and the daddy longlegs began to tiptoe down the walls, restless at my intrusion. I eased out of the cabin, keeping a close eye on them.

I picked at my dinner, sitting alone in my favorite booth at Rosie's restaurant half a block from my apartment. As usual, Rosie had bullied me into ordering according to her dictates. It's a phenomenon I don't seriously complain about. Beyond McDonald's Quarter Pounders with Cheese, I don't have strong food preferences, and I'm just as happy to have someone else steer me through the menu. Tonight she recommended the caraway seed soup with dumplings, followed by a braised pork dish, yet another Hungarian recipe involving meatstuffs overwhelmed by sour cream and paprika. Rosie's is not so much a restaurant as it is a funky neighborhood bar where exotic dishes are whipped up according to her whims. The place always feels as though it's on the verge of being raided by the food police, so narrowly does it skirt most public health regulations. The scent in the air is a blend of Hungarian spices, beer, and cigarette smoke. The tables in the center of the room are those chrome-and-Formica dinette sets left over from the 1940s. Booths hug the walls: stiff, high-backed pews sawed out of construction-grade plywood, stained dark brown to disguise all the knotholes and splinters.

It was not quite seven, and none of the habitual sports enthusiasts were in evidence. Most nights, especially in the summer months, the place is filled with noisy teams of bowlers and softball players in company uniforms. In winter, they're forced to improvise. Just this week a group of revelers had invented a game called Toss the Jockstrap, and a hapless example of this support garment was now snagged on the spike of a dusty marlin above the bar. Rosie, who is otherwise quite bossy and humorless, seemed to find this amusing and left it where it was. Apparently her impending nuptials had lowered her IQ several critical points. She was currently perched up on a bar stool, scanning the local papers while she smoked a cigarette. A small color television set was blaring at one end of the bar, but neither of us was paying much attention to the broadcast. Rosie's beloved William, Henry's older brother, had flown to Michigan with him. Rosie and William were getting married in a month, though the date seemed to drift.

The telephone rang from its place on the near end of the bar. Rosie glanced over at it with annoyance, and at first I thought she wouldn't answer it at all. She took her time about it, refolding the paper before she set it aside. She finally answered on the sixth ring, and after she'd exchanged a few brief remarks with the caller, her gaze jumped to mine. She held the receiver in my direction and then clunked it down on the bar top, probably devastating someone's eardrum.

I pushed my dinner plate aside and eased out of the booth, careful that I didn't snag a splinter in the back of my thigh. One day I'm going to rent a belt sander and give all the wooden seats a thorough scouring. I'm tired of worrying about the possibility of impaling myself on spears of cheap plywood. Rosie had moved to the far end of the bar, where she turned down the volume on the TV set. I crossed to the bar and picked up the receiver. "Hello?"

"Hey, Kinsey. Cheney Phillips. How are you?"

"How'd you know where I was?"

"I talked to Jonah Robb, and he told me you used to hang out at Rosie's. I tried your home number and your machine picked up, so I figured you might be having dinner."

"Good detective work," I said. I didn't even want to ask what had made him think to discuss me with Jonah Robb, who was working the Missing Persons detail at the Santa Teresa Police Department when I'd met him three years before. I'd had a brief affair with him during one of his wife's periodic episodes of spousal abandonment. Jonah and his wife, Camilla, had been together since seventh grade. She left him at intervals, but he always took her back again. It was love junior high school style, which became very tedious for those on the periphery. I hadn't known what the game was, and I didn't understand the role I'd been tagged to play. Once I got the message, I'd opted out of the situation, but it left me feeling bad. When you're single, you sometimes make those mistakes. Still, it's disconcerting to think your name is being bandied about. I didn't like the idea that I was the subject of conversation in the local police locker room.

"What are you up to?" I said to Cheney.

"Nothing much. I'll be going down to lower State Street later tonight, looking for a guy with some information I want. I thought you might like to ride along. An old girlfriend of Lorna's tends to hustle her butt in the same neighborhood. If we spot her, I can introduce you . . . if you're interested, of course."

My heart sank as visions of an early bedtime evaporated. "It sounds great. I appreciate the offer. How do you want to work it? Shall I meet you down there?"

"You can if you like, but it's probably better if I swing by and pick you up on the way. I'll be cruising a big area, and it's hard to know where I'll be."

"You know where I live?"

"Sure," he said, and rattled off my address. "I'll be there about eleven."

"That late?" I squeaked.

"The action doesn't even get rolling 'til after midnight," he said. "Is that a problem?"

"No, it's fine."

"See you then," he said, and hung up.

I glanced at my watch and noted with despair that I had about four hours to kill. All I really wanted was to hit the sack, but not if I was going to have to get up again. When I'm down, I like to stay down. Naps leave me feeling hungover without the few carefree moments of an intervening binge. If I was going to drive around with Cheney Phillips until all hours, I thought I'd be better off staying on my feet. I decided I might as well conjure up some work in the interim. I drank two cups of coffee and then paid Rosie for my dinner, taking my jacket and handbag as I headed out into the night.

The sun had set at 5:45, and the moon probably wouldn't be

rising until 2:00 A.M. At this hour, everybody in the neighborhood was still wide awake. In almost every house I passed, front windows glowed as if the rooms within were aflame. Night moths like soft birds batted ineffectually against the porch bulbs. February had silenced all the summer insects, but I could still hear a few hearty crickets in the dry grass and an occasional nightbird. Otherwise, the quiet was pervasive. It seemed warmer than last night, and I knew, from the evening paper, that the cloud cover was increasing. The winds were northerly, shaking through the thatch of dried palm fronds above me. I walked the half block to my apartment and let myself in briefly to check for messages.

There was nothing on my machine. I went out again before I yielded to the temptation to call Cheney and cancel tonight's big adventure. The squeak in the gate seemed like a melancholy sound, cold metal protesting my departure. I got in my car and turned the key in the ignition, cranking the lever for the heater as soon as the engine roared to life. There was no way the system could deliver hot air so soon, but I needed the illusion of coziness and warmth.

I headed out the 101 for half a mile and took the Puerta Street off-ramp. St. Terry's Hospital was only two blocks down. I found a parking space on a side street, locked the car, and walked the remaining half block to the front entrance. Technically, visiting hours didn't start until eight, but I was hoping the nursing director on the cardiac care unit would bend the rules a bit.

The glass doors slid open as I approached. I passed the hospital café to the left of the lobby, with its couches arranged in numerous conversational groupings. Several ambulatory patients, wearing robes and slippers, had elected to come down and sit with family members and friends. The area was rather like a large, comfortably furnished living room, complete with piped-in music and paintings by local artists. The scent in the lobby was not at all unpleasant but nonetheless reminded me of hard times. My aunt Gin had died here on a February night over ten years ago. I shut the door on the thought and all the memories that came with it.

The gift shop was open, and I did a quick detour. I wanted to buy something for Lieutenant Dolan, though I couldn't think quite what. Neither the teddy bears nor the peignoirs seemed appropriate. Finally I picked up an oversize candy bar and the latest issue of *People.* Entering a hospital room is always easier with an item in hand—anything to smooth your intrusion on the intimacies of illness. Ordinarily I wouldn't dream of conducting business with a man in his pajamas.

I paused at the information desk long enough to get his room number and directions to CCU, then hiked down countless corridors toward the bank of elevators in the west wing. I punched the button for three and emerged into a light, airy foyer with a glossy, snow-white floor. I turned left into a short hallway. The CCU waiting room was just to the right. I peered through the glass window set into the door. The room was empty and spare: a round table, three chairs, two love seats, a television set, pay phone, and several magazines. I moved over to the door leading into CCU. There was a phone on the wall and beside it a sign advising me to call in for permission to enter. A nurse or a ward clerk picked up the call, and I told her I wanted to see Lieutenant Dolan.

"Wait a minute and I'll check."

There was a pause, and then she told me to come on in. The curious thing about illness is that a lot of it looks just like you'd expect. We've seen it all on television: the activity at the nurses' station, the charts and the machinery designed to monitor the ailing. On the cardiac care unit, the floor nurses wore ordinary street clothes, which made the atmosphere seem more relaxed and less clinical. There were five or six of them, all young and quite friendly. Medical personnel could oversee vital signs from a central vantage point. I stood at the counter and watched eight different hearts beat, a row of green spiky hiccups on screens lined up on the desk.

The ward itself was done in southwestern colors: dusty pinks, mild sky blues, cool pale greens. The doors to each room were made of sliding glass, easily visible from the nurses' station, with draw drapes that could be pulled shut if privacy was required. The feel of the unit was as clean and quiet as a desert: no flowers, no artificial plants, all the laminate surfaces plain and spare. The paintings on the walls were of desert vistas, mountains rising in the distance.

I asked for Lieutenant Dolan, and the nurse directed me down the corridor. "Second door on the left," he said.

"Thanks."

I paused in the doorway of Lieutenant Dolan's room, which was sleek and contemporary. The bed he rested on was as narrow as a monk's. I was used to seeing him on the job, in a rumpled gray suit, grumpy, harassed, completely businesslike. Here he seemed smaller. He was wearing an unstructured, pastel cotton gown with short sleeves and a tie back. He sported a day's growth of beard, which showed prickly gray across his cheeks. I could see the tired, ropy flesh of his neck, and his once muscular arms were looking stringy and thin. A floor-to-ceiling column near the head of his bed housed the paraphernalia necessary to monitor his status. Cables pasted to his chest looped up to a plug in the column, where a screen played out his vital signs like a ticker tape. He was reading the paper, half-glasses low on his nose. He was attached to an IV. When he caught sight of me, he set the paper aside and took his glasses off. He gave the edge of the sheet a tug, pulling it across his bare feet.

He motioned me in. "Well, look who it is. What brings you down here?" He ran a hand through his hair, which was sparse at best and now looked as if it had been slicked back with sweat. He pushed himself up against the angled bed. His plastic hospital bracelet made his wrist seem vulnerable, but he didn't seem ill. It was as if I'd caught him on a Sunday morning, lounging around in his pajamas before church.

"Cheney told me you were laid up, so I thought I'd pop by. I hope I didn't interrupt your paper."

"I've read it three times. I'm so desperate I'm down to the personals. Somebody named Erroll wants Louise to call him, in case you know either one."

I smiled, wishing he looked stronger, knowing I'd look even worse if I were in his place. I held out the magazine. "For you," I said. "I figure nothing in your condition precludes an overdose of gossip. If you're really bored, you can always do the crossword puzzle in the back. How're you feeling? You look good."

"I'm not bad. I've been better. The doctor's talking about moving me off the unit tomorrow, which seems like a good sign." He scratched at the stubble on his chin. "I'm taking advantage by refusing to shave. What do you think?"

"Very devil-may-care," I said. "You can go straight from here to a life on the bum."

"Pull a chair over. Have a seat. Just move that."

The chair in the near corner had the rest of the paper and several magazines piled up on the seat. I set the whole batch aside and dragged the chair over toward the bed, aware that both Dolan and I were using chitchat and busywork to cover a basic uneasiness. "What are they telling you about going back to work?"

"They won't say at this point, but I imagine it'll be a while yet. Two, three months. I scared 'em pretty bad, from what everybody says. Hell, Tom Flowers ended up doing mouth-to-mouth, which he'll never live down. Must have been a sight for sore eyes."

"You're still with us, at any rate."

"That I am. Anyway, how are you? Cheney told me about Janice Kepler. How's it going so far?"

I shrugged. "All right, I guess. I've been on it less than a day. I'm supposed to meet Cheney later. He's going to cruise lower State, looking for a snitch, and offered to point out a chum of Lorna's while he's about it."

"Probably Danielle," Dolan said. "We talked to her at the time, but she wasn't much help. You know these little gals. The life they live is so damn dangerous. Night after night, connecting up with strangers. Get in a car and you have to be aware it might be the last ride you ever take. And they see *us* as the enemy. I don't know why they do it. They're not stupid."

"They're desperate."

"I guess that's what it is. This town is nothing compared to L.A., but it's still the pits. You take someone like Lorna, and it makes no sense whatever."

"You have a theory about who killed her?"

"I wish I did. She kept her distance. She didn't buddy up to people. Her lifestyle was too unconventional for most."

"Oh, I'll say. Has anybody told you about the video?"

"Cheney mentioned it. I gather you've seen it. I probably ought to take a look myself, see if I recognize any of the players."

"You better wait 'til you're home. It'll get your heart rate right up there. Janice Kepler gave me a copy. She's feeling very paranoid and made me swear I'd guard the damn thing with my very life. I haven't checked the dirty-book stores, but it wouldn't surprise me to see half a dozen copies in stock. From the packaging, it looks like it was manufactured up in the Bay Area someplace."

"You going up there?"

"I'd like to. Seems like it's worth a try if I can talk Janice into it."

"Cheney says you want to take a look at the crime scene photographs."

"If you don't object. I saw the cabin this afternoon, but it's been empty for months. I'd like to see what it looked like when the body was found."

Lieutenant Dolan's brow furrowed with distaste. "You're welcome to take a look, but you better brace yourself. That's the worst decomp case I ever saw. We had to do toxicology from bone marrow and whatever little bit of liver tissue we could salvage."

"There's no doubt it was her?"

"Absolutely none," he said. He lifted his eyes to the monitor, and I followed his gaze. His heartbeat had picked up, and the green line was looking like a row of ragged grass. "Amazes me how the memory of something like that can cause a physiological reaction after all these months."

"Did you ever see her in real life?"

"No, and it's probably just as well. I felt bad enough as it was. 'Dust to dust' doesn't quite cover it. Anyway, I'll call Records and get a set for you. When do you want to go over there?"

"Right now, if possible. Cheney doesn't pick me up for another three hours yet. I was up late last night, and I'm dead on my feet. My only hope is to keep moving."

"Photographs will wake you up."

Most of the departments at the police station close down at six. The crime lab was closed and the detectives gone for the day. In the bowels of the building, the 911 dispatchers would still be sitting at their consoles, fielding emergency calls. The main counter, where parking tickets are paid, was as blank as the ribs on a rolltop desk, a sign indicating that the window would open again at 8:00 A.M. The door to Records was locked, but I could tell there were a couple of people working, probably data-processing technicians entering the day's warrants into the system. The small front counter wasn't currently manned, but I managed to lean over, peering into the records department around the corner to the right.

A uniformed officer spotted me and broke away from a conversation with a civilian clerk. He moved in my direction. "Can I help you?"

"I just talked to Lieutenant Dolan over at St. Terry's. He and Detective Phillips are letting me look at some files. There should be a set of photographs he said I could take."

"The name was Kepler, right? Lieutenant just called. I have 'em right back here. You want to come on through?"

"Thanks."

The officer depressed a button, releasing the door lock. I went through into a back hallway and turned right. The officer reappeared in the doorway to Records and Identification. "We got a desk back here if you want to take a seat."

I read through the file with care, making notes as I went. Janice Kepler had given me much of the same material, but there were many interdepartmental memos and notes that hadn't been part of her packet. I found the witness interviews the police had conducted with Hector Moreno, J. D. Burke, and Serena Bonney, whose home address and phone number I jotted down. There were additional interviews with Lorna's family, her former boss, Roger Bonney, and the very Danielle Rivers I was hoping to meet on lower State Street tonight. Again, I made a note of home addresses and telephone numbers. This was information I could develop on my own, but why pass it up? Lieutenant Dolan had left word that I could photocopy anything I needed. I took copies of countless pages. I'd probably interview many of the same people, and it would be instructive to compare their current opinions and observations with those made at the time. Finally I turned my attention to the crime scene photographs.

In some ways, it's hard to know which is more sordid, the pornography of sex or the pornography of homicide. Both speak of violence, the broken and debased, the humiliations to which we subject one another in the heat of passion. Some forms of sex are as cold-blooded as murder, some kinds of murder as titillating to the perpetrator as a sexual encounter.

Decomposition had erased most of the definition from Lorna Kepler's flesh. The very enzymes embedded in her cells had caused her to disintegrate. The body had been invaded, nature's little cleaning crew busily at work—maggots as light as a snowfall and as white as thread. It took me many minutes before I could look at the photographs without revulsion. Finally I was able to detach myself. This was simply the reality of death.

I was interested in the sight of the cabin in its furnished state. I had seen it empty: sooty and forsaken, full of spiders and mildew, the fusty smell of neglect. Here, in full color and again in black and white, I could see fabric, crowded countertops in use, sofa pillows in disarray, a vase full of sagging flowers in an inch of darkened water, rag rugs, the spindle-lathed wooden chair legs. I could see a pile of mail on the sofa cushion where she'd left it. There was something distasteful about the unexpected glimpses of her living space. Like a houseguest arriving early, who sees the place before the hostess has had the chance to tidy up.

Aside from a few photographs meant to orient the viewer, Lorna's body was the prime subject of most eight-by-ten glossies. She lay on her stomach. Her posture was that of someone sleeping, her limbs arranged in the classic chalk outline that marks the position of the corpse in any TV show. No blood, no emesis. It was hard to imagine what she was doing when she went down—answering the front door, running for the telephone. She wore a bra and underpants, her jogging clothes tossed in a pile close by. Her long dark hair still carried its sheen, a tumble of glossy strands. In the light of the flashbulb, small white maggots glowed like a spray of seed pearls. I slipped the pictures back in the manila envelope and tucked them in my handbag.

7

I was leaning against my VW, parked at the curb in front of my place, when Cheney came around the corner in a VW that looked even older than mine. It was beige, very dinged up, an uncanny replica of the 1968 sedan I had run off the road nearly two years before. Cheney chugged to a stop, and I tried opening the car door on the passenger side. No deal. I finally had to put a foot up against the side of the car to get sufficient leverage to wrench the door open. The squawk it made sounded like a large, unruly beast breaking wind. I slid onto the seat and pulled futilely at the door, trying to close it. Cheney reached across me and wrenched it shut again. He threw the gears into first and took off with his engine rumbling.

"Nice car. I used to have one just like this," I said. I yanked at the seat belt, making a vain attempt to buckle it across my lap. The whole device was frozen, and I finally just had to pray he'd drive without crashing and burning. I do so hate to end an evening being flung through the windshield. At my feet I could feel a breeze blowing through a hole where the floor had rusted out. If it were daytime, I knew I'd see the road whipping past, like that small glimpse of track you see when you flush the toilet on a train. I tried to keep my feet up to avoid putting weight on the spot lest I plunge through. If the car stalled, I could push us along with one foot without leaving my seat. I started to roll down the window and discovered that the crank was gone. I opened the wing window on my side, and chilly air slanted in. So far, the wing window was the only thing on my side that functioned.

Cheney was saying, "I have a little sports car, too, but I figure there's no point in taking anything like that into the neighborhood we'll be in. Did you talk to Dolan yet?"

"I went over to St. Terry's to see him this evening. He was a doll, I must say. I went straight from the hospital to the station to look at files. He even provided me copies of the crime scene photographs."

"How'd he seem?"

"He was okay, I guess. Not as grouchy as usual. Why? What's your impression?"

"He was depressed when I talked to him, but he might have brought himself up for you."

"He has to be scared."

"I sure would be," Cheney said.

Tonight he was wearing a pair of slick Italian shoes, dark pants, a coffee-brown dress shirt, and a soft, cream suede windbreaker. I have to say he didn't look like any undercover cop I ever saw. He glanced over at me and caught the fact that I was conducting a visual survey. "What."

"Where are you from?" I asked.

"Perdido," he said, naming a little town thirty miles south of us. "What about you?"

"I'm local," I said. "Your name seems familiar."

"You've known me for years."

"Yes, but do I know you from somewhere else? Do you have family in the area?"

He made a noncommittal mouth sound that generally indicated "yes."

I looked at him closely. Being a liar myself, I can recognize other people's evasive maneuvers. "What's your family do?"

"Banks."

"What about banks? They make deposits? They do holdups?"

"They, mmm, you know, own some."

I stared at him, comprehension dawning like a big cartoon sun. "Your father is X. Phillips? As in Bank of X. Phillips?"

He nodded mutely.

"What is it, Xavier?"

"Actually, it's just X."

"What's your other car, a Jag?"

"Hey, just because he has big bucks doesn't mean I do. I have a Mazda. It's not fancy. Well, a little bit fancy, but it's paid for."

I said, "Don't get *defensive*. How'd you end up a cop?"

Cheney smiled. "When I was a kid, I watched a lot of TV. I was raised in an atmosphere of benign neglect. My mother sold high-end real estate while my father ran his banks. Cop shows made a big impression. More than financial matters, at any rate."

"Is your dad okay with that?"

"He doesn't have any choice. He knows I'm not going to follow in his footsteps. Besides, I'm dyslexic. To me, the printed page looks like gibberish. What about your parents? Are they still alive?"

"Please note. I'm aware that you're changing the subject, but I'm electing to answer the question you asked. They both died a long time ago. As it turns out, I do have family up in Lompoc, but I haven't decided what to do about them yet."

"What's to decide? I didn't know we had a choice about these things."

"Long story. They've ignored my existence now for twenty-nine years, and suddenly they want to make nice. It doesn't sit well with me. That kind of family I can do without."

Cheney smiled. "Look at it this way. I feel the same way about mine, and I've been in touch with them since birth."

I laughed. "Are we cynical or what?"

"The 'or what' part sounds right."

I turned my attention to the area we'd begun to cruise. It was not far from my place. Down along Cabana Boulevard, a left turn across the tracks. The condominiums and small houses began to give way to commercial properties: warehouses, "lite" industry, a wholesale seafood company, a moving-and-storage facility. Many buildings were long, low, and windowless. Tucked in along a side street was one of two "adult" bookstores. The other was located on the lower end of State Street, several blocks away. Here, small barren trees were spaced at long intervals. The streetlights seemed pale respite against the wide stretches of the dark. Looking off toward the mountains, I could see the smoky glow of the town washed up against the sky. The houses along the hillside were linked together in a fairyland of artificial lights. We began to pass small groups of people, five or six leaning against cars, clusters of the young whose sex was difficult to distinguish. Their eyes followed us without fail, conversations halted momentarily in the hopes that we would offer business of one sort or another. Sex or drugs, it probably didn't matter as long as money changed hands. Through the window, I could smell the dope as joints were passed from hand to hand.

The dull booming of a bass note signaled the proximity of the establishment we were looking for.

Neptune's Palace was a combination bar and pool hall with an open courtyard along one side, surrounded by a wide asphalt parking lot. Patrons had spilled out into both the courtyard and the parking lot. The yellow glow of mercury-vapor lights streamed across the gleaming tops of parked cars. Blasts of music spilled from the bar. Near the front of the place, girls were lounging against a low wall, their eyes following as a succession of vehicles cruised by in search of the night's adventure. The double doors stood open like the entrance to a cave, the rectangle of tawny light softened by a fog of cigarette smoke. We circled the block twice, Cheney peering out for sight of Danielle.

"No sign of her?" I asked.

"She'll be here someplace. For her, this is like the unemployment office."

We found a parking place around the corner, where the night air was quieter. We got out and locked the car, moving along the sidewalk past numerous same-sex couples who seemed to view us with amusement. Heterosexuals are so out of it.

Cheney and I pushed our way into the bar, merging with the shoals of inebriated patrons. Music blasted from the dance floor. The damp heat from all the bodies inside was nearly tropical in its nature. The very air smelled briny from the cheap beer on tap. The nautical theme was everywhere apparent. Big fishing nets were draped from the beams across the ceiling, where reflecting bulbs played like sunlight on surface water. Up there, a light show simulated twilight on the ocean, day fading into sunset, followed by the jet black of night. Sometimes the constellations were projected overhead, and sometimes ferocious cracks of lightning formed the apparition of a storm at sea. The walls were painted in a multitude of blues, shades graduating downward from the calm blue of a summer swell to the midnight hues of the deep. Sawdust on the concrete flooring created the illusion of the ocean's sandy bottom. The dance floor itself was defined by what looked like the prow of a sunken ship. So perfect was the fantasy of life beneath the sea that I found myself feeling grateful for every breath I took.

Tables were tucked into alcoves made to look like coral reefs. The lighting was muted, much of it emanating from massive saltwater aquariums in which large, pouty-mouthed groupers undulated endlessly in search of prey. Reproduction antique navigational charts were embedded in polyurethane on every tabletop, and the world they portrayed was one of vast unpopulated oceans with treacherous creatures lurking at the outer edges. Not so different from the patrons themselves.

In the occasional brief lull between cuts, I picked up the faint effects being played through the sound system: ship's bells, the creak of wood, sails flapping, the shriek of seagulls, the tinny warning of the buoys. Most eerie was the nearly undiscernible wails of drowning seamen, as if all of us were caught up in some maritime purgatory, in which alcohol, cigarettes, laughter, and pounding music served to ward off those faint cries creeping into the silence. All the waitresses were dressed in skintight, spangled body suits as shimmering as fish scales. I had to guess most had been hired on the basis of their androgyny: cropped hair, slim hips, and no breasts to speak of. Even the boys were wearing makeup.

Cheney stayed close behind me, his hand placed comfortably in the middle of my back. Once he leaned to say something, but the noise in the place obliterated his voice. He disappeared at one point and came back with a bottle of beer in each hand. We found an expanse of unpopulated wall with a largely unobstructed view of the place. We leaned there, people watching. The volume of the music would necessitate a hearing test later. I could picture all the cilia in my ear canal going flat. I'd once fired a gun from the depths of a garbage bin and ever since had been plagued by an intermittent hissing deep inside my head. These kids were going to need ear trumpets by the age of twenty-five.

Cheney touched my arm and then pointed across the room. His mouth formed the word "Danielle," and I followed his gaze. She was standing near the door, apparently alone, though I had to guess she wouldn't be for long. She was probably in her late teens, lying regularly about her age, else how would she get in here? She had dark hair long enough to sit on and long legs that seemed to go on forever. Even at that distance, I could see slim hips, a flat belly, and the breasts of early adolescence, a body type much admired by the postmenopausal male. She was wearing lime-green satin hot pants and a halter top with a lime-green bomber jacket over it.

We made our way across the room. At a certain point in our progress, she spotted Cheney's approach. He pointed toward the courtyard. She pivoted and went out in advance of us. Outside, the temperature dropped dramatically, and the sudden absence of cigarette smoke made the air smell like freshly cut hay. The chill felt like liquid pouring over my skin. Danielle had turned to face us, hands in her jacket pockets. Up close, I could see the skillful use of cosmetics in the battle she must have fought with her own youthful looks. She could have passed for twelve. Her eyes were the luminous green of certain tropical fish, and her look was insolent.

"We have a car parked around the corner," Cheney said without preamble.

"So?"

"So we could have a little talk. Just the three of us."

"About what?"

"Life in general, Lorna Kepler in particular."

Danielle's eyes were fixed on mine. "Who's she?"

"This is Kinsey. Lorna's mother hired her."

"This is not a bust," she said warily.

"Oh, come on, Danielle. It's not a bust. She's a private investigator looking into Lorna's death."

"Because I'm telling you, Cheney, you set me up for something, you could get me in real trouble."

"It's not a setup. It's a meeting. She'll pay your regular rates."

I gave Cheney a look. I'd have to pay the little twerp?

Danielle's gaze raked the parking lot and then strayed in my direction. "I don't do women," she said sullenly.

I leaned forward and said, "Hey, me neither. In case anybody gives a shit."

Cheney ignored me and addressed himself to her. "What are you afraid of?"

"What am I *afraid* of?" she said, finger pointing to her own chest. Her nails were bitten to the quick. "I'm afraid of Lester, for one thing. I'm afraid of losing my teeth. I'm afraid Mr. Dickhead's going to flatten my nose again. The guy's a bastard, a real prick . . ."

"You should have pressed charges. I told you that the last time," Cheney said.

"Oh, right. I should have gone ahead and checked into the morgue, saved myself that messy middle step," she snapped.

"Come on. Help us out," Cheney coaxed.

She thought about it, looking off into the dark. Finally, grudgingly, she said, "I'll talk to her, not to you."

"That's all I'm asking."

"I'm not doing it because you're *asking*. I'm doing it for Lorna. And just this once. I mean it. I don't want you to set me up like this again."

Cheney grinned seductively. "You're too perfect."

Danielle made a face, mimicking his manner, which she wasn't buying for a minute. She headed off toward the street, talking back across her shoulder. "Let's get it over with before Lester shows up."

Cheney walked us to the car, where we went through the requisite door-wrenching exercise. The ensuing squawk was so loud, a couple halfway down the block stopped necking long enough to see what kind of creature we were torturing. I took the passenger seat and let Danielle take the driver's side in case she needed to make a hasty getaway. Whoever Lester was, I was getting nervous myself.

Cheney leaned toward the wing window. "Back in a bit."

"You see Lester, don't you tell him where I'm at," she warned.

"Trust me," Cheney said.

"Trust him. What a joke," she said to no one in particular.

We watched him through the front windshield as he disappeared into the dark. I sat there hoping her Monday night rates were low. I couldn't remember how much cash I had on me, and I didn't think she'd take my Visa, which was maxed out anyway.

"You can smoke if you want," I said, thinking to ingratiate myself.

"I don't *smoke,*" she said, offended. "Smoking wrecks your health. Know how much we pay in this country for smoking-related illnesses? Fifteen billion a year. My father died of emphysema. It was like walking suffocation every day of his life. Eyes bugging out. He's breathing . . . he's like this . . ." She paused to demonstrate, hand on her chest. The sounds she made were a combination of rasping and choking. "And he can't get any air. It's a horrible way to die. Dragging around this old oxygen tank. You better quit while you're ahead."

"I don't smoke. I thought you might. I was being polite."

"Don't be polite on my account," she said. "I hate smoking. It's very bad for you, plus it stinks." Danielle looked around then, regarding the interior of the VW with distaste. "What a pigsty. You could get a disease sitting in this thing."

"At least you know he's not on the take," I said.

"Cops in this town don't take money," she said. "They have too much fun sticking people in the can. He's got a much nicer car, but he's too paranoid to bring it down here. So. Enough with the chit-chat, get-to-know-you bullshit. What do you want to know about Lorna?"

"As much as you can tell me. How long did you know her?"

Danielle's mouth pulled down in a facial shrug. "Couple of years. We met working for this escort service. She was a good person. She was like a mother to me. She was my what-do-you-call-'em . . . mentor . . . only now I see I should have listened to her more."

"How so?"

"Lorna killed me. She was great. She really blew me away. I was like totally in awe. She knew what she wanted and she went after it, and if you didn't like where she was coming from, then it was too bad for you."

"What did she want?"

"A million bucks, for starters. She wanted to retire by the time she was thirty. She could have done it, too, if she'd lived long enough."

"How'd she propose to do it?"

"How do you think?"

"That's a lot of time on your back," I said.

"Not at the rates she charged. After she left the escort service? She was making two hundred thousand dollars a year. Two hundred *thousand*. I couldn't believe it. She was smart. She invested. She didn't blow money the way I would've if I'd been in her shoes. I got no head for finance. What's in my pocket I spend, and when it's gone, I start over. At least I used to be that way until she straightened me out."

"What was she going to do when she retired?"

"Travel. Goof off. Maybe marry some guy who'd take care of her for life. Thing is . . . and here's what she kept hammering at me about . . . you got money, you're independent. You can do anything you want. Some guy mistreats you, you get the fuck out. You can walk. Know what I'm saying?"

"That's my philosophy," I said.

"Yeah, mine, too, now. After she died, I opened a little savings account, and I salt it away. It's not much, but it's enough, and I'm going to let it sit. That's what Lorna always said. You put it in the bank and you let it collect interest. She put a lot of her money in blue-chip stocks, municipal bonds, shit like that, but she did it all herself. She wasn't into this business about financial managers and people like that, because, for one thing, she said it's the perfect excuse for some asshole to come along and rip you off. You know stockbrokers? She called 'em portfolio pimps." She laughed at the phrase, apparently amused at the idea of procurers on Wall Street. "How about you? You got savings?"

"As a matter of fact, I do."

"Where is it? What'd you do with it?"

"I put it in CDs," I said, feeling faintly sensitive on the subject. It seemed strange defending my financial strategy to some girl who worked the streets.

"That's good. Lorna did some of that, too. She liked tax-free munis, and she had some of her money in Ginnie Maes, whatever they are. Listen to us. This is what I like. Talkin' about all this long-term stuff. You have money, that's power, and no guy can come along and punch your lights out, right?"

"You mentioned her making two hundred thousand. She pay taxes on the money?"

"Of course! Never fuck with the feds, was her first rule of thumb. That's the first thing she taught me. Anything you make, you declare. Know how they got Al Capone and those guys? Undeclared income. You cheat the feds, you end up in the can, like big time, and that's no lie."

"What about—"

"Just a minute," she cut in. "Let me ask you something else. How much do you earn?"

I stared at her. "How much do *I* earn?"

"Yeah, like last year. What was your annual income? What'd you pay taxes on?"

"That's getting pretty personal, isn't it?"

"You don't have to act like that. This is strictly between us. You say and then I will. We'll trade tit for tat, as it were."

"Twenty-five thousand."

Now it was her turn to stare. "That's *all?* I earned twice that. No fooling. Fifty-two thousand five hundred and change."

"You got your nose broken, too," I pointed out.

"Yeah, well, you had *your* nose broken. I can tell by looking. I'm not criticizing. No offense," she said. "You're not a bad-looking chick, but for twenty-five thousand, you get punched in the chops same as me, am I right?"

"I wouldn't look at it quite like that."

"Don't bullshit yourself. I learned that from Lorna, too. Take my word for it. Your job is dangerous the same as mine, with only half the pay. You ought to switch, in my opinion. Not that I'm promoting my line of work. I'm just telling you what I think."

"I appreciate your concern. If I decide to change careers, I'll come to you for job counseling."

She smiled, amused at the sarcasm or what she assumed was sarcasm. "I'll tell you something else she taught me. Keep your big mouth shut. You do a guy, you don't talk about it afterward. Especially in the crowd she's running in. She slipped up once and swore she'd never do it again. Some of those guys . . . whoo! You're better off forgetting you ever knew 'em."

"Do you travel in those circles? The real high-class stuff?"

"Well, not all the time. Not now. When she was alive, I did now and then. Like once in a while, she'd dress me up fancy and take me with her on a big one. Me and this other girl named Rita. What a hoot. Some guys like 'em young. You shave your pubes and act like you're about ten years old. Like this one night? I made over fifteen hundred dollars. Don't ask me doing what. That's something else you don't talk about. Lester would have killed me if he found out."

"What happened to all her money when she died?" I asked.

"Beats the hell out of me. You'd have to ask her folks about that. I bet she didn't have a will. I mean, what'd she need a will for? She was young. Well, twenty-five, which is not *that* old. I bet she thought she had years, and it turned out she had nothing."

"How old are you?"

"Twenty-three."

"You are not."

"I am *too*."

"Danielle, you're not."

She smiled slightly. "Okay, I'm nineteen, but I'm mature for my age."

I said, "Seventeen is probably closer, but we'll let that pass."

"You better ask more about Lorna. You're wasting your money when you ask about me."

"What was Lorna doing out at the water treatment plant? That doesn't sound like it was worth even the part-time pay."

"She had to do *something*. She couldn't tell her parents how she was earning her bread. They were real conservative; least her dad was. I met her mom at the funeral, and she seemed nice enough. Her old man was a butt, all the time on her case, checkin' up on her. Lorna was a wild one, and she didn't like to be controlled."

"I talked to her father earlier today, and he said Lorna didn't have many friends."

Danielle dismissed that with a toss of her head. "What does he know? Just because he never met any. Lorna liked night people. Everybody she knew came out of hiding when the sun went down. Like spiders and all those what-do-you-call-'em . . . nocturnal creatures. Owls and bats. You want to meet her friends, you better get used to staying out all night. What else? This is fun. I didn't realize I was so smart."

"What about the porno film? Why'd she do that?"

"Oh, same old, same old. You know how it is. Some guy came down from San Francisco. She met him one night in at the Edgewater and got to talking about that stuff. He thought she'd be dynamite, and I guess she was. At first she didn't want to do it, but then she figured, Hey, why not? She didn't get paid much, but she said she had a ball. What'd you hear about that?"

"I didn't hear about it. I saw it."

"You did not. You saw that?"

"Sure, I have a copy."

"Well, that's weird. That video was never released."

Now it was my turn to express skepticism. "Really? It never went into distribution? I don't believe it." We sounded like a couple of talking birds.

"That's what she said. She was pissed off about it, too. She thought it could be her big break, but there was nothing she could do."

"The cassette I saw was edited, packaged, the whole bit. They must have had a lot of money tied up in it. What's the story?"

"I just know what she said. Maybe the venture was undercapitalized, whatever the term is. How'd you get a copy?"

"Someone sent it to her mother."

Danielle barked out a laugh. "You're kidding. That's gross. What kind of jerk would do a thing like that?"

"I don't know yet. I'm hoping to find out. What else can you tell me?"

"No, no. You ask and I'll answer. I can't think of anything off the top of my head."

"Who's Lester?"

"Lester had nothing to do with Lorna."

"But who is he?"

She gave me a look. "What's it to you?"

"You're afraid of him, and I want to know why."

"Get off it. You're wasting your money."

"Maybe I can afford it."

"Oh, right. On what you make? That's bullshit."

"Actually, I don't even know what you're charging."

"Trick rates. Fifty bucks."

"An hour?" I yelped.

"Not an hour. What's the matter with you? Fifty bucks a trick. Nothing about sex takes an *hour*," she said contemptuously. "Anybody says it's an hour is rippin' you off."

"I take it Lester's your pimp."

"Listen to her. 'Pimp.' Who taught you to talk that way? Lester Dudley—Mr. Dickhead to you—is my personal manager. He's like my professional representative."

"Did he represent Lorna?"

"Of course not. I already told you, she was smart. She declined his services."

"You think he'd have any information about her?"

"Not a chance. Don't even bother. The guy's a real piece of shit."

I thought for a moment, but I'd covered the questions that came readily to mind. "Well. This should do for now. If you think of anything else, will you get in touch?"

"Sure," she said. "As long as you got the money, I got the mouth . . . so to speak."

I picked up my handbag and took out my wallet. I gave her a business card, jotting my home address and telephone number on the back. Ordinarily I don't like to give out that information, but I wanted to make it as easy for her as possible. I reviewed my cash supply. I thought maybe she'd be magnanimous and waive her fees, but she held her hand out, watching carefully as I counted bills into her palm. I had to make up the last dollar with the loose change in the bottom of my bag. Of course, I was short.

"Don't worry about it. You can owe me the dime."

"I'll give you an IOU," I said.

She waved the offer aside. "I trust you." She tucked the money in her jacket pocket. "Men are funny, you know? Big male fantasy about hookers? I see this in all these books written by men. Some guy meets a hooker and she's gorgeous: big knockers, refined, and she's got the hots for him. Him and her end up bonking, and when he's done, she won't take his money. He's so wonderful, she doesn't want to charge him money like she does everyone else. Now that's bullshit for sure. I never knew a hooker who'd do a guy for free. Anyway, hooker sex is for shit. If he thinks that's a gift, then the joke's on him."

8

It was close to one-thirty in the morning when I parked my VW in the little parking lot outside the emergency entrance to St. Terry's Hospital. After my conversation with Danielle, Cheney had dropped me back at my place. I moved in through the squeaking gate and around to the back. I heard Cheney give his horn a short toot, and then he took off. The night sky was still clear, bright with stars, but I could see patchy clouds collecting at the western edge as predicted. An airplane moved across my field of vision, a distant dot of red winking among the pinpricks of white, the sound trailing behind it like a banner advertising flight. The final quarter of the moon had narrowed to the curved silver of a shepherd's crook, a cloud like a wisp of cotton caught in its crescent. I could have sworn I still heard the booming music that had shaken Neptune's Palace. In reality, the club was less than a mile from my apartment, and I suppose it was possible the sound might have carried. It was more likely a stereo or a car radio in much closer range. Against the drumming of the high tide at the ocean half a block away, the faint

thump of bass was a muted counterpoint, brooding, silky, and in-
distinct.

I paused, keys in hand, and leaned my head briefly against the
door to my place. I was tired, but curiously disinterested in sleep.
I've always been a day person, thoroughly addicted to early rising
and morning sunshine in a nine-to-five world. I might work late on
occasion, but for the most part I'm home by early evening and
sound asleep by eleven. Tonight, yet again, I was nudged by rest-
lessness. Some long suppressed aspect of my personality was being
activated, and I could feel myself respond. I wanted to talk to
Serena Bonney, the nurse who'd discovered Lorna's body. Somewhere in the accumulating verbal portrait of Lorna Kepler was the
key to her death. I went back through the gate and closed it quietly
behind me.

The emergency room had an air of abandonment. The sliding glass
doors opened with a hush, and I moved into the quiet of the blue-
and-gray space. There were lights on in the reception area, but the
patient registration windows had been closed for hours. To the left,
behind a small partition with its wall-mounted pay telephones, the
waiting room was empty, the TV a square of blank gray. I peered to
the right, toward the examining rooms. Most were dark, with the
surrounding curtains pulled back and secured on overhead tracks. I
could smell freshly perked coffee wafting from a little kitchenette at
the rear of the facility. A young black woman in a white lab coat
came out of a doorway marked "Linens." She was small and pretty.
She paused when she spotted me, flashing a smile. "Oh, I'm sorry. I
didn't know anyone was here. Can I help you?"

"I'm looking for Serena Bonney. Is she working this shift?"

The woman glanced at her watch. "She should be back shortly.
She's on her break. You want to have a seat? The TV's on the
blink, but there's lots of reading material."

"Thanks."

For the next fifteen minutes, I read outdated issues of *Family
Circle* magazine: articles about children, health and fitness, nutri-

tion, home decorating, and inexpensive home-building projects meant for Dad in his spare time—a wooden bench, a treehouse, a rustic shelf to support Mom's picturesque garden of container herbs. To me, it was like reading about life on an alien planet. All the ads showed such perfect women. Most were thirty years old, white, and had flawless complexions. Their teeth were snowy and even. None of them had wide bottoms or kangaroo pouches that pulled their slacks out of shape. There was no sign of cellulite, spider veins, or breasts drooping down to their waists. These perfect women lived in well-ordered houses with gleaming floors, an inconceivable array of home appliances, oversize fluffy mutts, and no visible men. I guess Dad was relegated to the office between his woodworking projects. Intellectually I understood that these were all highly paid models simply *posing* as housewives for the purpose of selling Kotex, floor covering, and dog food. Their lives were probably as far removed from housewifery as mine was. But what did you do if you actually were a *housewife,* confronted with all these images of perfection on the hoof? From my perspective, I couldn't see any connection at all between my lifestyle (hookers, death, celibacy, handguns, and fast food) and the lifestyle depicted in the magazine, which was probably just as well. What would I do with a fluffy mutt and containers full of dill and marjoram?

"I'm Serena Bonney. Did you want to see me?"

I looked up. The nurse in the doorway was in her early forties, a good-size woman, maybe five feet ten. She wasn't obese by any stretch, but she carried a lot of weight on her frame. The women in her family probably described themselves as "hearty peasant stock."

I set the magazine aside and got to my feet, holding out my hand. "Kinsey Millhone," I said. "Lorna Kepler's mother hired me to look into her death."

"Again?" she remarked as she shook my hand.

"Actually, the case is still open. Can I take a few minutes of your time?"

"It's a funny hour for an investigation."

"I should apologize for that. I wouldn't ordinarily bother you at work, but I've been suffering insomnia for the last couple of nights, and I thought I might as well take advantage of the fact that you're working."

"I don't really know much, but I'll do what I can. Why don't you come on into the back? It's quiet at the moment, but that may not last long."

We moved past two examining rooms and into a small, sparsely furnished office. Like the nurses upstairs, she was dressed in ordinary street clothes: a white cotton blouse, beige gabardine pants, and a matching vest. The crepe-soled shoes marked her as someone who stood for long hours on her feet. Also her wristwatch, like a meat thermometer with a sweeping second hand. Serena paused at the door frame and leaned out into the hall. "I'll be in here if you need me, Joan."

"No problem," came the reply.

Serena left the door ajar, positioning her chair so she could keep an eye on the corridor. "Sorry you had to wait. I was up on the medical floor. My father was readmitted a couple of days ago, and I try to peek in at him every chance I get." She had a wide, unlined face and high cheekbones. Her teeth were straight and square, but slightly discolored, perhaps the result of illness or poor nutrition in her youth. Her eyes were light green, her brows pale.

"Is his illness serious?" I sat down on a chrome chair with a seat padded in blue tweed.

"He had a massive heart attack a year ago and had a pacemaker put in. He's been having problems with it, and they wanted to check it out. He tends to be a bit obstreperous. He's seventy-five, but *very* active. He practically runs the Colgate Water Board, and he hates to miss a meeting. He thrives on adrenaline."

"Your father isn't Clark Esselmann, by any chance?"

"You know him?"

"I know his reputation. I had no idea. He's always raising hell with the developers." He'd been involved in local politics for fifteen years, since he'd sold his real estate company and retired in splendor. From what I'd heard, he had a rough temper and a tongue that could shift from saltiness to eloquence depending on the subject. He was stubborn and outspoken, a respectable board member for half a dozen charities.

She smiled. "That's him," she said. She slid a hand through her hair, which was coppery, a cross between red and dark gold. It looked as though she'd had some kind of body permanent, because the curl seemed too pronounced to be entirely natural. The cut was short, the style uncomplicated. I pictured her running a brush through her hair after her morning shower. Her hands were big and her nails blunt cut but nicely manicured. She spent money on herself, but not in any way that seemed flashy. Suffering illness or injury, I'd have trusted her on sight.

I murmured something innocuous and then changed the focus of the conversation. "What can you tell me about Lorna?"

"I didn't know her well. I should probably say that up front."

"Janice mentioned that you're married to the fellow Lorna worked for at the water treatment plant."

"More or less," she said. "Roger and I have been separated for about eighteen months. I'll tell you, the last few years have been hellish, to say the least. My marriage fell apart, my father had a heart attack, and then Mother died. After that, Daddy's health problems only got worse. Lorna house-sat for me when I needed to get away."

"You met her through your husband?"

"Yes. She worked for Roger for a little over three years, so I'd run into her if I popped in at the plant. I'd see her at the employee picnics in the summer and the annual Christmas party. I thought she was fascinating. Clearly a lot smarter than the job required."

"The two of you got along?"

"We got along fine."

I paused, wondering how to phrase the question that occurred to me. "If it's not too personal, can you tell me about your divorce?"

"My divorce?" she said.

"Who filed? Was it you or your husband?"

She cocked her head. "That's a curious question. What makes you ask?"

"I was wondering if your separation from Roger had anything to do with Lorna."

Serena's laugh was quick and startled. "Oh, good heavens. Not at all," she said. "We'd been married ten years, and we both got bored. He was the one who broached the subject, but he certainly didn't get any grief from me. I understood where he was coming from. He feels he has a dead-end job. He likes what he does, but he's never going to get rich. He's one of those guys whose life hasn't quite come up to his expectations. He pictured himself retired by the age of fifty. Now he's past that, and he still hasn't got a dime. On the other hand, I not only have a career I'm passionate about, but I'll have family money coming to me one of these days. Living with that got to be too much for him. We're still on friendly terms, we're just not intimate, which you're welcome to verify with him."

"I'll take your word for it," I said, though of course I'd check. "What about the house-sitting? How'd Lorna end up doing that?"

"I don't remember exactly. I probably mentioned in passing that I needed someone. Her place was small and remarkably crude. I thought she'd enjoy spending time in a more comfortable setting."

"How often did she sit?"

"Five or six times altogether, I'd guess. She hadn't done it for a while, but Roger thought she was still willing. I could check my calendar at home if it seems relevant."

"At the moment I don't know what's relevant and what's not. Were you satisfied with the job she did?"

"Sure. She was responsible; fed and walked the dog, watered plants, brought in the newspaper and the mail. It saved me the kennel fees, and I liked having someone in the house while I was gone. After Roger and I split, I moved back in to my parents' house. I was interested in a change of scene, and Dad needed some unofficial supervision because of his health. Mother's cancer had already been diagnosed and she was doing chemo. This was an arrangement that suited all of us."

"So you were living at your father's at the time Lorna died?"

"That's right. He's been under doctor's care, but he's what they call a 'noncompliant' patient. I had plans to be out of town, and I didn't want him in the house alone. Dad was adamant. He swore he didn't need help, but I insisted. What's the point of a getaway weekend if I'm worried about him the whole time? As a matter of fact, that's what I was trying to set up when I went to her place and found her. I'd tried calling for days, and there was never any answer. Roger told me she was taking a couple of weeks' accrued vacation, but she was due back any day. I wasn't sure when she'd get in, so I thought I'd stop by and leave her a little note. I parked near the cabin, and I was just getting out of my car when I noticed the smell, not to mention the flies."

"You knew what it was?"

"Well, I didn't know it was her, but I knew it was something dead. The odor's quite distinct."

I shifted the subject slightly. "Everyone I've interviewed so far has talked about how beautiful she was. I wondered if other women regarded her as a threat."

"*I* never did. Of course, I can't speak for anyone else," she said. "Men seemed to find her more appealing than women, but I never saw her flirt. Again, I'm only talking about the occasions when I saw her."

"From what I hear, she liked living on the edge," I said. I introduced the matter without framing a question, interested in what kind of response I might get. Serena held my gaze, but she made no reply. So far she'd tended to editorialize on every question I asked. I ran the query one more round. "Were you aware that she was involved in other activities?"

"I don't understand the question. What kind of activities are you referring to?"

"Of a sexual nature."

"Ah. That. Yes. I assume you're referring to the money she made from the hotel trade. Humping for hire," she said drolly. "I didn't think it was my place to bring that up."

"Was it common knowledge?"

"I don't think Roger knew, but I certainly did."

"How did you find out?"

"I'm not sure. I really can't remember. Indirectly, I think. I ran into her at the Edgewater one night. No, wait a minute. I remember what happened. She came into the ER with a broken nose. She had some explanation, but it didn't make much sense. I've seen assault and battery often enough that I wasn't fooled. I didn't say so to her, but I knew *something* was going on."

"Could it have been a boyfriend? Someone she was living with?"

I could hear voices in the hallway.

She glanced over at the door. "I guess it could have been, but as far as I knew she was never in any kind of steady relationship. Anyway, the story she told seemed suspect. I've forgotten what it was now, but it seemed phony as hell. And it wasn't just the broken nose. It was that in conjunction with some other things."

"Such as?"

"Her wardrobe, her jewelry. She was subtle about it, but I couldn't help noticing."

"When was the incident that brought her to the emergency room?"

"I don't remember exactly. Probably two years ago. Check with Medical Records. They can give you the date."

"You don't know hospitals. I'd have better luck getting access to state secrets," I said.

A baby had begun to cry fretfully in the waiting room.

"Does it make a difference?"

"It might. Suppose the guy who punched her decided to make it permanent."

"Oh. I see your point." Serena's eyes strayed to the open door again as Joan went past.

"But she didn't confide in you when she came in?"

"Not at all. After I saw her at the Edgewater, I put two and two together."

"Seems like a bit of a leap."

"Not if you'd seen her the night I ran into her. Part of it, too, was the guy she was with. Older, very slick. Gold jewelry, gorgeous suit. Clearly a man who had money to burn. I saw them in the bar and later in the boutique where she was trying on clothes. He dropped a bundle that night. Four Escada outfits, and she was modeling a fifth."

"I assume Escada is expensive."

"Dear God." She laughed, patting herself on the chest.

Lights were going on in the examining cubicle across from us. I could hear the murmuring of voices: fussy baby, shrill mom speaking rapid-fire Spanish.

Serena went on. "It happened again within the month, as I remember. Same situation, different guy, same look. It didn't take a rocket scientist to figure it out."

"You think one of these guys knocked her around?"

"I think it's a better explanation than the one she gave. I'm not saying this is always true, but some guys in that age bracket start having trouble with impotency. They pick up high-priced call girls and spread the money around. Champagne and gifts, a gorgeous babe in tow. It looks good on the surface, and everybody thinks what a stud he is. What these men are looking for is a one-up relationship because they can't 'get it up' any other way. He's paying for the service, so if the equipment doesn't work, it's her fault, not his, and he can express his disappointment any way he likes."

"With his fist."

"If you want to look at it from his point of view, why not? He's paid for her. She's his. If he can't perform, he's got her to blame and he can paste her in the chops."

"Some deal. She keeps the cash and the clothes in exchange for the punishment."

"She doesn't always get punished. Some of these guys like to be punished themselves. Beaten, humiliated. They like to have their little fannies spanked for being bad, bad, bad."

"Did Lorna tell you this?"

"No, but I've heard it from a couple of other hookers on the local circuit. I also did some reading on the subject when I was getting my degree. I used to see them come in, and I'd be incensed at the way they were treated, furious because I didn't really understand what was going on. I'd jump to the rescue, trying to save them from the 'bad' guys. For all the good *that* did. In an odd way, I'm a better nurse if I can stay detached."

"And that's what you did with her?"

"Exactly. I felt compassion, but I didn't try to 'fix' her. It was none of my business. And she didn't see it as a problem, at least as far as I knew."

"You seem to spend a lot of time at the Edgewater. Is that where the singles hang out these days?"

"The singles in our age group, yes. I'm sure the kids would find it stuffy beyond belief and the prices astronomical. Frankly, it makes married life look pretty good."

"Do you happen to remember any dates when you saw her? If I check with the hotel, it helps to pin it down."

She thought about that briefly. "Once I was with a bunch of girlfriends. We get together to celebrate birthdays. That time it was mine, so it must have been early in March. We don't always manage to get together on the exact date, but it would have been a Friday or Saturday because that's when we play."

"That was last March?"

"Must have been."

"Was this before the broken nose or afterward?"

"I have no idea."

"Did Lorna know you knew?"

"Well, she saw me that night and maybe twice before that. Since Roger and I had separated, I was out with friends almost every weekend. Lorna and I didn't come right out and discuss her 'career,' but there were veiled references." Serena had used the fingers of both hands to form the quote marks around the word *career.*

"I'm just curious. How do you happen to remember in such detail? Most people can't recall what happened *yesterday.*"

"The police asked me most of this, and it stuck in my mind. Also, I've given it a lot of thought. I don't have a clue why she was murdered, and it bothers me."

"You believe she was murdered?"

"I think it's likely, yes."

"Were you aware that she was involved in pornography?"

Serena frowned slightly. "In what way?"

"She starred in a video. Someone sent the cassette to her parents about a month ago."

"What was it, like a snuff film? S and M?"

"No. It was fairly pedestrian in terms of the story and subject matter, but Mrs. Kepler suspects it may be linked to Lorna's death."

"Do you?"

"I'm not being paid to have opinions at this point. I like to keep my options open."

"I understand," she said. "It's like making a diagnosis. No point in ruling out the obvious."

There was a knock at the door frame and Joan peered in. "Sorry to interrupt, but we've got a baby over here I'd like you to take a look at. I've got a call in to the resident, but I think you should see him."

Serena rose to her feet. "Let me know if there's anything else," she said to me as she moved toward the door.

"I'll do that. And thanks."

I drove back to my place through deserted streets. I was beginning to feel at home in the late night world. The nature of the darkness shifts from hour to hour. Once the bars close down and traffic dissipates, what emerges is the utter stillness of three A.M. The intersections are empty. Traffic lights are bright O's of red and sea-foam green in a dazzling string that you can see for half a mile.

Clouds were pouring in. A dense ground fog, like cotton batting, was laid across the mountains, and the gray hills were pocked with streetlights against the backdrop of rolling mist. Most of the residential windows I saw were dark. Where an occasional light burned, I pictured students churning out last minute papers, the nightmares of the young. Or maybe the lights burned for recent insomniacs like me.

A police car cruised slowly along Cabana Boulevard, the uniformed officer turning to stare at me as I passed. I took a left onto my street and found a parking place. I locked the car. The sky was velvety with clouds now, the stars completely obscured. Darkness hugged the ground, while the sky was tinged with eerie light, like dark gray construction paper smudged with white chalk. Behind me, I heard the low hum of air moving swiftly through the spokes of a bike. I turned in time to see the man on the bicycle passing. From the rear, his taillight and the strips of reflecting tape on his heels made him look like someone juggling three small points of light. The effect was oddly unsettling, a circus act of the spirits performed solely for me.

I went through the gate and let myself into my apartment, flipping on the light. Everything was orderly, just as I'd left it. The quiet was profound. I could feel a little nudge of anxiety, made up of weariness, the late hour, empty rooms around me. I wasn't going to be able to sleep at this point. It was like hunger—once the peak moment passed, the appetite diminished and you could simply do without. Food, sleep . . . what difference did it make? The metabolism shifts into overdrive, calling up energy from some other source. If I'd gone to bed at nine or even ten o'clock, I could have slept through the night. But now my sleep permit had reached its expiration point. Having stayed awake this long, I was consigned to further wakefulness.

My body was both fatigued and fired up. I dropped my handbag and jacket on the chair by the door. I glanced at the answering machine: no messages. Did I have any wine on the premises? No, I did not. I checked the contents of the refrigerator, which showed nothing of culinary interest. My pantry was typically barren: a few stray cans and dried items that, singly or in combination, would never constitute anything remotely edible, unless you favored uncooked lentils with maple syrup. The peanut-butter jar had concentric swirl marks in the bottom, as if the rest of it had drained away. I found a kitchen knife and scraped the sides of the jar, eating the accumulated peanut butter off the blade as I walked around. "This is really pitiful," I said, laughing, but actually I didn't mind a bit.

Idly I flipped on the TV set. Lorna's video was still in the VCR. I touched the remote control, and the tape began to run again. I had no intention of watching any late night sex, but I went through the credits twice. The night before, I'd tried directory assistance in San Francisco, hoping for a telephone number for the production company Cyrenaic Cinema. In the credits, the producer, director, and film editor were all listed by name: Joseph Ayers, Morton Kasselbaum, and Chester Ellis respectively. What the hell, telephone operators are awake all night.

I tried the names in reverse order, bombing out on the first two. When I got to the producer, I picked up a hit. The operator sang, "Thank you for using AT and T," and a recording kicked in. A mechanical voice came on the line and recited Joseph Ayers's number for me twice.

I made a note, then picked up the phone and called directory assistance in San Francisco again, this time checking for a listing in the names of the other players, Russell Turpin and Nancy Dobbs. She wasn't listed, but there were two Turpins with the first initial *R*, one on Haight and one on Greenwich. I wrote down both numbers. At the risk of wasting my time and Janice Kepler's money, a trip north might actually be worth a shot. If the contacts didn't pan out, at least there was hope of eliminating the porno angle as a factor in her daughter's death.

I put a call through to Frankie's Coffee Shop, and Janice answered on the second ring. "Janice. This is Kinsey. I have a question for you."

She said, "Fire away. We're not busy."

I brought her up to date on my conversations with Lieutenant Dolan and Serena Bonney, and then filled her in on the minisurvey I'd done of the pornographic film crew. "I think it might be worthwhile to talk to the producer and the other actor."

"I remember him," she cut in.

"Yeah, well, between Turpin and this film producer, I'm hoping we can satisfy some questions. I'll try to contact both by phone in advance, but it looks like it'd make sense to make a quick trip. If I can set up a few appointments, I thought I'd hit the road."

"You're going to drive?"

"I'd thought to."

"Don't you have a dinky little VW? Why not fly? I would, if I were you."

"I guess I could," I said dubiously. "On a short hop like that, though, the plane fare will be outrageous. I'll have to rent a car up there, too. Motel, meals . . ."

"That sounds okay to me. Just save your receipts and we'll reimburse you when you get back."

"What about Mace? Did you tell him about the tape?"

"Well, I told you I would. He was shocked, of course, and then he got mad as hell. Not with her, but whoever put her up to it."

"What's his feeling about the investigation itself? He didn't seem that thrilled yesterday."

"He told me just what he told you," she said. "If this is what it takes to make me happy, he'll go along with it."

"Great. I'll probably fly up sometime tomorrow afternoon and talk to you as soon as I get back."

"Have a good flight," she said.

9

At 9:00 the next morning, I roused myself just long enough to call Ida Ruth, telling her I'd be in shortly in case anyone was looking for me. As I pulled the covers up, I checked the Plexiglas skylight above my bed. Clear, sunny skies, probably sixty-five degrees outside. To hell with the run. I awarded myself ten more minutes of rest. I next woke at 12:37, feeling as hungover as if I'd drunk myself insensible the night before. The tricky factor with sleep is that aside from the *number* of hours you put in, the body seems to hold you accountable for their position. Snoozing from four A.M. to eleven A.M. doesn't necessarily equate with the same number of hours logged between eleven P.M. and six. I had sketched in a full seven, but my regular metabolic rhythms were now decidedly off and required additional down time to correct themselves.

I called Ida Ruth again and was relieved to discover she was out at lunch. I left a message, indicating I'd been delayed by a meeting with a client. Don't ask why I fib to a woman who doesn't even cut my paycheck. Sometimes I lie just to keep my skills up. I staggered out of bed and into the bathroom, where I brushed my teeth. I felt as if I'd been anesthetized, and I was sure that none of my extremities would function. I propped myself against the wall in the shower, hoping the hydrotherapy would mend my skewed circuits. Once dressed, I found myself eating breakfast at one in the afternoon, wondering if I'd ever get myself back on track again. I put on a pot of coffee and dosed myself with caffeine while I made some phone calls to San Francisco.

I didn't get very far. Instead of Joseph Ayers, I got an answering machine that may or may not have been his. It was one of those carefully worded messages that bypasses confirmation of the party's name or the number called. A mechanical male voice said, "Sorry I wasn't here to take your call, but if you'll leave your name, number, and a brief message, I'll get back to you."

I left my name and office number and then left messages on answering machines for both R. Turpins. One voice was female, the other male. To both Turpins I chattered happily, "I'm not sure if this is the right Turpin or not. I'm looking for Russell. I'm a friend of Lorna Kepler's. She suggested I call if I was ever in San Francisco, and since I'm going to be up there in the next couple of days, I thought I'd say hi. Give me a call when you get this message. I'd love to meet you. She spoke so highly of you. Thanks." Through San Francisco information, I checked out the names of other members of the crew, working my way patiently down the list. Most were disconnects.

As long as I was home, I opened my desk drawer and pulled out a fresh pack of index cards, transcribing the information I'd picked up on the case to date—about four cards' worth. Over the last several years I've developed the habit of using index cards to record the facts uncovered in the course of an investigation. I pin the cards on the bulletin board that hangs above my desk, and in idle moments I arrange and rearrange the data according to no known plan. At some point I realized how different a detail can look when it's seen out of context. Like the pieces in a jigsaw puzzle, the shape of reality seems to shift according to circumstance. What seems strange or unusual can make perfect sense when it's placed in the proper setting. By the same token, what seems unremarkable can suddenly yield up precious secrets when placed against a different backdrop. The system, I confess, usually nets me absolutely nothing, but a payoff comes along just often enough to warrant continuing. Besides, it's restful, it keeps me organized, and it's a visual reminder of the job at hand.

I pinned Lorna's photograph on the board beside the cards. She looked back at me levelly with calm, hazel eyes and that enigmatic smile. Her dark hair was pulled smoothly away from her face. Slim and elegant, she leaned against the wall with her hands in her pockets. I studied her as if she might reveal what she had learned in the last minutes of her life. With the silence of a cat, she returned my gaze. Time to get in touch with Lorna's day self, I thought.

I drove along the two-lane asphalt road, past the low, rolling fields of dry grass, drab green overlaid with gold. Here and there, the live oaks appeared in dark green clumps. The day was darkly overcast, the sky a strange blend of charcoal and sulfur yellow clouds. The swell of mountains in the distance were a hazy blue, sandstone escarpments visible across the face. This section of Santa Teresa County is basically desert, the soil better suited for chaparral and sage scrub than productive crops. The early settlers in the area planted all the trees. The once sear land has now been softened and civilized, but there is still the aura of harsh sunlight on newly cultivated ground. Take away the irrigation systems, the drip hoses, and the sprinklers, and the vegetation would revert to its natural state—ceanothus, coyote brush, manzanita, and rolling grasses that in dry years yield a harvest of flames. If current predictions were correct and we were entering another drought, all the foliage would turn to tinder and the land would be cleared beneath a plow of fire.

Up ahead, on the left, was the Santa Teresa Water Treatment Plant, erected in the 1960s: red tile roof, three white stucco arches, and a few small trees. Beyond the low lines of the building, I caught sight of the maze of railings that surrounded concrete basins. To my right, a sign indicated the presence of the Largo reservoir, though the body of water wasn't visible from the road.

I parked out in front and went up the concrete stairs and through the double glass doors. The reception desk sat to the left of the front entrance, which opened into a big room that apparently doubled as class space. The clerk at the desk must have been Lorna's replacement. She looked young and capable, without a hint of Lorna's beauty. The brass plate on her desk indicated that her name was Melinda Ortiz.

I gave her my business card by way of introduction. "Could I have a few minutes with the plant supervisor?"

"That's his truck behind you. He just arrived."

I turned in time to see a county truck turn into the driveway. Roger Bonney emerged and headed in our direction with the preoccupied air of someone on his way to a meeting, focus already leapfrogging to the encounter to come.

"Can I tell him what this is in regards to?"

I looked back at her. "Lorna Kepler."

"Oh, her. That was awful."

"Did you know her?"

She shook her head. "I've heard people talk about her, but I never met her myself. I've only been here two months. She had this job before the girl I replaced. There might have been one more in between. Mr. Bonney had to go through quite a few after her."

"You're part-time?"

"Afternoons. I got little kids at home, so this is perfect for me. My husband works nights, so he can keep 'em while I'm gone."

Bonney entered the reception area, manila envelope in hand. He had a broad face, very tanned, tousled curly hair that had probably turned gray when he was twenty-five. The combination of lines and creases in his face had an appealing effect. He might have been too handsome in his youth, the kind of man whose looks make me surly and unresponsive. My second husband was beautiful, and that relationship had come to a demoralizing end . . . at least from my perspective. Daniel seemed to think everything was just swell, thanks. I was inclined now to disconnect from certain male types. I like a face marked by the softening processes of maturity. A few sags and bags are reassuring somehow. Bonney caught sight of me and paused politely at Melinda's desk lest he interrupt our conversation.

She showed him my card. "She asked to talk to you. It's about Lorna Kepler."

His gaze leapt to mine. The brown eyes were unexpected. With silver-gray hair and his fair coloring, I'd imagined blue.

"I'll be happy to make an appointment for later if this is not convenient," I said.

He looked at his watch. "I have the annual state health services inspection in about fifteen minutes, but you're welcome to come with me while I walk the plant. Shouldn't take long. I like to satisfy myself everything's in order before they come."

"That'd be great."

I followed him down a short corridor to the left, pausing while he stopped in his office and dropped the envelope on his desk. He wore a pale blue dress shirt, collar unbuttoned, tie askew, stone-washed blue jeans, and heavy work boots. With a hard hat and clipboard, you could place him at a construction site and mistake him for an engineer. He was a little under six feet tall, and he'd picked up the substantial look of a man in his mid-fifties. He wasn't fat by any means, but he was broad across the shoulders and heavy through the chest. My guess was that he controlled his weight now with constant exercise, probably tennis and golf, with an occasional fierce game of racquetball. He didn't have the lean muscle mass of a long-distance runner, and he somehow struck me as the sort who'd prefer competition while he kept himself in shape. I pictured him playing high school football, which in ten more years would inspire his joints to disintegrate.

I followed on his heels as we started off again. "I appreciate your talking to me on such short notice."

"It's no problem," he said. "Ever had a tour of the water treatment plant?"

"I never even knew it was here."

"We like to educate the public."

"In case the rates go up again, I'll bet."

He smiled good-naturedly as we pushed through a heavy door. "You want the spiel or not?"

"Absolutely."

"I was sure you would," he said. "Water from the reservoir across the road comes through the intake structure, passing under the floor of the reception area. You might have been aware of it if you'd known what to listen for. Fish screens and trash racks minimize the entry of foreign material. Water comes down through here. Big channel runs under this part of the building. We're about to shut down for a maintenance inspection in the next few days."

In the area we passed, a series of gauges and meters tracked the progress of the water, which was pouring through the facility with a low-level hum. The floors were concrete, and the pipes, in a tangled grid across the wall, were painted pink, dark green, brown, and blue, with arrows pointing in four directions. A floor panel had been removed, and Bonney pointed downward without a word. I peered into the hole. Down about four feet, I could see black water moving blindly through the channel like a mole. The hair along my arms seemed to crawl in response. There was no way to tell just how deep it was or what might be undulating in its depths. I stepped away from the hole, picturing a long suckered tentacle whipping out to grab my foot and drag me in. I'm nothing if not suggestible. A door closed behind us with a hollow clank, and I was forced to suppress a shriek. Bonney didn't seem to notice.

"When did you last talk to Lorna?" I asked.

"Friday morning, April twentieth," he said. "I remember because I had a golf tournament that weekend, and I was hoping to leave work early and get out to the driving range. She was due in at one, but she phoned and said she was suffering a real bad allergy attack. She was trying to get out of town anyway, you know, to find some relief from the pollen count, so I told her to go ahead and take the day off. There wasn't any point having her come in if she was feeling punk. According to the police, she died the next day."

"So she was supposed to be back at work May seventh?"

"I'd have to check the date. It would have been two weeks from Monday, and they'd found her by then." He reverted back to tour guide mode, talking about construction costs as we entered the next section of the plant. The low hum of rushing water and the smell of chlorine created an altered awareness. The general air of the place was of backwash valves and pressurized tanks on the verge of exploding. It looked as though one good jolt from the San Andreas fault and the whole facility would collapse, spewing forth billions of gallons of water and debris, which would kill both of us in seconds. I edged up closer to him, feigning an interest I didn't quite feel.

When I tuned in again, he was saying, "The water is pre-chlorinated to kill disease-causing organisms. Then we add coagulants, which cause the fine particles to clump together. Polymers are generally added in the coagulation process to improve the formation of insoluble flocs that can then be filtered out. We have a lab in the back so we can monitor the water quality."

Oh, great. Now I had to worry about disease-causing organisms on the loose in the lab. Drinking water used to be such a simple matter for me. Get a glass, turn the tap on, fill water to the brim, and gulp it down until you burped. I never thought about insoluble floc or coagulants. Barf.

Simultaneous with his explanation of the plant operation, which he must have done a hundred times in the past, I could see him scrutinize every inch of the place in preparation for the upcoming inspection. We clattered down a short flight of concrete steps and through a door to the outside. The day seemed curiously bright after the artificial light inside, and the damp air was perfumed with chemicals. Long walkways ran between blocks of open basins surrounded by metal railings, where still water sat as calm as glass, reflecting gray sky and the underside of the concrete grids.

"These are the flocculation and coagulation basins. The water's kept circulating to create a floc of good size and density for later removal in the sedimentation basins."

I was saying "Mmm"- and "Uhn-hun"-type things.

He talked on, taking the whole process for granted. What I was looking at (trying not to register my profound distaste) were still troughs where water sat with a viscous-looking liquid on its surface, bubble-coated and inky. The sludge was as black as licorice and looked as if it were made up of melted tires just coming to the boil. Perversely, I pictured a plunge into the tarry depths, wondering if you'd flail to the surface with your flesh in tatters from all the chemicals. Steven Spielberg could have a ball with this stuff.

"You're not with the police department?" he asked. He hadn't stopped walking once.

"I was, once upon a time. Temperamentally, I'm better suited to the private sector."

I was trotting at his heels like a kid on a field trip, irretrievably separated from the rest of the class. Out the backside of the plant, there was a wide, shallow reservoir of cracked black sediment, like a thawing pond of crud. Thousands of years from now, anthropologists would dig this up and imagine it was some kind of sacrificial basin.

He asked, "Are you allowed to say who you're working for? Or is that privileged information?"

"Lorna's parents," I said. "Sometimes I prefer not to give out the information, but in this case it's a straightforward matter. No big secret. I had this same conversation with Serena last night."

"My soon-to-be ex? Well, that's an interesting point of departure. Why her? Because she found the body?"

"That's right. I couldn't get to sleep. I knew she worked the night shift at St. Terry's, so I thought I might as well talk to her first. If I'd thought you were up, I'd have knocked on your door as well."

"Enterprising," he remarked.

"I'm getting paid fifty bucks an hour for this. Makes sense to work every chance I get."

"How's it going so far?"

"Right now, I'm at the information-gathering phase, trying to get a feel for what I'm dealing with. I understand Lorna worked for you for what, three years?"

"About that. Originally the job was full-time, but with the budget cuts, we decided we'd try getting by with twenty hours a week. So far it's been fine, not ideal, but doable. Lorna was taking classes over at city college, and the part-time employment really suited her schedule."

By now we'd circled back through the plant on some subterranean level. The entire underground space was dominated by massive pipes. We went up a long flight of stairs and suddenly emerged into a well-lighted corridor not that far from his office. He showed me in and indicated a chair. "Have a seat."

"You have time?"

"Let's cover what we can, and what we don't have time for, we can try another day." He leaned over and pressed the button on his intercom. "Melinda, buzz me if I'm not out there when the inspectors arrive."

I heard a muffled, "Yes, sir."

"Sorry for the interruption. Go ahead," he said.

"No problem. Was Lorna good at the job?"

"I had no complaints. The work itself didn't amount to much. She was largely a receptionist."

"Did you know much about her personal life?"

"Yes and no. Actually, in a facility like ours, where you have less than twenty employees on any given shift, we get to know each other pretty well. We're in operation twenty-four hours a day, seven days a week, so this is family to me. I have to say Lorna was a little bit standoffish. She wasn't rude or cold, but she was definitely reserved. Break time, she always seemed to have her nose in a book. Brought a sack lunch, sometimes sat out in her car to eat. She didn't volunteer a lot of information. She'd answer if you asked, but she wasn't forthcoming."

"People have described her as secretive."

He made a face at the term. "I wouldn't say that. 'Secretive' has a sinister implication to my way of thinking. She was pleasant, but somewhat aloof. The term *restrained* might be apt."

"How would you describe your relationship with her?"

"*My* relationship?"

"Yes, I'm wondering if you ever saw her outside of work."

His laugh seemed embarrassed. "If you mean what I think, I have to say I'm flattered, but she was strictly an employee. She

116

was a good-looking girl, but she was what . . . twenty-four years old?"

"Twenty-five."

"And I'm twice that. Believe me, Lorna had no interest in a man my age."

"Why not? You're nice-looking, and you seem personable."

"I appreciate your vote, but it doesn't mean much to a girl in her position. She was probably looking for marriage and a family, last thing in the world I have any interest in. In her eyes, I'd have been a slightly overweight old turd. Besides, the women I date, I like to have shared interests and intelligent conversation. Lorna was bright, but she never even heard of the Tet offensive, and the only Kennedys she knew about were Caroline and John-John."

"Just a possibility," I remarked. "I broached the same subject with Serena, wondering if Lorna was in any way associated with your divorce."

"Not at all. My marriage to Serena simply ran out of juice. Sometimes I think dissension would have been an improvement. Conflict has some spark to it. What we had was flat."

"Serena says you wanted the divorce."

"Well, that's true," he said, "but I've bent over backward to keep things friendly. It's like I said to my attorney: I feel guilty enough as it is, so let's not make matters worse. I love Serena. She's a hell of a nice gal, and I think the world of her. I'm just not ready to live without passion. I'd have to hope she represented the situation much in the same light."

"Actually, she did," I said, "but I thought it was worth exploring in the context of Lorna's death."

"I understand. Of course, I was sorry as hell when I found out what happened to her. She was honest, she was prompt, and as far as I know, she got along with everyone." I saw him ease a look at his watch under the pretext of adjusting the band.

I stirred on my chair. "I better let you go," I said. "I can see you're distracted."

"I guess I am, now that you mention it. I hope you don't think I'm rude."

"Not at all. I appreciate your time. I have to be out of town in the next couple of days, but I may get back to you, if that's okay."

"Of course. I'm sometimes hard to reach, but you can check with Melinda. We'll be closing down for maintenance and repairs on Saturday, so I'll be here if you need me then."

"I'll keep that in mind. In the meantime, if you think of anything pertinent, could you give me a call?"

"Certainly," he said.

I left another business card. We shook hands across the desk, and then he walked me out. Two inspectors were waiting by Melinda's desk. The guy wore a dress shirt, jeans, and tennis shoes. I noticed the woman inspector was dressed a lot better. Roger greeted them pleasantly, giving me a quick wave as he ushered them down the hall.

I drove to my office. It was midafternoon and faint rays of winter sun were pushing through the overcast. The sky was white, the grass a vivid shade of lime green. February comes to Santa Teresa in a tumble of hot pink geraniums, magenta bougainvillea, and orange nasturtiums. I was accustomed to functioning in the dark by now, and the light seemed harsh, the colors too glaring. Night seemed softer, like a liquid that surrounded everything, cool and soothing. At night, all the foliage was blended by shadow, fused and simplified, where daylight divided, setting objects in sharp contrast, at war with one another.

I let myself in the side entrance and then sat at my desk, shifting papers around, trying to behave as if I had some purpose. I was too tired to socialize and the lack of sleep was re-creating the sensation of being stoned. I felt as if I'd been smoking dope for the last two days. All my energy had seeped away, like sawdust leaking out through a hole in my shoe. At the same time, the infusion of coffee was causing a crackling sound in the center of my brain, like an antenna picking up radio signals from outer space. Any minute now Venusians would send warnings of the forthcoming invasion, and I'd be too out of it to call the police. I laid my head down on my desk and sank into unconsciousness.

An hour and five minutes into the nap to end all naps, the telephone rang. The sound cut through me like a chain saw. I jumped as if goosed. I snatched up the receiver and identified myself, trying to sound as though I were wide awake.

"Miss Millhone? This is Joe Ayers. What can I do for you?"

I couldn't think who the hell he was. "Mr. Ayers, I appreciate the call," I said enthusiastically. "Hang on one second." I put my hand across the mouthpiece. Joe Ayers. Joseph Ayers. Ah. The pornographic film producer. I shifted the phone to the other ear so I could make notes as we chatted. "I understand you were the producer of an art movie in which Lorna Kepler appeared."

"That's correct."

"Can you tell me about her involvement in the project?"

"I'm not sure what you're asking."

"I guess I'm not, either. Someone sent a video to her mother, and she asked me what I could find out. I noticed your name listed as the producer—"

Ayers cut in brusquely. "Miss Millhone, you're going to have to fill me in here. We have nothing to discuss. Lorna Kepler was murdered six months ago."

"It was actually ten months. I'm aware of that. Her parents are hoping to develop additional information." I was sounding pompous even to my own ears, but his irritation was irritating.

"Well, you're not going to develop anything from me," he said. "I wish I could help, but my contact with Lorna was extremely limited. Sorry I can't help you."

I checked my notes in haste, trying to talk fast enough to snag his interest. "What about the other two actors who were in the film with her, Nancy Dobbs and Russell Turpin?"

I could hear him shift with annoyance. "What about them?"

"I'd like to talk to them."

Silence. "I can probably tell you how to get to him," he said finally.

"You have a current address and telephone number?"

"I should have it somewhere." I heard him snapping through the pages of what I guessed was his address book. I tucked the phone in the crook of my neck and uncapped my pen.

"Here we go," he said.

He rattled out the information, which I made a note of. The Haight Street address corresponded with the one I'd picked up from directory assistance. I said, "This is terrific. I appreciate this. What about Miss Dobbs?"

"Can't help you there."

"Look, can you tell me what your schedule is for the next couple of days?"

"What does my schedule have to do with it?"

"I was hoping we could meet."

Through the phone, I could hear his brain cells whirring as he processed the request. "I really don't see the point. I hardly knew Lorna. I might have been in her company four days at best."

"Can you remember when you last saw her?"

"No. I know I never saw her after the shoot, and that'd be a year ago December. That was the one and only time we ever did business together. Matter of fact, that film was never even put in release, so I had no reason to contact her afterward."

"Why wasn't the film released?"

"I don't think that's any of your concern."

"What is it, some kind of secret?"

"It's not secret. It's just none of your business."

"That's too bad. I was hoping you could give us some help."

"Miss Millhone, I don't even really know who you are. You call me up, leave a message on my machine with an area code I don't even recognize. You could be anyone. Why the hell should I help you?"

"Right. You're right. You don't know me from Adam, and there's no way I can compel you to give me information. I'm down in Santa Teresa, an hour away by plane. I don't want anything in particular from you, Mr. Ayers. I'm just doing what I can to try to figure out what happened to Lorna, and I'd appreciate some background. I can't force you to cooperate."

"It's not a question of cooperation. I have nothing to contribute. Truly."

"I probably wouldn't even take an hour of your time."

I could hear him breathing while he took this in. I half expected him to hang up. Instead his tone became wary. "You're not trying to break into the business, are you?"

"The business?" I thought he was referring to the private eye trade.

"Because if you're some kind of bullshit actress, you're wasting your time. I don't care how big your tits are."

"I assure you I'm not. This is strictly legitimate. You can verify my credentials with the Santa Teresa police."

"You couldn't have caught me at a worse time. I just flew back from six weeks in Europe. My wife's having some kind of goddamn shindig I'm supposed to attend tonight. She's shelling out a fortune, and I don't know half the people she's invited. I'm dead on my feet as it is."

"What about tomorrow?"

"That's even worse. I've got business to take care of."

"Tonight then? I can probably be there in a couple of hours."

He was silent, but his annoyance was palpable. "Oh, shit. All right. What the hell," he said. "If you actually fly up, you can give me a call. If I feel up to it, I'll see you. If not, too bad. That's the best I can do, and I'll probably regret it."

"That's great. That's fine. Can I reach you at this same number?"

He sighed, probably counting to ten. I'd irritated him so desperately, we were almost friends. "Here's the number at the house. I might as well give you the address while I'm at it. You sound like you can be very obnoxious if you don't get what you want."

"I'm terrible," I said.

He gave me his home address.

"I'm going to bed," he said. I heard the phone banged down.

I put a call through to my travel agent, Lupe, and asked for reservations on the next flight out. As it happened, everything was booked until nine o'clock. She put me on standby status and told me to get on out to the airport. I went back to my place and flung a few items in a duffel bag. At the last minute, I remembered I hadn't told Ida Ruth where I'd be. I called her at home.

Here's what she said when she heard I was flying to San Francisco: "Well, I hope you're wearing something better than jeans and a turtleneck."

"Ida Ruth, I'm insulted. This is business," I said.

"Uhn-hun. Look down and describe what you have on. On second thought, don't bother. I'm sure you look stunning. You want to give me a number where you can be reached?"

"I don't know where I'll be staying. I'll call when I get there and let you know."

"Leave it on the office machine. I'll be in bed by the time you get to San Francisco," she said. "You be careful."

"Yes, ma'am. I promise."

"Take some vitamins."

"I will. See you when I get back," I said.

I tidied my apartment in case the plane went down, taking out the trash as a parting gesture to the gods. As we all know, the day I neglect this important ritual, the plane will auger in and everyone will think what a slob I was. Besides, I like order on the premises. Coming home from a trip, I like to be greeted with serenity, not sloppiness.

10

When I got to the airport, I left the VW in long-term parking and hiked back to the terminal. Like most public buildings in Santa Teresa, the airport is vaguely Spanish in appearance: one and a half stories of white stucco with a red tile roof, arches, and a curving stairway up the side. Inside the terminal, there are only five departure gates, with a tiny newsstand on the first floor and a modest coffee shop on the second. At the United counter, I picked up my ticket and gave my name to the agent in case a seat opened up on an earlier plane. No such luck. I found a seat nearby, propped my head on my fist, and snoozed like a vagrant until my flight was called. In the time I waited, I could have driven to San Francisco.

The plane was a little putt-putt with fifteen seats, ten of which were occupied. I turned my attention to the glossy airline magazine tucked in the seat pouch in front of me. This was my complimentary copy—it said so right on the front—the term *complimentary* meaning way too boring to spend real money on. While the engines were being revved up with all the high whine of racing mopeds, the flight attendant recited last rites. We couldn't hear a word she was saying, but the way her mouth was moving we got the general idea.

We took off with the aircraft bucking and shuddering, the flight smoothing out abruptly as we reached altitude. The attendant made her way down the aisle with a tray, dispensing clear plastic cups full of orange juice or Coca-Cola and childproof packets of—choose one—pretzels or peanuts. The airlines, extremely cunning at trimming costs these days, have now reduced the serving size of these peanuts to (approximately) one tablespoon per person. I broke each of mine in half, eating one piece at a time to prolong the experience.

As we droned up the coast through the night-blackened sky, communities below us appeared as a series of patchy, disconnected lights. At that altitude the towns looked like isolated colonies on an alien planet with dark stretches between what by day would be mountains. I was disoriented by the landscape. I tried to pick out Santa Maria, Paso Robles, and King City, but I had no clear sense of size or distances. I could see the 101, but the highway looked eerie and unfamiliar at that remove.

We reached San Francisco in a little under an hour and a half. Coming in, I could see the streetlights undulate across the hills, tracing the terrain like a contour map. We touched down at a commuter terminal so remote that a progression of ground agents had to be stationed along the tarmac to point us to civilization. We went into the building, up the back stairs like immigration deportees, and finally emerged into a familiar corridor. I stopped off at a newsstand and bought myself a decent city map, then found the rental car counter, where I filled out all the paperwork. By 11:05 I was on the 101, heading north toward the city.

The night was clear and cold, the lights of Oakland and Alameda visible to my right across the bay. Traffic moved swiftly, and the city began to take shape around me like a neon confection. Half a mile past Market Street, at Golden Gate Avenue, the 101 dwindled down to a surface road. I drove the short half block to Van Ness and turned left, eventually taking another left onto Lombard. Coffee shops and motels of every size and description lined both

sides of the four-lane thoroughfare. Not wanting to devote unnecessary energy to the project, I checked into the Del Rey Motel at
the first "Vacant" sign. I would only be there one night. All I
needed was a room clean enough that I wouldn't be forced to wear
shoes at all times. I asked for accommodations away from the traffic
noise and was directed to 343 at the back.

The Del Rey was one of those motels where the management
assumes you're going to steal everything in sight. All the coat hangers were designed so the hooks couldn't be removed from the
hanging rod. There was a notice on the television warning that
removal of the cord and any movement of the set would automatically sound an alarm beyond guest control. The clock radio was
bolted to the bed table. This was an establishment fully prepared to
outfox thieves and scam artists. I put an ear to the wall, wondering
who might be lurking in the room next to mine. I could hear snores
rattle against the quiet. That was going to be restful later when I
tried to sleep myself. I sat down on the edge of the bed and called
the office, leaving my telephone number for Ida Ruth. While I was
at it, I dialed my own answering machine, using the remote code to
check for messages. None. My winsome long-distance message had
netted me no response, which meant I'd have to go a-calling at
some point.

It was nearly midnight by now, and I could feel energy seeping
out through my pores. Since I'd given up my day life to conduct my
business by night, I'd noticed it was getting harder to predict the
plunges into exhaustion. I longed to fling myself backward on the
bed and fall asleep in my clothes. I roused myself before the notion
became too seductive. In the bathroom, a printed notice warned of
lingering drought conditions and begged motel guests to use as
little water as possible. I took a quick (guilt-ridden) shower, then
dried myself on a towel as rough as a sidewalk. I set my duffel on
the bed and pulled out clean underwear and panty hose. Then I
hauled out the wonder garment, my black all-purpose dress. Not
that long ago, this article had been a-fester with ditch water, smelling of mildew and assorted swamp creatures. I'd sent it to the
cleaners several times in the intervening months, and by now it was

as good as new . . . unless you sniffed really, really closely. The fabric represented the apex of recent scientific achievement: lightweight, wrinkle-defying, quick-drying, and indestructible. Several of my acquaintances rued this latter quality, begging me to dump the dress and add another to my wardrobe. I couldn't see the point. With its long sleeves and tucked front, the all-purpose dress was perfect (well, adequate) for all occasions. I'd worn it to weddings, funerals, cocktail parties, and court appearances. I gave it a shake and undid the zipper, managing to step into the dress and my black flats simultaneously. No one would mistake me for a fashion plate, but at least I could pass myself off as a grown-up.

According to the map and the address I'd been given, Joseph Ayers was living in Pacific Heights. I laid the map on the car seat and left on the interior light so I could see where I was going. I took a left on Divisadero and headed toward Sacramento Street. Once in the vicinity, I cruised the area. Even at this hour, the Ayers residence wasn't hard to spot. The house was ablaze with lights, and a steady stream of guests, both arriving and departing, were taking advantage of the "varlet" parking out in front. I turned my car over to one of the young men in black dress pants and white tuxedo shirts. There was a Mercedes ahead of me and a Jaguar pulling up behind.

The front gate was open, and late arrivals were being steered around the side of the house toward the garden in back. Entrance to the party was being monitored by a man in a tuxedo, who viewed my outfit with visible concern. "Good evening. May I see your invitation?"

"I'm not here for the party. I have a personal appointment with Mr. Ayers."

His look said this seemed doubtful; however, he was being paid to smile, and he gave me the minimum wage's worth. "Ring the front doorbell. One of the maids will let you in."

The house was surrounded by a narrow band of yard, generous by San Francisco standards, where houses were usually constructed smack up against each other. A high boxwood hedge had been planted just inside the wrought-iron fence to maximize privacy. I moved up the brick walk. The grass on either side was tender green and recently mowed. The house was a looming three stories of old red brick, aged to the color of ripe watermelon. All of the leaded-glass windows were framed in pale gray stone. The mansard roof was gray slate, and the entire facade was washed with indirect lighting. From the rear, I could hear the alcohol-amplified voices of numerous guests superimposed on the harmonies of a three-piece combo. Occasionally a burst of laughter shot upward like a bottle rocket, exploding softly against the quiet darkness of the neighborhood.

I rang the bell as instructed. A maid in a black uniform opened the door and stepped back to admit me. I gave her my name and told her Mr. Ayers was expecting me. She didn't seem to care one way or the other, and the black all-purpose dress apparently suited her just fine, thanks. She nodded and departed, allowing me a moment to take in my surroundings. The foyer was circular, with a black marble staircase curving up from the right. The ceiling rose a full two stories and was capped with a cascading chandelier of gilt and flashing prisms. One of these days an earthquake would send the weight of it crashing, and the maid would be flattened like a cartoon coyote.

Yet another man in a tuxedo appeared in due course and escorted me toward the back of the house. The floors were black-and-white marble squares, laid out like a gameboard. The ceilings in the rooms we passed were a good twelve feet high, rimmed with plaster garlands and strange imps peering down at us. The walls in the hallway were covered in dark red silk, padded to dampen sound. I was so intent on my survey, I nearly bumped into a door. The butler butled on, ignoring me discreetly when I yelped in surprise.

He ushered me into the library and pulled the double doors together as he left the room. A large Oriental rug spread a soft mauve pattern across the parquet floor. On the left, the room was anchored by a massive antique desk of mahogany and teak, inlaid with brass. The furniture—an oversize sofa and three solidly constructed armchairs—was upholstered in burgundy leather. The room was functional, fully used, not some tidy assemblage designed to impress. I could see file cabinets, a computer setup, a fax machine, a copier, and a four-line telephone. Mahogany shelves on three walls were lined with books, one section devoted to film scripts with titles inked across the visible end.

On the fourth wall, floor-to-ceiling windows overlooked the walled grounds in the rear, where the party was in full swing. The noise level had risen, but the brunt of it was muted by the mullioned panes. I stood at the windows and looked down at the crowd below. Sections of the immense garden had been tented for the occasion, the red canvas glowing with candlelight. Tall propane heaters had been placed along the perimeter to warm the chilly night air. Tiny bulbs had been strung through all the saplings on the property. Every branch was defined by pinpoints of illumination. Tables had been covered in red satin cloths. The centerpieces were arrangements of dark red roses and carnations. Folding chairs were swaddled in clouds of red netting. I could see the caterers were still setting up a cold midnight supper—blood sausage, no doubt.

The invitations must have specified the dress requirements. The men wore black tuxedos, and all the women wore full- or cocktail-length dresses in red or black. The women were slim, and their hair was ornamental, dyed that strange California blond affected by women over fifty. Their faces seemed perfect, though by dint of surgery they all appeared to be much the same age. I suspected that none of these people were the cream of San Francisco society. These folk were the rich milk who had risen as close to the top of the bottle as money and ambition permitted in the course of one generation. My guess was that even as they drank, eyeing the buffet tables, they were trashing the host and hostess.

"If you're hungry, I can have someone bring you something to eat."

I turned. "I'm fine," I said automatically. In truth I was starving, but I knew I'd feel disadvantaged grubbing down food in this man's presence. "Kinsey Millhone," I said as I held out my hand. "Thanks for seeing me tonight."

"Joseph Ayers," he replied. He was probably in his late forties, with the intense air of a gynecologist delivering embarrassing news. He wore glasses with large lenses and heavy tortoise-shell frames. He tended to keep his head down, dark eyes peering up somberly. His handshake was firm, and his flesh felt as slick as if he'd just donned rubber gloves. His forehead was lined, his face elongated, an effect exaggerated by the creases beside his mouth and down the length of his cheeks. His dark hair was beginning to thin on top, but I could see that he'd been vigorously handsome once upon a time. He wore the requisite tuxedo. If he was still exhausted from long hours in the air, he showed no signs of it. He gestured me onto one of the leather chairs, and I took a seat. He sat down behind the desk and placed a finger against his lips, tapping thoughtfully while he studied me. "Actually, you might look good on camera. You have an interesting face."

"No offense, Mr. Ayers, but I've seen one of your films. Faces are the least of it."

He smiled slightly. "You'd be surprised. There was a time when the audience wanted big, voluptuous women—Marilyn Monroe types—almost grotesquely well endowed. Now we're looking for something a little more realistic. Not that I'm trying to talk you into anything."

"This is good," I said.

"I have a film school background," he said as if I'd pressed for an explanation. "Like George Lucas and Oliver Stone, those guys. Not that I put myself in the same league with them. I'm an academic at heart. That's the point I was trying to make."

"Do they know what you do?"

He cocked his head toward the window. "I've always said I was in the business, which is true—or at least, it was. I sold my company a year ago to an international conglomerate. That's what I've been doing in Europe these past few weeks, tying up loose ends."

"You must have been quite successful."

"More so than the average Hollywood producer. My overhead was low, and I never had to tolerate union bosses or studio heads. If I wanted to do a project, I did it, just like that." He snapped his fingers to illustrate. "Every film I've done has been an instant hit, which is more than most Hollywood producers can say."

"What about Lorna? How'd you meet her?"

"I was down in Santa Teresa Memorial Day weekend, this would have been a couple of years ago. I spotted her in a hotel bar and asked if she was interested in an acting career. She laughed in my face. I gave her my card and a couple of my videocassettes. She called me some months later and expressed an interest. I set up the shoot. She flew up to San Francisco and did two and a half days' work, for which she was paid twenty-five hundred dollars. That's the extent of it."

"I'm still puzzled by the fact that the film never went into distribution."

"Let's just say I wasn't happy with the finished product. The film looked cheap, and the camera work was lousy. The company that bought me out ended up taking my entire library, but that one wasn't included in the deal."

"Did you know Lorna was working as a hooker on the side?"

"No, but it doesn't surprise me. Do you know what they call those people? Sex workers. A sex worker might do all manner of things: massage, exotic dance, out-call, Lesbian videos, hard-core magazines. They're like migrant pickers on the circuit. They go where the work is, sometimes city to city. Not that I'm saying she'd done related work. I'm filling you in on the big picture."

I watched his face, marveling at the matter-of-fact tone he was using. "What about you? What was your relationship with her?"

"I was in London when she was killed. I left on the twentieth."

I disregarded the nonsequitur, though it interested me. When we'd talked on the phone, he'd been vague about how long ago her death had occurred. Maybe he'd done an internal audit in anticipation of my arrival.

He opened a drawer and took out a slip of paper. "I checked the payroll roster for the film she did. These are the names and addresses of a couple of crew members I've been in touch with since. I can't guarantee they're still here in San Francisco, but it's a place to start."

I took the slip and glanced at it, recognizing the names from the list I'd checked. Both San Francisco numbers were now disconnects. "Thanks. I appreciate this." Worthless as it is, I thought.

He got up from the desk. "Now if you'll forgive me, I have to put in a quick appearance before I go to bed. Are you sure you wouldn't like a drink?"

"Thanks, but I'd better not. I have ground to cover yet, and I'm not in town that long."

"I'll walk you out," he said courteously.

I followed him down the wide white marble stairs, across the foyer, and through a vast empty room with a domed ceiling and pale, glossy, hardwood floors. At the far end, there was a small stage. "What will you do now that your business is sold?"

"This is the ballroom," he said, catching the curiosity in my look. "My wife had it refurbished. She gives charity balls for diseases only rich people get. To answer your question, I won't have to do anything."

"Lucky you."

"Not luck. This was my intention from the onset. I'm a goal-oriented person. I'd advise you to do likewise."

"Absolutely," I said.

In the foyer, we shook hands. I noticed he had the door closed before I reached the front walk. I retrieved my car, tipping the parking valet a buck. From his look of amazement, everybody else must have tipped him five.

I consulted my map. Russell Turpin's Haight Street address wasn't far. I headed south on Masonic and crossed the Panhandle section of Golden Gate Park. Haight was two blocks up, and the address I needed was only four blocks down.

The sidewalks were crowded with pedestrians. Remnants of the past glories of Haight-Ashbury were still in evidence: vintage dress shops and bookstores, funky-looking restaurants, a storefront clinic. The street was well lighted, and there was still quite a bit of traffic. The street people were decked out like the flower children of old, still wearing bell-bottoms, nose rings, dreadlocks, torn blue jeans, leather, face paints, multiple earrings, backpacks, and knee-high boots. Music tumbled out of bars. In half the doorways, kids loitered, looking stoned, though perhaps on drugs more exotic than grass or 'ludes.

I circled, driving an eight-block track—two down, two over, two up, two back—trying to find a place to tuck my car. San Francisco seems ill equipped to accommodate the number of vehicles within the city limits. Parked cars are squeezed into every available linear inch of curb, angled into hillsides, lined up on sidewalks, wedged against the buildings. Front bumpers are nosed in too close to fire hydrants. Back bumpers hang out into red-painted zones. Garage space is at a premium, and every driveway bristles with signs warding off the poachers.

By the time I found parking, it was nearly 1:00 A.M. I tucked my rental around the corner on Baker Street, whipping into a place as another vehicle pulled out. I fumbled in the bottom of my handbag until I found my penlight. I locked my car and hiked up the hill the half block to Haight. All of the buildings were close-packed, pastel, four and five stories tall. An occasional frail tree contributed a grace note of green. Many of the oversize windows were still lighted. From the street I could see, in a diminishing series of acute angles, fireplace mantels, bold, abstract paintings, white walls, bookshelves, hanging plants, and crown molding.

The address I had turned out to be a "modern" fourplex of shaggy brown shingles sandwiched between two Victorian frame houses. The streetlight was burned out, and I was left to surmise that one was painted dull red, the other an indigo blue with (perhaps) white trim. In the dark, both appeared to be shades of muddy gray. I talked to a painter once who worked on movie sets. For a film shot in black and white, he said the crew used brown paint in eleven different shades. My current surroundings had the same feel, an environment drained of color, reduced to tones of chestnut and dun. The gradations were infinite but visible only to night souls.

Turpin apparently occupied a second-floor apartment, and I was gratified to note that the hand-lettered card tucked in the slot actually specified "Russell" by name, along with a housemate named

Cherie Stanislaus. I peered through the glass door at a handsomely papered foyer with an apartment door on either side. At the rear, a stairway angled left and out of sight, probably doubling back on itself to an identical hallway above. I moved out to the street and looked up at the second-floor windows. The front rooms on both sides of the building were lighted, which suggested that the occupants were still awake.

As I moved up the stairs to the entrance, I could hear the tapping of high heels approaching from behind me. I paused, looking back. The blonde coming up the stairs wore makeup so pale, the effect was ghostly. Her eyes were elaborately done up with thick false eyelashes, two shades of eye shadow, and a black pencil line on both her upper and lower lids. Her forehead was high, and her hair was teased upward at the crown, held back with a gaudy rhinestone clip. The rest of her hair was long and straight, splitting at the shoulder so that half extended down her back. A cluster of long curls tumbled over her breasts. Her long dangle earrings were shaped like elongated question marks. She wore a dark leotard on top and a slinky black skirt that was split up one side. Her hips were narrow, her stomach flat. She took out a ring of keys and gave me a long, cool look as she unlocked the foyer door. "Looking for someone?"

"Russell Turpin."

"Well, you've come to the right place." Her smile was self-contained, not unfriendly, but less than warm I thought. "He's not here, but you can come up and wait if you want. I'm his roommate."

"Thanks. You're Cherie?"

"That's right. Who are you, pray tell?"

"Kinsey Millhone," I said. "I left a message on your machine. . . ."

"I remember that. You're Lorna's friend," she said. She pushed the door open, and I followed her in. She paused, making sure the door had latched shut again before she headed up the stairs. I trailed behind. Having lied on the phone, I now had to decide whether to play this straight.

"Actually, Lorna and I never met," I said. "I'm a private investigator looking into her death. You knew she'd been killed?"

"Yes, of course we did. I'm happy to hear you mention it. Russell wasn't looking forward to delivering the bad news about Lorna's death." Her stockings were black mesh, and her three-inch stiletto heels forced her calves into high relief. When we reached the second-floor landing, she unlocked the door to apartment C. She stepped out of her shoes with a little grimace of relief, then padded through the living room in her stocking feet. I thought she'd turn on a table lamp, but apparently she preferred the gloom. "Make yourself comfortable," she said.

"You have any idea what time he'll be home?"

"Any time, I'd imagine. He doesn't like staying out too late." She turned on a light in the kitchen, which was visible through bifold shutters resting on the countertop. She pushed the shutters open. Through the gap, I watched her take out two ice-cube trays, which she cracked and emptied into an acrylic ice bucket. "I'm having a drink. If you want one, speak up. I hate playing hostess, but I'm good for one round. I have a bottle of Chardonnay open, if you're interested. You look like a white wine kind of girl."

"I'd love some. You need help?"

"Don't we all?" she remarked. "You have offices in the city?"

"I'm from Santa Teresa."

She tilted her head, peering through the pass-through at me. "Why would you come all the way up to see Russell? He's not a suspect, I hope."

"Are you his girlfriend?" I thought it was time I posed the questions instead of her.

"I wouldn't say that. We're fond of each other, but we're not exactly an 'item.' He prefers to be thought of as footloose and fancy free. One of those types."

She plunked several ice cubes in a tall glass and splashed Scotch halfway up the side. She squirted in seltzer water, using one of those devices I'd seen in old thirties movies. She took a sip, shuddering slightly, and then set the glass aside while she found a wineglass in the cupboard. She held it up to the light and decided it wasn't clean enough. She rinsed and dried it. She took the Chardonnay out of the refrigerator and filled my glass, then put the bottle in a cooler and left it on the counter. I moved over to the pass-through and took the wineglass she handed me.

"I don't know if you're aware of this, but Russell's very screwed up," she said.

"Really. I've never met him."

"You can take my word for it. You want to know why? Because he's hung like a mule."

I said, "Ah." Having seen him in action, I could attest to that.

Cherie smiled. "I like the 'ah.' It's diplomatic. Come on back to my room and we can talk while I change. If I don't get out of this girdle, I'm going to kill myself very soon."

11

Cherie's bedroom furniture consisted of a fifties "sweet" of blond wood with curving lines. She sat down at a dressing table with a big round mirror in the center and two deep drawers on either side. She turned on a dressing table lamp, leaving the rest of the room shrouded in shadows. She had twin beds with blond-wood headboards, a blond bed table, an old forty-five record player with a fat black spindle, and a black canvas-and-wrought-iron butterfly chair covered with discarded clothing. My only choice for seating was one of the twin beds. I elected to lean against the door frame instead.

Cherie wriggled out of her girdle and panty hose and tossed them on the floor, then turned to study herself in the mirror. She leaned forward, checking the lines near her eyes with a critical gaze. She shook her head in disgust. "Isn't aging the pits? Sometimes I think I should just shoot myself and get it over with."

While I watched, she spread out a clean white towel and took out cold cream, a skin toner, cotton balls, and Q-tips, apparently in preparation for removing her makeup. I've seen dental hygienists who weren't as meticulous in assembling their instruments.

"Did you know Lorna?" I asked.

"I met her. I didn't 'know' her."

"What'd you think of her?"

"I was envious, of course. She was what they call 'a natural beauty.' All so effortless. It's enough to make you sick." Her eyes met mine in the mirror. "You don't wear a lot of makeup, so you probably can't relate to this, but I spend *hours* on myself, and to what end, I ask? Fifteen minutes on the street and it all evaporates. My lipstick's eaten off. My eye shadow ends up in this crease . . . look at this. My eyeliner gets transferred to my upper lid. Every time I blow my nose, my foundation comes off on the tissue like paint. Lorna was just the opposite. She never had to do anything at all." She peeled off a false eyelash and placed it in a small box, where it lay like a wink. She peeled off the other lash and placed it beside the first. Now it looked like two eyes closed in sleep. "What I wouldn't have given to have skin like hers," she said. "Oh, well. What's a poor girl to do?" She put a hand to her forehead and lifted off her hair. Under the wig, she wore what looked like a rubber bathing cap. She dropped her voice to its natural baritone, addressing my reflection. "Well! Here's Russell now. Nice to meet you," he said. Like a disappearing act, Cherie vanished, leaving a slightly gawky-looking man in her place. He turned and struck a pose. "Be honest. Which do you prefer?"

I smiled. "I like Cherie."

"So do I," he said. He turned and looked at himself again, squinting closely. "I can't tell you how obnoxious it is waking up every morning to a beard. And a penis? My gawd. Picture *that* in your lacy little underpants. Like a big old ugly worm. Scares me to death." He began to put cold cream on his face, wiping off foundation in swipes.

I couldn't take my eyes off him. The illusion had been perfect. "Do you do this every day? Dress up in women's clothes?"

"Most days. After work. From nine to five, I'm Russell: tie, sport coat, button-down collar, the whole bit. I don't wear wingtips, but the moral and spiritual equivalent."

"What sort of work do you do?"

"I'm the assistant manager at the local Circuit City, selling stereo systems. Nights, I can relax and do anything I want."

"You don't make a living from the acting?"

"Oh. You saw the film," he said. "I hardly made a dime, and it never went anywhere, which I must say was a relief. Think of the irony of getting famous as Russell, when I'm really Cherie at heart."

"I just talked to Joe Ayers at his place. He says he sold his company."

"Trying to turn respectable, I'd imagine." He raised his eyebrows, smiling slightly. His expression suggested there was no real chance of *that*. Foundation gone, he took a cotton ball and soaked it with skin toner. He began to wipe off the cold cream and any remaining traces of makeup.

"How many films did you make for him?"

"Just the one."

"Were you disappointed it was never released?"

"I was at the time. I've realized since then that I don't care to capitalize on my 'equipment.' I despise being male. I really hate all the macho posturing and bullshit, all the *effort* it takes. It's much more fun being female. Sometimes I'm tempted to do away with 'it,' but I can't bear to have myself surgically altered, as endowed as I am. Maybe an organ donor program would be interested," he said. He waved a hand airily. "But enough of my tacky problems. What else can I tell you about Lorna?"

"I'm not sure. I gather you really didn't know her that well."

"That depends on your frame of reference. We spent two days together while the film was being shot. We had an instant rapport and laughed our tiny asses off. She was *such* a kick. Kinky and fearless, with a wicked sense of humor. We were soul sisters. I mean that. I was heartbroken when I heard that she had *died,* of all things."

"That was the only time you saw her? During the filming?"

"No, I ran into her maybe two months later, up here shopping with that piggy-looking sister."

"Which one? She has two."

"Oh, really. I can't remember the name. Something odd, as I recall. She looked like an imitation Lorna: same face, but all porked out. Anyway, I saw them on the street down around Union Square, and we stopped to chat about nothing in particular. She looked spectacular as ever. That's the last I saw of her."

"What about the other actress, Nancy Dobbs? Was she a friend of Lorna's?"

"Oh, gawd. Wasn't she the worst? Talk about wooden."

"She was pretty bad," I admitted. "Has she done other films for Ayers?"

"I doubt it. In fact, I'm sure not. I think she just did that one as a lark. Someone else had been hired and opted out at the last minute. Lorna had *her* pegged. Nancy was terribly ambitious, without the talent or the body to get very far. She's one of those women who'd try to screw her way to the top, only no one would have her, so how far could she get? What a dog." Russell laughed. "Actually, she'd have screwed a dog if she'd thought it would help."

"How'd she get along with Lorna?"

"As far as I know, they never had any kind of *snit,* but privately each felt *in*finitely superior to the other. I know because they both took to confiding in me between takes."

"Is she still in the city? I'd like to talk to her."

Russell looked at me with surprise. "You didn't see her tonight? I thought you must have talked to her at Ayers's little soiree."

"What would she be doing there?"

"She's married to him. That's the point, isn't it? All during the shoot, she really flung herself at him. Next thing we heard . . . wahlah. She was Mrs. Joseph Ayers, noted socialite. It's probably why he dumped the porno flick. Imagine *that* getting out. He calls her 'Duchess,' by the way. Isn't that pretentious?"

"Was there ever a suggestion that Joe Ayers's relationship with Lorna was other than professional?"

"He was never involved with her sexually, if that's what you mean. It's really a bit of a cliché to imagine these guys are out 'sampling the merchandise.' Believe me, his only interest was in making a buck."

"Lorna's mother seems to think her death was related to the film somehow."

"Possible, I suppose, but why would anybody kill her for that? She might have been a star if she'd lived. As for those of us who worked on it, trust me, we got along. We were all so grateful for the opportunity, we made a point of it," he said. "How in the world did her mother find out?"

"Somebody sent her the tape."

Russell stared at my reflection in the mirror. "As an expression of condolences, that's in poor taste," he said. "You'd have to wonder at the motive."

"Ain't that the truth."

I went back to the motel, feeling wide awake. By two in the morning Santa Teresa has shut down. In San Francisco all the bars had closed, but numerous businesses were still open: gas stations, bookstores, fitness gyms, video rentals, coffee shops, even clothing stores. I changed out of my flats and the all-purpose dress, stripping off my panty hose with the same relief Cherie had expressed. Once in my jeans and turtleneck, I felt like I was back in my own skin again. I found an all-night diner two doors away from the Del Rey and ate a lavish breakfast. I returned to my room and put the chain on the track. I plunked off my Reeboks, propped all the pillows at my back, and checked Lorna's file again, leafing through the crime scene sketches and the accompanying pictures.

The photographer had shot the outside of the house, front yard and back, with views looking north, south, east, and west. There were shots of both the front and back porches, wood railings, windows. The front door had been closed, but unlocked, with no signs of forced entry. Within the cabin itself, there was no weapon visible and no evidence of a struggle. I could see colored smudges where the fingerprint technicians had been at work with their various powders. According to the report, elimination fingerprints and palm prints had been taken, and most latents on the premises had been accounted for. Many were Lorna's. Some were from family members, the landlord, her friend Danielle, a couple of acquaintances who'd been interviewed by homicide investigators. Many surfaces had been wiped clean.

The photographs of Lorna began in long shot, establishing her position relative to the front door. There were intermediate-range photos, close-ups with a six-inch ruler in evidence to indicate scale. The log showed an orderly progression through the area. I was frustrated by the flat, two-dimensional images. I wanted to crawl into the frame, examine all the items on the tabletops, open up the drawers, and pick through the contents. I found myself squinting, moving pictures closer to my face and then back again, as if the subject matter might suddenly leap into sharper focus. I would stare at the body, scanning the background, taking in items through my peripheral vision.

The cabin, when I'd seen it, had been stripped of all the furniture. Only the bare bones of Lorna's living space were left intact: empty cabinets and bathroom, plumbing, and electrical fixtures. It was good to see the pictures, to correct my mental process. In memory, I had already begun to distort the room sizes and relative distances. I went through all the pictures a second time and then a third. In the ten months since Lorna's death, the crime scene had been dismantled, and this was all that remained. If murder were ever proved and a suspect charged, the entire case could easily rest on the contents of this envelope. And what were the chances? What could I possibly hope to accomplish this late in the game? Basically, in my investigation, I was mimicking the spiral method of a crime scene search: starting at the center, moving outward and around in ever-widening circles. The problem was that I had no direction and no hard line to take. I didn't even have a theory about why she had died. I felt as though I were fishing, fly casting in the hopes that I'd somehow snag myself a killer. All *that* wily devil had to do was lie low, looking up at my lure from the bottom of the cove.

I sorted through the file while I let my mind wander. Aside from the random or the serial killer, the perpetrator of a homicide has to have a *reason,* some concrete motive for wanting the victim dead. In the case of Lorna Kepler, I was still uncertain what the reason was. Financial gain was a possibility. She'd had assets in her estate. I made a note to myself to check with Janice on that score. Given the assumption that Lorna had no living issue, Janice and Mace would be her legal heirs if she died intestate. It was hard to picture either one of them guilty of murder. For one thing, if it were Janice, she'd have to be a fool to turn around and bring me into it. Mace was a question mark. He certainly hadn't conformed to my notion of a grieving parent. Her sisters were another possibility, though neither struck me as sufficiently smart or sufficiently energetic.

I picked up the phone and dialed Frankie's Coffee Shop. This time Janice answered. I could hear jukebox music in the background, but not much else.

"Hi, Janice. This is Kinsey, up in San Francisco."

"Well, Kinsey. How are you? I'm always surprised to hear from you at such an hour. Did you find the fellow she was working for?"

"I talked to him this evening, and I also tracked down one of the other actors in the film. I haven't made up my mind about either one of them. In the meantime, something else has come up. I'm wondering if I could take a look at Lorna's financial records."

"I suppose so. Can you say why, or is that classified?"

"Nothing's classified between us. You're paying for my services. I'm trying to pin down a motive. Money's an obvious possibility."

"I guess that's true, but it's hard to see how it could apply in this case. None of us had any idea she had money until after she died and we went through her files. I'm still in shock. It was unbelievable, given *my* perception. I was forever slipping her a twenty just to make sure she'd eat right. And there she was with all those stocks and bonds and savings accounts. She must have had six. You'd think with that kind of money, she'd have lived a little better."

I wanted to tell her the money was part of Lorna's pension fund, but it seemed unkind somehow since she hadn't lived long enough to use it. "Did she have a will?"

"Well, yes. Just one sheet of paper that she'd written out herself. She left everything to Mace and me."

"I'd like to see that, if you don't object."

"You can see anything you want. When I get home from work, I'll find the box of Lorna's personal effects and leave it on Berlyn's desk. You can stop by when you get back and pick it up from her."

"I'd appreciate that. I want to talk to the two of them, in any event."

"Oh, shoot, and that reminds me. Have you talked to that woman Lorna used to house-sit for?"

"Once."

"Well, I wonder if you'd do me a favor. Last time I went through Lorna's things, I came across a set of house keys I'm sure belong to her. I've been trying to return them and haven't had a minute to take care of it."

"You want me to drop them off?"

"If you would. I feel like I should do it myself, but I just don't have time. And I'd appreciate it if you'd make sure I get everything back when you finish going through it. There's some dividend and interest statements I'm going to need to pass along to the probate attorney when he files her income taxes."

"Has the estate been settled yet?"

"It's still in the works. What I'm giving you is copies, but I'd still like to have them back."

"No problem. I can probably drop it all off to you day after tomorrow."

"That'd be fine." I could hear the swell of chatter in the background. She said, "Uh-oh. I got to go."

"See you tomorrow," I said, and hung up.

I looked around at the room, which was serviceable but glum. The mattress was as dense as mud, while the pillows were foam rubber and threatened serious neck damage. I'd made reservations for a noon flight out of San Francisco. It was now almost three A.M. I wasn't ready to sleep. If I junked my return ticket, I could drive the rental car back and drop it at the airport in Santa Teresa, where my VW was sitting in the long-term parking lot. The trip would take roughly six hours, and if I could manage to avoid dozing off at the wheel, I'd be back around nine.

I suddenly found myself energized by the notion of heading home. I swung my feet over the side of the bed, found my Reeboks, pulled them on, and left the laces dangling. I went into the bathroom, gathered up my toiletries, and shoved everything in the duffel. It took me longer to wake the night manager than it took me to check out. By 3:22 I was heading south on the 101.

There's nothing as hypnotic as a highway at night. Visual stimulation is reduced to the lines on the road, asphalt zipping past in a series of streaks. Any shrubbery at the side of the road is diminished to a blur. All the trailer trucks were in transit, semis carrying goods that ranged from new cars to furniture, from flammable liquids to flattened cardboard boxes. Off to the side, I caught sight of townlet after townlet encased in darkness, illuminated only by rows of street lamps. An occasional billboard provided visual distraction. At long intervals a truck stop appeared, like an island of light.

I had to stop twice for coffee. Having opted to head back, I now found the drive narcotic and was struggling to stay awake. The radio in the rental car was good company. I flipped from station to station, listening to a talk show host, classical and country music, and countless newscasts. Once upon a time I'd smoked cigarettes, and I could still remember the habit as a way of marking time on car trips. Now I'd rather drive off a bridge than light up. Another hour passed. It was nearly dawn and the sky was turning white, the trees along the road beginning to reclaim their color, now charcoal green and dark chartreuse. Dimly I was aware of the sun coming up like a beachball into my line of vision, the colors of the sky shading up from dark gray to mauve to peach to bright yellow. I had to flip down the visor to keep the glare out of my eyes.

By 9:14 I'd turned in the rental and picked up my VW and I was pulling into a parking place in front of my apartment. My eyes felt itchy and I ached from a weariness that felt like the flu, but at least I was home. I let myself in, checked to see that there were no messages, brushed my teeth, took my shoes off, and fell into bed.

For once, sleep descended like a blow to the head, and I went down, down, down.

I woke at 5:00 P.M. The eight hours should have been adequate, but as starved as I was for sleep, I felt I was dragging myself out of quicksand. I was still struggling to adjust to the inverted pattern my life had taken. In bed at dawn, up again in the afternoon. I was eating breakfast at lunchtime, dinner in the dead of night, though often that meal turned out to be cold cereal or scrambled eggs and toast, which meant I ate breakfast twice. I was vaguely aware of a psychological shift, a change in my perception now that I'd substituted night for day. Like a form of jet lag, my internal clock was no longer synchronized with the rest of the world's. My usual sense of myself was breaking down, and I wondered if a hidden personality might suddenly emerge as if wakened from a long sleep. My day life was calling, and I was curiously reluctant to answer.

I rolled out of bed, dumped my dirty clothes, took a shower, and got dressed. I stopped at a minimart where I grabbed a carton of yogurt and an apple, eating in my car as I headed over to the Keplers'. I could have used a couple more hours of sleep, but I was hoping to talk to Lorna's sisters before their mother woke up. Like me, her days and nights were turned around, and I felt a strange bond with her.

Mace's plumbing truck wasn't parked in the drive this time. I left my VW on the berm, by the white split-rail fence, and moved up the walk to the porch, where I knocked. Trinny answered the door, though it took her a while. "Oh, hi. Mom worked a double shift and she's not up yet."

"I figured as much. She said she'd tuck some information in a box and leave it with Berlyn."

"She's not here right now. She's running some errands. You want to come in and wait?"

"Thanks." I followed her through the small, densely furnished living room to the dining area, which was located at one end of the kitchen. Sunset wasn't far off, and the kitchen windows were getting dark, lending the lighted kitchen an artificial air of warmth. An ironing board had been set up, and the scent of freshly pressed cotton made me long for summer. "Mind if I take a look at Berlyn's desk? If the box is close to the surface, I can go ahead and get it."

Trinny took up the iron again. "It's right in there." She pointed toward the door that led into the den.

One corner of the room apparently doubled as the offices for Kepler Plumbing. I remembered seeing both the desk and the filing cabinet the night I talked to Mace. A banker's box with my name scrawled on top was sitting right in plain sight. For once I resisted any further urge to snoop. I lifted the lid to check the contents. A fragrance wafted up, some delicate combination of citrus and spice. I closed my eyes, wondering if this was Lorna's scent. I'd experienced it before—the very air saturated with someone's characteristic smell. With men it's after-shave, leather, or sweat. With women it's cologne. The house keys Janice had mentioned were sitting on top of a neatly packed collection of file folders, all in alphabetical order: bank statements, past income taxes, dividends, stocks, assorted annual reports. Tucked into one end of the box was a folded cashmere scarf. I pressed the length of it against my face, smelling cut grass, cinnamon, lemon, and clove. I hauled the box back to the kitchen and set it by one of the kitchen chairs, the scarf laid on top. "Is this Lorna's? It was in the box with her stuff."

Trinny shrugged. "I guess."

I folded it twice and tucked it back where it had been. "Mind if I sit down? I was hoping I'd have a chance to talk to you."

"Fine," she said. She slid the lever on the iron to the off position.

"I hope I'm not interrupting dinner preparations."

"I got a casserole in the oven. All I have to do is heat it and make a salad real quick."

I took a seat, wondering how to coax some information out of her. I wasn't even sure what I wanted to know, but I considered it a bonus to be alone with her. She was wearing the same cutoffs I'd seen her in before. Her legs looked solid, her bare feet tucked into rubber flip-flops. Her T-shirt this time must have been an XXL, the front emblazoned with a painted design. She moved from the ironing board to the kitchen table, where she sat down across from me and began squeezing a tube of paint in a Jackson Pollock–type design on the front of a new T-shirt. Dots and squiggles. Hanging from a knob on one of the kitchen cabinets was a completed work, its lines of paint puffed out in three dimensions. She caught my gaze. "This's puff paint," she said. "You put it on and let it dry, and when you iron it on the wrong side, it puffs out like that."

"That's cute," I said. I got up and moved closer to the kitchen cabinet, taking a moment to inspect the finished product. Looked dreadful to me, but what do I know? "You sell these?"

"Well, not yet, but I'm hoping. I made this one I got on, and whenever I go out everybody's like 'Oh, wow, cool T-shirt.' So I thought since I wasn't working I could set up my own business."

My oh my. She and her sister Lorna, both driven by the entrepreneurial spirit. "How long have you been doing this?"

"Just today."

I took my seat at the kitchen table again, watching Trinny work. I began to cast out my line. Surely there was something I could wheedle out of her. To my right was a stack of travel brochures, touting Alaskan cruises, ski holidays, and package tours to Canada and the Caribbean. I picked up a pamphlet and began to scan the copy: "The world's last unspoiled paradise . . . stunning white beaches . . . deep azure lagoons . . ."

Trinny saw what I was doing. "Those are Berlyn's."

"Where's she going?"

"She doesn't know yet. She says Alaska looks good."

"Are you going, too?"

She made a disappointed face. "I don't have the money."

"Too bad. It looks like fun," I said. "She doesn't mind traveling alone?"

"Nuh-uhn. She likes it. Not all the time, but if she has to, she says. She did the one trip already, in the fall."

"Really. Where'd she go then?"

"Acapulco. She loved it. She says she'll take me if she goes back."

"That's neat. I was in Viento Negro last summer, but that's as far south as I've been."

"I haven't even been that far. Berlyn's always liked to travel. I don't have the same bug. I mean, I like it and all, but there's stuff I'd rather do."

"Like what?"

"I don't know. Buy clothes and stuff."

I tried another tack. "Lorna's death must have been hard. Are you doing okay with that?"

"I guess so. It's been hard on them. I mean, Mom and Daddy used to be a lot closer. Once Lorna died, seems like everything changed. And now it's like Mom's the only one caught up in it. Lorna's all she talks about. Berlyn gets her feelings hurt. It really pisses her off. It's like, what about us? Don't we count for anything?"

"Were you close to Lorna?"

"Not really. Lorna wasn't close to anyone. She lived in her world and we lived in ours. She had that cabin, and she liked it private. She hated it if people stopped by without asking. A lot of times she wasn't even home. Nights especially she'd be out somewhere. She made it plain you should keep away unless you called first and got yourself invited."

"How often did you see her?"

"A lot over here, whenever she stopped by. But at the cabin, maybe once or twice in the three years she lived there. Berlyn liked to go over. She's kind of nosy by nature. Lorna was real mysterious."

"Like what?"

"I don't know. Like, why was she so picky about people dropping in? What's the big deal? She didn't have to worry about us. We're her *sisters*."

"Did you ever find out where she went at night?"

"Nuh-uhn. Probably wasn't any place special. After a while, I more or less accepted her for what she was. She wasn't sociable, like us. Berlyn and me are buddies. We like to pal around and double-date and stuff like that? Right now, like, neither of us has a boyfriend, so we see movies and go out dancing on the weekends.

Lorna never did the first nice thing for either one of us. Well, she did now and then, but you practically had to lay down and beg."

"How'd you find out about her death?"

"The police stopped by the house and asked to speak to Daddy. He was the one who told Mom, and she told us. It was kind of creepy. I mean, we thought Lorna was out of town. Off on vacation, is what Mom said. So we didn't think anything about it when we didn't hear from her. We just figured she'd give us a call when she got back. It's horrible to think she was just laying there, moldering."

"It must have been awful."

"Oh, God. I started screaming, and Berl got white as a ghost. Daddy was like in *shock*. Mother took it the worst. She still isn't over it. She was staggering around shrieking and crying, practically tearing her hair out. I've never seen her like that. She's usually the one holds the rest of us together. Like when Grandma died? This was her own *mother*. She kept real calm, made airline reservations, packed our bags so we could go back to Iowa to the funeral. We were all young kids, acting dumb, boo-hooing real pitiful. She got everything all organized, as cool as you please. When we found out about Lorna, she just fell to pieces."

"Most parents don't expect to outlive their kids," I said.

"That's what everybody says. It doesn't help that the police think she was murdered and all."

"What's your opinion?"

Trinny made a mute shrug with her mouth. "I guess she could have died from her allergies. I don't like to think about it. Too icky for my taste."

I shifted the subject. "Were you the one who went to San Francisco with Lorna last year?"

"That was Berlyn," she said. "Who told you about that?"

"I met the guy on the tape."

She glanced up from her work with interest. "Which one?"

12

She had the good grace to blush. Despite the dark brown hair, she was fair-complected, and the tint hit her cheeks like a heat rash. She dropped her gaze to the work in front of her, suddenly much busier than she'd been before. I could tell she was casting about for a way to change the subject. She bent over her work. I guess it was important to get the paint dots just right.

"Trinny?"

"What?"

"How'd you happen to see the tape? And don't say 'which tape' because you know exactly which tape I'm talking about."

"I didn't see the tape."

"Oh, come on. Of course you did. If you didn't, how'd you know there was more than one guy?"

"I don't even know what you're talking about," she said with pious irritation.

"I'm talking about the porno tape in which Lorna appeared. Remember? Your mother told you."

"Maybe Mom told us that, too. About the other guy, more than one."

I said, "Uhn-hun," in my most skeptical tone. "What happened, did Lorna give you a copy?"

"Nooo," she said, giving it two sliding syllables, high note to low, offended by the notion.

"Then how'd you know there was more than one man?"

"I *guessed*. What do you care?"

I stared at her. The obvious conclusion leapt to mind. "Were *you* the one who wrapped it and put it out in the mailbox?"

"No. And anyway, I don't have to answer." This time the tone was sullen, but the blush came up again. This was better than a polygraph.

"Who did?"

"I don't know anything about anything, so you might as well change the subject. This is not a court of law, you know. I'm not under oath."

An attorney in the making. For a moment I thought she'd put her fingers in her ears and start humming, just to shut me out. I cocked my head, trying to catch her eye. "Trinny," I sang. She was studiously engaged in the T-shirt in front of her, adding a gaudy orange spiral of puff paint. I said, "Come on. I don't *care* what you did, and I swear I will never say a word to your parents. I've been wondering who sent the tape to them, and now I know. In a way, you did us all a favor. If your mother hadn't been upset about it, she wouldn't have come to me, and the whole investigation might have died where it was." I waited and then gave her a line prompt. "Was it Berlyn's idea or yours?"

"I don't have to answer."

"How about a nod if I guess right?"

Trinny added some lime-green stars to the T-shirt. It was getting tackier by the minute, but I felt as though we were getting some-place.

"I'll bet it was Berlyn."

Silence.

"Am I right?"

Trinny lifted one shoulder, still without making eye contact.

"Ah. I'm assuming that little gesture means 'yes.' So Berlyn sent the tape. Now the question is, how'd she get it?"

More silence.

"Come on, Trinny. Please, please, please?" I learned this interrogation method back in grade school, and it's particularly effective when the subject matter is a cross-your-heart-type secret just between us girls. I could see her softening. Whatever our confidences, we're usually *dying* to tell, especially if the confession involves the condemnation of someone else.

Her tongue moved across her teeth as though she were testing for fuzz. Finally she said, "Swear you won't tell?"

I held up my hand as if taking an oath. "I won't say a word to another soul. I won't even mention that you *mentioned* it."

"We just got sick of hearing how wonderful she was. Because she wasn't all that great. She was pretty and she had a great bod, but big deal, you know?"

"Really," I said.

"Plus, she took money for *sex*. I mean, Berlyn or me would *never* have done that. So how come Lorna got elevated to the stars? She wasn't pure. She wasn't even *good.*"

"Human nature, I guess. Your mother doesn't get to have Lorna in her life, but she keeps that perfect picture in her heart," I said. "It's hard to let go when that's all you have."

Her voice had begun to rise. "But Lorna was a bitch. All she thought about was *herself.* She hardly gave Mom and Daddy the time of day. I'm the one helps out, for all the good it does. I'm as sweet as I know how, and it doesn't make any difference. Lorna's the one Mom loves. Berlyn and me are just bullshit." Emotion was causing her skin to change colors, chameleonlike. Tears rose like water suddenly coming to the boil. She put a hand to her face, which twisted as a sob broke through.

I reached out and touched her hand. "Trinny, that's just not true. Your mother loves you very much. The night she came to my office, she talked about you and Berlyn, all the fun you have, all the help around the house. You're a treasure to her. Honestly."

She was crying by then, her voice high-pitched and pinched. "Then why doesn't she tell us? She never says a word."

"Maybe she's afraid to. Or maybe she doesn't know how anymore, but that doesn't mean she isn't crazy about you."

"I can't stand it. I can't." She sobbed like a child, giving rein to her grief. I sat and let her work it through on her own. Finally the tears subsided and she sighed heavily. She fumbled in the pocket of her cutoffs, pulling out a ratty hankie, which she pressed against her eyes. "Oh, God," she said. She propped her elbows on the table and then blew her nose. She looked down, realizing she'd picked up the imprint of wet paint on her forearm. "Well, shit. Look at that," she said. A bubble of laughter came up like a burp escaping.

"What's going on?" Berlyn was standing at the front door, her expression blank with suspicion.

Both of us jumped, and Trinny let out a gasp. "Berl! You scared me half to *death*," she said. "Where did you come from?" She wiped her eyes in haste, trying to cover up the fact that she'd been crying.

Berlyn had a plastic carryall of groceries in one hand, her key ring in the other. She fixed Trinny with a look. "Pardon me for sneaking. I didn't know I was interrupting. I parked in the driveway big as life." Her gaze jumped to mine. "What's the matter with you?"

"Nothing," I said. "We were talking about Lorna, and Trinny got upset."

"Just what I need. I've heard enough about her. Daddy's got it right. Let's just drop the subject and get on to something else. Where's Mom? Is she up yet?"

"I think she's in the shower," Trinny said.

Belatedly, I became aware of water running somewhere.

Berlyn dumped her purse on a chair and moved over to the counter, where she began to unload grocery items. Like Trinny, she wore cutoffs, a T-shirt, and flip-flops, professional attire for the working plumber's helper. The roots on her blond hair were showing through. Despite the four-year age difference, her face was a projection of Lorna's in middle age. Maybe young death isn't bad, perfect beauty suspended in the amber of time.

Berlyn turned to Trinny. "Could you give me a hand?" she said, aggrieved. "How long has she been here?"

Trinny shot me a pleading look and went over to help her sister.

"Ten minutes," I supplied, though I hadn't been asked. "I just stopped by for the stuff your mother left. Trinny was showing me how to make T-shirts, and then we got talking about Lorna's death." I reached for the box, thinking to flee the premises before Janice emerged.

Berlyn studied me with interest. "So you said."

"Ah. Well. Fun as this is, I better be on my way." I got up, slung the strap of my handbag over my shoulder, and picked up the box, ignoring Berlyn. "Thanks for the painting lesson," I said to Trinny. "I'm sorry about Lorna. I know you loved her."

Her smile was pained. She said, "Bye," and gave me a half-hearted wave. Berlyn went into the den without a backward look, closing the door behind her with a decided snap. I stuck my tongue out at her and crossed my eyes, which made Trinny laugh. I mouthed, "Thank you," to Trinny and took my leave.

It was nearly six o'clock when I unlocked my office door and put the box of Lorna's files on my desk. Everybody else in the firm was gone. Even Lonnie, who usually works late, had packed it in for the day. All my tax forms and receipts were still sitting where I'd left them. I was disappointed the elves and fairies hadn't come along to finish up my work. I gathered all the bits and pieces and tucked them in a drawer, clearing space. I doubted Lorna's papers would yield any information, but I needed to take a look. I put some coffee on and sat down, set the lid of the box aside, and began to work my way through the manila folders. It looked as if someone had lifted Lorna's files directly from a desk drawer and placed them in the banker's box. Each file was labeled neatly. Tucked in the front were copies of various probate forms that Janice must have picked up from the attorney. It looked as though she were doing the preliminary work of culling and assembling, making penciled notes. I studied each sheet, trying to form a picture of Lorna Kepler's financial status.

An accountant could probably have made quick work of this stuff. I, on the other hand, having made a C minus in high school math, had to frown and sigh and chew my pencil. Janice had filled out a schedule of Lorna's assets, listing the cash in her possession at the time of her death, uncashed checks payable to her, bank accounts, stocks, bonds, Treasury bills, mutual funds. Lorna had no pension plan and no life insurance. She did have a small insurance policy for the jewelry she'd acquired. She hadn't owned any real property, but her liquid assets came to a little under five hundred thousand dollars. Not bad for a part-time clerk-harlot. Janice had included a copy of Lorna's will, which seemed clear enough. She'd left all her valuables, including jewelry, cash, stocks, bonds, and other financial assets, to her parents. Attached to the will was a copy of the completed "Proof of Holographic Instrument" that Janice had filed. In it, she attested that she was acquainted with the decedent for twenty-five years, had personal knowledge of her handwriting, that she had "examined the will and determined that its handwritten provisions were written by and the instrument signed by the hand of the decedent."

Danielle had speculated that Lorna wouldn't have a will, but the document seemed consistent with Lorna's systematic nature. Neither Berlyn nor Trinny had been left any money, but that didn't seem unusual. Two thousand bucks apiece might have gone a long way toward softening their attitudes, but she might not have understood the animosity they harbored. Or maybe she knew and felt the same about them. At any rate, the estate wasn't complicated. I didn't think it necessitated the services of an attorney, but the Keplers might have been intimidated by all the official paperwork.

I checked back through the last few years of Lorna's income tax. Her only W-2's were from the water treatment plant. Under "Your Occupation," she had listed herself as "secretary" and "mental health consultant." I had to smile at that. She'd been meticulous in reporting income, taking only standard deductions. She'd never donated a dime to charity, but she'd been (largely) honest with the government. To the recipient, I suppose the services of a prostitute might be classified under mental health. As for the payments themselves, I guess no one at the IRS had ever wondered why the bulk of her "consulting fees" were paid to her in cash.

Janice had notified the post office to forward Lorna's mail to her, and she'd tossed in a stack of unopened statements: windowed envelopes from various sources, all of them marked "important tax information." I opened a few, just to check the year end against my list. Among them was a statement from a bank in Simi Valley that I'd seen on her tax forms for the last two years. The account had been closed out, but the bank had sent her a 1099-INT, reporting the interest accrued during the first four months of the year. I tucked that in with the other statements. All the credit cards had been canceled and notices sent to each company. I sorted through some of the files Lorna'd kept: canceled checks, receipts for utilities, various credit card slips.

I laid out the canceled checks like a hand of solitaire. At the bottom, under "Memo," she'd dutifully written in the purpose of the payment: groceries, manicure, haircut, linens, sundries. There was something touching about the care she'd taken. She hadn't known she'd be dead by the time these checks came back. She hadn't known her last meal would be her last, that every action she'd taken and each endeavor she'd engaged in were part of some finite number that would soon run out. Sometimes the hardest part of my job is the incessant reminder of the fact we're all trying so assiduously to ignore: we are here temporarily . . . life is only ours on loan.

I put down my pencil and eased my feet up on the desk, rocking back on my swivel chair. The room seemed dark, and I reached over and flipped on the lamp on the bookshelf behind me. Among Lorna's possessions, there was no address book, no calendar, no appointment book of any kind. That might have sparked my curiosity, but I wondered if it didn't speak to Lorna's caution about her clients. Danielle had told me she was very tight-lipped, and I felt this discretion might extend to the keeping of written notes as well.

I reached for the manila envelope that held the crime scene photographs. I sorted through until I found the angles that showed the papers on her table and countertop. I pulled the light over closer, but there was no way to see if there was an appointment book visible. I glanced at my watch. I was dog-tired. I was also bored and hungry, but I could feel my senses quicken as the darkness gathered depth. Maybe I was turning into a vampire or a werewolf, repelled by sunlight, seduced by the moon.

I got up and shrugged into my jacket, leaving Lorna's papers on my desk. What was bothering me? I scanned the desktop. A fact . . . something obvious . . . had passed through my hands. The problem with being tired is that your brain doesn't work so hot. Idly I paused and moved a batch of papers aside, leafing through the forms. I looked at the holographic will and Janice's supporting statement. I didn't think that was it. In theory, it would seem self-serving that Janice was in a position to attest to the legitimacy of a will from which she largely benefited. However, the truth of it was that if Lorna had died with no will at all, the result would have been the same.

I picked up the bank notices and shuffled through them again, pausing when I got to the statement from the bank in Simi. The interest was minimal since she'd closed the account in April. Before that, she'd maintained a balance of roughly twenty thousand dollars. I looked at the closing date. The zero balance showed as of Friday, April 20. The day before she died.

I pulled out the files Lieutenant Dolan had given me. The personal property inventory mentioned all manner of items found on the premises, including Lorna's handbag and her wallet, containing all her credit cards and a hundred bucks in cash. Nowhere was there mention of twenty thousand dollars. I took the notice with me to the Xerox room around the corner, made a copy of the statement, and stuck it in my handbag. Serena Bonney had been the first person on the scene. I checked my notes for her father's address, packed up Lorna's papers with the crime scene photographs, and took the banker's box with me down the stairs to my car.

. . .

The address I'd picked up for Clark Esselmann turned out to be a sizable estate, maybe seven or eight acres surrounded by a low sandstone wall, beyond which the rolling lawns had been erased by the dark. Landscaping floods washed light across the exterior of the house, which was constructed in the French country style, meaning long and low with a steeply pitched roof. Mullioned windows formed a series of staunch yellow grids along the facade, while the tall fieldstone chimneys jutted up like black towers against the charcoal sky. Low-voltage lights defined the foliage and walkways, allowing me a fair sense of what it must have looked like by day. Interior lights winking in a small structure some distance from the main house suggested a guest house or perhaps maid's quarters.

When I reached the main entrance, I could see electronic gates. A key pad and intercom were planted at expensive-car window height. Naturally my VW left me disadvantaged, and in order to buzz I had to pull on the emergency brake, open the car door, and torque my whole body, risking vicious back spasms. I pushed the button, wishing I could order a Big Mac and fries.

A disembodied voice came in response. "Yes?"

"Oh, hi. I'm Kinsey Millhone. I have some house keys that belong to Serena Bonney."

There was no reply. What did I expect, a gasp of astonishment? Half a second later the two halves of the gate began to swing back in silence. I eased my VW up the circular driveway, lined with junipers. The entry was cobblestone, with a separate lane leading to the left and on around to the rear. I caught a glimpse of garages, like a line of horse stables. Just to be contrary, I bypassed the front door and drove around the side of the house to a brightly lighted gravel parking pad in back. The four-car garage was linked to the main house by a long, covered breezeway, beyond which I could see a short stretch of lawn intersected by a man-made reflecting pond, submerged lights tucked among its rocks. All across the property, lighting picked out significant landscape features: ornamental shrubs and tree trunks appearing like oils painted on black velvet. On the clear black surface of the pond, water lilies grew in clumps, breaking up a perfect inverted image of the house.

Night-blooming jasmine filled the air with perfume. I back-tracked to the front door and rang properly. Moments later Serena answered, dressed in slacks and a white silk shirt.

"I brought your keys back," I said, holding them out to her.

"Those are my keys? Oh, so they are," she said. "Where did these come from?"

"Lorna's mother came across them. You must have given Lorna a set when she was house-sitting for you."

"Thanks. I'd forgotten. Nice of you to return them."

"I've also got a question, if you can spare me a minute."

"Sure. Come on in. Dad's out on the patio. He just got out of the hospital today. Have you met him?"

"I don't think our paths have ever crossed," I said.

I followed her through the house and into a large country kitchen. A cook was in the process of preparing the evening meal, barely glancing up from her chopping board as we passed through. An informal dining table large enough to seat eight was located in a bay of French doors on the far side of the room. The ceiling rose a story and a half, with crisscrossing wooden beams. An assortment of baskets and bunches of dried herbs hung on wooden pegs. The floor was a pale, glossy pine. The layout of the room allowed space for two separate cooking islands about ten feet apart. One was topped with dark granite with its own inlaid hardwood cutting surfaces and a butler's sink. The second housed a full-size sink, two dishwashers, and a trash compactor. A fireplace on a raised hearth held a blazing fire.

Serena opened the French doors, and I followed her out. A wide flagstone patio ran the width of the house. Outside lights seemed to create an artificial day. A black-bottomed lap pool, a good seventy-five feet by twenty, defined its outer edge. The water was clear, but the black tile seemed to erase its inner dimensions. Pool lights picked up a shifting web of emerald green that somehow made the bottom look endlessly deep. Diving into that would be like a plunge into Loch Ness. God knew what creatures might be lurking in the abyss.

Clark Esselmann, in his robe and slippers, a stick in his hand, was teasing a black Labrador retriever into the ready position. "Okay, Max. Here we go now. Here we go."

The dog was full-grown, probably the same age in dog years as the old man himself. Max nearly quivered, totally focused on the game being played. As we approached, the old man threw the stick into the lap pool. The dog flung himself into the water, moving toward the stick, which was now bobbing in the water at the far end. I recognized Serena's father from numerous pictures that had appeared in the *Santa Teresa Dispatch* over the years. White-haired, in his seventies, he carried himself with an old-fashioned ramrod-straight posture. If his heart problems had affected him, it was hard to see how.

Serena smiled, watching them. "This is the first chance he's had to connect with Max. They usually go through this first thing in the morning, and what a sight they are. Dad swims in one lane and the dog swims in the other."

Vaguely I was aware of the telephone ringing somewhere inside the house. The dog collected the stick in his teeth and swam in our direction, scrambling up the stairs at the near end of the pool. He dropped it at the old man's feet and then barked once sharply. Esselmann threw the stick again. It sailed toward the deep end of the pool, landing with a faint splash. The dog flew off the side and swam, head high. The old man laughed and clapped his hands, urging the dog on. "Come on, Max. Come on."

The retriever clamped his mouth on the stick again and turned, paddling back to the stairs, where he scrambled out, water pouring off his oily coat. Max dropped the stick at Esselmann's feet and then shook himself vigorously. Water flew out in all directions. Both Serena and her father laughed. Esselmann brushed at the polka dots of water on his cotton robe. I could have sworn Max was grinning, but I might have been mistaken.

A maid in a black uniform appeared at the French door. "Mr. Esselmann? Phone for you."

The old man turned and glanced in that direction, then headed toward the house while the dog pranced sideways and barked, hoping for one more toss. Serena caught my eye and smiled. Clearly, her father's hospital discharge had lightened her mood. "Can I offer you a glass of wine?"

"I'd better not," I said. "Wine makes me sleepy, and I have work to do yet."

We moved back through the French doors into the kitchen, where the wood fire popped cheerfully. Esselmann was standing near the planning center, on the telephone. He glanced over his shoulder and raised a hand, indicating his awareness of our presence. Beyond him, the door to the hall was open, and the dog's wet footprints led to a second door that was now closed. I had to guess Max had been relegated to the basement until he managed to dry himself. I heard a scratching noise, and then the dog issued one of those brief barks intended to make his wishes known.

"Don't be ridiculous. Of course, I'll be there. . . . Well, I'm opposed, of course. We're talking about an allotment of twelve million gallons a year. I'm absolutely adamant about this, and I don't care who knows it." His manner shifted to something slightly less gruff. "I feel fine. . . . I appreciate that, Ned, and I hope you'll tell Julia I received the flowers she sent and they were lovely. . . . Yes, I'll do that. I don't have much choice. Serena keeps me on a very tight leash." He turned and rolled his eyes at her, knowing that she was nearby. "I'll see you at the meeting Friday night. Just tell Bob and Druscilla how I'm voting on this. We can talk about it then, but I hope we're in accord. . . . Thank you. I'll do that. . . . Same to you."

He hung up the handset with a shake of his head. "Damn fools. First time my back is turned, they get sweet-talked into something. I hate the oil companies. That Stockton fellow's not going to have his way on this."

"I thought you were in his corner."

"I changed my mind," he said emphatically. He held his hand out to me. "Please excuse my bad manners. I shouldn't keep you standing while I rant and rave. Clark Esselmann. You caught me in the middle of my daily romp with the dog. I don't believe we've met."

I introduced myself. His grip was firm, but I could detect a slight tremor in his fingers. Up close, I could see that his color was poor. He looked anemic, and the flesh on the back of his right hand was bruised from some medical procedure. Still, he had a certain hardy determination that seemed to prevail in the face of his recurring health problems.

"Dad, you're not seriously thinking of trying to make it to a board meeting."

"You can bet on it," he said.

"You just got home. You're in no shape. The doctor doesn't even want you driving yet."

"I can take a taxi if need be. Or I can have Ned pick me up."

"I don't mind driving you. That's not the point," she said. "I really think you ought to take it easy for a few days."

"Nonsense! I'm not so old or infirm that I can't make decisions about what I'll do on any given day. Now if you girls will excuse me, I'm going up to take a rest before dinner. It's been a pleasure, Miss Millhone. I hope the next time we meet, you'll find me decently dressed. I don't usually meet the public in my bathrobe."

Serena touched his arm. "You need help getting up the stairs?"

"Thankfully, I don't," he said. He moved from the room with a shuffling gait that nevertheless propelled him at nearly normal speeds. As he passed the basement, he reached over and opened the door. The dog must have been lurking at the top of the stairs because he appeared at once and trotted after the old man, glancing back at us with satisfaction.

As Serena turned back to me, she sighed in exasperation. "That man is so stubborn, he drives me nuts. I've never had children, but surely parents are worse. Ah, well. Enough. I'm sure you didn't come here to listen to my gripes. You said you had a question."

"I'm looking for some money Lorna might have had when she

died. Apparently she closed out a bank account on Friday of that week. As far as I can see, there's twenty thousand dollars unaccounted for. I wondered if you'd seen any cash on the premises."

Serena put a hand to her chest in surprise. "She had *that* kind of money? That's incredible."

"She actually had quite a bit more, but this is the only money that seems to be missing."

"I can tell I'm in the wrong business. Wait till Roger hears this."

"You didn't see any sign of it the day you found the body? Might have been a cashier's check."

"Not me. Ask her landlord. I didn't even go in."

"And he did?"

"Well, it was only for a minute, but I'm sure he did."

"He told me once he caught the smell, he turned right around and went back to his place and called the cops."

"That's true, but then while we were waiting for the police to show up, he opened the door and went in."

"To do what?"

Serena shook her head. "I don't know. I guess I thought he wanted to see what it was. I'd forgotten all about it till you brought it up."

13

When I got back to my apartment, Danielle was standing on my doorstep in a shallow pool of light. Her long legs were bare, capped by the shortest pink miniskirt on record. She wore black high heels, a black tank top, and a varsity letter jacket with a big black *F* across the back. Her hair was so long that it extended below the bottom of the jacket in the back. She smiled when she caught sight of me crossing the yard. "Oh, hey. I thought you were gone. I came to get my dime. The IRS says I'm short on my estimated income tax."

"Aren't you cold? It's really freezing out here."

"You must never have lived in the East. It's probably fifty degrees. With this jacket I got on, I'm as warm as toast."

"What's the *F* stand for?"

"What do you think?" she said drolly.

I smiled as I unlocked the door and flipped the lights on. She followed me in, pausing at the threshold to assess the premises. Her eyes looked enormous, the green offset by dark liner, her lashes beaded with mascara. Under all the makeup she had a smooth, baby face: snub nose, sulky mouth. She strolled the perimeter of my living room, tottering on her high heels as she peered at all the bookshelves. She picked up the framed photograph of Robert Dietz. "Well, he's cute. Who's this?"

"A friend."

She lifted her brows and gave me a look that suggested she knew what kind of friend he was. She put the picture down again and shoved her hands in her jacket pockets. I hung my own jacket across the back of a director's chair. She sat down on my sofa and rubbed a hand across the surface of the fabric as if to test the weight. Tonight her fingernails were long and perfect, painted a vivid fire-engine red. She crossed one long, bare leg across the other and swung a foot while she completed her survey. "This is not bad. They got any other units as good as this?"

"This is the only rental. My landlord's eighty-five."

"I don't discriminate. I like old guys," she said. "Maybe I could give him a discount."

"I'll pass the word along in case he's interested. What are you doing here?"

She got up and moved over to the kitchen, where she opened my cabinets to check the contents. "I was bored. I don't go in to work until eleven. It's a problem sometimes what to do before. Mr. Dickhead's in a bad mood, so I'm avoiding him."

"What's his problem?"

"Oh, who knows? He's probably raggin' it," she said. She flapped a hand in the air, dismissing his ill temper. She pulled a couple of teabags out of her jacket pocket and dangled them in the air. "You want some peppermint tea? I got some bags if you boil the water. It's good for digestion."

"I'm not worried about digestion. I haven't had dinner yet."

"Me neither. Sometimes all I have is tea if Lester's taken my money. He doesn't want me getting fat."

"What a pal," I said.

She shrugged, unconcerned. "I look after myself. I'm into megavitamins and high colonics and like that."

"There's a treat," I said. I filled the kettle with hot water and put it on the stove. I flipped the burner on.

"Laugh all you want. I bet I'm healthier than you."

"That wouldn't take much, the way I eat," I said. "Speaking of which, you want dinner? I don't cook, but I can have a pizza delivered. I have to go out in a bit, but you're welcome to join me."

"I wouldn't mind some pizza," she said. "If you just do the veggies, without all the sausage and pepperoni, it's not even bad for you. Try that place around the corner. I bonk the owner sometimes. He gives me a big discount because I chew his bone."

"I'll mention that when I call the order in," I said.

"Here, I'll do it. Where's the phone?"

I pointed to the phone on the table beside the answering machine. We both noticed the blinking light.

"You got a message," she said. She reached down automatically and pressed the replay button before I had a chance to protest. It seemed as rude for her to listen as to open my mail. A mechanical computer voice announced that I had one message. Beep.

"Oh, hi, Kinsey. This is Roger. I just wanted to touch base and see how things were going. Anyway, you don't have to call back, but if you have any more questions, you can reach me at home. Bye. Oh, I guess I better give you the number." He recited his home phone and then hung up with a click.

"Lorna's boss," she said. "You know him?"

"Sure. Do you?"

She wrinkled her nose. "I met him once." She picked up the phone and punched in a number she seemed to know by heart. She turned and looked at me while the phone rang on the other end. "I'm going to have 'em leave the cheese off. It cuts the fat," she murmured.

I left her to the negotiations while I made us each a cup of tea. The night I'd met her, she'd seemed wary, or maybe that was just her working persona. Tonight she seemed relaxed, nearly buoyant. Her mood was probably drug-induced, but there was actually something charming about her ingenuousness. She had a natural goodwill that animated every gesture. I heard her conducting business with the kind of poise that must come from "bonking" guys from every walk of life. She put a hand over the mouthpiece. "What's the address here? I forgot."

I gave her the number, which she recited into the telephone. I could have taken her to Rosie's with me, but I didn't trust Rosie to be polite. With William gone, I was worried she might revert to her former misanthropy.

Danielle hung up the phone and took off her jacket, which she folded neatly and put on one end of the sofa. She came over to the counter, clutching her oversize shoulder bag. Somehow she seemed as graceful as a colt, all arms and long legs and bony shoulders.

I passed her a mug of tea. "I have a question for you."

"Hold on. Let me say something first. I hope this is not too personal. I wouldn't want you to take offense."

"I really hate sentences that start that way," I said.

"Me too, but this is for your own good."

"Go ahead. You're going to say it anyway."

She hesitated, and the face she made conveyed exaggerated reluctance. "Promise you won't get mad?"

"Just say it. I can't stand the suspense. I have bad breath."

"That haircut of yours is really gross."

"Oh, thanks."

"You don't have to get sarcastic. I can help. Honestly. I was working on my license as a cosmetologist when I first connected up with Lester . . ."

"Mr. Dickhead," I supplied.

"Yeah, him. Anyway, I'm a great cutter. I did Lorna's hair all the time. Give me a pair of scissors and I can turn you into a vision. I'm not fooling."

"All I have is nail scissors. Maybe after dinner."

"Come on. We got fifteen minutes until the pizza gets here. And look at this." She opened up her shoulder bag and let me peek. "Ta-da." Inside she had a brush, a little hair dryer, and a pair of shears. She placed the hair dryer on the counter and clacked the scissors like a pair of castanets.

"You came over here with that stuff?"

"I keep it with me all the time. Sometimes at the Palace I do haircuts in the ladies' room."

I ended up sitting on a kitchen stool with a hand towel pinned around my neck, my hair wet from a dousing at the kitchen sink. Danielle was chatting happily while she trimmed and clipped. Snippets of hair began to tumble around me. "Now don't get scared. I know it looks like a lot, but it's just because the whole thing's uneven. You got great hair, nice and thick, with just the tiniest touch of curl. Well, I wouldn't call it curl so much as body, which is even better."

"So why didn't you get your license?"

"I lost interest. Plus, the money's not that hot. My father always said it'd be a great fallback position if the economy went sour, but hooking's better, in my opinion. A guy might not have the bucks to get his hair blown dry, but he's always got twenty for a BJ."

I mouthed the term *BJ* silently. It took me half a second to figure that one out. "What are you going to do when you get too old to bonk?"

"I'm taking classes at city college in financial management. Money's the only other subject that really interests me."

"I'm sure you'll go far."

"You gotta start somewhere. What about you? What will you do when you're too old to bonk?"

"I don't bonk now. I'm pure as the driven snow."

"Well, no wonder you get cranky. What a drag," she said.

I laughed.

For a while we were silent as she concentrated on her work. "What's the question? You said you had something you wanted to ask."

"Maybe I better check my cash supply first."

She pulled my hair. "Now don't be like that. I bet you're the kind who kids around to keep other people at a distance, right?"

"I don't think I should respond to that."

She smiled. "See? I can surprise you. I'm a lot brighter than you think. So ask."

"Ah, yes. Did Lorna mention pulling twenty grand out of a bank account before she was supposed to go out of town?"

"Why would she do that? She always traveled with a guy. She never spent her own money when she went someplace."

"What guy?"

"Anyone who asked," she said, still clipping away.

"You know where she was headed?"

"She didn't talk about that stuff."

"What about a diary or an appointment book?"

Danielle touched her temple with the tip of her scissors. "She kept it all up here. She said otherwise her clients didn't feel safe. Cops raid your place? They got a search warrant, you're dead, and so's everybody else. Quit wiggling."

"Sorry. Where'd the money go? It looks like she closed out the whole account."

"Well, she didn't give it to me. I wish she had. I'd have opened an account of my own just like that." She snapped the scissors near my ear, and seven hairs fell to earth. "I meant to do that," she added. She set the scissors on the counter and plugged in the hair dryer, picking up locks of hair on the bristles of the hairbrush. It's incredibly restful to have someone fooling with your hair like that.

I raised my voice slightly to compete with the noise. "Could she have paid off a debt or posted bail for someone?"

"Twenty G's in bail would be a hell of a crime."

"Did she owe anybody?"

"Lorna didn't have debts. Even credit cards she paid off before finance charges went on," she said. "I bet the money was stolen."

"Yeah, that occurred to me, too."

"Must have been after she was dead," she added. "Otherwise Lorna would have fought tooth and nail." She turned the dryer off and set it aside, stepping back to scrutinize her handiwork. She took a moment to fluff and rearrange individual strands and then nodded, apparently satisfied.

The doorbell rang, Mr. Pizza Man on the doorstep. I handed Danielle twenty bucks and let her conclude the deal while I ducked into the downstairs bathroom and checked myself in the mirror. The difference was remarkable. All the choppiness was gone. All the blunt, stick-out parts that seemed to go every which way were now tamed and subdued. The hair feathered away from my face in perfect layers. It even fell into place again if I shook my head. I caught sight of Danielle reflected in the mirror behind me.

"You like it?" she asked.

"It looks great."

"Told you I was good," she said, laughing.

We ate from the box, splitting a large cheeseless veggie pizza, which was tasty without causing all my arteries to seize up. At one point she said, "This is fun, isn't it? Like girlfriends."

"You miss Lorna?"

"Yeah, I do. She was a kick. After work, her and me would pal around downtown, find a coffee shop, have breakfast. I remember once we bought a quart of orange juice and a bottle of champagne. We sat out in the grass at my place and drank mimosas until dawn."

"I'm sorry I never got to meet her. She sounds nice."

At eight we folded the box and stuck it in the trash. Danielle put her jacket on while I got mine. Once outside, she asked me to drop her off at her place. I took a left on Cabana, following her directions as she routed me down a narrow alleyway not that far from Neptune's Palace. Her "hovel," as she referred to it, was a tiny board-and-batten structure at the rear of someone else's yard. The little house had probably been a toolshed at one time. She got out of the car and leaned back in the window. "You want to come in and see my place?"

"Maybe tomorrow night," I said. "I got some stuff to do tonight."

"Pop by if you can. I got it fixed up real cute. If business is slow, I'm usually home by one . . . provided Lester isn't bugging me to score. Thanks for dinner and the ride."

"Thanks for the cut."

I watched her clop off into the night, high heels tapping on the short brick walk to her front door, dark hair trailing down her back like a veil. I fired up my car and headed for the Keplers' house.

I parked in the driveway and made my way along the flagstone path leading to the porch. The porch light was off, and the yard was dark as pitch. I picked my way up the low front stairs, which were dimly illuminated by the light from the living room windows. Janice had told me they usually ate dinner at this hour. I tapped on the front door and from the direction of the kitchen heard a chair scrape back.

Mace answered my knock, his body blocking most of the light spilling out the door. I smelled tuna casserole. He had a paper napkin in one hand, and he made a swipe at his mouth. "Oh, it's you. We're eating supper right now."

"Is Janice here?"

"She's already left. She works eleven to seven every day, but some girl got sick and she went in early. Try tomorrow," he said. He was already moving to shut the door in my face.

"Mind if I talk to you?"

His face went momentarily blank, just a tiny flick of temper that wiped out any other expression. "Pardon?"

"I wondered if you'd object to a quick chat," I said.

"Yeah, I do. I work a long, hard day, and I don't like people watching while I eat."

I felt a flash of heat, as though somebody'd taken a blow torch to the back of my neck. "Maybe later," I said. I turned and moved down the porch steps. As the door closed behind me, he muttered something obscene.

I backed out of the drive with a chirp and threw the car into first. What a turd. I did not like the man at all. He was a horse's ass and a jerk, and I hoped he had itchy hemorrhoids. I drove randomly, trying to cool down. I couldn't even think what to do with myself. I would have gone to Frankie's to talk to Janice, but I knew I'd say spiteful things about her spouse.

SUE GRAFTON

Instead, I went to the Caliente Cafe, looking for Cheney Phillips. It was still early for a Wednesday night, but CC's was already crowded, sound system blasting and enough cigarette smoke to make breathing unpleasant. For a place with no Happy Hour, no two-for-one deals, and no hors d'oeuvres (unless you count chips and salsa as a form of canapé), CC's does a lively business from the time it opens at five P.M. until it closes at two in the morning. Cheney was sitting at the bar in a dress shirt, faded jeans, and a pair of desert boots. He had a beer in front of him and was talking with the guy sitting next to him. When he saw me, he grinned. Lordy, I'm a sucker for good teeth. "Ms. Millhone. How are you? You got your hair cut. It looks good."

"Thanks. You got a minute?"

"Of course." He picked up his beer and eased himself off the bar stool, scanning the place for a vacant table where we could talk. The bartender was moving in our direction. "We need a glass of Chardonnay," Cheney said.

We found a table on the side wall. I spewed for a while about my dislike of Mace Kepler. Cheney wasn't all that fond of the man himself, so he enjoyed my comments.

"I don't know what it is. He just gets me."

"He hates women," Cheney said.

I looked at him with surprise. "Is that it? Maybe that's what it is."

"So what else are you up to?"

I spent a few minutes filling him in on my trip to San Francisco, my talk with Trinny, her confession about the porno tape, and finally the money missing from the account. I showed him the bank statement, watching his face. "What do you think?"

By then he was slouched down on his spine, his legs stretched out in front him. He had one elbow propped up on the table, and he held the statement by one corner. He shifted on his seat. He didn't seem impressed. "She was going out of town. She probably needed money." He sat and studied the bank statement while he sipped at his Corona.

"I asked Danielle about that. She says Lorna never paid. She only traveled with guys who sported her to everything."

"Yeah, but it still isn't necessarily significant," he said.

"Of course it isn't *necessarily* significant, but it might be. That's the point. Serena says J.D. went into the cabin briefly while they were waiting for the cops. Suppose he lifted it."

"You think it's sitting right there, this big wad of dough?"

"Well, it could be," I said.

"Yeah, right. For all you know, Lorna was involved in off-track betting or she picked up a fur coat or bought a shitload of drugs."

"Uhn-hun," I said, cutting in on his recital. "Or maybe the cash was lifted by the first officer at the scene."

"There's an idea," he said, not liking the image of police corruption. "Anyway, you don't know it was cash. It could have been a check made payable to someone else. She could have moved the money over to her checking account and paid the balance on her Visa bill. Most people don't walk around with cash like that."

"I keep picturing a wad of bills."

"Well, try to picture something else."

"Serena might have taken it. She pointed a finger at J.D., but really, all we have is her word she didn't go into the cabin herself. Or maybe Lorna's parents found the stash and kept their mouths shut, figuring they'd have to have money for the funeral. I was going to ask about that, but Kepler pissed me off."

Cheney seemed amused. "You just never give up."

"I think it's interesting, that's all. Besides, I'm desperate for a lead. Mace Kepler doesn't have a record, does he? I'd love to get him on something."

"He's clean. We checked him out."

"Doesn't mean he isn't guilty. It just means he hasn't been caught yet."

"Don't get distracted." He pushed the statement across the table. "At least you know who mailed the porno tape to Mrs. K," he said.

"It doesn't lead anywhere."

"Don't sound so depressed."

"Well, I hate these raggedy-ass investigations," I said. "Sometimes the line is so clear. You pick up the scent and you follow it. It may take time, but at least you know you're going someplace. This is driving me nuts."

Cheney shrugged. "We investigated for months and didn't get anywhere."

"Yeah, I know. I don't know what made me think I could make a difference."

"What an egotist," he said. "You work on a case three days and you think, boom, you should be solving it."

"Is that all it's been? Feels like I've been on this sucker for weeks."

"Anyway, something will break. Killer's been sitting around all this time thinking he's in the clear. He's not going to like it that you're nosing around."

"Or she."

"Right. Let's don't get sexist about homicide," he said.

Cheney's pager went off. Until that moment I hadn't even been aware that he was toting one. He checked the number and then excused himself, going into the rear of the bar to use the pay phone. When he came back, he said he had to leave. One of his informants had been arrested and was asking for him.

After he left, I hung around long enough to finish my wine. Business was picking up, and the noise level was rising, along with the toxic levels of secondhand cigarette smoke. I grabbed my jacket and my shoulder bag and headed for the parking lot. It was not even midnight, but all the parking spaces were filled and cars were beginning to line the road out in front.

The sky was overcast. The lights from the city made the cloud cover glow. Across the road, at the bird refuge, a low mist was rising from the freshwater lagoon. A faint sulfurous smell seemed to permeate the air. Crickets and frogs masked the sounds of traffic on the distant highway. Closer at hand, an approaching freight train sounded its horn like a brief organ chord. I could feel the ground rumble faintly as the searchlight swept around the bend. The man on the bike went by. I turned and stared after him. The mounting thunder of the train made his passage seem as silent as a mime's. All I was aware of was the dancing of the lights, his juggling performance, for which I was an audience of one.

In the side lot, I spotted the rounded roofline of my VW where I'd parked it in a circle of artificial light. A shiny black stretch limousine was parked across the row of cars, blocking four vehicles, including mine. I peered toward the driver's side. The window was lowered soundlessly. I paused, pointing at my car to indicate that I was hemmed in. The chauffeur touched his cap but made no move to start his engine. Little Miss Helpful, I waited for half a second and then said, "Sorry to bother you, but if you can just move up about three feet, I think I can squeeze out. I'm the VW at the back." The chauffeur's gaze moved to a point behind me, and I turned to see what he was looking at.

The two men had emerged from the bar and were heading in our direction, feet crunching on gravel, their progress leisurely. I moved on toward my car, thinking to go ahead and unlock it and get in. No point in standing in the cold, I thought. The cadence of the footsteps picked up, and I turned to see what was going on. The two men appeared on either side of me, crowding in close, each man gripping an arm. "Hey!" I said.

"Please be very quiet," one of them murmured.

They began to walk me toward the limo, virtually hoisting me off the ground so that my feet barely touched as they hurried me along. I felt like a kid being held aloft by my parents, lifted over curbs and puddles. When you're little, this is fun. When you're big, it's scary stuff. The rear door of the limo opened. I tried to dig my heels in, but I had no purchase.

By the time I gathered myself and bucked, squawking, "Help!" I was in the back of the limo with the door slammed shut.

The interior was black leather and burled walnut. I could see a compact bar, a phone, and a blank television screen. Above my head, a band of varicolored lighted buttons controlled every aspect of the passengers' comfort: air temperature, windows, reading lights, the sliding moon roof. The interior glass privacy panel was rolled up between us and the chauffeur. I sat there, squeezed in between the two guys on the back bench seat, facing a third man across a spacious length of plush black carpeting. In the interest of personal safety, I made a point of looking straight ahead. I didn't want to be able to identify the two sidekicks. The guy facing me didn't seem to care if I looked at him or not. All three men were throwing out body heat, absorbed by the silence, which ate up all but the sounds of heavy breathing, largely mine.

The only lights on in the limo were small side bars. The floods from the parking lot were cut by the heavily tinted windows, but there was still ample illumination. The atmosphere in the car was tense, as if the gravitational field were somehow different here than in the rest of the world. Maybe it was the overcoats, the conviction I had that everybody in the car was packing except me. I could feel my heart thumping in my chest and the sick thrill of sweat trickling down my side. Often fear makes me sassy, but not this time. I felt excessively respectful. These were men who operated by a set of rules different from mine. Who knew what they'd consider rude or offensive?

The limo was so long that the man across from me was probably sitting eight feet away. He appeared to be in his sixties, short and blocky, balding on top. His face was dotted with miscellaneous moles, the skin as heavily lined as a pen-and-ink sketch. His cheeks bowed out almost to a heart shape, his chin forming the point. His eyebrows were an unruly tangle of white over dark, sunken eyes. His upper lids sagged. His lower lids were pouched into smoky poufs. He had thin lips and big teeth, set slightly askew in his mouth. He had big hands, thick wrists, and heavy gold jewelry. He smelled of cigars and a spicy after-shave. There was something distinctly masculine about him: brusque, decisive, opinionated. He held a small notebook loosely in one hand, though he didn't seem to be referring to it. "I hope you'll forgive the unorthodox method of arranging a meeting. We didn't intend to alarm you." No accent. No regional inflection.

The guys on either side of me sat as still as mannequins.

"Are you sure you have the right person?"

"Yes."

"I don't know you," I said.

"I'm a Los Angeles attorney. I represent a gentleman who's currently out of the country on business. He asked me to get in touch."

"Regarding what?" My heartbeat had slowed some. These were not robbers or rapists. I didn't think they were going to shoot me and fling my body out into the parking lot. The word M-A-F-I-A formed at the back of my mind, but I didn't allow it to become concrete thought. I didn't want confirmation, in case I was forced to testify later. These guys were professionals. They killed for business, not pleasure. So far, I *had* no business with them, so I figured I was safe.

The *alleged* attorney was saying, "You're conducting a homicide investigation my client has been following. The dead girl is Lorna Kepler. We'd appreciate it if you'd apprise us of the information you've acquired."

"What's his interest? If you don't mind my asking."

"He was a close friend. She was a beautiful person. He doesn't want anything coming to light that might sully her reputation."

"Her reputation was sullied before she died," I pointed out.

"They were engaged."

"In what?"

"They were getting married in Las Vegas on April twenty-first, but Lorna never showed."

14

I stared across the dark of the limousine at him. The claim seemed so preposterous that it might just be true. I'd been told Lorna met some heavy hitters in the course of her work. Maybe she fell in love with some guy and he with her. Mr. and Mrs. Racketeer. "Didn't he send someone up here to find her when she didn't show?"

"He's a proud man. He assumed she'd had a change of heart. Naturally, when he heard what had happened to her, the news was bittersweet," he said. "Now, of course, he wonders if he could have saved her."

"We'll probably never have the answer to that."

"What information do you have so far?"

I was forced to shrug. "I've only been working since Monday, and I haven't come up with much."

He was silent for a moment. "You spoke to a gentleman in San Francisco with whom we've had dealings. Mr. Ayers."

"That's right."

"What did he tell you?"

I paused. I wasn't sure whether Joe Ayers's cooperation or his failure to cooperate would generate disfavor in this crowd. I pictured Ayers hanging from his chandelier by his dick. Maybe the Mob didn't really do things that way. Maybe they'd picked up a bad rep these days. Living in Santa Teresa, we didn't have a lot of experience with these things. My mouth had gone dry. I was worried about my responsibility to the people I'd spoken with. "He was courteous," I said. "He gave me a couple of names and telephone numbers, but I'd already checked them out, so the information wasn't that useful."

"Who else have you spoken to?"

It's hard to sound casual when your voice starts to quake. "Family members. Her boss. She'd done some house-sitting for the boss's wife, and I talked to her." I cleared my throat.

"This was Mrs. Bonney? The one who found her?"

"That's right. I also talked to the homicide detective who handled the case."

Silence.

"That's about it," I added, sounding lame.

His eyes drifted down to his notebook. There was a glint of light when his gaze came up again. Clearly he knew exactly whom I'd spoken to and was waiting to see how candid I intended to be. I pretended I was in a courtroom on the witness stand. He was an attorney, according to *his* claim. If he had questions, let him ask and I'd answer. In the unlikely event that I knew more than he did, I thought it was better not to volunteer information.

"Who else?" he asked.

Another trickle of sweat slid down my side. "That's all I can think of offhand," I said. The car seemed hot. I wondered if they had the heater turned on.

"What about Miss Rivers?"

I looked at him blankly. "I don't know anyone by that name."

"Danielle Rivers."

"Oooh, yeah. Right. I did speak to her. Are you guys connected to that fellow on a bike?"

He ignored that one. He said, "You talked to her twice. Most recently tonight."

"I owed her some money. She came by to collect. She gave me a haircut and we ordered a vegetarian pizza. It was no big deal. Really."

His gaze was cold. "What has she told you?"

"Nothing. You know, she said Lorna was her mentor, and she passed along some of Lorna's financial strategies. She did mention her personal manager, a guy named Lester Dudley. You know him?"

"I don't believe Mr. Dudley is relevant to our discussion," he said. "What's your theory about the murder?"

"I don't have one yet."

"You don't know who killed her?"

I shook my head.

"My client is hoping you'll pass the name along when it comes into your possession."

Oh, sure, I thought. "Why?" I tried not to sound impertinent, but it was tough. It's probably smarter not to quiz these guys, but I was curious.

"He would consider it a courtesy."

"Ah, a courtesy. Got it. Like between us professionals."

"He could also make it worth your while."

"I appreciate that, but . . . mmm, I don't mean to sound rude about this, but I don't really want anything from him. You know, that I can think of at the moment. Tell him thanks for the offer."

Dead silence.

He reached into the inside breast pocket of his coat. I flinched, but all he did was take out a retractable ballpoint pen, which he clicked. He scribbled something on a business card and held it out to me. "I can be reached at this number at any hour."

The guy on my right moved forward, took the card, and passed it to me. No name. No address. Just the handwritten number. The attorney continued, his tone pleasant. "In the meantime, we'd prefer that you'd keep this conversation confidential."

"Sure."

"No exceptions."

"Okay."

"Including Mr. Phillips."

Cheney Phillips, undercover vice cop. I said, "Got it."

I felt cool air on my face and realized the limo door had been opened. The guy on my right got out, extending a hand to me. I appreciated the assist. It's hard to hump your way across a seat when the sweat on the back of your knees is causing you to stick to the upholstery. I hoped I hadn't wet myself. In this situation, I didn't even trust my legs to work. I emerged somewhat ungracefully, butt first, like a breech birth. To steady myself, I put a hand against the car parked next to mine.

The guy got back in the limo. The rear door closed with a click and the car eased away, gliding soundlessly out of the parking lot. I checked for the license plate, but the number had been obscured by mud. Not that I'd have had the plate run. I didn't really want to know who these guys were.

Under my jacket, the back of my turtleneck was cold and damp. An involuntary spasm scampered down my frame. I needed a hot shower and a slug of brandy, but I didn't have time for either. I unlocked my car and got in, slapping the lock down again as if pursued. I peered into the backseat to make sure I was alone. Even before I started the car, I flipped the heater on.

I sat in a back booth at Frankie's Coffee Shop, as far from the windows as I could get. I kept searching the other patrons, wondering if one of them was tailing me. The place was moderately full: older couples who'd probably been coming here for years, kids looking for some place to hang out. Janice had spotted me when I came in, and she appeared at the table with a coffeepot in hand. There was a setup in front of me: napkin, silverware, thick white ceramic cup turned upside down on a matching saucer. I turned the cup right-side up, and she filled it. I left it on the table so she couldn't see how badly my hands were shaking.

"You look like you could use this," she said. "You're white as a sheet."

"Can you talk?"

She glanced behind her. "Soon as the party at table five clears out," she said. "I'll leave you this." She put the pot down and moved back to her station, pausing to pick up an order from the kitchen pass-through.

When she returned, she was toting an oversize cinnamon roll and two pats of butter wrapped in silver paper. "I brought you a snack. You look like you could use a little jolt of sugar with your caffeine."

"Thanks. This looks great."

She sat down across from me, careful to keep an eye out in case customers came in.

I opened both pats and broke off a band of hot roll, which I buttered and ate, nearly moaning aloud. The dough was soft and moist, the glaze dripping down between the coils. Nothing like fear to generate an appetite for comfort foods. "Fantastic. I could get addicted. Is this a bad time for you?"

"Not at the moment. I may have to interrupt. Are you all right? You don't seem like yourself."

"I'm fine. I have a couple of things I need to ask." I paused to lick butter from my fingers, and then I wiped them on a paper napkin. "Did you know Lorna was supposed to get married in Las Vegas the weekend she died?"

Janice looked at me as if I had begun to speak a foreign language and she was waiting for subtitles to appear at the bottom of the screen. "Where in the world did you hear such a thing?"

"Think there's any truth to it?"

"Until this very second, I'd have said absolutely not. Now you mention it, I'm not so sure. It's possible," she said. "It might explain her attitude, which at the time I couldn't identify. She seemed excited. Truly, like she was wanting to tell me something, but was holding back. You know how kids are. . . . Well, maybe you don't. When kids have a secret, they can hardly keep it in. They want to tell so bad they can't stand it, so most of the time they just blab it right out. She was acting like that. At the time, I wasn't picking up on it consciously. I did notice, because that's what popped in my head the minute you said that, but at the time, I didn't press. Who was she going to marry? As far as I know, she didn't even date."

"I don't know the man's name. I gather it was some fellow from Los Angeles."

"But who told you? How did you find out about him?"

"His attorney got in touch with me a little while ago. Actually, it might have been the guy himself, playing games. It's hard to say."

"Why haven't we heard about him before now? She's been dead ten months and this is the first I've heard of it."

"Maybe we've finally started fishing in the right swamp," I said.

"You want me to ask the girls if she said anything to them?"

"I'm not sure it matters. I have no reason to believe the story's fabricated. It's a question of filling in some blanks."

"What else? You said there were a couple of things."

"On the twentieth of April—the day before she died—she closed out a savings account she kept down in Simi Valley. It looks like she withdrew approximately twenty thousand dollars, either in cash or check. It's also possible she moved the money to another account, but I can't find a record of it. Is this ringing any bells with you?"

She shook her head slowly. "No. I don't know anything about that. Mace or me didn't come across any substantial sums of money. I'd have turned it in, figuring it might be evidence. Besides, if it was Lorna's money, it'd be part of her estate and we might have to pay taxes on it. I don't cheat the government, not even the tiniest little bit. That's one thing I taught her. You don't fool around with the IRS."

"Could she have hidden it?" I asked.

"Why would she do that?"

"I have no idea. She might have closed out the account and then tucked the money away someplace until she needed it."

"You think someone stole it?"

"I don't even know if there was really any money in the first place. It looks like there was, but I can't be sure. It's possible her landlord might have taken it. At any rate, it's a detail I need to pin down."

"Well, I sure never saw it."

"Was she security conscious? I didn't see a lot of locks and bolts at her place."

"Oh, she was awful about that. She left the door wide open half the time. In fact, I've often thought somebody might have got in while she was jogging, which is why there wasn't any sign of forced entry. The police thought so, too, because they asked me about it more than once."

"Did she ever mention a safe in the house?"

Her tone was skeptical. "Oh, I don't think she had a safe. That doesn't seem like her at all. In that crappy little cabin? It wouldn't make any sense. She believed in banks. She had accounts everywhere."

"What about her jewelry? Where did she keep that? Did she have a safe-deposit box?"

"It was nothing like that. She kept a regular old jewelry box in her chest of drawers, but we didn't find anything expensive. Just some costume stuff."

"But she must have had good pieces if she went through all the trouble and expense to insure them. She even made a point of mentioning her jewelry in her will."

"I'll be happy to show you what we found, and you can see for yourself," Janice said.

"What about those home security devices where people hide their valuables—you know, fake rocks or Pepsi cans or phony heads of lettuce in the vegetable bin? Did she have anything like that?"

"I doubt it. The police never found anything in the house that I know of. I'm not sure about outside. I know they searched the yard around the cabin. If she had something like that, they'd have found it, wouldn't they?"

"You're probably right, but I may go back over there tomorrow and take a look. Feels like a waste of time, but I don't like loose ends. Anyway, it's not like I have any better ideas."

I went home to bed and slept fitfully, pricked by the awareness that I had work to do yet. While my body teetered toward exhaustion, my brain synapses fired at random. Ideas seemed to shoot up like rockets, exploding midair, a light show of impressions. By some curious metamorphosis, I was being drawn into the shadowy after-hours world Lorna Kepler had inhabited. Night turf, the darkness, seemed both exotic and familiar, and I felt myself waking to the possibilities. In the meantime, my system was operating on overload, and I didn't so much sleep as short myself out.

At five twenty-five in the evening, when I finally opened my eyes, I felt so anchored to the bed I could barely move. I closed my eyes again, wondering if I'd picked up a superfluous three hundred pounds in my sleep. I checked my extremities but found no evidence of massive overnight weight gain. I rolled out of bed with a whimper, pulled myself together with minimal attention to the particulars, and headed out my front door. At the first fast-food establishment I passed, I picked up an oversize container of hot coffee and sucked on it like a baby, effectively burning my lips.

By six, when ordinary folk were heading home from work, I was bumping down the narrow dirt lane that led to Lorna's cabin. I'd been driving with a constant eye on my rearview mirror, wondering if the fellows in the limousine were following. Whatever their tailing methods, they were experts. Since I'd started this case, I'd never been aware of being under surveillance. Even now I'd have been willing to swear there was no one watching.

I parked my car nose out, pausing as I had the first time to drink in the mossy perfume of the place. I set my empty cup on the floor and removed my flashlight and a screwdriver from the glove compartment. I got out of the car, pausing to assess the weather of the night. I was faintly aware of the ebb and flow of the freeway in the distance, a dull tide of passing cars. The air was soft and cold, the shadows shifting capriciously as if blown by the wind. I moved toward the cabin, stomach churning with uneasiness. It was amazing to me how much I'd learned about Lorna since I'd first seen the place. I'd reviewed the postmortem photographs so often, I could almost conjure up a vision of her as she'd been when she was discovered: softened, disintegrating, returning to the elements. If there were ghosts in this world, surely she was one.

The night was foggy, and I could hear the intermittent moaning of a foghorn sounding on the ocean. The night breeze had a saturated feel to it, rich with the scent of vegetation. I swept away the dark with the beam of my flashlight. The garden Leda'd planted was tangled and overgrown, tomato volunteers pushing up among the papery stalks of dead corn. A few onion sets had survived the last harvest. Come spring, even left to its own devices the garden might resurrect itself.

I stood in the front yard and studied the cabin, circling the outside. There was nothing to speak of: dirt, dead leaves, patches of dried grass. I went up the porch steps. The door was still off its hinges. I tapped to see if it was hollow, but it clunked back at me, dense and solid. I flipped on the overhead light. The dingy glow of a forty-watt bulb defined the interior spaces in a wash of faint yellow. I did a slow visual survey. Where would I hide twenty thousand dollars in cash? I started at the entryway and worked my way around to the right. The cabin was poorly insulated, and there didn't seem to be a lot of nooks and crannies. I tapped and poked, sticking the tip of my screwdriver in every crevice and crack. I felt like a dentist probing for cavities.

The kitchen seemed to suggest the greatest possibility for hiding places. I took drawers out, measured the depth of cabinets, looking for any discrepancies that might hint at an opening. I crawled along the floor, getting filthy in the process. Surely the cops had done exactly this . . . if they'd known what to search for.

I tried the bathroom next, shining my light up behind and inside the toilet tank, testing tiles for loose ones. I pulled out the medicine cabinet, peering down into the lathing behind it. I scrutinized the space in the alcove where she'd kept her bed, checked the metal floor plate in the living room on which the wood-burning stove had rested. There was nothing. Whatever Lorna did with her money, she didn't keep it on the premises. If she'd had jewelry or large sums of cash, she hadn't stuck it in a hidey-hole. Well, let's correct that. Whatever she'd done with her valuables, I didn't know where they were. Maybe someone else got to them first or maybe, as Cheney suggested, she'd used the money some other way. I finished up the search with a second survey, feeling dissatisfied.

By chance my gaze dropped to the Belltone box. The housing had been popped loose, and I leaned toward it, using my screwdriver to explore the space. For an instant I prayed a secret compartment would open up and a wad of bills would spill out. Optimist that I am, I always hope for things like that. There was nothing, of course, except the tag end of electrical wire. I'd never actually seen the working mechanism of a doorbell, but the wire seemed odd. I stood and stared at it for a moment and then leaned closer, squinting. What *was* that?

I went outside, down the creaking wooden steps. The front porch was hiked up on concrete supports, elevated about three feet, the space narrowing down to nothing where the ground sloped upward at the back. The intention must have been to keep moisture away from the floor joists, but the net effect was to create a cinder-strewn crawl space that had been screened with wooden lathing. I crouched beside the lathing and stuck my fingers through the holes. I gave a pull and a small section lifted away, allowing me to peer at the space underneath the cabin. It was pitch black. I raked the area with the beam of my flashlight and was treated to the bouncing of daddy longlegs as they warned me away.

There was a flat piece of plywood on the ground with a few garden tools laid on top. I stood up again, aligning my sights with the approximate location of the Belltone box. I adjusted my position and shone my flashlight up along the joists. I could see where the green wire came down through the floor. It was stapled along the joists at long intervals, running toward the edge of the porch close to me. I was going to have to inch my way under, not a happy thought given all the spiders lurking in the dark.

Gingerly I got down on my hands and the balls of my feet and duck-walked my way under. The spider kiddies viewed me with alarm, and many of them fled in what must have been spider fear and panic. Later they would have horrified conversations about the unpredictability of humans. "Eeew. All those fingers," they'd say. "And those big nasty feet. They always look like they're about to squish you." Spider mothers would console them. "Most humans are completely harmless, and they're just as scared of us as we are of them," they'd say.

I craned my head, sweeping the underside of the porch with the beam of my flashlight. Right at eye level a leather case had been stapled to the wood. I used the flat end of my screwdriver to force the staples out. The case was dusty and mealy where the leather had begun to deteriorate. I humped my way out from under the porch. I dusted my hands off, brushed gravel and dirt from my jeans, then flipped off the flashlight. I moved back into the cabin to examine my find. What I was holding looked like the carrying case for a little portable radio or tape recorder, complete with holes in the end into which an earphone or a mike could be plugged. There was a slit along one end for the volume control. It had to be a surveillance setup, not sophisticated by any means, but possibly effective. Somebody had planted something similar in my apartment a couple of years back, and I'd discovered it only by accident. In the meantime, the voice-activated recorder had captured my end of all phone calls, all incoming messages on my answering machine, both sides of any conversations I'd had on the premises.

Someone had been spying on Lorna. Of course, it was possible she'd planted the device herself, but only if she'd had a reason to keep an audible record of her conversations. If that were the case, I couldn't believe she wouldn't have planted the recorder inside the cabin, where reception would be good and the tapes easier to replace. Something like this, tacked to the underside of the cabin, was bound to pick up a lot of ambient noise.

Gosh-a-rudy, I thought, now who do I know who'd have access to all kinds of surveillance equipment? Could it be Miss Leda Selkirk, daughter of the PI who'd once had his license yanked for an illegal wiretap? I flipped my flashlight back on and turned the lights off in the cabin. I unlocked my car and turned the key in the ignition, easing the VW down the bumpy road toward the street.

I parked out in front of the Burkes' half-darkened house.

When Leda answered my knock, I was standing with the decrepit leather case dangling off the end of my screwdriver like the skin of some strange beast. Tonight, her midriff was bare. Here it was the middle of February and she was wearing an outfit that might have been suitable for a belly dancer: wrap-around sarong-style pants with wide legs in a thin floral fabric reminiscent of summer pajama bottoms. The top was a similar fabric, different print, with no sleeves and one button appearing right between her quite weensie breasts. I said, "Is J.D. here?"

She shook her head. "He's not home yet."

"Mind if I come in?" I pictured her playing dumb, a reaction ranging anywhere from denial to duh.

She looked at me and she looked at the leather case, apparently unable to think of a thing to say except, "Oh."

She stepped back from the door, and I went into the darkened hall, following as she led the way toward the kitchen at the rear. A glance to the left showed Jack, the sticky-fingered toddler, lying in a stupor on the couch, watching a cartoon video. The infant slept, slumped sideways in a well-padded portable car seat while colored images flickered across its face.

The kitchen still smelled like the sautéed onions and ground beef from dinner on Monday, which seemed like ages ago. Some of the dishes piled in the sink looked the same, too, though several other meals' worth had been piled on top. She was probably the type who waited until everything was used before she ventured into the washing process. "You want some coffee?" she asked. I could see a fresh pot on a Mr. Coffee stand, the mechanism still spitting out the last few drops.

"That'd be nice," I said. I sat down at the banquette and checked the kitchen table for sticky spots. I found a clear couple of inches and propped my elbow with care.

She took down a mug and filled it, then refilled hers before she put the pot back on the machine. In profile, her nose seemed too long for her face, but the effect in certain lights was lovely nonetheless. Her neck was long and her ears elfin, her short-cropped dark hair trimmed to wisps around her face. Her eyes were lined in smudged black, and her lip gloss was a brownish tint.

I put the leather case in the middle of the table.

She took a seat on the bench, pulling her feet up under her. She ran her hand through her hair, her expression somewhat sheepish. "I kept meaning to take that out, but I never got around to it. What a dork."

"You installed surveillance equipment?"

"Wasn't much. Just a mike and a tape recorder."

"Why?"

"I don't know. I was worried," she said. Her dark eyes seemed enormous, filled with innocence.

"I'm listening."

Color was rising in her face. "I thought J.D. and Lorna might be fooling around, but I was wrong." There was a baby bottle half-full of formula sitting on the table. She unscrewed the nipple and used the contents for cream. She offered me some, but I declined.

"What was it, voice-activated?"

"Well, yeah. I know it sounds kind of dumb in retrospect, but I'd just found out I was pregnant with the baby, and I was throwing up all day. Jack wasn't even out of diapers, and I was frantic about J.D. I knew I was being bitchy, but I couldn't help myself. I looked horrible and felt worse. And there was Lorna, slim and elegant. I'm not stupid. I figured out what she did for a living, and so did he. J.D. started finding excuses for going back there every other day. I knew if I confronted him, he'd laugh in my face, so I borrowed some of Daddy's stuff."

"*Were* they having an affair?"

Her expression was self-mocking. "He fixed her toilet. One of her screens had come loose, and he fixed that, too. The most he ever did was complain about me, and even that wasn't bad. She had a fit and chewed him out. She said he had a hell of a nerve when I was the one doing all the suffering and hard work. Also, she got on him because he didn't lift a finger with Jack. That's when he started cooking, which has been a big help. I feel bad I never thanked her, but I wasn't supposed to know she'd come to my defense."

"How'd you know how to install the bug?"

"I've watched Daddy do it. Lorna was gone a lot, so it wasn't hard. The doorbell never worked, but the box was there. I just drilled a hole in the floor and then crawled under the cabin. All I had to do was make sure the tape was close enough to the edge of the porch so I could switch it without a hassle. We kept the gardening tools under there. Any time I weeded, I would find a way to check the tape."

"How many tapes did you run?"

"I only used one tape, but the first time was a bust because the mike was defective and didn't pick up half the time. Second try was better, but the sound was distorted, so you couldn't hear too well. She had the radio on. She played this jazz station all the time. Up front there's this little fragment with her and J.D. I had to listen three times to be sure it was him. Then her drying her hair . . . that was entertaining. I got her end of a couple of phone calls, that whole business where she's cranking on J.D. Then more music, only country this time, then she's talking to some guy. That part's left over from the first round, I think."

"Did you tell the police?"

"There wasn't anything to tell. Besides, I was embarrassed," she said. "I didn't want J.D. to know I didn't trust him, especially when it turned out he's innocent. I felt like a fool. Plus, the whole thing's illegal, so why incriminate myself? I'm still worried they'll start thinking it was J.D. who killed her. It scared me silly when you started in on us, but at least this way I can prove the two of them were friends and got along okay."

I stared at her. "Are you trying to tell me you still *have* the tapes?"

"Well, sure, but there's only one," she said. "The first time was mostly static, so I went ahead and taped over it."

"You mind if I listen?"

"You mean right now?"

"If you don't mind."

15

She unfolded herself and got up from the table. She moved out into the hallway and disappeared from sight. Moments later she returned with an empty cassette box and a little tape recorder, the cassette already in place and visible through the oval window. "I guess I didn't have to keep this, but it made me feel better. Really, J.D. couldn't have killed her because he wasn't even in town. He took off Friday morning on a fishing trip. She wasn't killed until Saturday when he was miles away."

"Where were you that day?"

"I was gone too. I decided to go part of the way with him. He took me as far as Santa Maria and dropped Jack and me at my sister's on Friday. I spent a week with her and then came home on the bus."

"You have any objections to giving me her name and number?"

"You don't believe me?"

"Let's don't get into that, Leda. You're not exactly a Girl Scout," I said.

"Well, I know, but that doesn't mean I'd *kill* anyone."

"What about J.D.? Can he verify his whereabouts?"

"You can ask my sister's husband, Nick. That's who he went to Nacimiento with."

I made a note of the name and number.

Leda punched the play button on the recorder. After a brief interval of white noise, the sound seemed to jump out. The reception was dismal, filled with clunks and banging as people moved around. With the equipment so close, the knocking on the door sounded like lightning cracks. A chair scraped, and someone thunked across the floor.

"Oh, hi. Come on in. I got the check right here."

There were a couple of inaudible remarks between the two of them. The front door closed like a muffled explosion.

Footsteps clunking. *"How's Leda feeling?"*

"She's kind of down in the dumps, but she was this way last time. She gets to feeling fat and ugly. She's convinced I'm going out to screw around on her, so she busts out crying every time I leave the house."

I put out a hand. "Hold on a minute. That's J.D.'s voice?"

She pushed pause, and the recording stopped. "Yeah, I know. It's hard to recognize. I had to play it two or three times myself. You want to hear it again?"

"If you don't mind," I said. "I've never heard Lorna's voice, but I'm assuming you can identify her as well."

"Well, sure," Leda said. She punched the rewind button. When the tape stopped, she pressed play, and we listened to the opening again. *"Oh, hi. Come on in. I got the check right here."*

Again, muffled remarks between the two of them and the front door closed like a sonic boom.

Footsteps clunking. *"How's Leda feeling?"*

"She's kind of down in the dumps, but she was this way last time. She gets to feeling fat and ugly. She's convinced I'm going out to screw around on her, so she busts out crying every time I leave the house."

Lorna was saying, *"What's her problem? She looks darling."*

"Well, I think so, but she's got some girlfriend that happened to." Footsteps thunked across the floor and a chair scraped back, sounding like a lion roaring in the jungle.

"She only gained fifteen pounds with Jack. How could she feel fat? She doesn't even show. My mother gained forty-six with me. Now, that's uggers. I've seen pictures. Stomach hanging down to here. Boobs looked like footballs, and her legs looked like sticks." Laughter. Mumbles. Static.

"Yeah, well, it isn't real, so you can't talk her out of it. You know how she is. . . . [mumble, mumble] *. . . insecure."*

"That's what you get for hooking up with someone half your age."

"She's twenty-one!"

"Serves you right. She's an infant. Listen, you want me to keep Jack while you two go out to dinner?" More mumbles.

"xxxxxxx" The response here was completely missing, blotted out by static.

". . . problem. He and I get along great. In exchange, you can do me a favor and fog the place for me next time I go out of town. The spiders are getting out of control."

"Thanks. . . . ceipt in your mailbox." Chairs scraping. Clump, clump of footsteps crossing the cabin. Muffled voices. The conversation continued outside and then stopped abruptly. Silence. When the tape picked up again, there were strains of country music with the high whine of a hair dryer running over it. A phone began to ring. The hair dryer was turned off. Clump, clump, clump of footsteps like a series of gunshots. The phone was picked up, and Lorna raised her voice in greeting. After that, much of her end of the call was a series of short responses . . . *uhn-hun, sure, right, okay, that's great.* There was a fragmentary mention of the Palace that made me think she might be talking to Danielle. Hard to tell with the competing strains of country music overlaid. There was a second conversation between J.D. and Lorna, which was much as Leda indicated. J.D. complained, and Lorna chewed him out because he never helped at home.

Leda pressed the stop button impatiently. "It goes on like that. Pissed me off they were always talking about me behind my back. Lot of the rest is just mumbling, and most you can't even hear."

"Too bad," I said.

"Yeah, well, the equipment was kind of dinky. I didn't want to get into anything elaborate because it was too much trouble. The amplification was minimal. You get a lot of distortion that way."

"When was this done? Any way to pin down the date?"

"Not really. Lorna sat with Jack a couple different times, but I never wrote it down. It wasn't any special occasion. Just us popping out for a bite to eat. With a toddler at home, an hour by yourself feels like heaven."

"What about the month? It must have been early in the pregnancy because he mentions you're not showing yet. And wasn't there mention of a receipt? In that first conversation, it sounds like he's stopped by to pick up the rent."

"Oh. Maybe so. You could be right about that. I mean, Jeremy was born in September, so that must have been . . . I don't know . . . April sometime? She paid the first of the month."

"When did you start the taping?"

"Around then, I guess. Like I said, the first tape was all static. This is the second one I did. I think he actually had the exterminator out for all the spiders and bugs. He probably has a record of it if you want me to look it up."

"What else is on here?"

"Mostly junk, like I said. The batteries went dead about halfway through, and after that all you hear is the stuff still on there from the first time I taped." She pulled the tape out and tucked it back in the empty cassette box. She got up from the table as if to leave the room.

I caught her casually by the arm. "Mind if I take that?"

She hesitated. "What for?"

"So I can hear it again."

She made a face. "Nnn, I don't know. I don't think that's a good idea. This's the only one I got."

"I'll bring it back as soon as possible."

She shook her head. "I'd rather not."

"Come on, Leda. What are you so worried about?"

"How do I know you won't turn it over to the cops?"

"Oh, right. So they can listen to people clump around making small talk? This is not incriminating stuff. They're talking about the fuckin' *bugs*," I said. "Besides, you can always claim you had permission. Who's going to contradict you?"

She gave that consideration. "What's your interest?"

"I was hired to do this. This is my job," I said. "Look. From what you've said, this tape was made within a month of Lorna's death. How can you be sure it's not significant?"

"You'll bring it right back?"

"I promise."

Reluctantly she put the cassette on the table and pushed it over to me. "But I want to know where to call in case I need it back," she said.

"You're a doll," I said. I took out a business card and made a note of my home phone and my home address. "I gave you this before, but here it is again. Oh, and one more thing."

Sounding crabby, she said, "What?"

Every time I manipulate people, it seems to make them so *cross*. "Has J.D. come into any money in the last few months?"

"J.D. doesn't have money. If he does, he never told me. You want me to ask when he gets in?"

"It's not important," I said. "Anyway, if you mention it, you might have to tell him what we were talking about, and I don't think you want to do that."

From the expression on her face, I thought maybe I could trust her discretion.

I stopped at a minimart on the way back to my place. Somewhere I had a tape recorder, but the batteries were probably dead. While I was at it, I bought myself a king-size cup of coffee and a nasty-looking meat sandwich wrapped in cellophane. From the pink stuff peeking out the side, it was hard to imagine what cow part this was thin slivers of. I ate driving home, feeling too starved to wait. It was not quite eight o'clock, but this was probably lunch.

Home again, I spent some time getting organized. The tape recorder was right where it was supposed to be, in the bottom drawer of my desk. I changed the batteries and found the headphones, a pencil, and a legal pad. I played the tape through, listening with my eyes closed, the headphones pressed against my ears. I played the tape back again, taking notes this time. I transcribed what I could hear clearly and left a series of dots, dashes, and question marks where the sound was garbled or inaudible. It was slow going, but I finally reached a point where I'd gleaned as much as I could.

As Leda had indicated, toward the end of the tape, after sixty minutes of boring talk, her machine had gone dead, leaving a fragment from the first taping she'd done. The one voice was Lorna's. The other voice was male, but not J.D.'s as far as I could tell. There was a segment of country music playing on the radio. Lorna must have turned it off because the silence was abrupt and punctuated by static. The guy spoke up sharply, saying, *"Hey . . ."*

Lorna sounded annoyed. *"I hate that stuff. . . . xxxxxxx. xxxxxxxxx . . ."*

"Oh, come on. I'm just kidding. But you have to admit, it's xxxxxxxxxx. She goes in xxxxxxxxxxxxx day . . . xxxxxx . . ."

"Goddamn it! Would you stop saying that? You're really sick. . . ."

"People shouldn't xxxxxxxx . . . [clatter . . . clink] *. . ."*

Sound of water . . . squeaking . . .

". . . xxxxxxxxx . . ."

Thump, thump . . .

"I'm serious . . . by—"

"xxxxx . . ."

Laughter . . . chair scrape . . . rustle . . . murmur . . .

There was something quarrelsome in the tone, an edginess in Lorna's voice. I played the tape twice more, writing down everything I heard clearly, but the subject of the conversation never made any sense. I took the headphones off. I pinched the bridge of my nose and rubbed my hands across my face. I wondered if the guys in the forensics lab had a way to amplify sound on a tape like this. As a private investigator, I was not exactly into high-tech equipment. A portable typewriter was about as state-of-the-art as I could boast. The problem was, I didn't see how I could ask for police assistance without an explanation of some kind. Despite my assurances to Leda, she was guilty of withholding, if not evidence, then information that might have been relevant to the police investigation. Cops get very surly when you least expect it, and I didn't want them to take an interest in something that wasn't mine to begin with.

Who else did I know? I tried the Yellow Pages in the telephone book under "Audio." The businesses listed offered laser home theaters, giant-screen TVs, custom design and installation of audio systems, and presentation graphics, followed by the ads for hearing aids, hearing evaluations, and speech therapists. I tried the section entitled "Sound," which was devoted in large part to designing wireless drive-through intercoms and residential and commercial sound systems. Oh.

I checked my watch: quarter after nine. I flipped back to the White Pages under K-SPL and called Hector Moreno at the local FM station. It was probably too early to reach him, but I could at least leave a message. The phone was picked up after three rings. "K-SPELL. This is Hector Moreno."

"Hector? I can't believe it's you. This is Kinsey Millhone. Aren't you there awfully early?"

"Well, hey. How are you? I switch shifts now and then. Keeps me from getting bored. What about you? What are you up to?"

"I have a tape recording with very poor sound quality. Would you have any way to clean it up?"

"That depends on what you got. I could try," he said. "You want to drop it off? I can leave the door unlocked."

"I'll be right there."

En route, I made a stop at Rosie's, where I told her about Beauty and begged for doggie bones. Earlier she'd boiled up two pounds of veal knuckle for the stock she makes. I had to pick through the trash to get them, but she wrapped two in paper with the usual admonishment. "You should get a dog," she said.

"I'm never home," I replied. She is always on me about this. Don't ask me why. Just a piece of aggravation, in my opinion. I took the packet of bones and began to back away, hoping to curtail discussion.

"A dog is good company, and protection, too."

"I'll think about it," I said as the kitchen door swung shut.

"Get a fella while you're at it."

At the station, I let myself in. Hector had left the door ajar and the foyer lights on. I went down into the twilight of the stairwell with my paper packet of bones. Beauty was waiting for me when I reached the bottom. She was the size of a small bear, her dark eyes bright with intelligence. Her coat was red gold, the undercoat puffy and soft. When she saw me, her fur seemed to undulate and she emitted a low, humming growl. I watched her lift her head at the scent of me. Without warning she pursed her lips and howled, a soaring note of ululation that seemed to go on for minutes. I didn't move, but I could feel my own fur bristle in response to her keening. I was rooted to the bottom step, my hand on the rail. Something primitive in her singing sent ice down along my spine. I heard Hector call her, then the quick thump of his crutches as he swung along the corridor.

"Beauty!" he snapped.

At first she refused to yield. He called her again. Her eyes rolled back at him reluctantly, and I could see her debate. She was willful, intent. As strong as her urge toward obedience, she didn't want to comply. Her complaints were sorrowful, the half-talk of dogs in which sentiment is conveyed in the insistent language of canines. She howled again, watching me.

I murmured, "What's the matter with her?"

"Beats me."

"I brought her some bones."

"It's not that." He leaned down and touched her. The howling became a low cry, filled with such misery that it broke my heart. He held his hand out. I passed him the packet of veal knuckles.

Hector looked at me oddly. "You smell like Lorna. Have you been handling something of hers?"

"I don't think so. Just some papers," I said. "There was a scarf of hers in the banker's box, but that was yesterday."

"Sit down very carefully on the steps where you are."

I eased myself down into a sitting position. He began to talk to Beauty, his tone full of comfort. She watched me with a mixture of hope and confusion, thinking I was Lorna, knowing I was not. Hector offered her the bones, which failed to interest her. Instead, carefully, she extended her blunt snout and sniffed at my fingers. I could see her nostrils work as she sifted and analyzed the components of my personal scent. He scratched her ears, massaging her meaty shoulders. Finally she seemed to accept that she had erred somehow. She hung her head, watching me with puzzlement, as if at any minute I might turn into the woman she was waiting for.

Hector straightened up. "She's okay now. Come on. Here. Why don't you take these," he said, passing the bones back to me. "She might decide she likes you yet."

I followed him into the same small studio. Beauty had resumed her wary guardianship, and she positioned herself between the two of us. She put her head down on her feet. Occasionally she gave me a look, but she was clearly depressed. Hector had made fresh coffee, which he offered from a jug thermos sitting on the counter beside a cardboard box and a leather photo album. I let him pour me a cup, figuring I couldn't feel much worse. He perched up on his stool, and I watched while he phased out the jazz number that was playing. He extemporized a commentary, feigning casual knowledge from the liner notes in the CD. His voice was deep and melodious. He slipped in another cassette, adjusted the sound levels, and then turned to me. "Let's try the bones," he said. "Beauty needs a lift, poor girl."

"I feel bad," I said. "I was wearing those jeans when I went through Lorna's files."

I opened the paper packet and hunkered next to Beauty. He coached me through the process. She finally relented, allowing me to stroke her densely furred head. She took one of the knuckle

SUE GRAFTON

bones between her feet and licked it thoroughly before she tested with her teeth. She made no particular objection when I rose again and perched up beside Hector on a second stool. Hector, meanwhile, was sorting through a stack of old black-and-white photographs with white fluted rims. He had a box of gummed corners and was mounting selected snapshots in an album fat with photographs.

"What are those?"

"My dad's got a birthday coming up, and I thought he'd get a kick. Most of these were taken during World War Two."

He passed me a snapshot of a man in pleated pants and a white dress shirt, standing in front of a microphone. "He was forty-two. He'd tried to enlist, but Uncle Sam turned him down. Too old, bad feet, punctured eardrum. He was already working as an announcer at radio station WCPO in Cincinnati, and they told him they needed him for the war effort, keep morale up here at home. He used to take me with him. Probably how I got the bug." He set the album aside. "Let's see what you have."

I took the cassette from my bag and passed it over to him. "Someone was doing a little eavesdropping. I'd rather not say who."

He turned it over in his hand. "I probably can't do much with this. I was hoping you were talking eight- or multitrack. Know how this works?"

"Not at all," I said.

"This is Mylar ribbon, coated on one side with a bonding material containing iron oxide. Signal passes through a coil in a recording head, and that causes a magnetic field to form between the poles of the magnet. Iron particles get magnetized in something called domains. No point in boring you to death," he said. "The point is, professional recording equipment is going to give you far better fidelity than a little tape like this. What was it, some kind of little dingus running off batteries?"

"Exactly. There's a lot of ambient noise, mumbling and static. You can't hear half of it."

202

"Doesn't surprise me. What'd you use for playback, same thing?"

"Probably the equivalent," I said. "I gather you can't help."

"Well, I can put it on my machine at home and see if that gives you anything. If the sound wasn't laid down in the first place, there's never going to be a way to pick it up on playback, but I got good speakers and could maybe filter out some frequencies, play around with bass and treble, and see what that does."

I pulled out the notes I'd made. "This is what I picked up so far. Anything I couldn't hear, I left blank with a question mark."

"Can you leave the tape with me? I can take a crack at it when I get home tonight and call you sometime tomorrow."

"I'm not sure about that. I swore I'd guard it with my life. I'd hate having to admit I left the tape with you."

"So don't tell. Someone asks for it back, just give me a call and come pick it up."

"You're a very devious person, Hector."

"Aren't we all?"

He took the page of notes I'd made and went into the other room to make a copy while I waited. I gave him my business card with my home address and phone jotted on the back. By the time I left the studio, Beauty had apparently decided I was part of her pack, though much lower in the pecking order and therefore in need of protection. She very kindly walked me to the stairwell, matching her footsteps to mine, and watched as I went up the steps and out into the foyer. I peeked back and found her still standing there, looking up, her gaze fixed on mine. I said, "Good night, Beauty."

Pulling out of the K-SPL parking lot, I caught a glimpse of a lone man on a bike streaking across the intersection. He took the corner wide and disappeared from sight, reflectors on his spokes making circles of light. For a moment I could feel a mounting roar in my ears, darkness gathering at the edges of my vision. I rolled down the window and pulled fresh air into my lungs. A wave of clamminess climbed my frame and passed. I pulled into the empty intersection and slowed, peering right, but there was no sign of him. The street lamps receded in a series of diminishing uprights that narrowed to a point and vanished.

I headed down to lower State Street, cruising Danielle's turf. I needed company or a good night's sleep, whichever came first. If I found Danielle, maybe the two of us would buy champagne and orange juice, drink a toast to Lorna just for old times' sake. Then I'd head for home. I pulled into the parking lot at Neptune's Palace and got out of my car.

From the far end of the parking lot, the noise level was considerably louder than I'd experienced before. The crowd was boisterous. The side doors were opened onto the parking lot, and a knot of revelers had spilled out. Some guy toppled sideways, taking two women with him. The three of them lay on the asphalt, laughing. This was Thursday night trade, nearly manic in its energy, everyone determined to party, gearing up for the coming weekend. Music pounded against the walls. Cigarette smoke drifted on the frigid night air in wisps and curls. I heard the shattering of glass, followed by maniacal laughter as if a genie had been released. I caught sight of a patrol car in the parking lot. The black-and-whites usually come down here every couple of hours. The beat officer parks and works his way through the place in search of liquor violations and petty criminals.

I steeled myself and pushed through the door. I traveled the length of the bar like a fish swimming upstream, scanning the assembled patrons for Danielle. She'd said she usually started work at eleven, but there was always the chance she'd stop at the bar first to have a drink. There was no sign of her at all, but I did see Berlyn on her way to the dance floor. She was wearing a short black skirt and a red satin top with spaghetti straps. Her hair was slightly too short for the topknot she affected, so that more seemed to hang down than was secured above. Her earrings were big double rhinestone hoops that glittered and bounced against her neck as she moved. At first I thought she was unaccompanied, but then I saw a fellow pushing through the crowd in front of her. The other bobbing dancers closed around her, and she was gone.

I made my way back to the front door and checked the parking lot without luck. I fired up the VW and cruised the neighborhood, pausing at all the street corners where the hookers hung out. Ten more minutes of this shit and I was heading home. Finally I pulled in at the curb, leaned over, and rolled my window down. A rail-thin brunette, wearing a T-shirt, miniskirt, and cowboy boots, separated herself from the wall she was leaning on. She ambled over and opened the door on the passenger side. I could see the puckering of goose bumps on her frail, bare arms.

"You want company?" She was strung out on something, throwing off that odd crackhead body odor. Her eyes kept sliding upward out of focus, like the roll on a TV picture.

"I'm looking for Danielle."

"Well, hon, Danielle's busy, so I'm covering her act. What you want, I can get, and that's an actual fact."

"Did she go home?"

"It's possible that Danielle has gone back to her place. Give me ten dollars more and I'll sit on your face."

I said, "Rhyming. Very nice. Meter's a little off, but otherwise you're Longfellow."

"Baby, don't be strange. You got any change?"

"I'm fresh out," I said.

"I won't pout." She pushed away from the car and sauntered back to her post. I pulled away, hoping I hadn't unleashed a fit of iambic pentameter. It hadn't occurred to me that Danielle might hang out at her place before going to work.

I headed up two blocks and hung a left, turning into the narrow alleyway where Danielle had her digs. I pulled even with the property and peered through the gap in the shrubs, my gaze moving up the brick walk that led to her door. Her curtains had been drawn, but I could see the glow of lights on inside. I really had no idea whether she brought johns back to her place or not. It was close enough to the Palace to be practical, but there were also a couple of fleabag hotels in the area, and she might have preferred to take her business there. I saw a shadow pass the window, which seemed to suggest she was on her feet. My car engine chuffed noisily, headlights slicing through the dark like blades. I could feel myself vacillate. She might be alone and glad of company. On the other hand, she might be occupied. I really didn't want to see her in a business context.

While I debated, I killed the engine and flicked out my headlights. The alley disappeared in pitch blackness, night insects chirring in the heavy silence. Within a minute my eyes were accustomed to the dark, and the landscape began to reassemble itself in shades of charcoal. I got out of the car and locked it behind me. Maybe I'd knock once. If she was busy, so be it. I felt my way from the alley to the brick walk, holding one hand in front of me lest I stumble over trash cans.

I reached her doorstep and cocked my head, listening for the sound of voices or canned laughter from the television. I gave a tentative knock. From the other side of the door, I heard low moans, sensuous and repetitive. Uh-oh. I remembered the first trailer I'd moved into after the death of my aunt. Coming in late one summer night, I'd heard a pregnant neighbor woman making sounds like that. Ever the good citizen, I'd gone over to her window, where I'd tapped and asked if she needed help. I'd thought she was in labor, realizing too late the process I'd interrupted was the one that *made* babies, not delivered them.

Behind me, someone moved out of the shadows near the alley and eased through the shrubs. Leisurely footsteps scritched on the pavement and gradually faded. Danielle's moaning was renewed, and I backed up a step. I stared out at the alleyway with puzzlement. Was that her john I'd just seen? I leaned my head against the door. "Danielle?" No response.

I knocked again. Silence.

I tried the knob. The hinges made no sound at all as the door swung inward. At first, all I saw was the blood.

16

The emergency room at St. Terry's was bedlam, a glimpse into purgatory. There had been a six-car accident on the highway, and all of the examining rooms were filled with the injured and dying. In each cubicle, against the hot white cloth of the surrounding screens, I could see a shadow play of medical procedures against a backdrop of supply carts, wall-mounted oxygen, the hanging bags of blood and glucose, X-ray machinery. Once in a while the low hum of activity would be cut by hellish shrieks from the patient on the gurney. On one stretcher, unattended, the victim writhed as if licked by flames, crying, "Mercy . . . have mercy." An orderly came by and moved him into a newly vacated examining room.

Doctors, nurses, and med techs had been mustered from every corner of St. Terry's. I watched them work in perfect concert, actions urgent and precise. What the medical soap operas on TV conveniently omit is all the pain and the puke, body functions gone bad, needles piercing flesh, the bruises and the trembling, the low cries for help. Who wants to sit there and stare at real life? We want all the drama of hospitals without the underlying anguish.

In the waiting room, the faces of the relatives who'd been notified of the collision were gray and haggard. They spoke in hushed voices, family members huddled in small groups, their postures bent with dread. Two women clung together, weeping hopelessly. On the other side of the glass doors, at one end of the parking lot, the nicotine addicts had collected in a cloud of cigarette smoke. I'd seen Serena Bonney soon after Danielle was brought in, but she'd been swallowed up by the commotion.

When I'd first pushed open Danielle's front door, she was lying on the floor naked, her face as pink and pulpy as seedless watermelon. Blood spurted from a jagged laceration in her scalp, and she moved her limbs aimlessly as if she might crawl away from her own internal injuries. I'd disconnected my emotions, doing what I could to stem the bleeding while I grabbed the phone off her bed table. The 911 dispatcher had alerted a patrol car and an ambulance, both of which arrived within minutes. Two paramedics had gone to work, administering whatever first aid they could.

The bruises on her body formed a pattern of dark, overlapping lines that suggested she'd been pounded with a blunt instrument. The weapon turned out to be a rag-wrapped length of lead pipe that her assailant had tossed in the bushes on his way out. The patrol officer had spotted it when he arrived and left it for bagging by the crime scene investigators, who showed up shortly afterward. Once the officer secured the scene, we moved out onto the small front porch, standing in a shallow pool of light while he questioned me, taking notes.

By then the alleyway was choked with vehicles. A stutter of blue lights punctuated the darkness, the police radio contributing a deadpan staccato murmur broken up by rasping intervals of static. A clutch of neighbors had assembled in the side yard in a motley assortment of sockless jogging shoes, bedroom slippers, coats, and ski jackets pulled on over nightclothes. The patrol officer began to canvass the crowd, checking to see if there were any other witnesses aside from me.

A sporty bright red Mazda pulled up in the alley with a chirp of tires. Cheney Phillips emerged and strode up the walk. He acknowledged my presence and then exchanged brief words with the uniformed officer, identifying himself before he moved into Danielle's cottage. I saw him halt on the threshold and back up a step. From the open door he did a slow survey of the bloody scene, as if clicking off a sequence of time-lapse photographs. I imagined the view as I had seen it: the rumpled bedding, furniture knocked sideways and toppled. In the meantime, Danielle had been wrapped in blankets and shifted onto the gurney. I stepped aside for the paramedics as they brought her through the front door. I made eye contact with the older of the two. "Mind if I ride along?"

"Fine with me, as long as the detective doesn't object."

Cheney caught the exchange between us and gave a nod of assent. "Catch you later," he said.

The gurney was eased into the back of the ambulance.

I left my car where it was, parked to one side of the alley behind Danielle's house. I sat beside her blanket-covered form in the rear of the ambulance, trying to stay out of range of the young paramedic, who continued to monitor her vital signs. Her eyes were bruised and as swollen as a newly hatched bird's. From time to time I could see her stir, blind with pain and confusion. I kept saying, "You're going to be okay. You're fine. It's over." I wasn't even sure she heard me, but I had to hope the reassurances were getting through. She was barely conscious. The flashing yellow lights were reflected in the plate-glass storefronts as we sped up State Street. The siren seemed somehow disassociated from events. At that hour of the night the streets were largely empty, and the journey was accomplished with remarkable dispatch. It was not until we reached the emergency room that we heard about the multicar wreck out on 101.

I sat out in the waiting room for an hour while they worked on her. By then most of the accident victims had been tended to, and the place was clearing out. I found myself leafing through the same *Family Circle* magazine I'd read before: same perfect women with the same perfect teeth. The July issue was looking dog-eared. Certain articles had been torn out, and someone had annotated the article on male menopause, penning rude comments in the margin. I read busy-day recipes for backyard barbecues, a column of readers' suggestions for solving various parental dilemmas involving their children's lying, stealing, and their inability to read. Gave me a lot of faith in the generation coming up.

Cheney Phillips walked in. His dark hair was as curly as a standard poodle's, and I noticed that he was impeccably dressed: chinos and sport coat over an immaculate white dress shirt, dark socks, and penny loafers. He moved to the reception desk and flipped out his badge, identifying himself to the clerk, who was frantically typing up admissions forms. She made a quick phone call. I watched while he followed her into the treatment room where I'd seen them take Danielle. Moments later he stepped out into the corridor, again in conversation with one of the ER doctors. Two orderlies emerged, maneuvering a rolling gurney between them. Danielle's head was swaddled in bandages. Cheney's expression was neutral as she was rolled away. The doctor disappeared into the next cubicle.

Cheney glanced up and saw me. He came out into the waiting room and took a seat next to me on the blue tweed couch. He reached for my hand and laced his fingers through mine.

"How's she doing?" I asked.

"They're taking her up to surgery. Doctor's worried about internal bleeding. I guess the guy kicked the shit out of her as a parting gesture. She's got a broken jaw, cracked ribs, damage to her spleen, and God knows what else. Doctor says she's a mess."

"She looked awful," I said. Belatedly I could feel the blood drain away from my brain. Clamminess and nausea filled me up like a well. Ordinarily I'm not squeamish, but Danielle was a friend, and I'd seen the damage. Hearing her injuries cataloged was too vivid a reminder of the suffering I'd witnessed. I put my head down between my knees until the roaring ceased. This was the second time I'd found myself fading, and I knew I needed help.

Cheney watched with concern. "You want to go find a Coke or a cup of coffee? It'll probably be an hour before we hear anything."

"I can't leave. I want to be here when she comes out of surgery."

"Cafeteria's down the hall. I'll tell the nurse where we are, and she can come get us if we're not back by then."

"All right, but make sure Serena knows. I saw her back there a little while ago."

The cafeteria had closed at ten, but we found a row of vending machines that dispensed sandwiches, yogurts, fresh fruit, ice cream, and hot and cold drinks. Cheney bought two cans of Pepsi, two ham-and-cheese sandwiches on rye, and two pieces of cherry pie on Styrofoam plates. I sat numbly at an empty table in a little alcove off to one side. He came back with a tray loaded down with the food, straws, napkins, plastic cutlery, paper packets of salt and pepper, and pouches of pickle relish, mustard, ketchup, and mayonnaise. "I hope you're hungry," he said. He began to set the table, arranging condiments on matching paper napkins in front of us.

"Seems like I just ate, but why not?" I said.

"You can't pass this up."

"Such a feast," I said, smiling. I was too tired to lift a finger. Feeling like a kid, I watched while he unwrapped the sandwiches and began to doctor them.

"We have to make these really disgusting," he said.

"Why?"

"Because then we won't notice how bland they are." He tore at plastic packets with his teeth, squeezing gobs of bright red and yellow across the meat. Salt, pepper, and smears of mayonnaise with a scattering of relish. "You want to tell me about it?" he said idly while he worked. He popped the lid on a can of Pepsi and passed an amended sandwich to me. "Eat that. No arguments."

"Who can resist?" I bit into the sandwich, nearly weeping, it tasted so good. I moaned, shifting the bite to my cheek so I could talk while I was eating. "I saw Danielle last night. We had dinner together at my place. I told her then I might see her tonight, but I really went by on a whim," I said. I put a hand against my mouth, swallowing, and then took a sip of Pepsi. "I didn't know if she had company, so I sat there in the car with the engine running, checking it out. I could see she had her lights on, so I finally decided to go knock on her door. Worst-case scenario, she'd be with some guy and I'd tiptoe away."

"He probably saw your headlights." Cheney had eaten half his sandwich in about three bites. "Our moms would kill us if they saw us eating this fast."

I was bolting food down the same as he was. "I can't help it. It's delicious."

"Anyway, keep talking. I didn't mean to interrupt."

I paused to wipe my mouth on a paper napkin. "He must have heard me, if nothing else. That car makes a racket like a power mower half the time."

"Did you actually see him leaving her place?"

I shook my head. "I only caught a glimpse of him as he was walking away. By then I was on the porch, and I could hear her moan. I thought she was 'entertaining' from the sounds she made. Like I'd caught her in the throes of passion, maybe faking it for effect. When I saw the guy out in the alley, it occurred to me something was off. I don't know what it was. On the face of it, there was no reason to think he was connected to her, but it seemed odd somehow. That's when I tried the knob."

"He probably would have killed her if you hadn't showed."

"Oh, geez, don't say that. I was this close to leaving when I spotted him."

"What about a description? Big guy? Little?"

"Can't help you there. I only saw him for a second, and it was largely in the dark."

"You're sure it was a man?"

"Well, I couldn't swear to it in court, but if you're asking what I thought at the time, I'd say yes. A woman doesn't usually whack another woman with a lead pipe," I said. "He was white, I know that."

"What else?"

"Dark clothes, and I'm sure he was wearing hard shoes because I heard his soles scratching on the pavement as he walked away. He was cool about it, too. He didn't run. Nice, leisurely pace, like he was just out for a stroll."

"How do you know he wasn't?"

I thought about it briefly. "I think because he didn't look at me. Even in the dark, people are aware of each other. I sure spotted him. In a situation like that, someone looks at you, you turn and look at them. I notice it most when I'm out on the highway. If I stare at another driver, it seems to catch their attention and they turn and stare back. He kept his face to the front, but I'm sure he knew I was watching."

Cheney hunched over his plate and started in on his pie. "We had a couple of cars cruise the area shortly after the call came in, but there was no sign of him."

"He might live somewhere down there."

"Or had his car parked nearby," he said. "Did she say she had a date tonight?"

"She didn't mention an appointment. Could have been Lester, come to think of it. She said he'd been in a foul mood, whatever that consists of." The pie was the type I remembered from grade school: a perfect blend of cherry glue and pink, shriveled fruit, with a papery crust that nearly broke the tines off the fork. The first bite was the best, the pie point.

"Hard to picture Lester doing something like this. If she's beat up, she can't work. Mr. Dickhead's all business. He wouldn't tamper with his girls. More likely a john."

"You think she pissed some guy off?"

Cheney gave me a look. "This wasn't spur of the moment. This guy went prepared, with a pipe already wrapped to hide his fingerprints."

I finished my pie and ran the fork around the surface of the Styrofoam plate. I watched the red of the cherry pie filling ooze across the tines of the plastic fork. I was thinking about the goons in the limousine, wondering if I should mention them to Cheney. I'd been warned not to tell him, but suppose it was them? I really couldn't see the motivation from their perspective. Why would an attorney from Los Angeles want to kill a local hooker? If he was so crazy about Lorna, why beat the life out of her best friend?

Cheney said, "What."

"I'm wondering if this is related to my investigation."

"Could be, I guess. We'll never know unless we catch him."

He began to gather crumpled napkins and empty Pepsi cans, piling empty plastic packets on the tray. Distracted, I pitched in, cleaning off the tabletop.

When we got back to the emergency room, Serena called the OR and had a chat with one of the surgical nurses. Even eavesdropping, I couldn't pick up any information. "You might as well go on home," she said. "Danielle's still in surgery, and once she comes out, she'll be in the recovery room for another hour. After that, they'll take her to intensive care."

"Will they let me see her?" I asked.

"They may, but I doubt it. You're not a relative."

"How bad is she?"

"Apparently she's stable, but they're not going to know much until the surgeon gets finished. He's the one to give you details, but it's going to be a while yet."

Cheney was watching me. "I can run you home, if you like."

"I'd rather stick around here than go home," I said. "I'll be fine if you want to go. Honest. You don't have to baby-sit."

"I don't mind. I got nothing better at this hour anyway. Maybe we can find a couch somewhere and let you grab a nap."

Serena suggested the little waiting room off ICU, which was where we ended up. Cheney sat and read a magazine while I curled up on sofa slightly shorter than I was. There was something soothing about the snap of paper as he turned the pages, the occasional clearing of his throat. Sleep came down like a weight pressing me to the couch. When I woke, the room was empty, but Cheney'd draped his sport coat across my upper body, so I didn't think he'd gone far. I could feel the silky lining on his jacket, which smelled of expensive after-shave. I checked the clock on the wall: it was 3:35. I lay there for a moment, wondering if there was some way to stay where I was, feeling warm and safe. I could learn to live on a waiting room couch, have meals brought in, tend to personal hygiene in the ladies' room down the hall. It'd be cheaper than paying rent, and if something happened to me, I'd be within range of medical assistance.

From the corridor I heard footsteps and the murmur of male voices. Cheney appeared in the doorway, leaning against the frame. "Ah. You're back. You want to see Danielle?"

I sat up. "Is she awake?"

"Not really. They just brought her down from surgery. She's still groggy, but she's been admitted to ICU. I told the charge nurse you're a vice detective and need to identify a witness."

I pressed my fingers against my eyes and rubbed my face. I ran my hands through my hair, realizing that for once—because of Danielle's cutting skills—every strand wasn't standing straight up on end. I gathered my resources and let out a big breath, willing myself back to wakefulness. I pushed myself to my feet and brushed some of the wrinkles out of my turtleneck. One thing about casual dressing, you always look about the same. Even sleeping in a pair of blue jeans doesn't have much effect. From the corridor, we used the house phone to call into the ICU nurses' station. Cheney handled the formalities and got us both buzzed in.

"Am I supposed to have a badge?" I murmured to him as we moved down the corridor.

"Don't worry about it. I told 'em you're working undercover as a bag lady."

I gave him a little push.

We waited outside Danielle's room, watching through the glass window while a nurse checked her blood pressure and adjusted the drip on her IV. Like the layout in the cardiac care unit, these rooms formed a U shape around the nurses' station, patients clearly visible for constant monitoring. Cheney had chatted with the doctor, and he conveyed the gist of her current situation. "He took her spleen out. Orthopedic surgeon did most of the work, as it turns out. Set her jaw, set her collarbone, taped her ribs. She had two broken fingers, a lot of bruising. She should be all right, but it's going to take a while. The cut on her scalp turned out to be the least of it. Mild concussion, lots of blood. I've done that myself. Bang your head on the medicine cabinet, it looks like you're bleeding to death."

The nurse straightened Danielle's covers and came out of the room. "Two minutes," she said, lifted fingers forming a V.

We stood side by side, in silence, looking down at her like parents taking in the sight of a newborn baby. Hard to believe she belonged to us. She was nearly unrecognizable: her eyes blackened, jaw puffy, her nose packed and taped. One splinted hand lay outside the covers. All of her bright red acrylic nails had popped off or broken, and it made her poor swollen fingers look bloody at the tips. The rest of her was scarcely more than a child-size mound. She was drifting in and out, never sufficiently alert to be aware of us. She seemed diminished by machinery, but there was something reassuring about all the personnel and equipment. As battered as she was, this was where she needed to be.

Leaving ICU, Cheney put his arm around my shoulders. "You okay?"

I leaned my head against him briefly. "I'm fine. How about you?"

"Doing okay," he said. He pressed the down arrow for the elevator. "I had the doctor leave orders. They won't give out any information about her condition, and no one gets in."

"You think the guy would come back?"

"It looks like he tried to kill her once. Who knows how serious he is about finishing the job?"

"I feel guilty. Like this is somehow connected to Lorna's death," I said.

"You want to fill me in?"

"On what?" The elevators opened. We stepped in and Cheney pressed 1. We began to descend.

"The piece you haven't told me. You're holding something back, are you not?" His tone was light, but his gaze was intent.

"I guess I am," I said. I gave a quick sketch of my conversation in the limousine with the Los Angeles attorney and his sidekicks. As we emerged from the elevator, I said, "You have any idea who the guy could be? He said he represented someone else, but he might have been talking about himself."

"I can ask around. I know those guys come up here for R and R. Give me the phone number and I'll check it out."

"I'd rather not," I said. "The less I know, the better. Are they running prostitutes up here?"

"Maybe something minor. Nothing big time. They probably control local action, but that may not mean much more than skimming off the profits. Leave the nuts and bolts to the guys under them."

Cheney had parked on a side street closer to the front entrance than the emergency room. We reached the lobby. The gift shop and the coffee shop were both closed, shadowy interiors visible through plate-glass windows. At the main desk, a man was engaged in an agitated conversation with the patient information clerk. Cheney's manner underwent a change, his posture shifting into cop mode. His expression became implacable, and his walk took on a hint of swagger. In one smooth motion he'd flipped his badge toward the clerk, his gaze pinned on the fellow giving her such grief. "Hello, Lester. You want to step over here? We can have a chat," he said.

Lester Dudley modified his own behavior correspondingly. He lost his bullying manner and smiled ingratiatingly. "Hey, Phillips. Nice to see you. Thought I caught sight of you earlier, down around Danielle's place. You hear what happened?"

"That's what I'm doing here, otherwise you wouldn't see me. This's my night off. I was home watching TV when the dispatcher rang through."

"Not alone, I hope. I hate to see a guy like you lonely. Offer still stands, day or night, male or female. Anything you got a taste for, Lester Dudley provides. . . ."

"You pandering, Lester?"

"I was just teasing, Phillips. Jesus, can't a guy make a little joke? I know the law as well as you do, probably better, if it comes right down to it."

Lester Dudley didn't suit my mental image of a pimp. From a distance he had looked like a surly adolescent, too young to be admitted to an R-rated movie without a parent or guardian. Up close I had to place him in his early forties, a flyweight, maybe five four. His hair was dark and straight, slicked back away from his face. He had small eyes, a big nose, and a slightly receding chin. His neck was thin, making his head look like a turnip.

Cheney didn't bother to introduce us, but Lester seemed aware of me, blinking at me slyly like an earth-burrowing creature suddenly hauled into daylight. He wore kid's clothes: a long-sleeved cotton knit T-shirt with horizontal stripes, blue jeans, denim jacket, and Keds. He had his arms crossed, hands tucked into his armpits. His watch was a Breitling, probably a fake, riddled with dials, and far too big for his wrist. It looked more like something he might have acquired sending off box tops. "So how's Danielle doing? I couldn't get a straight answer from the broad at the desk."

Cheney's pager went off. He checked the number on the face of it. "Shit. . . . I'll be right back," he murmured.

Lester seemed to bounce on his heels, ill at ease, staring after Cheney as he moved over to the desk.

I thought I ought to break the ice. "You're Danielle's personal manager?"

"That's right. Lester Dudley," he said, holding out his hand.

I shook hands with him despite my reluctance to make physical contact. "Kinsey Millhone," I said. "I'm a friend of hers." When you need information, you can't afford to let personal repugnance stand in your way.

He was saying, "Clerk's giving me a hard time, wouldn't give me information even after I explained who I was. Probably one of those women's liberation types."

"No doubt."

"How's she doing? Poor kid. I heard she really got the shit

kicked out of her. Some crackaholic probably did it. They're mean sonsa bitches."

"The doctor left before I had a chance to talk to him," I said. "Maybe the clerk was under orders not to give out information."

"Hey, not her. She was having way too much fun. Enjoying herself at my expense. Not that it bothers me. I'm always taking flak from these women's libber types. Can you believe they're still around? I thought they gave it up by now, but no such luck. Here just last week, this bunch of ball busters? Came down on me like a ton of bricks, claimed I was engaged in white slavery. Do you believe that? What a crock. How can they be talking about white slavery when half my girls are black?"

"You're being too literal. I think you miss the point," I said.

"Here's the point," he said. "These girls make good money. We're talking big bucks, megadollars. Where these girls going to get employment opportunities like this? They got no education. Half of 'em's got IQs in double digits. You don't hear *them* whining. Do they complain? No way. They're living like queens. I'll tell you something else. This bunch of ball busters isn't offering a damn thing. No jobs, no training, not even public assistance. How concerned could they be? These girls have to earn a living. You want to hear what I told 'em? I said, 'Ladies, this is *business*. I don't create the market. It's supply and demand.' Girls provide goods and services, and that's all it is. You think they care? You know what it's about? Sexual repression. Male-bashing bunch of fuzz-bumpers. They hate guys, hate to see anyone get their jollies with the opposite sex. . . ."

"Or," said I, "they might object to the idea of anyone exploiting young girls. Just a wild guess on my part."

"Well, if that's their position, what's the beef?" he asked. "I feel the same way as them. But they treat me like the enemy, that's what I don't get. My girls are clean and well protected, and that's the truth."

"*Danielle* was well protected?"

"Of course not," he said, exasperated that I was being so dense. "She shoulda listened to me. I told her, 'Don't take guys home.' I

SUE GRAFTON

told her, 'Don't do a guy without I'm outside the door.' That's my job. This is how I earn my percentage. I drive her when she goes on appointments. No crazy's going to lay a hand on her if she's got an escort, for cripe's sake. She don't call, I can't help. It's as simple as that."

"Maybe it's time she got out of the life," I said.

"That what she's saying, and I go, 'Hey, that's up to you.' Nobody forces my girls to stay in. She wants out, that's her business. I'd have to ask how she's going to earn a living . . ." He let that one trail, his voice tinged with skepticism.

"Meaning what? I'm not following."

"I'm just trying to picture her working in a department store, waitressing, something like that. Minimum-wage-type job. Beat-up like that, it'd be tough, of course, but as long as she don't mind coming down in the world, who am I to object? You got scars on your face, might be a trick to get employment."

"Nobody's said anything about facial scars," I said. "Where'd you get that idea?"

"Oh. Well, I just assumed. Word on the street is she got busted up bad. Naturally, I thought, you know, some unfortunate facial involvement. It's a pity, of course, but a lot of guys try to do that, interfere with a poor girl's ability to make a living, undercut their confidence, and shit like that."

Cheney reappeared, his gaze shifting with curiosity from Lester's face to mine. "Everything okay?"

"Sure, fine," I said tersely.

"We're just talking business," Lester said. "I never did hear how Danielle is. She going to be all right?"

"Time to go," Cheney said to him. "We'll walk you out to your car."

"Hey, sure thing. Where they got her, up in orthopedics? I could send some flowers'f I knew. Someone told me her jaw's broke. Probably some coked-up lunatic."

"Skip the flowers. We're not giving out information. Doctor's orders," Cheney said.

220

"Pretty smart. I was going to suggest that myself. Keeps her safe from the wrong types."

I said, "Too late for that," but the irony escaped him.

Once we reached the street in front of St. Terry's, we did a parting round of handshakes as though we'd just had a business meeting. The minute Lester's back was turned, I wiped my hand on my jeans. Cheney and I waited on the sidewalk until we saw him drive away.

17

It was close to four in the morning as Cheney's little red Mazda droned through the darkened streets. With the top down, the wind whipped across my face. I leaned my head back and watched the sky race by. On the mountain side of the city, the shadowy foothills were strung with necklaces of streetlights as twinkling as bulbs on a Christmas tree. In the houses we passed, I could see an occasional house light wink on as early morning workers plugged in the coffee and staggered to the shower.

"Too cold for you?"

"This is fine," I said. "Lester seemed to know a lot about Danielle's beating. You think he did it?"

"Not if he wanted her to work," Cheney said.

The sky at that hour is a plain, unbroken gray shading down to the black of trees. Dew saturates the grass. Sometimes you can hear the spritzing of the rainbirds, computers programmed to water lawns before the sun has fully risen. If the cycle of low rainfall persisted as it had in the past, water usage would be restricted and all the lush grass would die. During the last drought, many home owners had been reduced to spraying their yards with dense green paint.

On Cabana Boulevard, a kid on a skateboard careened along the darkened sidewalk. It occurred to me that I'd been waiting to see the Juggler, the man on the bike, with his taillight and pumping feet. He was beginning to represent some capricious force at work, elfin and evil, some figment of my imagination dancing along ahead of me like the answer to a riddle. Wherever I went, he'd eventually appear, always headed somewhere in a hurry, never quite arriving at his destination.

Cheney had slowed, leaning forward to check the skateboarder as we passed him. Cheney raised a hand in greeting, and the kid waved back.

"Who's that?" I asked.

"Works night maintenance at a convalescent home. He had his driver's license pulled on a DUI. Actually, he's a good kid," he said. Moments later he turned into Danielle's alley, where my car was still parked. He pulled in behind the VW, shifting into neutral to minimize the rumble of his engine. "How's your day looking? Will you have time to sleep?"

"I hope so. I'm really bushed," I said. "Are you going to work?"

"I'm going home to bed. For a couple of hours, at any rate. I'll give you a call later. If you're up for it, we can get a bite to eat someplace."

"Let me see how my day shapes up. If I'm not in, leave a number. I'll get back to you."

"You going into the office?"

"Actually, I thought I'd go over to Danielle's and clean. Last I saw, the place was covered with blood."

"You don't have to do that. The landlord said he'd have a crew come in first thing next week. He can't get 'em till Monday, but it's better than you doing it."

"I don't mind. I'd like to do something for her. Maybe pick up her robe and slippers and take 'em over to St. Terry's."

"Up to you," he said. "I'll watch 'til you take off. Make sure your car starts and the boogeyman don't get you."

I opened the car door and got out, reaching down for my handbag. "Thanks for the ride and for everything else. I mean that."

"You're welcome."

I slammed the door, moving over to my car while Cheney hovered like a guardian angel. The VW started without a murmur. I waved to demonstrate that everything was okay, but he wasn't ready to let go. He followed me home, the two of us winding up and down the darkened streets. For once, I found a parking space right in front of my place. At that point he seemed to feel I was safe. He shifted into first and took off.

I locked the car, went through the gate, and walked around to the back, where I unlocked my front door and let myself in. I scooped up the mail that had been shoved through the slot, flipped a light on, set my bag down, and locked the front door behind me. I started peeling off my clothes as I climbed the spiral stairs, littering the floor with discarded articles of clothing like those scenes in romantic comedies where the lovers can hardly wait. I felt that way about sleep. Naked, I staggered around, closing the blinds, turning off the phone, dousing lights. I crawled under the quilt with a sigh of relief. I thought I was too tired to sleep, but as it turned out I wasn't.

I didn't wake until well after five P.M. For a moment I thought I'd slept all the way around the clock until the next dawn. I stared up at the clear Plexiglas dome above my bed, trying to orient myself in the half-light. Given the early February sunsets, the day was already draining away like gray water from the bottom of a bathtub. I assessed my mental state and decided I'd probably had enough sleep, realized I was starving, and hauled myself out of bed. I brushed my teeth, showered, and shampooed my hair. Afterward I pulled on an old sweatshirt and worn jeans. Downstairs, I collected a plastic bucket full of rags and cleaning products. Now that the immediate crisis had passed, I found myself tuning into the rage I felt for her assailant. Men who beat women were almost as low as the men who beat kids.

I tried Cheney's number, but he was apparently already up and out. I left a message on his machine, indicating the time of day and the fact that I was too hungry to wait for him. When I opened my front door, a manila envelope dropped out of the frame where it had been tucked. Across the front, Hector had scrawled a note: "Friday. 5:35 p. Knocked but no answer. Amended transcript and tape enclosed. Sorry I couldn't be more help. Give me a call when you get back." He'd jotted down his home number and the number for the studio. He must have stopped by and knocked while I was in the shower. I checked the time. He'd apparently been there only fifteen minutes before, and I had to guess it was too soon to catch him at either number. I tucked both the tape and the transcript in my handbag and then took myself to a coffee shop where breakfast was served twenty-four hours a day.

I studied Hector's notations while I made a pig of myself, hastily consuming a plate full of the sorts of foodstuffs nutritionists forbid. He hadn't managed to decipher much more than I had. To my page of notes, he'd added the following:

"Hey . . . I hate that stuff.' . . . myself think. You're not . . ."

"Oh, come on. I'm just kidding. . . . [laughter] But you have to admit, it's a great idea. She goes in at the same time every day . . . deify . . ."

"You're sick. . . ."

"People shouldn't get in my . . . [clatter . . . clink]"

Sound of water . . . squeak . . .

"If anything happens, I'll . . ."

Thump, thump . . .

"I'm serious . . . stubby—"

"No link . . ."

Laughter . . . chair scrape . . . rustle . . . murmur . . .

At the bottom of the page, he'd scrawled three big question marks. My sentiments exactly.

When I reached Danielle's cottage, I parked in the alleyway near the hedge as I had the night before. It was dark by then. At this rate I might never see full sun again. I took out my flashlight and checked the batteries, satisfied that the beam was still strong. I spent a few minutes walking along the borders of the alleyway, using the blade of light to cut through the weeds on either side. I didn't expect to find anything. I wasn't really looking for "evidence" as such. I wanted to see if I could figure out where Danielle's assailant might have gone. There were any number of places where he might have hidden, yards he could have crossed to reach the streets on either side. In the middle of the night, even a slender tree trunk can provide cover. For all I knew, he'd taken up a position within easy viewing distance, watching the ambulance and all the cop cars arrive.

I went back to Danielle's cottage, where I crossed the backyard to the main house. I climbed the back steps and knocked on the lighted kitchen window. I could see Danielle's landlord rinsing dinner dishes before he placed them in the rack. He caught sight of me at just about that time and came to the back door, drying his hands on a dish towel. I got a key from him, pausing to chat for a few minutes about the assault. He'd gone to bed at ten. He said he was a light sleeper, but his bedroom was on the second floor, the street side of the house, and he'd heard nothing. He was a man in his seventies, retired military, though he didn't say which branch. If he knew how Danielle made a living, he made no comment. He seemed as fond of her as I was, and that was all I cared about. I professed ignorance of her current status, except to indicate that she'd survived and was expected to recover. He didn't press for specifics.

I walked back along the brick path to Danielle's small porch. The crime scene tape had been removed, but I could still see traces of fingerprint powder around the doorknob and frame. The rag-wrapped length of bloody pipe would probably be tested for fingerprints, but I doubted it would yield much. I let myself into the cottage and flipped on the overhead light. The splattered blood was like a Rorschach, a dark red pattern of smears and exclamation marks where the force of the blows had flung blood in two tracks across the wall. The bloodstained rug had been removed, probably tossed in the trash can at the rear of the lot. The blood on the baseboard looked like teardrops of paint.

The entire apartment was barely a room and a half and cheaply constructed. I toured the premises, though there wasn't much to see. Like mine, Danielle's living quarters occupied a very small space. It looked as though Danielle's battle with her assailant had been confined to the front room, most of which was taken up with a sitting area and a king-size bed. The sheets and comforter were a Laura Ashley print, pink-and-white floral polished cotton with matching drapes, and a correlating pink-and-white-striped paper lined the walls. Her kitchen consisted of a hot plate and a microwave oven sitting atop a painted chest of drawers.

The bathroom was small, painted white, with tiny old-fashioned black-and-white tiles on the floor. The sink was skirted in the same Laura Ashley print she'd used in the bedroom. She'd bought a matching polished-cotton shower curtain, with a valance covering the rod. The wall opposite the john was a minigallery. A dozen framed photographs were hung close together, many sitting crooked on the hangers. Danielle must have been flung up against the connecting wall during the assault. Several had been knocked off the wall and lay facedown on the tile floor. I lifted them with care. Two of the frames had smashed on impact, and the glass in all four was either badly cracked or broken. I stacked the four damaged pictures together, tossed glass shards in the trash, and then straightened the remaining photographs, pausing to absorb the subject matter. Danielle as a baby. Danielle with Mom and Dad. Danielle at about nine, in a dance recital with her hair done up.

I went back into the front room and found a thick sheaf of brown grocery bags tucked in the slot between the wall and the chest of drawers. I put the damaged framed photographs in the bag and set them by the front door. I'd seen similar frames at the drugstore for a couple of bucks apiece. Maybe I'd stop by and pick up some replacements. I pulled all the linens off the bed and set them out on the porch. Even the dust ruffle had picked up a spray of blood posies. I'd make a trip to the cleaners in the morning. I filled my bucket with hot water, mixing a potent brew of cleaning solutions. I wiped down the walls, scrubbed the baseboards and floors until the soapy water turned a frothy pink. I dumped that lot, refilled the bucket, and started over again.

When I'd finished, I pulled out the transcript and sat down on the bed, using Danielle's phone to try Hector at his home number. He answered promptly.

"This is Kinsey here. I'm glad I caught you at home. I thought you might be on your way to the studio."

"Not this early, and today not at all. I work Saturday through Wednesday, so Thursday and Friday nights are usually my weekend. Last night was an exception, but I try to keep those to a minimum. I got hot plans tonight. I give Beauty a bath, and then she gives me one. You got the transcript, I take it."

"Yeah, and I'm sorry I missed you. I was in the shower when you dropped it off." We spent a few minutes commiserating with one another about the poor quality of the tape recording. "What'd you make of it?"

"Not much. I picked up a couple of words, but nothing that made any sense."

"You have any idea what they're talking about?"

"Nope. Lorna sounds upset with him, is mostly what I pick up."

"You're sure it's Lorna?"

"I couldn't swear, but I'm pretty sure it was her."

"What about the guy?"

"I didn't recognize his voice. Doesn't sound like anyone I'm familiar with. You ought to listen again yourself and see what you hear. Maybe we can take turns filling in the missing pieces like a jigsaw puzzle."

"We don't have to make it our life's work," I said. "I'm not even sure it's relevant, but I'll have another go at it when I get home." I glanced down at the annotated transcript. "What about this word *deify*. That seems odd, doesn't it? Deify who?"

"I wasn't real sure about that one, but it's the only word I could think of. Phrase I keep running through my head is that business about 'she goes in at the same time every day.' I don't know what the hell that's about."

"And why 'stubby'? Lorna says that, I think."

"Well, this may sound odd, but I'll tell you the hit I got on that. I don't think she's using 'stubby' as an adjective. There's a guy here in town with the nickname Stubby. She could be talking about him."

"That's an interesting possibility. This was someone she knew?"

"Presumably. His real name is John Stockton. Call him Stubby because he's a little short fat guy. He's a developer—"

"Wait a minute," I cut in. "I just heard that name. I'm almost sure Clark Esselmann referred to him . . . assuming there's only one. Is he a member of the Colgate Water Board?"

Hector laughed. "Whoa, no chance. They'd never let him on the board. Talk about a conflict of interests. He'd vote himself into half a dozen get-rich schemes."

"Oh. Then it's probably not related. Was she talking to or about him?"

"About him, I'd guess. Actually, there could be some marginal connection. Stockton would have to apply to the water board if he were trying to get a permit for some kind of development. Since Lorna 'baby-sat' with Esselmann, she might have heard about Stubby in passing."

"Yeah, but so what? In a town like this, you hear about a lot of things, but that doesn't get you killed. How hard is it to get a permit?"

"It's not hard to *apply,* but with the current water shortage, it'd take a hell of a project to get them to say yes."

I said, "Well." I ran the idea around a couple of laps, but it didn't seem to produce any insights. "I don't know how that pertains. If they're talking about water, it might tie in somehow with 'she goes in at the same time every day.' Maybe that reference is to swimming. I know Lorna jogged, but did she also swim?"

"Not that I ever heard. Besides, if the guy's talking to Lorna, why refer to her as 'she'? He's gotta be talking about someone else. And Stockton doesn't have anything to do with swimming pools. He does malls and subdivisions," he said. "With a phrase like that, they could be talking about work. She goes in 'to work' at the same time every day. Or she goes in 'to bed' at the same time every day."

"True. Oh, well. Maybe something will occur to us if we give it a rest. Anything else strike you?" I asked.

"Not really. Just that Lorna sounded pissed."

"I thought so, too, which is why I listened so carefully. Whatever the guy's saying, she didn't like it a bit."

"Ah, well. Like you say, if it's ever going to make any sense, you'll probably have to leave it alone for a while. If I have a brainstorm, I'll give you a buzz."

"Thanks, Hector."

By the time I locked up and returned the key to Danielle's landlord, it was close to 6:45 and the place was looking better. The smell of ammonia suggested an institutional setting, but at least Danielle wouldn't have to come home to a shambles. I went out to my car, arms loaded with odds and ends. I set the plastic bucket on the front seat on the passenger's side and stuck the bundle of bedclothes on the backseat, along with the paper bag holding the broken picture frames. I slid in behind the steering wheel and sat for a moment, trying to think what to do next. Hector's suggestion about Stubby Stockton as the subject of Lorna's taped conversation was mildly intriguing. From what I'd overheard of Clark Esselmann's comments on the phone, Stockton would be present at the upcoming board meeting, which was tonight by my calculations. With luck, maybe I'd run into Serena and I could quiz her again on the subject of the missing money.

I found a public phone at the nearest gas station and looked up the number for the Colgate Water District. It was way past working hours, but the message on the answering machine gave details about the meeting, which was scheduled at seven in the conference room at the district offices. I hopped in the car, fired up the engine again, and hit the highway, heading north.

Fourteen minutes later I pulled into the parking lot behind the building, uncomfortably aware of a steady stream of cars both ahead of me and behind. Like some kind of car rally, we nosed into parking slots one after the other. I shut my engine down and got out, locking the car behind me. It was easy enough to determine where the meeting was being held simply by following the other attendees. At the back end of the building, I could see lights on, and I trotted in that direction, starting to feel competitive about the available seating spaces.

The entrance to the conference room was tucked into a small enclosed patio. Through the plate-glass window, I could see the water board members already in place. I went in, anxious to get settled while there were still seats left. The meeting room was drab and functional: brown carpet, walls paneled in dark wood veneer, an L of folding tables up front, and thirty-five folding chairs for the audience. There was a big coffee urn on a table to one side, a stack of cups, sugar packets, and a big jar of Cremora. The lighting was fluorescent and made all of us look yellow.

The Colgate Water Board consisted of seven members, each with an engraved plate indicating name and title: counsel for the water district, the general manager and chief engineer, the president, and four directors, one of whom was Clark Esselmann. The board member named Ned, whom he'd talked to by phone, was apparently Theodore Ramsey, now seated two chairs away. The "Bob" and "Druscilla" he'd mentioned in passing were Robert Ennisbrook and Druscilla Chatham respectively.

Appropriately enough, the water board members had been provided big pitchers of iced water, and they poured and drank water lustily while discussing its scarcity. Some of the members I knew by name or reputation, but with the exception of Esselmann, I didn't recognize any of their faces. Serena was in the front row, fussing with her belongings and trying to act as if she weren't worried about her father. Esselmann, in a suit and tie, looked frail but determined. He was already engaged in conversation with Mrs. Chatham, the woman to his left.

Many people had already assembled, and most of the available folding chairs were filled. I spotted an empty chair and claimed it, wondering what I was doing here. Some attendees had briefcases or legal pads. The man next to me had written out a commentary in longhand, which he seemed to be refining while we waited for the meeting to begin. I turned and checked the rows behind me, all of which were occupied. Through the plate-glass window, I could see additional people seated at the picnic table or lounging against the ornamental fence. Speakers on the patio allowed the overflow crowd to hear the proceedings.

Copies of the agenda were stacked up front, and I left my seat briefly so that I could snag one for myself. I gathered that members of the audience would be free to address the board. To that end, requests were filled out and submitted. There were many consultations back and forth, people who seemed to know one another, some in small groups representing a particular petition. I wasn't even sure what the issues were, and the agenda I scanned made it all sound so tedious, I wasn't sure I cared. I wondered if I'd be able to identify Stubby Stockton on sight. A lot of us look short and fat while seated.

At 7:03 the meeting was called to order, with a roll call of board members present. Minutes of the previous meeting were read and approved without modification. Various items on the consent agenda were approved without discussion. Much rustling and coughing and throat clearing throughout. Everyone seemed to speak in a monotone, so that every subject was reduced to its most boring components. Service policies were discussed among the board members in the sort of dry style reserved for congressional filibusters. If anything was actually being accomplished, it was lost on me. What struck me as curious was that Clark Esselmann, in his telephone conversation with Ned at the house, had seemed quite passionate. Behind the scenes, feelings apparently ran high. Here, every effort was made to neutralize emotion in the interest of public service.

One by one members of the audience were able to approach the podium, addressing the board members with prepared statements. These they read aloud in their best singsong public speaking voices, managing somehow to deliver their comments without any sponta-

neity, humor, or warmth. As in church, the combination of body
heat and hot air was bringing the surrounding air temperature up
to anesthetic levels. For someone as sleep-deprived as I'd been for
the last five days, it was hard to keep from toppling off my chair
sideways.

I'm ashamed to confess I actually nodded off once, a sort of dip
in consciousness that I became aware of only because my head
dropped. It must have happened again, because just as I began to
enjoy a much needed snooze, I was jerked upright by a heated
verbal exchange. Belatedly, I realized I'd missed the opening
round.

Clark Esselmann was on his feet, stabbing a finger at the man at
the podium. "It's people like you who're ruining this county."

The man he was addressing *had* to be John "Stubby" Stockton.
He was maybe five feet tall and very heavyset, with a round baby
face and dark thinning hair. He was a man who perspired heavily,
and throughout the interchange he mopped at his face with his
handkerchief. "People like me? Oh, really, sir. Let's leave personalities out of this. This is not about me. This is not about you. This is
about jobs for this community. This is about growth and progress
for the citizens of this county, the—"

"Hogwash! This is about you making money, you damn son of a
bitch. What do you care about the citizens of this county? By the
time this . . . this abomination comes to pass, you'll be well out of
it. Counting your profits while the rest of us are stuck with this
eyesore for centuries to come."

Like lovers, Clark Esselmann and John Stockton, having once
engaged, seemed to have eyes only for each other. The room was
electrified, a ripple of excitement undulating through the audience.

Stockton's voice was syrupy with loathing. "Sir, at the risk of
offending, let me ask you this. What have *you* done to generate
employment or housing or financial security for the citizens of
Santa Teresa County? Would you care to answer that?"

"Don't change the subject—"

"Because the answer is nothing. You haven't contributed a stick, not a nickel or a brick to the fiscal health and well-being of the community you live in."

"That is untrue . . . that is *untrue!*" Esselmann shouted.

Stockton forged on. "You've blocked economic growth, you've obstructed employment opportunities. You've denounced development, impeded all progress. And why not? You've got yours. What do you care what happens to the rest of us? We can all go jump in the ocean as far as you're concerned."

"You're damn right you can jump in the ocean! Go jump in the ocean."

"Gentlemen!" The president had risen.

"Well, let me tell you something. You'll be long gone and the opportunity for growth will be long gone, and who's going to pay the price for your failure of imagination?"

"Gentlemen! Gentlemen!"

The president was banging his gavel on the table without any particular effectiveness. Serena was on her feet, but her father was waving her aside with the kind of peremptory motion that had probably intimidated her from childhood. I saw her sink back down while he shouted, trembling, "Save your speeches for the Rotary, young man. I'm sick of listening to this self-serving poppy-cock. The truth is, you're in this for the almighty buck, and you know it. If you're so interested in growth and economic opportunity, then *donate* the land and all the profits you stand to make. Don't hide behind rhetoric—"

"*You* donate. Why don't *you* give something? You've got more than the rest of us put together. And don't talk to me about hiding behind rhetoric, you pompous ass. . . ."

A uniformed security guard materialized at Stockton's side and took him by the elbow. Stockton shook him off, enraged, but a business associate appeared on the other side of him, and between the two of them he was eased out of the room. Esselmann remained on his feet, his eyes glittering with anger.

In the general swell of side conversations that followed, I leaned over to the man next to me. "I hate to seem ignorant, but what was that about?"

"John Stockton's trying to get water permits for a big parcel of land he wants to turn around and sell to Marcus Petroleum."

"I thought stuff like that had to go through the county board of supervisors," I said.

"It does. It was approved last month by a five–oh vote on the condition that they use reclaimed water from the Colgate Water District. It looked like it was going to pass without opposition, but now Esselmann is mounting a counterattack."

"But why all the heat?"

"Stockton's got some land the oil companies would love to have. All worthless without water. Esselmann supported him at first, but now he's suddenly opposed. Stubby feels betrayed."

I thought back to the phone call I'd overheard. Esselmann had mentioned the board's being sweet-talked into some kind of deal while he was in the hospital. "Was Stockton working on this while Esselmann was out ill?"

"You bet. Damn near succeeded, too. Now that he's back, he's using every ounce of influence to get the application turned down."

The woman in front of us turned and gave us a look of reproach. "There's still business going on here, if you don't mind."

"Sorry."

The president of the board was trying desperately to establish order, though the audience didn't seem particularly interested.

I put my hand across my mouth. "Have they voted on this?" I said in a lower tone.

The guy shook his head. "This issue came up a year ago, and the water board set up a blue-ribbon panel to investigate and make recommendations. They had environmental impact studies done. You know how it is. Mostly a stalling technique in hopes the whole thing would go away. The matter won't actually come to a vote until next month. That's why they're still hearing testimony on the subject."

The woman in front of us raised a finger to her lips, and our conversation dwindled.

In the meantime, Esselmann sat down abruptly, his color high. Serena went around the end of the table and joined him on his side, much to his displeasure. Stubby Stockton was nowhere to be seen, but I could hear him on the patio, his voice still raised in anger. Someone was trying to calm him, but without much success. The meeting picked up again, the president moving adroitly to the next item on the agenda, a fire sprinkler system agreement that didn't upset anyone. By the time I slipped out, Stockton was gone and the patio was empty.

18

I drove over to St. Terry's, stopping to fill my car with gas on the way. I knew I'd reached the hospital after visiting hours had ended, but ICU had its own set of rules and regulations. Family members were allowed one five-minute visit out of every hour. The hospital was as brightly lit as a resort hotel, and I was forced to circle the block, looking for a parking space. I moved through the lobby and took a right turn, heading for the elevators to the intensive care unit upstairs. Once I reached the floor, I used the wall-mounted phone to call into the ward. The night shift nurse who answered was polite but didn't recognize my name. She put me on hold without actually verifying Danielle's presence on the ward. I studied the pastel seascape hanging on the wall. Moments later she was back on the phone with me, this time using a friendlier tone. Cheney had apparently left word that I was to be admitted. She probably thought I was a cop.

I stood in the hallway and watched Danielle through the window to her room. Her hospital bed had been elevated to a slight incline. She seemed to doze. Her long dark hair fanned out across the pillow and trailed over the side of the bed. The bruising on her face seemed more pronounced tonight, the white tape across her nose a stark contrast to the swollen, sooty-looking black-and-blue eye sockets. Her mouth was dark and puffy. Her jaw had probably been wired shut because there was none of the slack-jawed look of someone sleeping. Her IV was still in place, as was her catheter.

"You need to talk to her?"

I turned to find the nurse from the night before. "I don't want to bother her," I said.

"I have to wake her up anyway to take her vital signs. You might as well come in. Just don't upset her."

"I won't. How's she doing?"

"She's doing pretty well. She's on a lot of pain medication, but she's been awake off and on. In another day or two we could probably move her down to medical, but we think she's safer up here."

I stood quietly beside the bed while the nurse took Danielle's blood pressure and her pulse, adjusting the drip on her IV. Danielle's eyes came open in that groggy, confused fashion of someone who can't quite remember where she is or why. The nurse made a note in the chart and left the room. Danielle's green eyes shone stark in the cloudy mass of bruises around her eyes.

I said, "Hi. How are you?"

"I been better," she said through her teeth. "Got my jaw wired shut. That's why I'm talkin' like this."

"I figured as much. Are you in pain?"

"Naw, I'm high." She smiled briefly, not moving her head. "I never saw the guy, in case you're wondering. All I remember is opening the door."

"Not surprising," I said. "It may come back in time."

"Hope not."

"Yeah. Tell me if you get tired. I don't want to wear you down."

"I'm okay. I like the company. What've you been up to?"

"Not much. I'm on my way home from a meeting at the water board. What a zoo. The old guy Lorna used to sit for got into a big shouting match with a developer named Stubby Stockton. The rest of the meeting was such a bore until then, it nearly put me to sleep."

Danielle made a murmuring sound to show she was listening. Her lids seemed heavy, and I thought she was close to nodding off herself. I'd hoped Stubby's name would spark some recognition, but maybe Danielle didn't have a lot of spark to spare. "Did Lorna ever mention Stubby Stockton to you?" I wasn't sure she even heard me. There was quiet in the room, and then she seemed to rouse herself.

"Client," she said.

"He was a client?" I said, startled. I thought about that for a moment, trying to process the information. "That surprises me somehow. He didn't seem like her type. When was this?"

"Long time. I think she only saw him once. Other guy's the one."

"What other guy?"

"Old guy."

"The one what?"

"Lorna screwed."

"Oh, I don't think so. You must have him mixed up with somebody else. Clark Esselmann is Serena Bonney's *father*. He's the old guy she baby-sat . . ."

She moved her good hand, plucking at the bedclothes.

"You need something?"

"Water."

I looked over at the rolling bed table. On it was a Styrofoam pitcher full of water, a plastic cup, and a plastic straw with an accordion section that created a joint about halfway down. "You're okay to drink this? I don't want you cheating because I don't know any better."

She smiled. "Wouldn't cheat . . . here."

I filled the plastic cup and bent the straw, then held the cup near her head, turning the straw at an angle until it touched her lips. She took three small sips, sucking lightly. "Thanks."

"You were talking about someone Lorna was involved with."

"Esselmann."

"You're sure we're talking about the same guy?"

"Boss's father-in-law, right?"

"Well, yeah, but why didn't you tell me before? This could be important."

"Thought I did. What difference does it make?"

"Fill me in and we'll see what difference."

"He was into kinky." She winced, trying to rearrange herself slightly in the bed. A spasm of pain seemed to cross her face.

"You okay? You don't have to talk about this right now."

" 'm fine. Ribs feel like shit, is all. Rest a minute."

I waited, thinking, "Kinky"? I pictured Esselmann getting his fanny spanked while he cavorted around in a garter belt.

I could see Danielle struggle to pull herself together. "She went there after his heart attack, but he came on to her. Said she about fell over. Not that she gave a shit. Buck's a buck, and he paid her a fortune, but she didn't expect it when he seemed so . . . proper."

"I'll bet. And his daughter never knew?"

"No one did. Then later, Lorna let the information slip. She said word got back and that's the last she saw of him. She felt bad. Daughter wanted to hire her, but old guy wouldn't have it."

"What do you mean, word got back? Who'd she let the information slip to?"

"Don't know. After that she was tight-lipped. Said you only have to learn *that* lesson once."

Behind me someone said, "Excuse me."

Danielle's ICU nurse was back. "I don't mean to seem rude about this, but could you wrap it up? The doctors really don't want her having more than five-minute visits."

"I understand. That's fine." I looked back at Danielle. "We can talk about this later. You get some rest."

"Right." Danielle's eyes closed again. I stayed with her for another minute, more for my sake than hers, and then I eased out of the room. The aide at the nurses' station watched my departure.

I found myself uncomfortably trying to conjure up an image of Lorna Kepler with Clark Esselmann. And kinky? What a thought.

It wasn't his age so much as his aura of formality. I couldn't find a way to reconcile his respectability with his (alleged) sexual proclivities. He'd probably been married to Serena's mother for fifty years or more. This all must have happened before Mrs. Esselmann died.

I made a six-block detour to Short's Drugs, where I purchased four eight-by-ten picture frames to replace the broken frames I'd brought with me from Danielle's. Lorna and Clark Esselmann, what an odd combination. The drugstore seemed filled with the same conflicting images: arthritis remedies and condoms, bedpans and birth control. While I was at it, I picked up a couple of packs of index cards, and then I went back to my place, trying to think about something else.

I parked, flipped the driver's seat forward, and hauled the banker's box full of Lorna's papers from under Danielle's blood-spattered bedclothes. For someone obsessive about the tidiness in my apartment, I seem to have no compunction at all about the state of my car. I piled my purchases on the box and anchored the load with my chin while I let myself in.

I settled in at my desk. I hadn't transcribed and consolidated my notes since the second day I was on the job, and the index cards I'd filled then seemed both scanty and inept. Information accumulates and compounds, layer upon layer, each affecting perception. Using my notebook, my calendar, gas slips, receipts, and plane ticket, I began to reconstruct the events between Tuesday and today, detailing my interviews with Lorna's boss, Roger Bonney, Joseph Ayers and Russell Turpin up in San Francisco, Trinny, Serena, Clark Esselmann, and the (alleged) attorney in the limo. Now I had to add Danielle's contention about Lorna's involvement with Clark Esselmann. That one I'd have to check out if I could figure out how. I could hardly ask Serena.

Actually, it cheered me to see how much ground I'd covered. In five days I'd constructed a fairly comprehensive picture of Lorna's lifestyle. I found myself getting absorbed in my recollections. As fast as I filled cards, I'd tack them on the board, a hodgepodge of miscellaneous facts and impressions. It was when I went back through Lorna's finances, transferring data from the schedule of assets, that I caught something I'd missed. Tucked into the file with her stock certificates was the itemized list of the jewelry she'd insured. There were four pieces listed—a necklace of matched garnets, a matching garnet bracelet, a pair of earrings, and a diamond watch—the appraised value totaling twenty-eight thousand dollars. The earrings were described as graduated stones, one-half- to one-carat diamonds, set in double hoops. I'd seen them before, only Berlyn had been wearing them, and I'd assumed they were rhinestones. I checked the time. It was nearly eleven, and I was startled to discover I'd been working for almost two hours. I picked up the phone and called the Keplers' house, hoping it wasn't too late. Mace answered. What a dick. I hated talking to him. I could hear some kind of televised sporting event blasting away in the background. Probably a prizefight, from the sound of the crowd. I stuck a finger up one nostril to disguise my voice. "Hi, Mr. Kepler, is Berlyn there, please?"

"Who's this?

"Marcy. I'm a friend. I was over there last week."

"Yeah, well, she's out. Her and Trinny both."

"You know where she's at? We were supposed to meet up, but I forgot where she said."

"What'd you say your name was?"

"Marcy. Is she over at the Palace?"

There was an ominous silence from him while in the background someone was really getting pounded. "I'll tell you this, Marcy, she better not be over there. She's over at the Palace, she's in big trouble with her dad. Is that where she said to meet?"

"Uh, no." But I was willing to bet money that's where she was. I hung up. I pushed the paperwork aside, shrugged into my jacket, and found my bag, pausing only long enough to run a comb through my hair.

When I opened my front door, a man was standing just outside.

I leapt back, shrieking, before I saw who it was. "Shit J.D.! What are you doing out here? You scared the hell out of me!"

He'd jumped, too, about the same time I had, and he now sagged against the door frame. "Well, damn. You scared *me*. I was all set to knock when you came flying out." He had a hand to his chest. "Hang on. My heart's pounding. Sorry if I scared you. I know I should have called. I just took a chance you'd be here."

"How'd you find out where I live?"

"You gave Leda this card and wrote it right here on the back. You mind if I come in?"

"All right, if you can keep it brief," I said. "I was on my way out. I've got something to take care of." I moved back from the door and watched him edge his way in. I don't like the idea of just anyone waltzing through my place. If I hadn't had some questions for him, I might have left him on the doorstep. His outfit looked like the one I'd seen him in before, but then again, so did mine. Both of us wore faded jeans and blue denim jackets. He still sported cowboy boots to my running shoes. I closed the door behind him and moved to the kitchen counter, hoping to keep him away from my desk.

Like most people who see my apartment for the first time, he looked around with interest. "Pretty slick," he said.

I indicated a stool, sneaking a look at my watch. "Have a seat."

"This is okay. I can't stay long anyway."

"I'd offer you something, but about all I've got is uncooked pasta. You like rotelli, by any chance?"

"Don't worry about it. I'm fine," he said.

I perched on one stool and left the other for him, in case he changed his mind. He seemed ill at ease, standing there with both hands stuck in the back pockets of his jeans. His gaze would hit mine and then flicker off. The light in my living room wasn't as kind to his face as the light in his own kitchen. Or maybe the unfamiliar surroundings had created new lines of tension.

I got tired of waiting to hear what he had to say. "Can I help you with something?"

"Yeah, well, Leda said you stopped by. I got home around seven, and she's pretty upset."

"Really," I said, giving it no inflection. "I wonder why."

"It's this business about the tape. She'd like to have it back, if you don't mind."

"I don't mind a bit." I moved over to the desk and removed it from the manila envelope Hector had tucked it in. I passed it over to J.D., and he put it in his jacket pocket without really looking at it.

"You have a chance to listen?" he asked. He was being way too casual.

"Briefly. What about you?"

"Well, I know pretty much what's in it. I mean, I knew what she was doing."

I said, "Ah," with a noncommittal nod. Inside, a little voice was going, *Wow, what's this about? This is interesting.* "Why was she upset?"

"I guess because she doesn't want the police to find out."

"I told her I wouldn't take it to them."

"She's not very trusting. You know, she's kind of insecure."

"That much I get, J.D.," I said. "I'm just wondering what's got her so uneasy she'd send you all the way over here."

"She's not uneasy. She doesn't want you thinking it was me." He shifted his weight from one foot to the other, smiling with embarrassment, using his very best "aw, shucks" routine. "Didn't want you puttin' the hairy eyeball on me. Scrutinizing." If there'd been a little dirt on the floor, he'd have stubbed the toe of his boot in it.

"I scrutinize everyone. It's nothing personal," I said. "In fact, since you're here, I have a question for you."

"Hey, you go right ahead. I got nothing to hide."

"Someone mentioned you went into Lorna's cabin before the cops showed up."

He frowned. "Somebody said that? Wonder who?"

"I don't think it's any secret. Serena Bonney," I said.

He nodded. "Well. That's right. See, I knew Leda'd put the mike in there. I knew about the tape, and I didn't want the cops to spot it, so what I did, I opened the door, leaned down, and clipped the mike off the wire. I wasn't even in there a minute, which is why I never thought to mention it."

"Did Lorna know she was being taped?"

"I never said anything. Tell you the truth, I was embarrassed by Leda's behavior. You know, by her attitude. She treated Lorna kind of snippy. She's young and immature, and Lorna's already giving me a hard time about her. If I told her Leda was spying on us, she'd have either laughed her butt off or gotten pissed, and I didn't think it would help their relationship."

"They had a bad relationship?"

"Well, no. It wasn't *bad,* but it wasn't that good."

"Leda was jealous," I suggested.

"She might have been a little jealous, I guess."

"So what are you here to tell me? That really everything's all right between you and Leda, and neither one of you had any reason to want Lorna out of the way, right?"

"It's the truth. I know you think somehow I had something to do with Lorna's death. . . ."

"How could I think that? You told me you were out of town."

"That's right. And she was, too. I was set to go fishing with my brother-in-law, and at the last minute she decided to go up to Santa Maria with me while I picked him up. Said she'd rather hang out with her sister than stay here by herself."

"Why are you repeating all this stuff? I don't get it."

"Because you act like you don't believe us."

"Gosh, J.D., how could I fail to believe you when you provide such nice alibis for each other?"

"It's not an alibi. Now, goddamn it. How can it be an alibi when all I'm doing is telling you where we were?"

"Whose vehicle did you take to go to Lake Nacimiento?"

He hesitated. "My brother-in-law has a truck. We took that."

"Santa Maria's an hour away. How do you know Leda didn't drive back in your car?"

"I don't for sure, but you could ask her sister. She'd tell you."

"Right."

"No, she would."

"Oh, come on. If you'd lie for Leda, why wouldn't her sister lie, too?"

"Somebody else must have seen her on Saturday. I think she

said they had a makeup party that morning. You know, where some cosmetic saleslady comes and does facials on everyone so they'll buy Mary Jane products or whatever it is. You don't have to get mad."

"Mary Kay. But you're right. I shouldn't get mad. I told Leda I'd verify all of this. I haven't had a chance to do it, so it's my fault, not yours."

"Now see? I don't know how you do that. Even when you apologize, you make it sound like you don't mean it. Why are you being so cranky with me?"

"J.D., I'm cranky because I'm in a hurry and I don't understand what you're up to."

"I'm not up to anything. I just came to get the tape. I thought while I was here, I'd . . . you know, discuss it. Anyway, you're the one that asked me. I didn't volunteer. Now it seems like I made it worse."

"Okay. I accept that. Let's let it go at that. Otherwise we'll be standing around all night explaining ourselves to one another."

"Okay. As long as you're not mad."

"Not a bit."

"And you believe me."

"I never said that. I said I accept it."

"Oh. Well, okay, then. I guess that's okay."

I could feel my eyes begin to cross.

It was twenty after eleven when I pushed my way through the crowd at Neptune's Palace. The illusion of the ocean depths was profound that night. Watery blue lights shaded down to black. A pattern of light played across the dance floor like the shimmer at the bottom of a pool. I raised my gaze to the ceiling, where a storm at sea was being projected. Lightning forked in a faux sky, and an unseen wind whipped across the ocean's surface. I could hear the cracking of the ship's timbers as the rain lashed the mast, the screams of drowning men set against a rock-and-roll backdrop.

Dancers swayed back and forth, their arms undulating in the smoke-heavy air. The music was so loud, it was almost like no sound, like silence, in the same way that black is every color intensified into nothing.

I found a perch at the bar and bought myself a beer while I scanned the crowd. The boys wore mascara and black lipstick while the girls sported punk haircuts and elaborate tattoos. I kept my gaze carefully averted. The music stopped abruptly, and the dance floor began to clear. I caught a glimpse of a familiar blond head I could have sworn was Berlyn's. She disappeared from view. I eased off the bar stool and circled to the right, peering over the roiling mob to the point where I thought I'd seen her. She was nowhere in sight, but I didn't think I was mistaken.

I lingered near a massive saltwater tank where a flat eel with vicious teeth was devouring a hapless fish. Suddenly I spotted her, sitting at a table with a beefy guy in a tank top, fatigue pants, and heavy army boots. His head had been shaved bald, but his shoulders and forearms were still thick with fur. Any body part not covered with hair seemed to be adorned with some kind of tattoo, dragons and snakes. I could see the ridges in his skull and rolls of flesh along his neck. I've often thought of fat backs as the portion of the human body that aliens would most prefer to eat.

Berlyn sat in profile. She'd shrugged off her leather jacket, which was now hanging over the back of her chair, anchored by her shoulder bag. She was wearing the earrings, two diamond-encrusted hoops dangling down on either side. Her skirt was green satin and, like her black one, short and tight. While she talked, she made frequent reference to the earrings, touching first one and then the other, reassuring herself that both were still in place. She seemed self-conscious, perhaps unaccustomed to wearing such ornate jewelry. The light from the candle in the middle of her table caught the myriad facets of the stones.

Booming music broke the air, and the two got up to dance again. Berlyn wore the same high, spiky heels, perhaps in hopes of lending grace to ankles that were otherwise as shapeless as porch posts. She had a butt on her like a loaded backpack tied around her waist. The table next to theirs had emptied, and I slid onto the chair next to hers.

Trinny suddenly appeared to my right. I'd have avoided the contact, but I knew she'd already spotted me.

"Hi, Trinny. How're you? I didn't know you came here."

"Everybody comes here. This is hot." She was glancing around as she spoke, snapping her fingers while she did some kind of chin thrust in time to the music. I wondered if this was mating behavior.

"You here by yourself?"

"Nuh-uhn, I came with Berl. She has a boyfriend she meets here because Daddy dudn't like him."

"Really, Berlyn's here, too? Where'd she go?"

"Right out on the dance floor. She was sitting right here."

She pointed in the general direction of the dance floor, and I peered dutifully. Berlyn was doing a bump-and-grind number with the beefy boyfriend. I could see his shaved head towering above the other heads bobbing on the dance floor.

"That's the guy your dad dudn't like? I can't imagine."

Trinny shrugged. "It's his hair, I think. Daddy's kind of conservative. He doesn't think guys should shave their heads."

"Yeah, but what difference could it make when he's got so much hair everywhere else?" I said.

Trinny made a face. "I don't like guys with hairy backs."

"Nice earrings Berlyn's wearing. Where'd she get 'em? I wouldn't mind a pair of those myself."

"They're just rhinestones."

"Rhinestones? That's cool. They look like real diamonds from here, don't you think?"

"Oh, right. Like she's really going to wear diamonds."

"Maybe she got 'em at one of those stores that sells look-alike jewels. You know, emeralds and rubies and like that. I look at that stuff and I can't tell the difference."

"Yeah, maybe."

I looked up. A fellow doing chin thrusts and a lot of finger popping was standing near Trinny's chair. She got up and started bumping and grinding on the spot. I waved at the air, trying to watch the dance floor around their flailing arms. "Do you mind?"

The two of them began to bebop in the direction of the dance floor. I found Berlyn again with her beau. I kept my eyes pinned on their heads bobbing on the dance floor. I leaned over as if to tie my shoe and slid my hand down into her purse. I felt her wallet, cosmetic bag, hairbrush. I sat up again and then simply extracted the handbag from the back of the chair where she'd hung it, leaving mine in its place. I hefted the strap across one shoulder and moved off to the ladies' room.

There were five or six women at the basins, makeup paraphernalia scattered across the shelving provided. All were engaged in a frenzy of hair ratting, blusher brushes, and lip pencils, not even looking up as I went into a stall and slid the bolt across. I hung the bag over a hook that had been thoughtfully provided by the management and began to search in earnest.

Berlyn's wallet was not that educational: driver's license, a couple of credit cards, a few folded credit card receipts shoved down among the currency. Her checkbook showed a series of deposits at weekly intervals, which I assumed represented paychecks from Kepler Plumbing, Inc. Chick was seriously underpaid. Scanning back over the last several months, I spotted an occasional deposit of twenty-five hundred dollars, usually followed by checks made out to Holiday Travel. That was interesting. I found the small velvet jeweler's box in which the earrings were probably kept.

I tried the interior zippered compartment, sorting through old grocery lists, Thrifty drugstore receipts, deposit slips. I pulled out passbooks for two different savings accounts. The first had been opened with a nine-thousand-dollar deposit about a month after Lorna's death. I could see intermittent withdrawals of twenty-five hundred dollars, bringing the current balance down to fifteen hundred. The second account held another six thousand dollars. There was probably a third account somewhere else. Berlyn had tucked the carbons of her deposit and withdrawal slips in the back of one passbook—information she didn't dare leave at home. If Janice had

SUE GRAFTON

discovered her cache of hidden funds, sticky questions would arise. I lifted a carboned slip from each passbook.

Someone knocked on the stall. "Are you dead in there?"

"Just a minute," I called.

I depressed the toilet handle, letting the toilet flush noisily while I shoved everything back in the handbag. I emerged from the stall with the bag over my shoulder. A black girl with a seventies Afro moved into the stall I'd vacated. I found an empty basin and gave my hands a vigorous scrub, feeling like they needed it. I left the restroom and returned to the table in haste just as the dance music came to a blasting finale. There was tumultuous applause from the dance floor, complete with piercing whistles and foot stompings. I slid onto my chair, snagged my bag from Berlyn's chair, and slipped hers into place.

Berlyn was approaching, the big guy right in her wake. Her chair tilted perilously. I grabbed for it, but not quickly enough to prevent her bag and leather jacket from tumbling on the floor in a heap.

19

I'd caught a glimpse of Berlyn's mouth, which opened with annoyance when she realized the chair had toppled over. She was looking sweaty and cross, her perpetual state, I suspected. I turned my back abruptly so I was facing the bar. I drank my beer, heart thumping. I heard her exclamation of surprise. "Look at this. Gaaaad . . ." She dragged the profanity out into three musical notes as she scooped up her belongings, apparently pausing to check the contents of her purse. "Somebody's been *in* here."

"In your bag?" the guy said.

"Yes, Gary, in my bag," she said, voice heavy with sarcasm.

"Anything missing?" He seemed concerned, but not freaked out. Maybe he was used to her tone of voice.

She said, "Hey."

I could tell she was speaking in my direction.

She poked me in the shoulder. "I'm talking to you."

I turned, feigning innocence. "Excuse me?"

"Oh, my God. What the hell are you doing here?"

"Well, hi, Berlyn. I thought it might be you," I said. "I saw Trinny a minute ago and she said you were around someplace. What's the problem?"

She gave the bag a shake as if it were a naughty pup. "Don't give me that bullshit. Have you been in here?"

I put a hand on my chest and looked around with puzzlement. "I've been in the ladies' room. I just sat down," I said.

"Ha ha. Very funny."

I looked up at the guy with her. "Is she on drugs?"

He rolled his eyes. "Come on now, Berl, settle down, okay? She wasn't bothering you. Give the chick a break."

"Shut up." Her blond hair looked nearly white in the flickering light from above. Her eyes were darkly lined, mascara separating her lashes into tiny rows of spikes. She fixed me with a look of singular intensity, swelling the way a cat does when it senses a threat.

I let my gaze roam across her face, resting on the diamond hoop earrings, which fairly quivered at her ears. I kept my smile pleasant. "Do you have something to hide, perchance?"

She leaned forward aggressively, and for a moment I thought she might snatch me up by the front of my turtleneck. She put her face so close to mine that I could smell her beery breath, which was not that big a treat. "What did you say?"

I spoke clearly, enunciating. "I said, your earrings are nice. I wonder where you got them."

Her face went blank. "I don't have to talk to you."

I shot a look at the guy just to see how he was taking this. He didn't seem all that interested. Already I found I liked him better than her. "How about this? You want to tell me how you acquired so much money in your savings accounts?"

The beefy guy looked from me to her and back, apparently confused. "You talkin' to me or her?"

"Actually, to her. I'm a private investigator, working on a job," I said. "I don't think you want to get in the middle of this, Gary. Right now we're fine, but it's going to get ugly in a minute."

He held up his hands. "Hey, you two have a beef, you can settle it without me. See you round, Berl. I'm outta here."

I said, "Bye-bye," to him and then to Berlyn, "My car's outside. You want to talk?"

We sat in my car. The parking lot outside Neptune's Palace seemed to have as much going on as the interior. Two beat cops were having a solemn chat with a kid who seemed to have trouble standing upright. In the aisle ahead of us and two cars over, a young girl was clinging to someone's fender while she emptied the contents of her stomach. The temperature was dropping, and the sky above us seemed clear as glass. Berlyn wasn't looking at me.

"You want to start with the earrings?"

"No." Sullen. Uncooperative.

"You want to start with the money you stole from Lorna?"

"You don't have to take that attitude," she said. "I didn't exactly *steal*."

"I'm listening."

She seemed to squirm, considering how much to "share" with me. "I'm telling you this in strictest confidence, okay?" she said.

I held a hand up Scout-style. I love confidences, and the stricter the better. I'd probably rat her out, but she didn't have to know that.

She weaseled around some more, mouth working while she decided how to put it. "Lorna called and told Mom she was going out of town. Mom didn't mention it to me 'til later, right before she went to work. I was upset because I had to talk to Lorna about this cruise to Mazatlán. She said she might be able to help me out, so I went over there. Her car was there, but her lights were out, and she didn't answer my knock. I figured she was out somewhere. I went back first thing in the morning, hoping I could catch her before she left."

"What time was this?"

"Maybe nine, nine-thirty. I was supposed to take the money to the travel agent by noon or I'd lose my deposit. I'd already given them a thousand dollars, and I had to have the balance or I'd forfeit everything I'd paid."

"That was for the cruise you took last fall?"

"Uhn-hun."

"What made you think Lorna had money?"

"Lorna always had money. Everybody knew what she did. Sometimes she was generous and sometimes not. It depended on her mood. Besides, she told me she'd help. She just about *promised*."

I started to quiz her on the subject but decided it would be better to let that pass for now. "Go on."

"Well, I knocked on the door, but she never answered. I saw her car was still there, and I thought maybe she was in the shower or something, so I opened the door and peeked in. She was on the floor. I just stood there and stared. I was so shocked I couldn't even think."

"Was the door locked or unlocked the night before?"

"I don't know. I didn't try. I didn't even think of it. Anyway, I touched her arm and she was really cold. I knew she was dead. I could tell just by looking. Her eyes were wide open, and she was staring. It was really gross."

"What next?"

"I just felt awful. It was horrible. I sat down and started crying." She blinked, staring through the windshield, which was a little dusty for my taste. I figured she was trying to conjure up a quick tear to impress me with the sincerity of her anguish.

"You didn't call the police?" I asked.

"Well, no."

"Why not? I'm just curious about your frame of mind."

"I don't know," she said grudgingly. "I was afraid they'd think I did it."

"Why would they think that?"

"I couldn't even prove where I was earlier because I was at home by myself. Mom was there, but she was sleeping, and Trinny still had a job back then. I mean, what if I was arrested? Mom and Daddy would have *died*."

"I understand. You wanted to protect them," I said blandly.

"I tried to think what to do. I was really screwed, you know? I'd just been praying for the money, and now it was too late. And poor Lorna. I felt so sorry for her. I kept thinking about all the things she wouldn't get to do, like get married, or have a baby. She'd never get to travel to Europe—"

"So you did what?" I said, cutting in on her recital. Her voice was getting quavery.

She took out a ratty tissue and dabbed at her nose. "Well. I knew where she kept her bank books, so I borrowed her driver's license and this passbook. I was so confused and upset, I didn't know what to do."

"I can imagine. Then what?"

"I got in my car and drove down to the valley and took some money out her savings."

"How much?"

"I don't remember. Quite a bit, I guess."

"You closed the account, didn't you?"

"What else was I supposed to do?" she said. "I figured once they found out she was dead, they'd freeze all her accounts like they did with my gramma. And then what good would it do? She *promised* she'd help. I mean, it wasn't like she'd turned me down or anything like that. She wanted me to have it."

"What about her signature? How'd you manage that?"

"We write alike anyway because I taught her myself before she went to kindergarten. She'd always imitated my writing, so it wasn't that hard to imitate hers."

"Didn't they ask for identification?"

"Sure, but we look enough alike. My face is fuller, but that's about the only difference. You know, hair color, but everybody changes that. Later, when the news hit the paper, nobody seemed to put it together. I don't even think her picture ran in the paper down there."

"What about the bank? Wasn't there a closing statement sent out?"

"Sure, but all the mail comes to me at home. Everything from them I pulled out and threw away quick."

"Well, almost everything," I said. "Then what?"

"That's all."

"What about the earrings?"

"Oh, yeah. I probably shouldn't have done that." She made a face meant to signify regret and other profound emotional responses. "I've been thinking I should put the rest of it back."

"Back where?"

"We still have some of her clothes and stuff. I thought I could stick the jewelry in an old purse, like that was where she kept it. In the pocket of her winter coat or something, and then, you know, discover it and act all amazed."

"That's certainly a plan," I said. I was missing something, but I couldn't figure out what. "Could we get back to the money for just a minute here? After you drove back from Simi, you still had Lorna's driver's license along with the cash. I'm trying to understand what you did next. Just so I can get a picture."

"I don't understand. What do you mean?"

"Well, her driver's license was listed on the police report, so you must have put it back."

"Oh, sure. I put the license right back where it was. Yeah, that's right."

"Uhn-hun. Like in her wallet or something?"

"Right. Then I realized I better make it look like she'd closed the account herself, you know, like she took some money out before she left town."

"I'm with you so far," I said with caution.

"Well, everybody thought she was already gone, so all I had to do was create the impression that she was alive all day Friday."

"Wait a minute. I thought this was Saturday. This all happened Friday?"

"It had to be Friday. The bank's not even *open* on Saturday, and neither is the travel agent."

My mouth did not actually drop open, but it felt as though it did. I turned to stare at her fully, but Berlyn didn't seem to notice. She was caught up in her narrative and probably wasn't tuned to my look of astonishment. She was really the most amazing mix of cunning and stupidity, and way too old to be so unaware.

"I went on home. I was really really upset, so I told Mom I had the cramps and went to bed. Saturday afternoon, I went back to her place and brought the mail in with the morning newspaper. I couldn't see any harm. I mean, dead is dead, so what difference did it make?"

"What'd you do with the bank book?"

"Kept it. I didn't want anybody to know the money was gone."

"So you waited a month and opened a couple of savings accounts." I was monitoring myself, trying to keep from using what an English teacher would probably refer to as the screaming accusative verb tense. Berlyn must have picked up on it to some extent because she nodded, trying to look humble and repentant. Whatever she'd told herself in the ten months since Lorna died, I suspect it sounded different now that she was explaining it to me.

"Weren't you worried about your fingerprints showing up at her place?" I said.

"Not really. I wiped off everything I touched so my prints wouldn't show, but even if I slipped up, I figured I had a right to be there. I'm her sister. I've been there lots of times. Anyway, how can they prove when a fingerprint was made?"

"I'm surprised you didn't buy yourself some new clothes or a car."

"That wouldn't be right. I didn't ask her for that stuff."

"You didn't ask her for the jewelry, either," I said tartly.

"I figure Lorna wouldn't mind. I mean, why would she care? I was so heartbroke when I found her." She ceased making eye contact, and her expression took on a troubled cast. "Anyway, why would she begrudge me when there wasn't anything she could do by then?"

"You do know you broke the law."

"I did?"

"Actually, you broke quite a few laws," I said pleasantly. I could feel my temper beginning to climb. It was like being on the verge of throwing up. I should have kept my mouth shut because I could feel myself losing it. "But here's the point, Berlyn. I mean, aside from grand theft, withholding evidence, tampering with a crime scene, obstructing justice, and God knows what other laws you managed to violate, you've completely fucked up the investigation of your own sister's murder! Some asshole's out there walking around free as a bird right this minute because of you, do you get that? What kind of fuckin' twit are you?"

That's when she finally started crying in earnest.

I leaned across the car and opened the door on her side. "Get out. Go home," I said. "Better yet, go to Frankie's and tell your mother what you did before it shows up in my report."

She turned to me, nose red, mascara streaking down her cheeks, nearly breathless from my betrayal. "But I told you in strictest confidence. You said you wouldn't *tell*."

"I didn't actually say that, but if I did, I lied. I'm really a wretched person. I'm sorry you didn't understand that. Now get out of my car."

She got out and slammed the door, her grief having turned to fury in ten seconds flat. She put her face close to the window and yelled, "Bitch!"

I started the car and backed out, so mad I nearly ran her down in the process.

I started cruising the neighborhood, hoping to run into Cheney Phillips somewhere. Maybe he was on call, doing vice rounds like a doctor. Mostly I was looking for a way to keep occupied while I sorted through the implications of what Berlyn had said. No wonder J.D. was nervous, doing everything he could to fix the day and time of his departure with Leda. If Lorna was murdered Friday night or Saturday, they were in the clear. Run it back a day and everything was up for grabs again.

I cut down along Cabana and headed toward CC's. Maybe Cheney was hanging out there. It was not quite midnight. The wind had picked up, moaning through the trees, blowing as if there were a storm in progress, though no rain fell. The surf was being churned up, a wild spray coming off the waves as they boomed against the shore. From a side street, to my left, I could hear a car alarm crying, and the sound seemed to carry like the howling of a wolf. Out of the corner of my eye, I caught the flight of a dried palm frond that hurtled down from a tree and skittered across the road in front of me.

There were very few cars in the parking lot at the Caliente Cafe. The place was quiet for a Friday night, with just a smattering of patrons and no sign of Cheney. Before I left, I used the pay phone and tried to reach Cheney at home. He was either out or not answering, and I hung up without leaving a message on his answering machine. I wasn't really sure what bothered me more, the story Berlyn had told me or Danielle's revelation about Lorna and Clark Esselmann.

I took a detour through Montebello, feeling unsettled. The Esselmann estate was on a narrow lane, without sidewalks or streetlamps. My headlights whitewashed the road ahead. The wind was still blowing. Even with my car windows up, I could hear it whuffling through the grass. A big limb was down, and I had to slow to avoid it, my eyes following the low wall that edged along the property. All the landscape lights were out, and the house sat in darkness, its angular black shape discernible against the clay-colored sky. There was no moon at all. An owl sailed across the road, touching down briefly in the grassy field on the other side, rising up again with a small dark bundle in its grip. Some death is as silent as the flight of a bird, some prey as unprotesting as a knot of rags.

The front gates were closed, and I could see little beyond the dark shapes of the junipers along the drive. I backed up and turned around, idling my engine while I debated what to do. Later, I'd wonder what might have happened if I'd actually gone ahead and pressed the intercom button and announced myself. It probably wouldn't have made a difference, but one can never be sure. Finally I put the car in gear and headed back to my place, where I crept into bed. Above me, the wind blew dry leaves across the domed skylight like the scratchings of tiny feet, something pricking at my conscience while I tossed in sleep. Once, in the dead of night, I could have sworn a cold finger touched the side of my face, and I woke with a start. The loft was empty, and the wind had died to a whisper.

My phone rang at noon. I'd been awake for an hour but unwilling to stir. Having completed my transmigration into the nocturnal realms, I found the notion of getting up any time before two repugnant. The phone rang again. It wasn't that I needed more sleep, I simply didn't want to face daylight. On the third ring, I reached for the phone and pulled it into bed with me, tucking the receiver up between my ear and pillow. "Hello."

"This is Cheney."

I propped myself on one elbow and ran a hand through my hair. "Well, hey. I tried calling you last night, but I guess you were out."

"No, no. I was here," he said. "My girlfriend was over, and we turned the phone off at ten. What's going on with you?"

"Oh, man, we gotta talk. All kinds of shit is coming down on this investigation."

"You ain't heard the half of it. I just got a call from a buddy in the sheriff's department. Clark Esselmann died this morning in a freak accident."

"He what?"

"You're never going to believe this. The guy was electrocuted in his swimming pool. Dove in to swim some laps and got fried, I guess. The gardener was killed, too. Fellow jumped in to try to save him and died the same way he did. Esselmann's daughter said she heard a scream, but by the time she got out there, they were both dead. Luckily she figured out what was going on and flipped the circuit breaker."

"That's really weird," I said. "Why didn't the breaker cut out to begin with? Isn't that what it's for?"

"Don't ask me. They've got an electrician out there now, checking all the wiring, so we'll see what he comes up with. Anyway,

Hawthorn's at the house with the crime scene boys, and I'm on my way over. Want me to swing by and pick you up?"

"Give me six minutes. I'll be waiting out in front."

"See you."

When Cheney and I reached the entrance to Clark Esselmann's estate, he pressed the button and announced our arrival to a hollow-sounding someone on the other end. "Just a minute and I'll check," the fellow said, and clicked off. During the drive, I'd told Cheney as much as I could about Esselmann's confrontation with Stubby Stockton at the meeting the night before. I'd also told him about my conversation with Berlyn and Danielle's claim about Esselmann's relationship with Lorna.

"You've been busy," he remarked.

"Not busy enough. I came over here last night thinking I should talk to him. I don't have any idea what I intended to say, but as it turned out, the place was dark, and I didn't think I should rouse the household to quiz him about his rumored kinkiness."

"Well, it's too late now."

"Yeah, isn't it," I said.

The gates swung open, and we started up the winding driveway, which was bordered with vehicles: two unmarked cars, the electrician's truck, and a county car that probably belonged to the coroner. Cheney parked the Mazda behind the last car in line, and we approached on foot. A fire department rescue vehicle and an orange-and-white ambulance were parked out front, along with a black-and-white patrol unit from the county sheriff's department. A uniformed sheriff's deputy left his post near the front door and moved to intercept us. Cheney flashed his badge, confirming his identity, and the two spoke together briefly before the deputy waved us through.

"How come you're allowed in?" I murmured as we crossed the porch.

"I told Hawthorn there might be a peripheral connection to a case we've been working. He's got no problem with it as long as we don't interfere," Cheney said. He turned and pointed a finger at my face. "You make any trouble and I'll wring your neck."

"Why would I make trouble? I'm as curious as you are."

At the front door we paused, stepping aside for the two paramedics from the fire department who were packed up and departing, presumably no longer needed.

We moved into the house and through the big country kitchen. The interior was quiet. No audible voices, no droning of the vacuum, no ringing telephones. I didn't see Serena or any of the household staff. The French doors stood open, and the patio, like a movie set, seemed crowded with people whose status and function were not immediately clear. Most loitered at a respectful distance from the pool, but the relevant members of the team were hard at work. I recognized the photographer, the coroner, and his assistant. Two plainclothes detectives were taking measurements for a sketch. Now that we'd been admitted, no one seemed to question our right to be present. From what we could ascertain, it hadn't yet been established that a crime had been committed, but the scene was being treated with meticulous attention because of Esselmann's high standing in the community.

Both Esselmann's body and that of the gardener had been removed from the water. They lay side by side, covered discreetly with tarps. Two sets of feet were visible, one bare and one shod in work boots. The bottoms of the bare feet were marked by an irregular pattern of burns, the flesh blackened in places. There was no sign of the dog, and I assumed he'd been locked up somewhere. The second set of paramedics stood together quietly, probably waiting for the okay from the coroner to transport the bodies to the morgue. It was clear they had no further business to conduct.

Cheney left me to my own devices. He was only marginally more entitled to be there than I was, but he felt free to circulate, while I thought it was smarter to keep a low profile. I turned and looked off toward the adjacent properties. By day, the rolling lawns were patchy, the grasses interseeded with a mix of fescue and Bermuda, the latter currently dormant and forming stretches of tatty brown.

The flowering shrubs that surrounded the patio formed a waist-high wall of color. I could see exactly where the gardener had been working that morning because the hedge he'd been clipping was crisply trimmed across one section and shaggy after that. His electric clippers lay on the concrete where he must have dropped them before he jumped into the water. The lap pool looked serene, its dark surface reflecting a portion of the steeply pitched roof. Perhaps it was an artifact of my overactive imagination, but I could have sworn the faint scent of cooked flesh still lingered in the morning air.

I wandered across the patio toward the breezeway that connected the four garages to the house, and then I ambled back. I didn't see how Esselmann's death could be an accident, but neither did I understand how it could be connected to Lorna's death. It was *possible* he'd killed her, but it didn't seem likely. If he felt remorse for their relationship, or if he feared exposure, he might have elected to commit suicide, but what a bizarre way to go about it. For all he knew, Serena might have been the one who happened on the scene, and she'd have died along with him.

I noticed activity at the side of the house closest to the pool: the electrician talking with the two detectives. He gestured his explanation, and I could see all of them looking from the electrical panel to the equipment shed that housed the pump, the filter, and the big heater for the pool. The electrician moved over to the side of the pool near the far end. He hunkered, still talking, while one of the detectives peered down into the water, squinting. He got down on his hands and knees and leaned closer. He asked the electrician a question and then took off his sport coat and rolled up his sleeve, reaching into the depths. The photographer was summoned, and the detective began to detail a new set of instructions. She reloaded her camera and changed the lens.

The other detective crossed to the coroner's assistant, and they conferred. The coroner had stepped back, and the two paramedics began to prepare the bodies for removal to the ambulance. From where I was standing, I could see the news ripple across the assembled personnel. Whatever the information, it spread from twosome to twosome as the group rearranged itself. The detective moved off, and I eased my way toward the coroner's assistant, knowing if I were patient, the news train would eventually reach my little station. The electrician had left his toolbox on the patio table, and he came over to pick it up. In the meantime, the deputy was talking to the fingerprint tech, who hadn't had much work to do so far. The three of them began to chat, looking back toward the pool. I overheard the electrician use the word *deify,* and my thoughts jumped to the transcript I'd been discussing with Hector.

I laid a hand on his arm, and he glanced back at me. "Excuse me. I don't mean to butt in, but *what* did you say?"

"I said there's a problem with the GFI. Wire's come loose, which is why the circuit breaker didn't trip like it should have. One of the pool lights is busted out, and that's what sent current through the water."

"I thought the term was GFCI, ground fault circuit interrupter."

"Same thing. I use both. GFI's easier, and everybody knows what you mean." The electrician was a clean-cut kid in his twenties, one of that army of experts who make the civilized world run a little more smoothly. "Damnedest thing I ever saw," he remarked to the deputy. "Break an underwater flood like that, you'd have to take a stick and poke it out from on top. Detective's going to find out when the pool was last serviced, but somebody really blew it. We're talking a big lawsuit. And I mean big."

The fingerprint technician said, "Think the gardener could have done it?"

"Doing what? You don't punch out a pool light by accident. I told the detective, that glass is tough. It takes work. If it'd been at night with the pool lights on, somebody might have noticed. Daytime like this and all that black tile, you can hardly see the near end, let alone the far."

From the other side of the patio, the detective motioned the electrician back, and he moved in that direction. Where I was, the deputy and the fingerprint technician had shifted the discussion to somebody who'd been electrocuted by his electric lawn mower because his mother, trying to be helpful, stuck the three-pronged plug into a two-pronged extension cord. The insulation on the neutral wire was defective, which caused direct contact between the cord and the metal handle of the mower. The deputy went into quite a bit of detail about the nature of the damage, comparing it to another case he'd seen where a child bit through an electric cord while standing in a puddle of water in the bathroom.

I kept thinking about the tape recording, thinking about the phrase *she goes in at the same time every day*. Maybe Esselmann wasn't the intended victim. Maybe Serena was meant to die instead. I looked for Cheney but couldn't seem to find him. I approached the nearest of the two detectives. "Would you have any objection if I talked to Mr. Esselmann's daughter? It won't take but a minute. I'm a friend of hers," I said.

"I don't want you discussing Mr. Esselmann's death. That's my job."

"It's not about him. This is about something else."

He studied me for a moment and then glanced away. "Keep it brief," he said.

20

I went through the kitchen toward the front of the house. In the foyer, I took a right and headed up the stairs. I had no idea how the bedrooms were laid out. I moved down the hallway from room to room. At the end of the corridor, there was an intersecting T with a sitting room on the right and a bedroom on the left. I could see Serena lying on a four-poster bed, covered with a light blanket. The room was sunny and spacious, yellow-and-white paper on the walls in a tiny rosette print. There were white curtains at the window, and all the woodwork was done in white.

Serena didn't seem to be asleep. I knocked on the door frame. She turned her head and looked at me. I didn't think she'd been crying. Her face was pale, unmarked by tears, the expression in her eyes more one of resignation than sorrow, if one can make that distinction. She said, "Are they finished out there?"

I shook my head. "It'll probably be a while. You want me to call anyone?"

"Not really. I called Roger. He's coming over as soon as he can get away from the plant. Did you want something?"

"I need to ask you a question, if you can tolerate the intrusion."

"That's all right. What is it?"

"Do you use the pool on a daily basis?"

"No. I never liked swimming. That was Daddy's passion. He had the lap pool put in about five years ago."

"Does someone else here swim? One of the maids, or the cook?"

She thought about it briefly. "Occasionally a friend might call and ask to use the pool, but no one else," she said. "Why?"

"I heard a taped conversation under circumstances I'd prefer not to go into. Lorna was talking to a man who used the phrase *she goes in at the same time every day.* I thought the reference might be to swimming, but at the time it made no sense. I was just wondering if there was a 'she' on the premises who went in 'at the same time every day.' "

She smiled wanly. "Just the dog, and she only goes in when Dad does. You saw her the other night. They play fetch, and then when he does his laps, she swims alongside him."

I could feel a flicker of confusion. "I thought the dog was a male. Isn't his name Max?"

"It's Maxine. Max for short," she said. "Actually, her real name's much longer because she's pedigreed."

"Ah, Maxine. How's she doing? I didn't see her downstairs. I thought she might be up here with you."

Serena struggled into a sitting position. "Oh, heavens. Thanks for reminding me. She's still at the groomers. I took her over first thing this morning. The shop owner even came in early to accommodate the appointment. I was supposed to pick her up at eleven, but it completely slipped my mind. Ask Mrs. Holloway if she'd go over there; at least call and let them know what's happened. Poor Max, poor girl. She's going to die without Daddy. The two of them were inseparable."

"Mrs. Holloway's the housekeeper? I haven't seen her, either, but I can call if you like."

"Please. Maybe Roger can pick her up on his way over here. It's Montebello Pet Groomers in the lower village. The number's on the planning center in the kitchen. I don't want to put you to any trouble."

"It's no trouble," I said. "Are you okay?"

"Really, I'm fine. I just want some time alone, and then I'll be down. I'll probably have to talk to the detective again, anyway. I can't believe this is happening. It's all so grotesque."

"Take your time," I said. "I'll tell the pet groomers someone's picking Max up later. You want this closed? It might be quieter."

"All right. And thank you."

"That's all right. I'm sorry about your father."

"I appreciate that."

I left the room, pulling the door shut behind me. I went down to the kitchen and put a call through to the grooming shop. I identified myself as a friend of Serena's, indicating that her father had died unexpectedly. The woman was extremely gracious, expressing her condolences. The shop was closing at three, and she said she could just as easily drop Max off on her way home. I left a note to that effect, assuming that Mrs. Holloway or Serena would spot it.

By the time I returned to the patio, the bodies had been removed and the photographer had packed up and left. There was no sign of the electrician, the coroner, or his assistant. The fingerprint technician was now working over by the pool equipment. At the near end of the pool, I saw Cheney talking to the younger of the two detectives, his buddy Hawthorn, I gathered, though he never introduced us. When he spotted me, he finished up his conversation and crossed the patio to meet me. "I was wondering where you went. They're nearly done here. You want to head out?"

"We might as well," I said.

We didn't say much until we'd left the house, walking down the driveway to the spot where Cheney's car was parked. I said, "So what's the current theory? It couldn't have been an accident. That's ludicrous."

Cheney unlocked the door and held it open for me. "Doesn't look like it on the surface, but we'll see what they come up with."

He closed the door on my side, effectively cutting off communication. I leaned over and unlocked the door on his side, but I had to wait until he'd gone around and let himself in. He slid under the steering wheel.

"Quit being such a stickler and play the game," I said. "What do you think?"

"I think it's dumb to guess."

"Oh, come on, Cheney. It had to be murder. Somebody busted out the pool light and then disconnected the GFI. You don't believe it was an accident. You're the one who told Hawthorn there might be a peripheral connection between Lorna's death and Esselmann's."

"What connection?" he said perversely.

"That's what I'm asking you!" I said. "God, you're aggravating. Okay, I'll go first. Here's what I think."

He rolled his eyes, smiling, and turned the key in the ignition. He put his arm across the seat and peered out of his rear window, backing out of the gate with a breathtaking carelessness. When he reached the road, he threw the gear into first and peeled out. On the way back to my place, I told him about Leda's surreptitious tape recording. I didn't have the transcript with me, but the text was so sketchy that it wasn't difficult to recollect. "I think the guy is telling her about his scheme. He's come up with a way to kill Esselmann, and he's feeling clever. Maybe he thought she'd find it amusing, but she obviously doesn't. You ought to hear her on the tape. She's pissed off and upset, and he's trying to act like it's all a big joke. The problem is, once he's told her, he's left himself open. If he actually intends to go through with it, she'll know it was him. Given her reaction, he can't trust her to keep quiet."

"So what's your theory? Bottom line," he said.

"I think she was killed because she knew too much."

He made a face. "Yeah, but Lorna died back in April. If the guy wanted to kill Esselmann, why wait this long? If the only thing that worried him was her blowing the whistle, why not kill the old guy the minute she's dead?"

"I don't know," I said. "Maybe he had to wait until things cooled down. If he'd moved too quickly, he might have called attention to himself."

He was listening, but I could tell he wasn't convinced. "Go back to the murder scheme. What's the guy intend to do?"

"I think he's talking about a variation on what actually happened. Clark and Max go through the same routine every morning. He throws a stick into the lap pool and she fetches. She's a retriever. She was born for this stuff. After they play, the two swim. So here's the deal. Suppose the pool's been electrified. He throws the stick. She leaps in and takes a big jolt. He sees she's in trouble. He goes in after her and he dies, too. It looks like an accident, some freaky set of circumstances everyone feels bad about. Poor guy. Tried to save his doggie and died in the process. In reality, Serena took the dog to the groomer's, so Clark went in swimming by himself. Instead of Clark and the dog, you have Clark and the gardener, but the setup's the same."

Cheney was quiet for a moment. "How do you know it's Lorna on the tape?" he said. "You've never heard her voice. The guy could be talking to Serena."

"Why would she be there in the first place?" I asked promptly. I noticed it was more fun to ask questions than to have to answer them.

"Haven't made that part up yet. The point is, Serena's upset because she doesn't want the dog used as bait, so she takes Max off to the groomer's to get her out of the way."

"I've talked to Serena. The voice didn't sound like hers."

"Wait a minute. That's cheating. You told me the voices were distorted. You've talked to J.D. and you said it didn't sound like him, either."

"That's true," I said reluctantly. "But you're suggesting Serena killed her own father, and I don't believe it. Why would she do it?"

"The guy's got a lot of money. Doesn't she inherit his estate?"

"Probably, but why kill him? He'd already had a heart attack, and his health was failing. All she had to do was wait, and probably not very long at that. Besides, I've seen her with him. There was nothing but affection. An occasional complaint about his stubbornness, but you can tell she admired him. Anyway, I'll see if I can get the tape back and you can hear it for yourself."

"Who has it?"

"Leda. She sent J.D. over to pick it up last night. Or that was his claim. Actually, in the suspect department, they're not bad candidates. Both of them were nervous I'd give the tape to the police. Neither has an alibi. And you know what J.D. does for a living? He's an electrician. If anybody'd know how to hot-wire a lap pool, he would."

"The town's full of people who'd know enough to do that," he said. "Anyway, if your theory's correct, then whoever killed Esselmann had to be someone who knew the house, the pool, and the routine with the dog."

"That's right."

"Which brings us back to Serena."

"Maybe," I said slowly. "Though Roger Bonney's another one who'd know all that."

"What's his motive?"

"I have no idea, but he's certainly the link between Lorna and Esselmann."

"Well, there you have it," Cheney snorted. "Now if Roger knows Stubby, the circle will be complete, and we can charge him with murder." Cheney was being facetious, but he'd made a good point, and I could feel a ripple of uneasiness.

My thoughts veered to Danielle and the man who'd walked off into the darkness of the alleyway. "How do we know this isn't the same guy who went after Danielle? Maybe the attack on her connects up to everything else."

Cheney had reached my place, and he slowed to a stop. He pulled on the brake and put the car in neutral, turning to face me, his smile gone. "Do me a favor and think about something else. It's a fun game, but you know as well as I do it doesn't mean jack."

"I'm just trying on theories, like throwing dinner plates against the wall to see if one will stick."

He reached over and gave my hair a little tug. "Just watch yourself. Even if you're right and all these things are related, you can't go tearing off on your own," he said. "This case belongs to the county sheriff. It's got nothing to do with you."

"I know."

"Then don't give me that look. It's nothing personal."

"It is personal. Especially when it comes to Danielle," I said.

"Would you quit worrying? She's safe."

"For how long? Any day now they'll move her out of ICU. Hospitals aren't exactly high security. You ought to see the people walking in and out of there."

"You're right about that. Let me think some and see what I can do. We'll talk soon, okay?" He smiled, and I found myself smiling in return.

"Okay."

"Good. I'll give you the number for my pager. Let me know if anything turns up."

"I'll do that," I said. He recited the number and had me repeat it back to him before he put the car in gear again.

I stood at the curb and watched the Mazda pull away and then moved through the gate and went around to the rear. It was Saturday afternoon, close to three o'clock. I let myself into my apartment. I made a note of Cheney's pager number and left it on my desk. I felt I was in a state of suspended animation. The answer was hovering somewhere on the periphery, like spots in my field of vision that moved sideways every time I turned to look. There had to be some chain of events, something that linked all the pieces of the puzzle. I needed a way to distract myself, setting all the questions aside until a few answers came. I went up the spiral stairs to the loft and changed clothes, pulling on my sweatsuit and my jogging shoes. I tucked the house key in my pocket and trotted over to Cabana Boulevard.

The day was crisp and clear, the midafternoon sun pouring over the distant mountains like a golden syrup. The ocean was a dazzling carpet of diamonds, the air freshly scented with the briny smell of the sea. The run was a pleasure, bringing back in full measure the joys of physical activity. I did four miles, feeling strong, and when I came back I took a shower and started over, eating cereal and toast while I read the paper I hadn't had time for that morning. I went out and ran an errand or two, picking up groceries, stopping at a wine store. It was close to six o'clock when I finally felt relaxed enough to sit down at my desk and flip the light on.

I went back to my index cards. I was going through the motions, not really on the track of anything in particular, just trying to keep busy until I figured out what to do next. I glanced down at the sack that held the broken picture frames. Shit. Of course, I'd forgotten to take Danielle's bedding to the cleaners before it closed, but at least I could switch the frames. I moved over to the kitchen counter with the new frames I'd picked up. I put the wastebasket nearby and pulled the photographs from the paper bag. There were four eight-by-ten enlargements, all in color. I removed the frame and the matting from the first, pausing to study the image: three cats lounging on a picnic table. A sleek gray tabby was in the process of jumping down, apparently not that happy about the photographic immortality. The other two cats were long-haired, one pale cream and one black, staring at the camera with expressions of arrogance and disinterest respectively. On the back she'd written the date and the cats' names: Smokey, Tigger, and Cheshire.

As I removed the photo from the cracked frame, the glass separated into two pieces. I tucked both in the trash can and tossed the frame in after them. I pulled out a new frame and peeled off the price tag, sliding the mat and the cardboard backing out of the frame. I tucked the photo between the backing and the mat, turning it over to make sure the image was straight. I eased the three layers—mat, photo, and backing—into the space between the glass and the series of staples that were sticking out of the frame. I turned it back again. It looked good.

I picked up the second photograph and went through the same process. The glass was only cracked across one corner, but the frame itself was unsalvageable. This photograph showed two young men and a young woman on a sailboat, everyone with beer cans, sunburns, and wind-tangled hair. Danielle had probably taken the picture herself. It must have been a good day with good friends at a time in her life when she was still in possession of her innocence. I've been on outings like it. You come home dog-tired and dirty, but you never forget.

In the third picture, Danielle was posed under a white trellised arch in the company of a young clean-cut guy. From the dress she was wearing, complete with an orchid on her wrist, I guessed this was taken at her high school prom. It was nice getting a glimpse of her private life, images of her as she'd been before. She had entered the life as surely as a novice entering a convent, with a gap just as wide between past and present.

The last picture had been rematted, a wide band of gray reducing the framed image to its two central figures: Danielle and Lorna dressed up and sitting in a booth. It looked like a commercial photograph, taken by a roving photographer who made a living snapping pictures on the spot. Hard to tell where this was taken, Los Angeles or Vegas, some glitzy nightclub, with dinner and dancing. In the background, I could see a portion of a bandstand and a potted plant. Champagne glasses on the table in front of them. The frame was cheap, but the wide gray matting was a nice choice for the subject matter, isolating the two of them.

Both women were looking elegant, seated at a round table in a black leather-padded booth. Lorna was so beautiful: dark-haired, hazel-eyed, with a perfect oval face. Her expression was grave, with just the smallest hint of a smile on her lips. She wore a black satin cocktail dress, with long sleeves and a square, low-cut neckline. The diamond hoop earrings sparkled at her ears. Danielle wore kelly green, a form-fitting sequined top, probably with a miniskirt, if I knew Danielle's taste. Her long dark hair had been smoothed into a French roll. I imagined Lorna getting her all dolled up for a kind of high-class date: two call girls on the town. Along the back of the booth, I could see a man's hand and arm extending behind Lorna. I could feel my heart begin to thump.

I extracted the photograph from the frame and turned it over. With the matting removed, I could see all four people who'd been sitting at the table that night: Roger, Danielle, Lorna, and Stubby Stockton. Oh, man, this is it, I thought. This is it. Maybe not everything, but the heart of the riddle.

I carried the photo with me to the telephone and called Cheney's pager number, punching in my own telephone number and the # sign at the sound of the tone. I hung up. While I waited for him to return my call, I sat at my desk and sorted through my notes, pulling all the index cards on which Roger was mentioned. Most were from my initial interview, with additional notes from my conversation with Serena. I scanned the cards on the bulletin board, but there were no further references. I laid the cards out on my desk like a tarot reading. I found the notes I'd scribbled to myself after my meeting with him. Roger had told me Lorna called him Friday morning. I circled the day and added a question mark, affixing the card to the photograph with a paper clip.

The phone rang. "Kinsey Millhone," I said automatically.

"This is Cheney. What's up?"

"I'm not sure. Let me tell you what I came across, and you tell me." I told him briefly how I'd acquired the photographs, and then I detailed the one I was looking at. "I know you were kidding when you talked about Roger and Stubby, but they *did* know each other, and well enough to go whoring together somewhere out of town. I also went back through my notes and came across an interesting discrepancy. Roger told me Lorna called him Friday morning, but she couldn't possibly have done that. She was dead by then."

There was a brief silence. "I don't see where you're going with this."

"I have no idea. That's why I'm calling you," I said. "I mean, suppose Roger and Stubby were in business together. If Lorna told Roger about her relationship with Esselmann, they could have been using the information to pressure him. Esselmann balked. . . ."

"So Stubby killed him? That's ridiculous. Stubby's got a lot of irons in the fire. This deal doesn't work, he's got another one lined up, and if that fails, he's got more. Believe me, Stockton is in business to do business. Period. If Esselmann dies, that only sets him back because now he's gotta wait until someone's appointed to take Clark's place, yada, yada, yada . . ."

"I'm not saying Stockton. I think it's Roger. He's the one who had access to that pool equipment. He had access to Lorna. He had access to everything. Plus, he knew Danielle. Suppose he and Stockton talked business that night. Danielle's the only witness."

"How're you going to prove it? All you have is speculation. This is all air and sunshine. You've got nothing concrete. At least, nothing you could take to the DA. He'd never go for it."

"What about the tape?"

"That's not proof of anything. It's illegal for starters, and you don't even know it's Lorna. They could be talking about anything. You ever heard the concept of 'fruit of the poisonous tree'? I've been thinking about this whole business ever since I dropped you off. You got people tampering with the crime scene, tampering with evidence. Any good defense attorney would rip you to shreds."

"What about Roger's claim Lorna called him Friday morning?"

"So the guy was mistaken. She called some other day."

"What if I went in with a wire and had a talk with him. Let me ask—"

Cheney cut in, his tone a mixture of impatience and outrage. "Ask him what? We're not going to wire *you*. Don't be asinine. What are you proposing, you go knock on his door? 'Hi, Rog. It's Kinsey. Who'd you kill today? Oh, no reason, just curious. Excuse me, would you mind speaking into this artificial flower I'm wearing in my lapel?' This is not your job. Face it. There's nothing you can do."

"Bullshit. That's bullshit."

"Well, it's bullshit you're gonna have to live with. We really shouldn't even be discussing this."

"Cheney, I'm tired of the bad guys winning. I'm sick of watching people get away with murder. How come the law protects them and not us?"

"I hear you, Kinsey, but that doesn't change the facts. Even if you're right about Roger, you got no way to nail him, so you might as well drop it. Eventually he'll screw up, and we'll get him then."

"We'll see."

"Don't give me 'we'll see.' You do something stupid and it's your ass, not his. I'll talk to you later. I got another call coming in."

I hung up on him, steaming. I knew he was right, but I really hate that stuff, and his being right only made it worse. I sat for a minute and stared at the photograph of Lorna and Danielle. Was I the only one who really cared about them? I held the missing piece of the puzzle, but there were no options open to me, no means of redress. There was something humiliating about my own ineffectiveness. I crossed the room and paced back, feeling powerless. The phone rang again and I snatched up the receiver.

"This is Cheney . . ." His voice was oddly flat.

"Hey, great. I was hoping you'd call back. Surely, between us, there's a way to do this," I said. I thought he was calling to apologize for being such a hard-ass. I expected him to offer a suggestion about some action we might take, so I was completely unprepared for what came next.

"That was St. Terry's on the line. The ICU nurse. We lost Danielle. She just died," he said.

I felt myself blink, waiting for the punchline. "She died?"

"She went into cardiac arrest. I guess they coded her, but it was too late to pull her back."

"Danielle *died?* That's absurd. I just saw her last night."

"Kinsey, I'm sorry. The call just came in. I'm as surprised as you are. I hate to be the one to tell you, but I thought you should know."

"Cheney." My tone was rebuking while his had become compassionate.

"You want me to come over?"

"No, I don't want you to come over. I want you to quit fucking with my head," I snapped. "Why are you doing this?"

"I'll be there in fifteen minutes."

The line clicked out and he was gone.

Carefully, I set the receiver in the cradle. Still standing, I put a hand across my mouth. What was this? What was happening? How could Danielle be dead while Roger was beyond reach? At first, I felt nothing. My initial response was a curious blank, no sensation at all attached. I took in the truth content of what Cheney had told me, but there was no corresponding emotional reaction. Like a monkey, I plucked up this bright coin of information and turned it over in my hand. I believed in my head, but I couldn't comprehend with my heart. I remained motionless for perhaps a minute, and when feelings finally crept back, what I experienced wasn't grief, but a mounting fury. Like some ancient creature hurtling up from the deep, my rage broke the surface and I struck.

I picked up the receiver, put my hand in my jeans pocket, and pulled out the card I'd been given in the limousine. The scribbled number was there, some magical combination of digits that spelled death. I dialed, giving absolutely no thought to what I was doing. I was propelled by the hot urge to act, by the blind need to strike back at the man who had dealt me this blow.

After two rings, the phone was picked up on the other end. "Yes?"

I said, "Roger Bonney killed Lorna Kepler."

I hung up. I sat down. I felt my face twist with heat, and tears spilled briefly.

I went into the bathroom and looked out the window, but the street beyond was dark. I went back to my desk. Oh, Jesus. What had I done? I picked up the phone and dialed the number again. Endless rings. No answer. I put the phone down. Hands shaking, I pulled my gun from the bottom drawer and popped in a fresh clip. I eased the gun into the waistband at the back of my jeans and pulled on my jacket. I grabbed my handbag and car keys, turned out the lights, and locked the door behind me.

I hit the 101, heading out toward Colgate. I kept checking my rearview mirror, but there was no sign of the limousine. At Little Pony Road, I took the off-ramp and turned right, continuing past the fairgrounds until I reached the intersection at State. I stopped at the traffic light, drumming my fingers on the steering wheel in impatience, checking my rearview mirror again. Along the main thoroughfare there was only one touch of color, words written out in red neon on the drugstore I spotted. *SAV-ON,* the sign said. The shopping mall to my left was apparently having a gala all-night sale. Klieg lights pierced the sky. White plastic flags were strung from pole to pole. At the entrance to the parking lot, a clown and two mimes were motioning for passing cars to turn in. The two mimes in whiteface began a playlet between them. I couldn't tell what silent drama the two were enacting, but one turned and looked at me as I pulled away from the light. I checked back, but all I saw was the painted sorrow on his downturned mouth.

I sped past a darkened service station, the bays and gasoline pumps shut down for the night. I could hear a burglar alarm clanging, apparently in a shop close by, but there was no sign of the police and no pedestrians running to see what was wrong. If there were actually burglars in the place, they could take their sweet time. We're all so accustomed to alarms going off that we pay no attention, assuming the switches have been tripped in error and mean nothing. Six blocks beyond, I crossed a smaller intersection heading up the road that led to the water treatment plant.

The area was largely unpopulated. I could see an occasional house on my right, but the fields across the road were scruffy and dotted with boulders. Coyotes yipped and howled in the distance, driven down from the hills by the need for water. It seemed too early in the evening for predators, but the pack was obeying a law of its own. They were hunting tonight, on the scent of prey. I pictured some hapless creature flying across the ground, in fear of its life. The coyote kills quickly, a mercy for its victim, though not much consolation.

I turned into the entrance to the treatment plant. Lights were on in the building, and there were four cars out front. I left my handbag in the car, locking it behind me. There was still no sign of the limousine. Then again, the guy wouldn't use his limo to make a hit, I thought. He'd probably send his goons, and they might well check Roger's place first, wherever that might be. A county-owned truck had been parked in the drive. As I passed, I put a hand out. The hood was still warm to the touch. I went up the stairs to the lighted entry. I could feel the reassuring bulk of the handgun in the small of my back. I pushed through the glass doors.

The receptionist's desk was empty. Once upon a time Lorna Kepler had sat there. It was curious to imagine her working here day after day, greeting visitors, answering the telephone, exchanging small talk with the control technician and senior treatment mechanics. Maybe it was her last shred of pretense, the final gesture she'd made toward being an ordinary person. On the other hand, she might have found herself genuinely interested in aeration maniforms and flash mix basins.

The interior of the building seemed quiet at first. Fluorescent lights glowed against the polished tile floors. The corridor was deserted. From one of the rear offices, I picked up the strains of a country music station. I could hear someone banging on a pipe, but the sound came from deep in the bowels of the building. I moved quickly down the hallway, glancing left into Roger's office. The lights were on, but he was nowhere to be seen. I heard footsteps approaching. A fellow in coveralls and a baseball cap came around the corner, moving in my direction. He seemed to take my presence for granted, though he took his cap off politely at the sight of me. His hair was a mass of curly gray mashed into a cap-shaped line around his head. "Can I help you with something?"

"I'm looking for Roger."

The fellow pointed down. "That's him you hear whumping on the sample lines." He was in his fifties, with a wide face, and a dimple in his chin. Nice smile. He reached out a hand and introduced himself. "I'm Delbert Squalls."

"Kinsey Millhone," I said. "Could you let Roger know I'm here? It's urgent."

"Sure, no problem. Actually, I'm just on my way down. Whyn't you follow me?"

"Thanks."

Squalls retraced his steps and opened the glass-paneled door into the area I'd seen before: multicolored pipes, a wall of dials and gauges. I could see the gaping hole in the floor. Orange plastic cones had been set across one end, warning the unwary about the dangers of tumbling in.

I said, "How many guys you have working tonight?"

"Lemme see. Five, counting me. Come on this way. You're not claustrophobic, I hope."

"Not a bit," I lied, following him as he crossed to the opening. On my previous visit, I'd seen a moving river of black water down there, silent, smelling of chemicals, looking like nothing I'd ever seen before. Now I could see lights and the bleak walls of concrete, discolored in places where the water had passed. I felt the need to swallow. "Where'd all the water go?" I asked.

"We shut the sluice gates, and then we have a couple of big basins it drains into," he said conversationally. "Takes about four hours. We do this once a year. We got some postaeration sample lines in the process of repair. They'd almost completely corroded. Been clogged for months until this shutdown. We got ten hours to get the work done, and then back she comes."

A series of metal rungs affixed to the wall formed a ladder, leading down into the channel. The banging had stopped. Delbert turned around and edged his foot down into the opening and then proceeded to descend. *Tink, tink, tink* went the soles of his shoes on the metal rungs as he sank from sight. I moved forward, turning myself. Then I descended as he had to the tunnel below.

Once we reached bottom, we were twelve feet underground, standing in the influent channel through which millions of gallons of water had passed. Down here it was always night, and the only moon shone in the form of a two-hundred-watt bulb. The passage smelled damp and earthy. I could see the sluice gate at the dark end of the tunnel, streaks of sediment on the floor. This felt like spelunking, not a passion of mine. I spotted Roger, with his back to us, working on an overhead line. He was standing on a ladder about fifteen feet away, the big lightbulb, in a metal guard, hooked on the pipe near his face. He wore blue coveralls and black rubber hip boots. I could see a denim jacket tucked across the ladder's brace. It was chilly down here, and I was glad I had my jacket.

Roger didn't turn. "That you, Delbert?" he said over his shoulder.

"That's me. I brought a friend of yours. A Miss . . . what is it, Kenley?"

"It's Kinsey," I corrected.

Roger turned. The light glittered in his eyes and bleached all the color from his flesh. "Well. I was expecting you," he said.

Delbert had his hands on his hips. "You need some help with that?"

"Not really. Why don't you find Paul and give him a hand?"

"Will do."

Delbert started up the ladder again, leaving us alone. His head disappeared, back, hips, legs, boots. It was very quiet. Roger came down from the ladder he was on, wiping his hands on a rag, while I stood there trying to decide how to go about this. I saw him pick up the jacket and check a pocket in front.

"This is not what you think," I said. "Listen, Lorna was getting married the weekend she was murdered. Earlier this week a fellow picked me up in a limo with a couple of flunkies in bulging over-coats . . ." I felt my voice trail off.

He had something in his hand about the size of a walkie-talkie: black plastic housing, a couple of buttons on the front. "You know what this is?"

"Looks like a taser gun."

"That's right." He pressed a button, and two tiny probes shot out on electrical wires that carried a hundred and twenty thousand volts. The minute the probes touched me I was down, my whole body numb. Couldn't move. Couldn't breathe. After a few seconds, my brain started to work. I knew what had happened, I just didn't know what to do about it. Of all the responses I'd imagined him making, this was not on the list. I lay on my back like a stone, trying to find a way to heave oxygen into my lungs. None of my extremities responded to cues. In the meantime, Roger patted me down, coming up with my gun, which he tucked in the pocket of his coveralls.

I was making a sound, but it probably wasn't very loud. He moved to the wall and climbed the ladder. I thought he was going to leave me down there. Instead he flipped the trap door so that it came down on the hole. "Thought we might like a little privacy," he said as he descended. He found a plastic bucket that had been tossed to one side. He turned it upside down and took a seat not that far from me. He leaned close. Mildly he said, "Fuck with me, I'll smother you with this jacket. Weak as you are, it's not going to leave any marks."

That's what he did with Lorna, I thought. Shot her with a stun gun, put a pillow across her face. Wouldn't have taken long. I felt like a baby in the early stages of development, moving my limbs randomly in an attempt to turn. Grunting, I managed to roll over on my side. I lay there breathing, looking at the wet pavement from the corner of my eye. My cheek rested on something gritty: anthracite, sludge, small shells. I collected myself, inching my right arm up under me. I heard the trap door open, and Delbert Squalls called down, "Roger?"

"Yes?"

"Guy up here to see you."

"Oh, hell," he breathed. And then to Delbert, "Tell him I'll be right there."

I rolled an eye at him, unable to speak, and saw a grimace of impatience cross his face. He got his arms under me and hauled me into a sitting position, propping me against the wall. Like a rag doll, I sat with my legs straight out in front of me, feet tilted together, my shoulders slumped. At least I was breathing. Above me, I could hear someone walking around. I wanted to warn him. I wanted to tell him he was making a terrible mistake. While I made grunting noises, Roger was going up the ladder, his feet going *tink, tink, tink,* head and shoulders disappearing. I felt tears fill my eyes. My limbs were deadened from the electrical jolt. I tried moving my arms, but the result was the same ineffectual feeling as discovering your extremities "asleep." I began to flex one fist, trying to get the blood to circulate. My whole body felt oddly anesthetized. I listened, straining, but heard nothing. I struggled and finally managed to topple sideways, turning over on my hands and knees, where I remained, breathing hard, until I could gain my feet. I don't know how long it took. All was silence above. I reached for the ladder and clung to the closest rung. After a moment, I began my ascent.

By the time I climbed out, there was no sign of anyone in the corridor. I forced myself forward. I'd begun to navigate better, but my arms and legs still felt oddly disconnected. I reached his office, where I peered in the door, leaning on the frame. There was no sign of him. My gun had been placed neatly in the center of his blotter. I crossed to the desk and picked it up, tucking it into the small of my back again.

I left the office, moving into the reception area. Delbert Squalls was sitting at the desk, leafing through the telephone book, probably ordering pizzas for the night crew. He looked up as I passed.

I said, "Where'd Roger go?"

"Don't tell me he left you down there? Man's got no manners. You just missed him. He took off with that guy in the overcoat. Said he'd be right back. You want to leave him a note?"

"I don't think that's necessary."

"Oh. Well, suit yourself." He went back to his search.

"Good night, Delbert."

" 'Night. Have a good evening," he said, reaching for the phone.

I emerged from the building into the chill night air. The wind had picked up again, and the sky, though cloudless, bore the fragrance of a distant rain heading in this direction. There was no moon, and the stars looked as though they'd been blown up against the mountains.

I went down the stairs to the slot where my car was parked. I let myself into the VW and turned the key in the ignition, pulling out onto the road that led back to town. As I crossed the intersection, I thought I caught sight of a limousine slipping into the dark.

EPILOGUE

Roger Bonney hasn't been seen since that night. Only a few people understand what really happened to him. I spent a long time in conversation with Lieutenant Dolan and Cheney Phillips and, for once, I told the truth. Given the enormity of what I'd done, I felt I had to accept the responsibility. In the end, after much consideration, they decided no purpose would be served in pursuing the matter. They did go through the motions of a missing persons investigation, but nothing came of it. And so it rests.

Now, in the dead of night, I ponder the part I played in Lorna Kepler's story, in the laying to rest of those ghosts. Homicide calls up in us the primitive desire to strike a like blow, an impulse to inflict a pain commensurate with the pain we've been dealt. For the most part, we depend upon judicial process to settle our grievances. Perhaps we've even created the clumsy strictures of the courts to keep our savageries in check. The problem is that so often the law seems pale in its remedies, leaving us restless and unfulfilled in our craving for satisfaction. And then what?

As for me, the question I'm left with is simple and haunting: Having strayed into the shadows, can I find my way back?

Respectfully submitted,
Kinsey Millhone

About the Author

Sue Grafton lives in Santa Barbara, California.

Sue Grafton

Published by Fawcett Columbine.
Available at your local bookstore, or call
toll free 1-800-793-BOOK (2665) to order by phone
and use your major credit card. Or use this coupon
to order by mail.

___ "G" IS FOR GUMSHOE	449-00062-1	$11.00
___ "H" IS FOR HOMICIDE	449-00063-X	$11.00
___ "I" IS FOR INNOCENT	449-00064-8	$11.00
___ "J" IS FOR JUDGMENT	449-00065-6	$11.00
___ "K" IS FOR KILLER	449-00066-4	$11.00
___ "L" IS FOR LAWLESS	449-00067-2	$11.00

Name _____

Address _____

City _____ State _____ Zip _____

Please send me the Fawcett Columbine I have checked above.

I am enclosing $_____
          plus
Postage & handling* $_____
Sales tax (where applicable) $_____
Total amount enclosed $_____

* Add $4 for the first book and $1 for each additional book.

Please send check or money order (no cash or CODs) to
Fawcett Mail Sales, 400 Hahn Road, Westminster, MD 21157.

Prices and numbers subject to change without notice.
Valid in the U.S. only.
All orders subject to availability.